The Earl, the Debutante, And the Infamous Widow

LIZZIE B ANDREWS

The Earl, the Debutante, and the Infamous Widow
© Lizzie B Andrews 2024

ISBN: 978-1-923163-61-4 (Paperback)

A catalogue record for this work is available from the National Library of Australia

Cover Design: Clark & Mackay
Format and Typeset: Clark & Mackay
Published by Lizzie B Andrews with assistance from Clark & Mackay

Proudly printed in Australia by Clark & Mackay

Chapter One

The Earl

London 1812

There are many reasons why, during their lives, a person may find it necessary to change course from the path they had previously chosen to follow. For Major Alexander Wilde, this happened when he unexpectedly became the heir to his uncle's earldom.

Until that point, Alex had enjoyed a career in the armed forces, following in his father's footsteps and had never considered a different future for himself. Yet now, here he was, the Sixth Earl of Tenby, about to enter Almack's ballroom, known as the marriage mart, to be introduced to the girl his mother, Lady Wilde, had chosen as the most fitting candidate to be his wife and countess!

"Don't look so miserable," his mother said, looking up at him. "We are not going to a funeral! And if you don't like her, we can always find someone else for you. Just promise me that you will give her a chance."

Alex sighed. "I have already promised you that I will consider her, Mother, if you remember."

"But I don't want you to put her off by frowning at her all evening. Try to enjoy yourself."

Enjoy himself? How was he supposed to do that? Looking around, he saw that all those around them were smiling and chatting excitedly and he knew that it was not easy to gain an invitation to Almack's. His mother was probably right. He should be more enthusiastic about being here. After all, only the cream of society was able to gain vouchers for Almack's, entitling them to purchase tickets for the ball in King's Street. It was where each Wednesday evening during the Season a subscription ball and supper were held for the purpose of introducing daughters to eligible sons. Yet, while everyone else in the room may be thrilled to be there, Alex was not! However, he knew it was now his responsibility to marry and produce an heir, so here he was. How had it come to this?

He had never considered it a possibility that he may inherit the earldom, nor had he ever coveted it. Even though his uncle had remained childless, Alex had been only third in line after his two older brothers. He remembered pitying Ted, the eldest of the three, for being heir. Not for him a life of adventure. He would have to learn the mundane tasks involved with managing an estate.

Alex recalled how Ted had always been considered the irresponsible one of the family and knew it unlikely that he would have been suited to the task of looking after the estate and the welfare of the numerous tenants and other estate workers but felt it grossly unfair that he had been denied the chance to try.

Ted had died in a hunting accident on the day he reached his majority. Alex's elder brother, Oliver, loved the land, and would have been ideal as earl, but he had died of a fever just over a year and a half ago, making Alex the heir at the age of twenty-nine. Alex, the most adventurous one of the three boys, the one many would have believed the most likely of the sons to die young, had lived an almost charmed life, receiving very few injuries during his career in the army, none of which were life threatening. A career he had wanted from as far back as he could remember, inspired by his mother's stories of his deceased father's exploits in the light cavalry resulting in him being posthumously awarded a knighthood for services to the crown.

Joining the army as soon as he was old enough, Alex had been thrilled to learn of his posting to the Peninsula where he had acquitted himself well in the fight against Napoleon's forces, being mentioned in dispatches on more than one occasion and being promoted in rank from Captain to Major.

His future had looked secure.

And then everything changed when his brother Oliver died. As soon as it became known that Alex was now the heir, his superiors decided to recall Major Wilde to England, deeming it inappropriate for the sole heir to an earldom to be in the line of fire. Something Alex strenuously resisted but without success.

He had found himself posted to the South of England, involved in the training of new recruits. And that was where he had remained until the demise of his uncle six months ago, making him the new Earl of Tenby, giving him the responsibility for Knopton Manor, the large estate in Surrey he had inherited, along with all the obligations that entailed. He also had inherited a substantial town house in London and a large portfolio of very profitable investments. Yet, given the chance, he would much rather still be a soldier fighting for his country.

His mother, Prudence, Lady Wilde, squeezed his arm in reassurance, smiling at him warmly as they waited to be admitted to the ballroom. He tried to smile in response, knowing that she was aware of his reluctance to accept his fate, and how he disliked being forced to the altar. But both knew he had to marry and produce an heir or heirs since there was no-one else of the line to inherit the title. If he failed in his duty the estate would pass to the crown.

He supposed that he should try to like this girl his mother had found for him but expected her to be no better than the others she had persuaded him to meet. As soon as the official mourning period for his brother, Oliver, had ended, his mother had begun holding dinner parties, inviting friends who had daughters who were either enjoying their first or second seasons for him to consider. While he always attended these dinners, he resisted all his mother's attempts at matchmaking, describing the young ladies as unappealing and insipid.

The trouble was that he liked the life of a bachelor. Shortly after returning to England, he had been introduced to a charming lady who had been happy to warm his bed and become his mistress. He remembered Jeanette fondly but had accepted the end of their relationship six months ago, after he became the earl. He had then travelled to the estate he had inherited and hardly had time to miss her, so busy was he getting acquainted with his tenants and learning from the steward all he needed to know. Just as well, really, he now accepted. No loose ends to deal with.

At last, he and his mother found themselves walking through the door of the ballroom. Alex took a deep breath feeling decidedly uncomfortable as he surveyed the room, looking for a girl who fit the description given to him by his mother.

"Over there, Alex," his mother told him, nudging him discreetly with her elbow while indicating with a tilt of her head. "The dark-haired girl standing next to that short, grumpy looking woman in grey, who happens to be Lady Dawson, Miss MacDonald's chaperone, by the way."

"Hmm, she is pretty enough at any rate," Alex told his mother, after thoroughly inspecting what he considered to be 'the merchandise'.

"You'll like Penelope, Alex," Lady Wilde said confidently. "She really is the best of this season's bunch in my opinion. A very nicely brought up girl, despite losing her parents so young. She became the ward of the Marquess of Frome, you know, who I believe has provided the girl with a substantial dowry."

"If she's such a paragon, Mother, why is she still free? You keep telling me how advanced the season is, and yet this prize is still available. There must be something that's putting off potential admirers."

"Her guardian's sister! Lady Dawson. She's the fly in the ointment. How can you get to know a girl without talking with her privately? Yet Lady Dawson stays by her charge's side and never allows Penelope to speak privately with anyone. She told me that, in her opinion, a gentleman should make his intentions clear before being allowed to be alone with a lady, even in an open carriage in the park. How old-fashioned is that! And Penelope is completely overshadowed by her chaperone - hardly says a word. Yet, you can take it from me, she does not lack spirit or intelligence. I have spent several evenings having a quiet cose with her, and on her own, she is a delightful companion, full of gaiety and charm. But as soon as Lady Dawson appears on the scene, especially when male company is present, Penelope clams up. It can only be her chaperone's presence that changes her, I'm sure."

"Or the presence of men!"

"Oh, no, Alex, I doubt that. When I told her a bit about you ... don't mind me singing your praises, do you?" Without pausing to hear his reply, she continued, "she said she was looking forward to being introduced to you this evening and told me how fond she was of a soldier's uniform."

"Ah, so she knows why I am here."

His mother shrugged. "Perhaps. But not that you are here only to meet her. However, she does know that you are looking for a wife."

"I suppose that is obvious. Why else would I be here? But, if she is fond of uniforms, I will likely disappointment her. I'm not in uniform now, Mother. She'll have to make do with a plain black and white outfit."

"Plain black and white? What rubbish! You look perfectly splendid, Alex. Why, it must have taken Jenkins a good hour to tie that cravat of yours. And the cut of your coat? Why, Beau Brummell himself would be envious."

Alex laughed and put his arm round his mother's shoulders. "You're biased, my dear. But thank you, all the same." He gave her shoulder an affectionate squeeze. "And may I compliment you on your attire. Another new outfit, I presume?"

"Yes, it is, and don't flatten my petal-shaped sleeves, dear boy. They're the latest style, you know."

His mother was wearing an Indian muslin high-waisted gown in pale lilac, with a richly embroidered hem and bodice. Even though she had now turned fifty, she had kept her trim figure and Alex still thought her to be as beautiful as she had been when she was younger. Her skin was smooth and unblemished, having few lines except those produced by smiles, and her hair, though now showing streaks of grey, was elegantly styled in a becoming upswept creation.

Before moving further into the ballroom, she suddenly turned towards Alex, reaching out to stroke his high velvet collar, as though it needed attention. But Alex noticed she had tears in her eyes. "What is wrong?" he asked, concern for her overshadowing all else. The bond between them had always been close and, although they hadn't lived together for many years, their relationship had remained strong.

"Oh Alex, you look so like your father. You were always my favourite child, you know, even though I did my best not to show it. I loved Edward and Oliver as well, but you were born after your father's death, and I was thrilled when it turned out that you had the same fair, curly hair and the bluest of eyes. You looked so like him, how could I not adore you? And now that you are thirty and it is time for you set up your own household, part of me feels as if I am about to lose your love to another!"

"Never!" Alex protested. "You will always be important to me."

"I know, I am being silly. Don't mind me. I don't know what came over me. I really do want you to find someone you can love." She stiffened her spine. "Come on, Alex, time to meet your fate."

Alex dutifully followed his mother across the room for the introductions to be made, feeling somewhat like a lamb going to the slaughter! He was not expecting to find love, being totally unfamiliar with that emotion, except in relation to family. If love did exist between a man and a woman, he considered it would be something that developed over time if one was lucky, not something that hit you between the eyes at first sight. Lust, on the other hand, was a very different matter. He knew quite a bit about that!

No, he was not looking for love. It was his duty to marry and all he was hoping for was someone who would make a good countess and mother, whilst also being a pleasant companion and bed mate. That would be enough. His mother considered that Miss MacDonald would make a suitable countess, so now it was up to him to decide if she met his other requirements.

And indeed, his first impression of the young lady was decidedly encouraging. He found himself delighted with both her looks and her manner. Without being aware of it, a smile lit his face reflecting his thoughts, eliciting a similar response from her. And instead of the warning bells sounding in his head as was usual with him whenever a young lady looked at him with such interest, this time he found himself pleased to find her so apparently taken with him. After the usual general pleasantries were exchanged, Alex requested the pleasure of partnering Miss MacDonald in the next set of country dances without the slightest qualm.

During their time on the dance floor, there was little chance for conversation, but their eyes communicated interest and admiration. Once or twice, Alex noticed her look away and tried unsuccessfully to follow her gaze. Probably wanting her friends to notice her success with the new earl, he surmised. He was only too aware of the interest being shown in him since inheriting the title. And not only by those with daughters of marriageable age. All seemed interested in examining and evaluating the new earl of Tenby.

Alex decided that Miss MacDonald wasn't as shy with men as his mother had led him to believe; she looked at him directly and showed no sign of nervousness at the attention he was giving her.

She seemed to him like an exquisitely graceful sprite in her white, flimsy, diaphanous gauze evening gown with its frills and flounces. So slim and lovely. Her fair, flawless skin was complimented by dark brown curls, arranged artfully in the Grecian style, and her eyes were large and brown, with the longest, thickest lashes he had ever seen. She had a neat figure, with small, firm breasts and delicate hands and feet. Truly delightful.

At the end of the set, he returned her to her chaperone, only to find this lady in what appeared to him to be an intimate conversation with his mother. No doubt talking about him, he thought, guessing that the two ladies were probably swapping notes! If he wanted out, now was the time to politely withdraw. But then he looked again at his partner and decided that he would be interested in getting to know her a little better. Perhaps a drive in the park together? And then he remembered his mother telling him that Lady Dawson would be unlikely to approve of such a scheme without going along with them!

However, while he was deciding on the next step to take, he found that he had little chance to say anything, for Lady Dawson immediately took complete command of the conversation, chattering on aimlessly without even pausing for breath, it seemed to him. Alex wanted to ignore her and engage Penelope in conversation, but, short of being rude to Lady Dawson, he had no opportunity to do so.

Another gentleman then came and claimed Penelope's hand for the next dance. Alex watched as she left his side quietly, her eyes downcast and her head bent, noticing only too clearly the change in her demeanour, as though she would have much preferred to have remained by his side.

For some reason he found himself feeling inordinately proud of her interest in him rather than in any other, even to the extent that she had felt confident enough when dancing with him to glance at him flirtatiously, whereas now, she looked most uncomfortable in the company of his rival. Penelope MacDonald's preference for Alex seemed also to have been noted by Lady Dawson, for, as soon as Penelope was out of earshot, that lady turned to address him.

"My young cousin seems quite taken with you, my lord."

"She is a delightful young lady, ma'am," Alex responded, his tone and smile conveying the truth of his words. It seemed that his mother and Lady Dawson had decided to take a hand in this courtship! On the one hand, that could make things a little easier for him, but on the other, he didn't want his decision to be forced or rushed.

"Yes indeed. I was saying to your mother while you two danced what a nice couple you made. Do you plan to be in town long, my lord?"

"For the foreseeable future, ma'am."

Both ladies were looking at him expectantly, it seemed, and he knew he needed to decide then and there whether to take the next step. But really what was there to decide? After all, why not? "Lady Dawson, I would very much like to call on Miss MacDonald in the morning, if this would meet with your approval, of course," he found himself saying.

"Oh, certainly, my lord. Penelope would be honoured by a visit from you, I'm sure," she said, her eyes gleaming with delight. Alex knew what she was thinking and began to wonder if he was the girl's only suitor. She was such a pretty girl, he doubted that, but anyway, he was now committed to calling on her.

And so it was that the next day, Alex arrived at the appointed hour carrying a large bouquet of roses. He was shown into a drawing room where he found both Miss MacDonald and her chaperone awaiting him. He stayed only for the prescribed fifteen minutes making stilted conversation but found it difficult to converse naturally with Penelope while Lady Dawson kept interrupting. Miss MacDonald acted as a demure young lady should, her eyes usually lowered in the appropriate manner, although she did occasionally peer at him through her lashes, he noted. She responded politely to his questions and conversations without introducing any topics of her own.

Despite this disappointing beginning, Alex continued with his courtship, but while making sure he claimed the maximum of two dances at the balls they attended during the following weeks, calling on her after each event, he learned little more about her. They had progressed to using first names at least, and he managed to discover that she enjoyed playing the piano and had been attached to the pony her guardian had given her. But her conversation seemed to be confined to the sort of things young, inexperienced ladies would talk about. Most of the time, she asked him questions. About his time in the army, his estate, and his town house. But she seemed unwilling to talk about herself in any meaningful way.

He knew his mother favoured the match, and Penelope seemed happy to be courted by him. Perhaps she was even beginning to imagine herself in love with him? But what about his feelings. Would she make him happy? He knew so little about her, and his mother only knew the basics. It would be good to speak confidentially with someone else but unfortunately, he didn't know anyone he would trust enough to keep his confidences. His cousin Percy would have been the best one to speak with, as he seemed to know everyone, but Alex knew that Percy was currently out of town at a country house party. Percy, a cousin on his mother's side, was his senior by five years, but the two had become close after Alex had returned to England.

It had been Percy who had introduced him to his favourite club, Boodles, where the two sometimes met up for dinner, and he had taken Alex around town, introducing him to some of his friends. Alex had been away from the London scene for too long to have built up a circle of close friends of his own in town and had needed that helping hand. It would be good to seek Percy's advice about his courtship when he returned to town.

Unfortunately for Alex, before he could consult with his cousin, Lady Dawson took him aside, wanting to know his intentions towards her charge. What could he say? There seemed no alternative but to assure her that his intentions were honourable and that he was courting her with a view to matrimony.

"I am glad to hear that," she said. "Otherwise, I would have to put an end to these visits of yours, since it has come to my attention that your names are being linked. Yet, I know that Penelope is quite taken with you and am confident that she will accept a proposal from you if my brother gives his consent. But first you need to gain permission from Claude, something I suppose I should have insisted upon much sooner. It is Claude - Lord Frome, you know - from whom you must seek consent. And I'm afraid he is unlikely to give it without seeing you in person. You know he resides in Yorkshire?"

"Yes, Miss MacDonald has spoken to me a little of her time in Yorkshire. But could I not speak to Miss MacDonald first, even if you wish to remain with us?"

"I am afraid not, my Lord. You have my support for what it is worth, but I have no legal authority over the girl. Her mother and I were merely first cousins, making Penelope a first cousin once removed, I think. No, her legal guardian is my brother, and it is he who must give his permission before you can approach his ward with an offer of marriage. And he never comes to London. You will have to go to him, I'm afraid."

"Oh, I am sorry if my attentions to your charge have put you in an awkward position and will of course do as you say and write to Lord Frome today about the matter. If, as you believe, he requires me to travel to Yorkshire, then that is what I shall do."

Or he could forget all about it and simply walk away. He didn't like being cornered! Lady Dawson had caused his hackles to rise, but he knew he should have expected something like this to happen. Often, a suitor couldn't even *begin* a courtship without first obtaining permission from a girl's guardian. He forced himself to smile and took his leave, trying to convince himself that he was making the right decision.

Chapter Two

Three days later, while waiting to hear from Lord Frome, Alex learned that his cousin Percy had returned to town, so went to Boodle's club that evening in the hope of running into him. Alex always enjoyed catching up with his cousin Percy, who he viewed as a charming but irresponsible rogue; not too handsome, not too much of a gamester, and not too much of a ladies' man. Percy was a well-travelled man, sought after by many hostesses as a reliable, entertaining guest. He only had a small, regular income, but was so much in demand as a house guest that he never had to be troubled over a shortage of funds. It would be good to sound out Percy about his intended. After all, Percy knew just about everybody.

Boodles was situated in St James's Street and was renowned as one of the best men's clubs in London, so, even if he didn't see Percy, Alex knew he would still enjoy dining there. Every man of substance in London belonged to at least one such club. It was a place where they could go to relax alongside others of their own ilk. A place where they could find entertainment or just simply escape for a while from their many responsibilities. Alex expected that, even after he married, he would still frequent a club or clubs, especially when parliament was sitting.

When Alex entered the club rooms, he looked around and immediately spotted his cousin who was luckily on his own. Percy looked up from the paper he was reading almost as if he sensed that someone he knew had entered. "I say, Alex," he said enthusiastically, discarding the newspaper, "this is the first time I've seen you since you became the earl. Come, take a drink with me to celebrate your new-found status." Percy immediately signalled to a waiter who took his order for a bottle of champagne.

"Thank you, Percy," Alex responded, smiling at his cousin while settling into the comfortable leather chair next to him. "It's good to see you again. I hoped I might find you here. How are you keeping?"

"Couldn't be better," Percy replied. "And you and Aunt Prue?"

By the time all the familial enquiries on both sides had been put and answered, the champagne had arrived, and Percy promptly proposed a toast to the new earl. Alex tried to smile as he accepted his cousin's good wishes, but truly thought there was little to celebrate. As he drank the champagne, he thought it more as drowning his sorrows, his mind reflecting on what he was leaving behind. The army, his comrades-in-arms and his *chere amie*, Jeanette.

Maybe the sadness must have shown in Alex's expression, if Percy's next comment was anything to go by. "It must have been hard for you to leave the army after all these years," Percy observed soberly, "even to become an earl. I know how much soldiering meant to you. Do you miss it terribly?"

Alex sighed. "I try not to but must admit that I do. It was my chosen career, after all. And even though I had to serve in a less rewarding posting after becoming my uncle's heir, I still hoped that it would be years before I became the earl. However, I am doing my best to accept the situation, and believe I am making headway. After all, I have no other choice, have I?"

"I suppose not. And I hear you have begun living the life of a country gentleman since the old earl died."

"Yes, I have spent time on the estate trying to come to grips with my responsibilities. That is my future now."

"I suppose so, but I hear you've even ditched that lovely mistress of yours. That's taking things a bit far, isn't it, old boy?"

"Jeanette ditched me, if you want the truth," Alex replied, leaving Percy to wonder what had happened while waiting for their glasses to be refilled.

"Jeanette ditched you?" Percy repeated as soon as they were alone again. "I find that hard to believe."

Alex sighed in resignation, not liking to discuss his personal relationships with anyone, but deciding that in this case, he had better elaborate a little.

"Well, it is true, my friend. You see, Percy, she chose to accept the offer of a new protector who could pay more attention to her than I am now able to do. I suppose it is probably just as well, you know, since the time has come for me to marry and set up my nursery."

"What a pity. About Jeanette, I mean. She seemed a devilishly attractive bit of fluff, if you don't mind me saying so, and seemed completely devoted to you. Never mind, old boy, you'll soon find another, I have no doubt."

"No, Percy, I am looking for a wife now, not a mistress."

"Can't imagine you staying faithful to a wife," commented Percy, frowning from the mere thought of it. "You're not going to change your lifestyle to that extent, are you, old man?"

Alex laughed. "Well, I'm going to try, at any rate."

"So, what I have heard is probably true, then."

"And just what *have* you heard?"

"Only that you are about to get yourself hitched. I understand you have already approached the young lady's guardian."

"Good Lord, Percy, how did you hear about that?"

Percy tapped the side of his nose. "A little bird told me all about it," he said with a chuckle. "You can't keep anything secret in this town. You should know that by now."

"Well, I doubt the rumour mill has got the story completely right. I haven't spoken with Penelope's guardian yet. Miss MacDonald, I suppose I should say. To do things properly, it seems that first off, before I can propose to her, I've got to ride to Yorkshire to speak to Lord Frome who is her guardian."

"Oh," Percy exclaimed, clearly surprised. "No, I haven't heard about that."

"What amazes me is how you have learned *anything* about it. How on earth has the story managed to get out so soon?"

"Can't help you there. It must have been at least third hand by the time I heard of it. So, you're off to Yorkshire, are you? God, but you're gullible, Alex. Get yourself the earldom, and before you know it, you settle down to matrimony! Do whatever your mother tells you, don't you, old boy?"

"No, Percy. I know what Mother wants, but I don't always follow her advice. However, in this, she is right. I am thirty now and have more responsibilities. One of which is to produce an heir. And since that must be my fate, I may as well marry someone who looks good enough to eat. Have you seen my intended, Percy? She is the sweetest girl in the world."

Percy laughed. "There are sweet-looking girls everywhere, old boy, as you know. We could go to visit that club where you met Jeanette and I could introduce you to some other lovely, very sweet morsels this very night, and you could have them any time you wanted, no thought of matrimony involved. Fancy it, Cos?"

"Not now, Percy, thanks all the same. Let me keep my illusions for a while at least," Alex said, laughing. His expression then changed. "But really Percy, that's why I am so pleased to see you. You seem to know all there is to know about everyone, and I need to pick your brains. Before

I head off to Yorkshire, I was wondering if you knew anything about my intended or her guardian, the Marquess of Frome."

"Only sought me out for advice, did you? Not for my company. I am cut to the quick! But, really Alex, you can't be that sure of her if you need my advice. Marriage is a serious step to take, old boy. Maybe you should slow down a bit. Take the time to make sure."

"You know how these things work, Percy. I have called on her several times, but she is difficult to get to know when she is so closely chaperoned. And anyway, that dragon of a chaperone of hers has told me that I cannot call on her again without her guardian's permission."

"Well, Alex, what can I say? I don't know the chit at all, I'm afraid. Only know she is an orphan who has been living with her guardian in Yorkshire for three or four years. Apparently, before that, she lived with an aunt. Don't know anything about her parents, I'm afraid, except that they weren't rich. I've never met her guardian, the Marquess of Frome, either. Even though he lives at Hoddam Hall, close to where friends of mine reside as it happens. But he doesn't go into society much. He never married, I believe, and from what I have heard he is a rather boring fellow, more interested in his inventions than in people. Can't imagine him being much fun to live with. Especially for a young girl."

"Well, I expect I shall be meeting the fellow soon, boring or not. Hopefully, my journey will not be wasted. Thank you, Percy."

"I doubt I have said anything to help you, so I don't know why you are thanking me."

"It is what you *haven't* said that has been the most helpful. If there were any scandal surrounding the girl, I am sure you would have heard something about it."

"Probably," Percy agreed. "And your wife would have to be free of scandal, wouldn't she?"

"But of course. Another thing, Percy. Perhaps you could help me with the arrangements for my journey, assuming he invites me, that is. How to get to Lord Frome's seat and the best route to take. Where to stay and that sort of thing. I am right in thinking you are familiar with that part of the world, aren't I?"

"You certainly are old thing. You have come to the right man for that kind of information. And I don't know why you are doubting the success of your suit. Of course you'll be accepted. Why, the girl hasn't even got a title. And as I told you, the news is already out. If you really do have any doubts, Alex, you must be the only one who has!"

Percy didn't pause to hear Alex's response, proceeding instead to explain the best route to take to Hoddam Hall, before adding, "And if you wish a little dalliance on the way, you will be passing close to Lady Margaret Greene's place. Heard of her, haven't you?"

"No, indeed I haven't. And as I have already told you, I am not looking for any more dalliances."

"Well, if you change your mind…"

"I won't, so stop trying to tempt me."

Percy shrugged. "Oh well, it's up to you, but she is reputed to be quite a beauty. Well-endowed if you know what I mean. And, although she lives a supposedly quiet life with her widowed mother and her young daughter, I know for a fact that she has entertained several gentlemen over the years, and all of them have returned to town with a smirk on their faces and such stories of passion! And you can have this little liaison without anyone knowing. That's the beauty of it, old boy. For she never comes to town. Wouldn't be received if she did. The scandal of her divorce, you know."

"Good Lord, Percy! Far from tempting me, you have offended me if you think I would be interested in a woman with a young girl who carries on with a series of men under the same roof. You had better tell me where this lady of dubious virtue resides so I can make sure to stay well away from her district."

"Oh, you crafty dog!" Percy said, amidst a gale of laughter, "Pretending to be such a puritan, aren't we? But I will tell you where she lives, old boy, and you can keep the reason for knowing to yourself."

After giving Alex the information, Percy added, "And I repeat, no-one need ever know if you choose to spend a little time with a beautiful and available woman while you are in the north."

"And *I* repeat. I am not interested. What age is this divorced woman's daughter, anyway.? Old enough to know what is going on? And what about the mother? What has she to say about it?"

"Hold on, Alex. How am I supposed to know? I haven't been one of her paramours, more's the pity. But she wasn't actually divorced. Her husband died before matters were finalised. Otherwise, she wouldn't have been allowed to have custody of her daughter. I believe the daughter is about ten, and the mother is a chronic invalid, if I remember correctly."

"Heavens, Percy. This obliging widow must be nearing thirty at least! Hardly in the first blush of youth! And I suppose her husband sued for divorce because he was cuckolded!"

"Well yes, in a way. The daughter's parentage isn't in doubt, apparently. But she was caught in bed with one of his best friends, of all people."

"Must have killed that friendship, if friendship it was."

"On the contrary. The two men remained the best of friends. Both belonged to a set of neck-or-nothing young blades if I remember it rightly."

"Some sort of marriage that must have been if a friendship took precedence. I can't imagine remaining friends with anyone who treated a wife of mine with such disrespect."

Percy agreed, and soon their interest in the subject waned. They spent the rest of the evening discussing politics, the latest gossip, and military campaigns.

* * *

The day after the awaited invitation from the Marquess of Frome arrived Alex set out, accompanied by his valet, Jenkins, who he had inherited from the previous earl, and two coachmen. He also took with him his favourite mount, Firefly, a chestnut roan which he rode for as much of the journey as he could. After all, he wasn't in any hurry to seal his fate. He decided that he may as well make the best of the trip north, especially as the weather was now getting warmer and the days longer. Alex managed to enjoy a good gallop every day on Firefly, travelling in the coach with his valet for the remainder of the time, stopping frequently at the inns recommended to him by Percy.

The Marquess had suggested Alex spend at least three nights at Hoddam Hall, presumably to give him enough time to decide whether he approved of the match and, assuming he did approve, for the settlements to be drawn up. After that, Alex would have to consider himself to be as good as betrothed, subject to Penelope's acceptance, which meant he was committed and could not back out. A gentleman could never withdraw from a marriage contract. Not without ruining his reputation once and for all.

He understood how the system worked and knew that, if their betrothal followed the expected pattern, he and Penelope would rarely be left alone before their wedding. Only then, when they were thrust into each other's company on a wedding trip, would they have the chance to really get to know one another. The system was enough to fill any sane man with trepidation.

Despite what he had told Percy, he had little doubt about being accepted by Penelope's guardian. Even though Lord Frome had a more exalted title than Alex's earldom, Alex had inherited a prosperous estate with a generous income from that and other investments. He wasn't a gamester, he was aware of no hidden family scandals, and more importantly in his opinion, Penelope was apparently in favour of the match, as was his mother. He also liked the girl, finding her a little shy, perhaps, but with a promise of warmth in her dark brown eyes.

By the time he reached Hoddam Hall, Alex had prepared himself mentally for the many questions he was sure his host would ask him, but this interrogation did not eventuate. The Marquess met Alex on the steps of Hoddam Hall, greeting him with a beaming smile of welcome. He was a portly gentleman who must have been on the wrong side of fifty, Alex guessed. His affable nature and smiling countenance immediately made Alex feel welcome and before long he found himself very comfortably settled in a spacious apartment with rooms for himself and his valet, plus an attached bathroom which contained a fitted bath and toilet! Were these Lord Frome's inventions? he wondered.

At dinner that first evening, Lord Frome explained that he felt no need to examine Alex's credentials further because, besides the letter written by Alex, he had also received one from his sister. "She sang your praises, I can tell you," the Marquess told Alex cheerfully, before relating just what the lady had said about him.

If Alex was surprised by Lady Dawson's effusive recommendation, it was nothing compared to the shock he received later that evening when the two gentlemen had retired to the library with a brandy for a discussion of the settlements. When Alex learned of the size of Penelope's dowry, he was astounded. It was more than generous and had obviously been provided by her guardian.

"Good gracious!" Alex exclaimed. "Had that been known she would have had every bachelor in town seeking her hand. Perhaps by the time I return, she may have found another suitor."

Lord Frome immediately waved aside this as a possibility. "Oh no, now that you have my consent to ask for her hand, the matter is settled as far as I am concerned."

Alex demurred no more, and as soon as the details of the marriage contract were finalised the two men then sat back, appreciating the good brandy.

"I must confess my relief at being able to shortly hand over my responsibility for my ward to another," Lord Frome admitted to Alex.

"Not that I don't care for the girl," he hastened to add. "But I am one of those people who like my own company and prefer a quiet life. Never married, you know. Not in the petticoat line, I'm afraid. Luckily, my brother and heir has produced several sons, securing the line of succession for the future."

"And does your brother reside nearby?" Alex probed.

"No, he resides on another inherited property in the South-west. Rarely see him, but that suits us both. I am not one of those who like frivolous entertainments, and I find his wife rather overbearing. She refused to take young Penelope under her wing, you know. Very unkind of her in my view since Penelope is a cousin of ours in a way and has few living relatives. Her mother was an only child and her father, Iain MacDonald, had only the one sibling, a sister, the aunt Penelope lived with until her death. I would still have been her guardian but believe it would have been better for someone else to have had the task of her general care. Not that I was unhappy to do it, of course."

"It sounds as if you have been her guardian for a longer time that I had assumed," Alex commented.

"Ever since her parents tragically died," he confirmed. "I was appointed as her Godfather when she was born and was happy to do that as well. She only had one grandparent living, Iain's father, but he lived in the wilds of Scotland, and apparently, he and his son didn't get along. Not sure why, but these things happen in families as I am sure you know.

"I had no idea that I had been named as her guardian in her father's will, but then, nobody thought that the provision would ever be required I suppose. Came as a bit of a shock to me, I can tell you. But I knew my duty and was very glad to learn that the aunt she was already living with wanted to continue to care for

Penelope, so I stayed out of the picture except for the financial and legal stuff." Lord Frome stopped then and took a sip of his brandy before continuing.

"When her aunt died, I asked both my sister and brother to have her live with them, but Celia couldn't help at that time and my brother refused to help, so Penelope came to live with me, along with her governess and a maid. I must confess I had little to do with her at first, leaving her in the hands of her governess for most of the time. During the past year, I took more of an interest in the girl, feeling it was my duty to socialise with my neighbours; parties and all that nonsense, you know. Not things I enjoy as you will have guessed. I prefer to spend my time with my inventions. You have probably noticed one of them already. I hope you like the bathroom attached to your bedchamber?"

"I do indeed."

"And did you notice that the bath is plumbed in?"

"I did but haven't tried it yet. Is it one of your inventions then?"

"Well, I can't take all the credit as I did adapt an existing invention. But it is better than the usual hip bath brought in by servants, eh?"

"Indeed, it is a most rare luxury, as is the fixed water closet. Another of your ideas?"

This enquiry gave Lord Frome the opening he needed to talk at length about his hobby, promising to take Alex round the estate the following morning including to the shed where he worked on his inventions, and Alex listened politely until he felt it late enough to retire for the night.

During the following two days, Lord Frome happily gave Alex a tour of Hoddam Hall and the extensive gardens, with Alex finding himself impressed by the history of the place. The outside stonework of the hall had vigorous vines clinging to the thick walls, flourishing so well that they were even encroaching on some of the small, mullioned windows. The gardens included both formal and informal areas, the latter laid out with shrubs and trees amidst vast areas of well-kept lawns. Further afield, Alex could see that the lawns led down to a large, artificial lake and beyond the lake were hills, fields, and forested areas disappearing into the distance.

Lord Frome was also very keen to show Alex the shed where he worked on his inventions which included a grass cutting machine. Alex heard at length about the rotating blades and every aspect of the latest version being developed, realising just how passionate and dedicated the marquess was about his hobby, almost to the exclusion of all else. Could Penelope have been happy living with the Marquess? Somehow, he doubted it.

But getting Lord Frome to talk about Penelope proved to be a lot more difficult than talking about his own interests, and it wasn't until his last evening at the Hall that Alex decided to force the issue by asking direct questions about Penelope's life in Yorkshire. The first thing he learned was that six months after Penelope came to live with her guardian, her governess left.

"Penelope persuaded me not to employ a new governess and even turned up her nose at the idea of me hiring a companion for her," Lord Frome told Alex.

"Why did she do that?" Alex asked, genuinely perplexed.

"No idea. I suppose she preferred just having her maid and visiting tutors. She had several of those at one time or another, including a riding instructor, art teacher, dancing instructor, piano teacher and one for general stuff like deportment and all that nonsense. She seemed happy enough but as she grew older, I knew I had to introduce her to the neighbourhood so she could get used to mixing socially with the local gentry."

"And did she make any friends?"

"Not that I know of. There were a couple of younger girls in the neighbourhood, but she never invited them here."

"Did she have any admirers?'

"Oh, I am sure she did, but most of my neighbours are older people, married and settled in life. There were no eligible bachelors around." The Marquess looked slightly embarrassed as he spoke, and Alex wondered at the cause.

The Marquess coughed and put down his napkin at this point, suggesting that since the meal was over, they should retire to the billiard room for a game. Alex got the impression the Lord Frome was deliberating trying to avoid speaking about Penelope's social life so instead asked about her parents. He already knew that she was the daughter of one of Lord Frome's female cousins, but knew little about her father, who had been described to him as a charming Scot by the name of Captain Iain MacDonald.

"He served in India with Lord Wellesley, the elder brother of the Duke of Wellington, you know."

Alex raised his eyebrows in surprise. "No, I did not know. How extraordinary!"

"What is extraordinary about it?"

"Well Miss MacDonald and I seem to have more in common than I had thought. Not only are we both the offspring of soldiers, but both our fathers served in India at one time, and the two may even have been acquainted."

"Unlikely," Lord Frome said, shaking his head. "Both Penelope's parents died shortly after arriving in India, struck down by a tropical disease."

"Goodness, that is terrible. How did Penelope cope with such devastating news?"

"Pretty cut up I would imagine. But she wasn't with them, you know. Her parents had chosen to leave her in England in the care of her maiden aunt when they sailed to India. That's the same woman Penelope lived with until she came here to Yorkshire. So, I don't think it likely that your father and Penny's ever met. Possible, but not probable, I'd say."

"It does seem unlikely, I agree."

Later that night, as Alex prepared for bed, he thought over all he had learned about his intended and wondered how she must have felt, an only child separated from her parents. Then the news of their deaths, followed only two years later by the death of her substitute mother. One move after the other, ending up with a fusty middle-aged bachelor, albeit a wealthy one. He decided that he would have to do his best to supply more stability and joy in her life. Which also meant that he must have finally made peace with the idea of marriage to Penelope, he realised.

The morning of Alex's departure finally arrived, but before he set out, Lord Frome extended an open invitation to both him and his mother, saying he hoped they would be his houseguests during the Christmas season. "I know it's a long way off," he added, "but it will give you and Penny the opportunity to meet each other in an informal setting. I hope my sister, Celia, will allow Penny to stay with her in London for a while longer. After all, a girl like her is bound to prefer the life there. But when she does return here, know that there is a welcome for you here as well."

Alex thanked his host for his generosity while explaining that since he had spent little time at Knopton yet, he would need to retire there at the end of the season to continue learning about its management. "But when Penelope returns here, I will no doubt accompany her as her escort. Then, at the end of the year, I should be only too pleased to accept your hospitality if my mother is agreeable. Thank you, Lord Frome, you have been most welcoming and kind."

"Don't mention it, dear boy. You are welcome here any time. And when next you come, I may have made some more progress with my grass cutter, eh? Although I expect you'll be giving all your attention to young Penny and won't want to spend time with an old twaddler like me!"

Alex politely assured his host of his interest in the grass cutter, thanked him again for his hospitality, and departed on horseback, his preferred mode of travel. Unlike on his journey north, Alex had been able to reserve rooms at the various hostelries for the return trip, and was therefore able to send his servants, chaise, and portmanteaux on ahead, allowing himself the indulgence of enjoying a quiet, cross-country ride.

The weather that day was mild with a gentle, cooling breeze and Alex made good time, travelling across country as much as possible, giving his horse his head. He stopped for a light luncheon at a pleasant inn in Tadcaster, remaining for sufficient time to rest his horse, before continuing at a more leisurely pace in the afternoon. He had no intention of hurrying home, where a life of duty awaited him.

He would formerly propose to Penelope on his return to London, the wedding would be arranged and afterwards he and Penelope would begin their married life on his estate. Eventually they would have children, he hoped, with one of them being a little boy, his heir.

His thoughts continued to linger on what his future might look like as he continued his journey, taking little interest in the scenery as he cantered along a narrow lane which wound through a thicket of trees. Suddenly, he lurched to the side, clutching his horse's mane, as that animal charged down the lane, through a village and across open fields, frantic after being frightened by a loud retort that had made him bolt and his master slump in the saddle.

Alex felt himself losing consciousness and struggled to hang on to his galloping steed. Bloody hell, he thought, I've been hit in the back by a bullet! Safe in battle and now felled by a bloody footpad or highwayman!

He knew he would not have the strength to sit straight in the saddle and instead talked to his horse, Firefly, calming the animal sufficiently for it to slow to a walk. No-one had caught up with him so far, he reasoned, so maybe his horse had outrun the attacker. Alex tried to raise his head to see if anyone was following him and to make out the lay of the land, but dizziness assailed him, and he had no choice but to cling on to Firefly and allow the animal to take him where it would.

His last conscious thought was that he must be somewhere in the vicinity of Percy's infamous Lady Margaret Greene!

Chapter Three

The Widow

"Where is the child now?" complained Lady Margaret Greene's mother for the third time. "I don't know why you allow her to go off on her own all the time, Meg. It isn't proper!"

Meg sighed in resignation. She had heard this argument many times before. Her mother may have lost the use of her legs, but she still had a sharp tongue!

"Yes Mama, I know how you feel about it. You've told me often enough. But she is my child, and I'll bring her up as I wish."

"I don't know how she is going to end up, really I don't," mumbled the older woman, "what with one thing and another. Buried here in the country, with no suitable friends. Not even a governess! I sometimes think it would have been better if she had stayed with *his* family. But then, they obviously didn't love her as we do, or they wouldn't have returned her to you, I suppose."

"Yes Mama, I know your views, only too well." Meg continued with her task of mending the hem of her unmentionables. "But if you think I would have given Emily up without a fight, you are very wrong. She belongs with me, and wants to be with me, which is more to the point."

"Who wouldn't want to stay here, spoiled as she is."

Meg opened her mouth to respond to this diatribe, but then thought better of it. Her mother was just letting off steam, as usual. Meg knew her mother loved Emily dearly and that she would be devastated if her granddaughter was ever wrenched from them again.

Getting no reply, her mother turned her attention to her daughter's behaviour instead. "And that's another thing. Why do you do your own mending? You know it's Alice's job. Just because she is too lazy to put in a good day's work, you shouldn't do it for her. Lazy piece, she is. Don't know why you keep her on."

"You know perfectly well why we keep her on, Mama. She has been with us for years. And stayed loyal, throughout all the scandal and everything. Few did, you know. Stay loyal to me, that is. I'm not going to repay her by replacing her. And anyway, she is not lazy. I am mending because I enjoy mending. I find it soothing. It takes my mind off other things."

"That's as may be, but if you ask me, you need your mind *on* other things. What's going to happen to us, that's what I worry about. Emily is growing up a savage. And no one will want to marry a girl whose mother .... well, you know what I mean. The least you could do is teach her ladylike behaviour."

Meg had heard these words so many times over the years that she rarely let them bother her, but today, for some reason, they did. Yet, deep down, she believed that she was doing what was right for her daughter. Like many others of the time, Meg was impressed with the Rousseau theory of education, which advocated that children up to the age of twelve learn more through physical activity and play, and through the example set by their parents, rather than by the study of formal school subjects.

Meg believed Rousseau's words, *"To learn to think we must exercise the limbs, senses and organs, which are the instruments of intellect"*. Whether she was influenced at all by her concern that a reputable governess may not wish to accept a post in her employ, she preferred not to contemplate, but she was certainly hoping that in a few more years, when Emily was twelve, enough time would have passed to lessen the chance of someone connecting her name with scandal.

As to the second part of her mother's complaint, Meg knew that *her* scandal was not the only skeleton in her family's closet! But she also knew her past was bound to affect Emily. It would always be there to haunt them all.

And knowing that her own mother couldn't bring herself to talk openly about the past didn't help. She bit her trembling lower lip to control her emotions, needing to at least appear unruffled, otherwise she feared she might scream her outrage aloud.

After she had calmed sufficiently to think clearly, but not enough to let the matter drop, she responded to her mother's latest attack. "Emily is naturally ladylike, Mama. And I will teach her all she needs to know at the right time. She is only nine, for goodness' sake. Let her have a childhood. At least I have some things to be thankful for through all the hurt. Lucas' parents have left me alone. In their hearts, I believe they know the truth, but I also know they will never admit it. Not to me, not to anyone."

"No need to get into a temper with me, Meg. I don't know why you must bring up the past all the time. I only want Emily to behave like other young girls, that's all."

"You brought up the past, Mama," Meg said, but added when she saw her mother's disbelieving expression, "All right. I'm sorry. And I'm not in a temper with you."

Meg knew it was useless to argue with her mother. And she knew she shouldn't. Her mother was only concerned, after all. And her sharp words were merely her way of dealing with life's disappointments. Just as her own often were. She knew her mother perceived herself as being a useless invalid, and Meg therefore tried very hard not to be impatient or angry with her, especially as Emily hated to see the two most important people in her life arguing with each other.

It wasn't as if Meg wasn't used to her mother's tirades by now. She had been this way for as long as Meg could remember. Ever since the riding accident which left her mother paralysed from the waist down. Meg had been barely five at the time, but all along had seemed to understand that her mother's anger was really directed at herself, not at others. Meg also suspected that if her mother lost the anger, she would likely go into a decline.

Chiding herself on her short temper, Meg put her mending aside, saying cheerfully as she moved to the door, "I'll go and see about dinner. What would you like?"

Her mother seemed to be considering the question but before she could answer, her granddaughter rushed into the room, looking dishevelled and leaving a trail of mud behind her as she ran to her mother.

"Mama, Mama, you must come ... at once ..." the child gasped out between breaths, while tugging at her mother's skirt. "Pleeeease ... hurry. There's a man ... and he's ... covered in blood ..."

Meg held her daughter's shoulders trying to pacify her. "Emily, darling, slow down. I will come but please wait a moment. Tell me what's happened," she asked as calmly as she could.

"I haven't time. Mama, you must come ... now ... he needs help. I'll tell you about it later."

Meg looked anxiously across at her mother, who was too dumbfounded to speak, and then allowed her daughter to pull her out of the door. As they rushed through the hallway, Meg called, "Alice, Alice. Get Jed and tell him to follow me. Someone is injured. Quick, Alice, do you hear me?"

"Lordy me," exclaimed a flustered Alice, appearing from the direction of the kitchen, wiping her hands on her apron, "What did you say? Who's injured?"

"Never mind, Alice. Just get Jed to follow me." And without waiting to listen to any further comment, she rushed from the house after her daughter, who was racing down to the stream, calling for her mother to hurry.

"Hurry Mama, hurry ... He came out of those trees, struggling to walk, but he kept falling ... oh there he is ... do you see?"

And indeed, there was a man, trying to walk towards them. But he only managed to stagger, being barely able to stand.

As they approached, he saw them and called to them, holding out one hand which was dripping blood, "Ma'am ... sor...sorry ... to trouble you ... been shot ... in the back."

Meg and Emily reached him, and immediately Meg took his other arm, also soaked in blood, and wrapped it across her shoulders, behind her head, trying to take his weight as she hung on to his hand. "Come, lean on me," she said, "we must get you to the house."

She had no concern for her safety, sensing from the way he had approached them that he meant them no harm. Apart from which, he was badly injured and wouldn't be able to stand for much longer, let alone attack anyone. But where had he come from and what had caused him to be shot? Time for that later, she decided. She could see a dark red, wet patch and a small hole in the fabric of the man's coat confirming to her that he had indeed been shot and that he had obviously lost a lot of blood. He needed help urgently.

As did she, she soon discovered. She was finding it almost impossible to make any headway and looked up in relief as she saw Jed lumbering down the slope. Meg saw that he was taking in the situation as he ran, noticing the man and, in the distance, a saddled horse which he pointed out to her. "That horse must belong to the gentleman," he called out as he drew near. "I will help you with this fellow, milady. As soon as I can, I will send young Peter to get the horse."

Meg nodded, knowing that Peter, the young lad who helped with the gardening, was passionate about horses and would relish such a task. By that time, Jed had reached them, and, without hesitating, he picked the man up in his arms, carrying him like a baby, while being careful to avoid pressing on the man's wound. "You should 'ave waited for me, milady. Look at you, all covered in blood now as well. I'll get him to the house. You look after Emily."

Emily, of course, didn't want to be looked after. She skipped on ahead, excitedly leading the way. "Will he die?" she said, turning towards them and running backwards, looking a bit worried.

"No," was Meg's immediate response, even though she did not know that for sure. She did not think that Emily understood what death really was even though her father had died. Emily still sometimes referred to her father as though he were still alive, although that happened less and less as the years passed, but Meg believed it may be better for Emily to think of her father as just not being there with them. Of course, Emily had seen a few dead animals, as one would expect, living as she did in the country, but like other children of her age, Meg was not sure that she understood all the implications of death.

"Shall I run and tell Grandmama?"

"No, you will wait for me." Meg quickly caught up with her daughter, taking her hand while giving her a reassuring smile. "We'll go together. It is up to us to clear the way so that Jed can bring the injured gentleman to a bedchamber. I think he's going to need to rest, don't you?"

"Oh yes," Emily approved, "and then we'll have to wash all that horrible blood off him, won't we?"

"Well, he'll certainly have to be washed," agreed Meg, amazed that her daughter seemed so unaffected by seeing a man bleeding so badly. "But not by us, Emily. Alice can see to him while Jed rides for the physician. You can come with me, and we can clean ourselves up."

Emily frowned at that suggestion. "But Mama, can't I stay with Alice? I'm sure I'll be able to help."

"I'm sure you could help, Emily. You have already helped, haven't you? It was you who found him and sought help for him."

"I did, didn't I?" Emily agreed, grinning with pride.

"Yes, but we now must see to ourselves. Alice will ask for our help if she needs it. We can go and see him when we have changed. All right?"

Emily seemed happier with these words, and as by then they had reached the house, they rushed past Alice, who was keeping the door open for them, and dashed up the stairs to the linen cupboard, Meg grabbing some sheets and taking them to a spare bedchamber where Alice met them. Between the three of them, the bed was prepared for their patient by the time Jed entered the room, panting only a little from his exertions.

He was a big man, and had the strength of an ox, or so it seemed. Being married to Alice, he had also been employed by the family for many years and loved his mistress as if she were one of his own. He was originally a gardener, but acted now more like a steward, or factotum, not only in charge of the stables and the gardens, but also the maintenance of the house, employing outside help to do most of the manual labour.

He laid the injured man carefully on the bed. "He'll be making a mess, I'm thinking. But leave him to me and Alice. We'll have him cleaned up and the sheets changed. I'm thinking he will be needing a doctor, milady. Shall I go to Tadcaster after I have him settled? It's a fair ride and I doubt I will be back before nightfall."

"Thank you, Jed. Those were my thoughts as well. And perhaps you should inform the magistrate while you are there. Not that he will be able to do anything about it," she added. She then turned to her daughter. "You see Emily, we're not needed here. Come, let's go and change."

Emily couldn't take her eyes off the man on the bed. "But we can't leave now," she protested, "we must find out who he is and what happened. Isn't he lovely, Mama? Look at all those blond curls."

"Yes, Emily, he does have nice curls, and we will find out who he is, but not now. He needs to have his wounds tended to first." Meg then took her daughter's hand, leading her from the room.

Meg had also noticed his blond curls, and his strong, angular, handsome features and could remember the warmth of him as she had held him earlier. She hadn't touched a man for so long. His body was hard and muscular as well as warm, she knew. While one hand had supported his arm, her other hand had gone around his back. Broad shoulders too, she remembered. Her heart was beating faster even thinking about him. She gave herself a mental shake. *I'm not going to touch him again*, she resolved. *Or even think of him as a man.* After all, she reminded herself, a man was the last thing she needed.

Alex was still conscious, but only just. The effort he had made to stumble towards the nearest buildings had taken their toll, and now he lay there on a bed, silent, allowing the words to wash over him. He loved the voice of the woman who had come to his aid, and vaguely remembered some of her words. She had been speaking to a little girl, clearly her daughter. And then he had heard them leave the room.

Just as well, because the two older people in the room then began to remove his clothing. He knew he should make the effort to talk to his rescuers, telling them who he was and how he came to be there, but instead, he gave in to his fatigue, closing his eyes, allowing his rescuers to undress him and tend to his wound as they saw fit.

Alex knew the woman was talking to him as they tried to make him comfortable but found himself only half listening. He vaguely remembered her introducing herself as Alice and her husband as Jed, explaining their position in the household to him. But when Alice told him that the name of their mistress was Lady Margaret Greene, Alex found himself paying much more attention! Lady Margaret Greene! Great heavens!

He tried to hide his sudden interest, which luckily turned out to be easier than he would have imagined, because he found himself feeling decidedly light-headed and tired. As well as suffering from a substantial amount of pain.

He felt considerably better after his wound had been dressed, he was glad to note, and found himself alone with Alice sitting by his bed, her husband having left the room. Alex listened as she told him that it was Lady Margaret Greene who had come to his aid along with her daughter, Emily. After a while he felt alert enough to have a conversation with Alice, trying to explain what had happened to him, but soon tiredness overcame him again.

He must have slept, because the next thing he became aware of was the mother and daughter returning. Lady Margaret Greene and Emily. He knew it was them even though he couldn't see them. He was lying on his stomach, naked now to the waist, with a sheet covering his lower body.

Alex could hear the rustle of skirts and was aware of a floral fragrance that pleased his senses.

"How is he, Alice?" Lady Margaret asked as she approached the bed.

"He'll live," Alice replied. "As you can see, we have dressed his wound as best we could with a wad of gauze, and the bleeding has stopped."

Alice's words made him try to turn his head to see what this supposed beauty looked like. He had hardly glanced at her earlier, but knew she was younger than he had thought she would be, and remembered she had deep auburn tresses which had been covered by a silly looking, but delightful, lace cap. He winced with pain from the effort of moving his head, letting it fall back to the pillow.

"Stay where you are, young man," chided Alice in a firm, but kindly voice. "You will likely start the bleeding again if you move. And I don't want to have to change the sheets a third time."

"Sorry," Alex murmured.

Alice then turned to Lady Margaret, asking her if her mother knew what was happening. Ah, the invalid mother that Percy had told him about, Alex thought.

"Yes, Emily and I popped in to see her and told her all we knew. I've had to promise to go back as soon as I can," she added with a smile.

"Well, this young man has been telling me what happened ... at least, what he knows of it, anyway. It seems he was riding along, minding his own business, when a single shot rang out. Luckily for him, it didn't get him in the middle of his back, but up there, near his right shoulder. The ball didn't go right through, which could mean trouble, but we will have to wait and see what damage it has done. Obviously missed all vital organs though, thank the Lord," she added.

"He has introduced himself, and to save him the effort, for he's mighty tired, you know, I'll tell you who he is. Lord Tenby is his name. Ever heard of him? Says he's only recently come into his title, so you probably haven't. Wilde is his family name. Alexander Wilde."

"No, I don't think we have ever met, have we, my lord?" Lady Margaret began, as she walked round the bed so that he could see her. "My name is Margaret Greene, and this is my daughter, Emily. I believe you already know my friend and housekeeper, Alice here, and her husband, Jed. He's the one who carried you to this room."

Alex heard her voice before she came into view, loving the sound, thinking it as smooth as honey. It was a voice he knew he would never get tired of hearing. And then she came into view, and he first noticed the skirt of her dress, it being on the same level as his eyes. It was made of a rather plain brown material, he noted. Then he focussed on her hands. Finely boned, delicate hands, folded together tightly for some reason. No rings on her fingers, and no fancy bracelets on her wrists.

Slowly, as his eyes travelled up her body, they came to rest for a brief time on her magnificent bosom, and, despite his fatigue, he felt his body respond! Even though she was wearing a lace modesty shawl, and the waistline of her dress was not as high as the latest fashion dictated, nor the neckline as low, she couldn't disguise the fact that she had been blessed with the most stunning breasts. He quickly forced his eyes higher, and was struck by her almost translucent skin, pale as porcelain.

He then took in her long, graceful, slender neck, before travelling upwards to her face. First, he noticed her strong, square jaw, which suggested stubbornness. Yet the rest of her face was purely feminine. It was a beautiful face, he thought. Somehow, the combination of the two facets of her face, softness, and strength, had between them created a woman of incredible beauty.

Then his eyes met hers. Dark blue eyes looking into startled grey ones, their light grey centre ringed with a distinct, dark grey border. Their eyes connected for only a moment, but immediately his body responded again. This time, he felt himself begin to harden, and almost smiled despite the pain in his shoulder - he wasn't dead yet!

Unable to resist, he then purposefully lowered his gaze to her bosom again and noticed that she was clearly disturbed by his perusal, her rapid breaths evident in the rise and fall of her chest. Was she merely embarrassed or did she perhaps also like what she saw?

Shifting his now sensuous gaze back to her face, he noticed that her cheeks had suddenly changed colour. She was blushing! A blush from such an experienced woman? How strange, he thought. As strange as her simple gown and lack of jewellery. Not at all what he had expected.

Chapter Four

Meg noticed his scrutiny, of course, and felt her colour rising, in part due to the unwanted effect his bold look was having on her body. She tried to hide her embarrassment by continuing to speak to him as calmly as she could. "I have sent for a physician, but it will be a while before he arrives, I'm afraid. Perhaps you would like me to send word to someone, my lord? I expect there is someone who will start worrying about you when you don't arrive at your destination on time."

She was glad when he responded to her question without any hint of disrespect. "My valet. Yes. He can be found at the Fox and Hounds in Selby. Could I let him know to come here with some of my things? There are two others as well, accompanying my baggage."

"That will be no problem. We have room here for all of them. But what about letting your family know?"

"God, no," he managed to say. "I was on my way to my town house in London, returning after a brief visit with The Marquess of Frome. On no account must my mother be told. She would be frantic with worry. I'm her only surviving son, you see," he explained, having to pause between every few words to get his breath.

"But surely, when you fail to arrive home, she will be frantic with worry anyway. At least if we send word to her that you are alive, it will be better than leaving her having to guess the reason for your delay."

Alex frowned, clearly considering her words. He didn't answer immediately, but after a while said, "You are right, of course. I should send word. But not that I have been shot. Or even that I have had an accident. Either of those two messages would have my mother heading this way without further thought. No, I'll just say I met up with an old army friend and decided to use the opportunity to visit with him and catch up with old times. I will conveniently 'forget' to add my whereabouts in my message. That way, she will just have to accept the tale." He laughed then, before pain turned the sound into a groan. "Sorry. I was suddenly struck by the thought of how she will receive the news. She will think it typical of me, gadding around the countryside neglecting my responsibilities and failing to tell her where I am."

"Is there anyone else we should tell? What about this Lord Frome you were visiting?"

"No, no. Definitely not. I believe I had overstayed my welcome as it is. No, if I can just get word to my valet and my mother, that will be more than enough."

Meg nodded and turned to her daughter, finding her staring at the earl. She appeared to be fascinated with him, particularly at his half naked body. "Emily, will you go and fetch some writing paper and pen and ink for Lord Tenby, dear?"

Meg had to admit that she was equally fascinated by the man, her eyes lingering on the movement of the muscles in his back, shoulders, and arms. So powerful and virile. And then she quickly pulled herself together. She had no right to think of her uninvited guest in those terms!

"Yes, of course," Emily agreed. "But what about his horse?"

Meg noticed that Emily still had not taken her eyes off the earl!

Meg tried not to smile at her daughter's obvious fascination. "His horse? Oh, Jed saw to his horse, Emily. But thanks for reminding me about it." She turned to Lord Tenby, finding that he had closed his eyes. She hoped he hadn't fallen asleep. "My lord, sorry to bother you again, but I am sure you must be worried about your horse. He is now safely in the stables."

Alex opened his eyes, seemingly with reluctance. "Firefly? Oh, thank you again. I doubt he would have gone far as I managed to stay on his back until shortly before your daughter found me. I am afraid I have put you all to a great deal of trouble."

"Can I go and look at Firefly, Mama?"

Meg smiled, explaining to Lord Tenby about her daughter's love of horses.

"Perhaps after you get the writing materials, Emily" she said.

"All right, Mama." Then she turned back to the earl. "I would love to see you ride him, sir. Even better, I would love to ride by your side!"

"Now you are being fanciful, Emily," her mother chided. "Go and fetch the writing materials, and then you may look at the horse while his lordship's notes are being written, but I want you back here to take them to the village. I need you to ask Mr Bennett to ride to Selby with the note to his lordship's valet and leave the letter for London at his shop. Tell Mr Bennett that it is urgent and that I will sort it out with him later. It would be a great help to me if you did that for us, darling."

Emily smiled, clearly liking the thought of playing an even more important role in this saga. "Yes Mama," she readily agreed before running off to complete the first of her mother's requests.

Alice had been listening to this exchange with interest. "Perhaps it would be better if I were to take the letters to the village," she suggested to Meg. "And if not me, perhaps you could take the letters to the village yourself. Personally, I believe that I should be the one to stay with the earl. It isn't right for you to look after him."

Meg looked closely at Alice, wondering what she was thinking. Was Alice saying that because she was the head of the household, it would be beneath her to sit with a sick man? Or was she implying that it would be improper for her and the earl to be left alone together? Meg guessed it would be the latter. Perhaps Alice had noticed the look that had passed between herself and the earl, albeit very briefly. Oh dear!

"Don't be silly, Alice. I am happy to do my bit, and anyway, you saw how delighted Emily was when asked to run the errand for us. No, I will be fine staying here while the earl writes his notes, but could you go and find out what is delaying Emily please? She may need help in finding the writing materials. And after that, it might be wise to alert the stable hand about Emily's visit."

"If you say so, but I still say it's not a good idea for you to be left alone with the earl," Alice complained, but grudgingly went on her way.

"I am causing you too much trouble," Alex said to Meg, trying to stay awake, but beginning to lose the battle.

"You are not putting us to too much trouble, my lord. And I was thinking that it may be better for me to write down what you want to say," Meg suggested. "You are looking very tired and weak."

"I hate to impose on you, but perhaps you could do the one to my valet for me, if it is not too much trouble, but *I* must write to Mother," he stressed.

Within minutes, Emily came running in with the writing materials, gave them to her mother and dashed off again to see the horse, returning in time to leave on her second errand. In the meantime, the notes had been written and Alice had returned. With the letters on their way and Alice back in the room, Meg was free to tend to her other duties, leaving Alice to look after Lord Tenby. Meg felt a twinge of regret as she left the room despite telling herself repeatedly that he was nothing to her.

She went first to her mother and then to the kitchen to arrange for extra food to be prepared. Firstly, a nourishing Flemish soup for the patient, to be followed by poached fish served with a selection of garden vegetables and Hollandaise sauce. She knew that her mother would want only the fish, as she did herself, but Emily always had a hearty appetite and would eat all put before her, so also requested that a treacle tart be made.

After arranging for dinner to be delayed until six o'clock, an hour later than usual, to make up for the time lost in tending to the earl, Meg organised the rooms for her unexpected guest's servants, preparing the bedchamber adjoining his own for his valet, and another room on the third floor for the other two servants to share. Luckily, there were plenty of empty rooms for both guests and servants, due to the way she chose to live. She was well able to afford to employ as many servants as she wished, having inherited an income of over five thousand pounds a year from her husband's estate. But she knew he would never have settled such an amount on her if he had lived to complete the divorce proceedings, and she, therefore, spent as little as possible, living in a far smaller house than someone of her station would do normally, intending to pass on most of the fortune to her daughter, in addition to the generous settlement already set aside for her. She managed with few servants, most of those coming in daily from the village nearby. Only Alice, Jed and Sally, her mother's personal maid, lived in.

Of course, she knew that in a few years' time she would need to attempt to re-enter society, and this would entail spending lavishly on all the trappings of a fashionable lifestyle, probably firstly in Bath, where she hoped to be accepted as a respectable widow by the influential dowagers living there. She felt that, so long as she led a blameless existence, Emily should be able, one day, to contract a suitable marriage, all past scandals forgotten. After all, not only would she be a substantial heiress, but a beautiful one, Emily having inherited the same dark straight hair, the same large, deep brown eyes, and classic features of her handsome father.

Meanwhile, Meg was determined to live quietly in Wharfe House, her current home in Yorkshire, away from the *haut ton* and the gossipmongers, content to be with her family and her loyal servants.

Wharfe House had formerly been part of the Greene estates, but was unencumbered, and, as it was a good distance from the principal seat, her husband's family had allowed her to purchase both it and the small amount of land surrounding it.

It was a strange looking building which had originally been built by a local landowner who had decided to construct the main entrance in the shape of a Gothic arch, and to have a crenelated roof line, aiming to give it the appearance of being a small castle. The front section of the house, named after the river by which it stood, was three storeys' high and its facade was of white rendered stone, whilst at the back was a one storey high brick section. The whole was a bit of a mishmash, if truth be told, the back having been a later addition, constructed when the need for more kitchen and scullery space eventuated. However, despite these drawbacks, the house fitted in well with the landscape, with its row of poplar trees on one side of the long driveway, and set as it was on its own, amongst the gently sloping hills.

Even though Meg had lived in the house for over four years, she had made few changes to either the outside or inside. She found the place comfortable enough for their needs and had allowed a rather conservative interior decorator to furnish the rooms with solid, utilitarian pieces, leaving the rather dark wood-panelled walls intact. To Meg, the house was a refuge, not a permanent home.

She had made no close friends in the district, being unwilling to risk rejection, but was polite to those she met and felt that she was respected by those who knew her. Alice once told her that the locals considered her to be a charming, but self-contained person who liked her privacy. If true, Meg was content with that.

As for her husband's family, they preferred to pretend she didn't exist, blaming her for the death of their only son. She knew she would never be welcome at their home. Her daughter, Emily, went to them for a short visit each year, taken there and back by Alice. Meg knew that Emily was fond of her paternal grandparents, having lived with them during the scandal of the divorce, but also knew she had been eager to return to her mother when they eventually relinquished their claim on her after their son's death.

Meg had once tried to mend the rift between herself and Sir Henry and Lady Greene for Emily's sake, but to no avail. They seemed to believe that if she had been a better wife, their son would still be alive. Somehow, they had reasoned that their beloved Lucas would never have left her to follow his friends' reckless lifestyle if he had been happier at home. They were blind to the truth, she knew, and would never admit that the fault lay with their perfect son. Yet they had certainly done all they could to get her into the family, she observed cynically. Even though she had been so young at the time. Only fifteen, in fact. Far too young to marry. But Lucas would have only her. And she had been dazzled by his good looks and flattering attentions.

She remembered how wonderful she had thought him. This tall, dark, and handsome friend of her brothers. Before long she was hopelessly in love with him. Well, that is what she thought at the time, but realised later that she had really been in love with the man she imagined him to be.

At the time, however, she was only too eager for the match and encouraged her brother to negotiate on her behalf, he having become her guardian on the death of their father. She had not then been aware that her brother's eagerness for the match had nothing to do with Meg's best interests but only his own.

The deal was simple, his sister's hand in exchange for money. Enough money to clear him of all his many pressing debts as well as to set him up so that he could live in grand style for years to come. Sir Henry Greene was a mere baronet. He knew that an earl's daughter, even one tainted by scandal, would be considered a good catch for their son.

Meg pulled her thoughts back from her distressing past, took one last look around the room she had just prepared, decided she had not forgotten anything, and went to keep her mother company while waiting for the doctor to arrive. The hours drifted by, but with no sign of the doctor. Meg became more and more restless. The dinner hour came and went, but, despite Meg's preparations, their visitor did not wake. Dinner had to be served eventually, but Meg found she had little appetite for it. The only one to really appreciate it had been Emily!

The hour was late when Jed finally returned, and when Meg discovered that he had not brought the doctor with him, she let her frustration be known. It took Jed quite a while to get her to listen to his explanation, but eventually accepted the reason for the doctor's decision to wait until the following morning before operating on the patient. He had apparently asked Jed a series of questions, enough to ascertain that the patient's bleeding was under control, before announcing that it would be wiser for him to remove the ball in daylight as no matter how many candles were able to be provided, he wouldn't be able to see as well at night as during the day.

"Meanwhile," Jed continued to a now attentive listener, "he instructed me to ensure that the patient be given lots of water to drink and then be allowed to rest with the help of a sleeping draught." At that point, Jed produced a small bottle from his pocket which he handed to Meg.

"Thank you, Jed, and I'm sorry for that unseemly outburst. I wasn't angry at you, you know."

"I never thought so for a minute, ma'am," he said, "You was just worried, I know."

Meg thanked him again and suggested he go to the kitchen to get some food. After he had left, she looked at her mother. "I suppose I'd better see he gets this, then," she announced. "And something to drink."

"Doctors!" her mother said scathingly, "Let you die before they'd put themselves out!"

Meg tended to agree but didn't want her mother being rude to the man when he finally did arrive. "Now Mama, we must be reasonable. I can even see his point now that it has been explained to me." She sighed. "I won't be long, Mama. I'll be back as soon as I have taken his medicine to Alice. I wonder how long it will be until his servants arrive. I suppose I had better wait up for them."

"Don't see why you should have to wait on servants," her mother complained. "Let Alice wait."

"But Alice is sitting with Lord Tenby," she explained.

"Well, I'm going to bed, that's for sure. Call Jed to carry me up, will you?"

"Mama, let Jed rest and eat. He's only just arrived back. I'll come back in a moment and let you know how our guest is faring. Then we'll ask Jed to carry you up. All right?"

A "humph," and a shrug of the shoulders was the only reply Meg received.

On reaching the bedchamber, Meg asked Alice quietly if all was well. "He's as quiet as a lamb," Alice replied, keeping her voice just above a whisper. "He stirred a couple of times saying he was thirsty, but he would only drink water, not the soup you had left for him. He's been sleeping soundly for a while now."

"The physician gave Jed a sleeping draught for him, but I don't think we should wake him up to give it him now, do you?"

Alice chuckled at the suggestion, then covered her mouth with her hand to smother the noise, clearly concerned that she may wake him.

"Jed is back with the doctor, then?"

"Jed just got back but the doctor isn't coming till the morning. Hence the sleeping draught. I've sent Jed to get something to eat. You can go to him if you like. I'll sit here for a while."

"And the doctor's not coming till tomorrow? Well, I never. A lazy sod, he must be, then."

"No, not really. I was angry when Jed arrived back without him, but what he said made sense. Says he needs daylight to operate safely, and that Lord Tenby should be all right till the morning so long as he drinks plenty of fluids and rests."

"Well, he's had a fair amount to drink, at any rate. And a fair amount of rest. Maybe the doctor's right. I hope so, anyway. Wouldn't like to think he might die from lack of attention. I'll just stay here till his man arrives, then. Shouldn't be much longer, should it?"

"I hope not, Alice," Meg replied.

Meg returned to her mother and called for Jed to carry her up to her room before settling herself down with her sewing basket to wait for the earl's servants to arrive. Eventually she felt too tired to sew and she put her basket aside, sitting back and closing her eyes. Hopefully she would not have too much longer to wait.

In fact, it was almost midnight before the valet, Jenkins, arrived at their door, carrying a portmanteau. Meg jerked awake when she heard the knock, knowing that Jed would open the door for the new visitors. Nevertheless, she rushed to the hallway in time to see the door close behind the only person who had entered. She was about to ask where the others were when he apologised for arriving at such a late hour, introducing himself as the earl's valet and explaining that he had instructed the two coachmen to head to the stables before going to the servants' entrance.

After alerting Jed about the other staff, who assured her that he would see to them, Meg led the valet to the earl's bedchamber. On the way she ascertained that he had eaten and needed no refreshments.

As soon as he entered the room, he rushed to the bed, looked closely at the wounded man, then at Alice. "Thank God!" he exclaimed, and then sighed, adding, "And I thank you all for saving him. I can tell from his colour that although he is pale, he is not dying. Thank you, all of you."

After a pause, he went on, "But I can take care of him now. If you'll allow it, I'll make myself a pallet on the floor here. I don't want to put you to any more trouble, but if you would be kind enough to provide me with a blanket and perhaps a pillow, I shall be more than comfortable."

"That won't be necessary," Meg responded. "I have already prepared this room for you." Meg then showed him the adjoining room, eliciting further thanks. In fact, he kept saying thank you to Meg repeatedly, bowing frequently. Meg tried not to smile but couldn't help thinking that if he continued to bow so quickly, he would be in danger of losing his hairpiece!

She then apprised him of the doctor's instructions and advised him of his probable time of arrival, before taking her leave, accompanied by Alice. In the hallway, Meg turned to Alice. "I also have to thank you, Alice, as well as Jed, for all you have done, but hope that one thankyou will be enough."

"You had better save your breath, you cheeky lass, for there will be even more to do on the morrow."

Awaking the following morning, Meg felt as if she had had little sleep. Despite being someone who normally retired most nights shortly after ten, Meg had found herself still awake hours after retiring. Images of her uninvited guest had danced before her eyes. Inappropriate images that she was unable to dispel, no matter how hard she tried. A picture of his naked torso had come to mind, and she had imagined what it would feel like to touch it. Never had she had thoughts of that nature before. Not even with her husband.

Eventually, she must have dozed off again, for she woke from a deep sleep, noting the sunshine seeping into the room through the curtains. She lay there for a while but soon became restless to begin the day. On rising, she found the morning was already warm, so dressed herself in a light cream coloured muslin day gown, arranging her hair neatly on the top of her head, covering it with a clean mob cap made of the finest lace.

Emily arrived just before eight o'clock with a breakfast for two, comprised of hot chocolate and bread and butter. This was their normal, daily routine. Breakfast at eight in Meg's bedchamber. Ellen, Meg's mother, on the other hand, always spent the morning in her own rooms, tended to by Sally, her personal maid, until it was time for luncheon to be served.

Of course, that morning Emily wanted to talk about the earl making her desire to see him again perfectly clear, but Meg explained that he was waiting to see the doctor, who was due to arrive shortly, and that Emily would just have to show restraint. Meg told her about the events of the night before and promised her daughter that she would be allowed to pay their guest a visit if the doctor agreed to it.

Normally, Emily and her mother would go for a long walk after breakfast, looking at plants and birds, and anything else that took Emily's interest. They would then return home for Emily to draw or paint what they had seen, after which Meg would encourage her to read more about subjects that interested her. She would then spend time writing in her journal. Today, however, Meg felt she should stay indoors so she could be ready to assist the doctor if her help was needed, and when she explained this to Emily, the child was only too eager to agree.

"That doesn't mean you can visit the earl, Emily. Or that you can escape from your studies. You can spend time in the library reading."

Emily frowned. "What do I have to read?"

"Choose any book you like."

Emily seemed happy with that and was soon ensconced in the library reading a book about King Arthur and Sir Lancelot.

Eventually, the physician arrived, and Meg took him to his patient. She found Jenkins in quite a temper. He explained to Meg that the earl had awoken several hours earlier after a drugged sleep - having needed the sleeping draught in the middle of the night after all – but was soon wracked by pain again. "I didn't want to give Lord

Tenby any more of the sleeping draught in case it was the wrong thing to do, and so he has been left to cope with the pain as best he could. I hope the doctor will now get on with his job!" With that he glowered at the doctor.

But the doctor seemed to have other ideas, telling Jenkins he could assist by plying the patient with brandy, explaining it would help with deadening the pain, while he prepared the area for the operation.

Meg immediately offered to get the brandy and returned shortly with two bottles of excellent cognac, handing them to Jenkins. "Please let me know what else I can do," she said to the physician.

"Your help will not be necessary, my lady," the physician replied. "But perhaps the help of one of the servants could be useful if you could spare one."

Meg felt a bit peeved at not being considered suitable help and was about to express her opinion on the matter when she saw that visitors had arrived!

Alice and Jed appeared in the doorway, and behind them, Meg could see Emily, who must have sneaked up behind them without them knowing.

Any thought of helping the doctor herself vanished from her mind the moment she saw her daughter. The need to get Emily away from the room before the gruesome task of removing the bullet began took precedence.

"I only need the help of one other person," the doctor decreed, his impatience with this interruption apparent to all. He then pointed at Alice. "You!" he declared. "The rest of you can go!"

What an arrogant man, Meg thought as she took her daughter firmly by the hand, leaving quietly without voicing her protest, merely lifting her chin a little to indicate her disapproval of the doctor's officious manner. Jed followed suit and returned to his duties.

A seemingly endless wait followed, but when, eventually, the doctor appeared in the cosy drawing room, he informed Meg that his patient was now sleeping peacefully, after having been given some soup. He repeated the instructions he had given to Jenkins which were to continue giving him a lot of fluids to drink, and to ensure his patient got plenty of rest.

"If any sign of fever is noted, you must send for me to return. The aftereffects are usually more dangerous than the wound," he informed them. "A man can stand losing a fair amount of blood, but it weakens him. If a fever develops in such cases, it often proves fatal, I'm afraid," he warned them.

"But he is a strong, young man, and should survive," he quickly added. "We can only pray the good Lord will spare him. He will suffer considerable pain for a few days and can be given more of the sleeping draught if necessary. He should have complete rest for four or five days and won't be fit to travel any distance for at least ten days." So saying, he presented Meg with his bill, then, without giving her time to think of any questions to ask him, promptly hurried off in his elegant chaise.

Chapter Five

Ten days at least before the patient could leave. Great Heavens! The news spread rapidly throughout the household, each person viewing the situation differently.

When Ellen heard the news, her first thought was that his stay was going to be most inconvenient, but then decided that she looked forward to meeting the man. Having someone new to talk with may be a nice change, so long as he was a nice young man who did not expect everyone to pander to his every wish.

Emily, on the other hand, had no reservations. She thought it was wonderful news. Her hero would be able to talk with her and maybe even ride with her.

To Alice, it meant more work for her and the other servants with four extra people to cater for, even though she knew the earl's man Jenkins would see to his master's personal needs.

Jed took a different view. He saw the advantage to him of using Lord Tenby's two other servants to help in the stables and gardens. There was certainly plenty of work for them to do.

Luckily, the two men seemed only too happy to oblige. The situation was disclosed to them as they were taking refreshments in the kitchen, and it didn't take much persuading for Jed to get them to agree to helping around the place Soon they were both busy; one seeing to his master's horses while the other set about weeding one of the many garden beds.

So, while most people in the household received the news of the earl having to remain at Wharfe House for at least ten more days with acceptance at least, Meg heard the news with some confusion. Of course, she was happy to help another human in difficulty, but she didn't like the effect he had on her senses. She didn't like how often she caught herself thinking about him either, or why those thoughts caused such strange sensations to course through her body.

He was only a man, after all. And she was not just out of the schoolroom! She didn't know anything about him, and, in any case, he was only here while he recovered from his wound. It was no use getting any silly ideas. Even if he was attracted to her and she allowed him to get close, he would only end up using her like all the other men in her life had done. Didn't she know by now that men were not to be trusted? After all, she had enough examples to learn from. Her father, her brother, her husband... and one or two more came to mind. No, she must stay away from him, and get him off her property as soon as possible.

By noon that same day, when the earl's staff were summoned to the kitchen for their main meal of the day along with the other servants, Meg went to the earl's bedchamber to inform Jenkins of the meal awaiting him. She didn't intend to stay, but when Jenkins seemed reluctant to leave, she discovered that the earl was restless with the aftereffects of the brandy and the operation. There seemed nothing for it but to offer to stay with the patient while he was away. At first, Jenkins tried to object, informing her somewhat shyly that his master was still very drunk and was sometimes using language not fitted for a lady's ears, but finally left after Meg had assured him that she was sure she had heard worse.

Meg told herself that the only reason she had offered to stay with the earl was because no one else was available, but she knew she was not being entirely honest with herself. Her heart was not beating this wildly simply because she had climbed a flight of stairs! Somehow the stranger stirred her emotions in a way she found decidedly unsettling, so it was with some trepidation that she moved to sit in the chair Jenkins had vacated.

It took even more courage for her to look across at the man responsible for her disquieting thoughts, finding him lying on his back, and although he was covered by a sheet, his restlessness had caused the sheet to slip down revealing his bandaged shoulder and bare torso. She wanted to go to him and pull the sheet higher but was reluctant to go that near to him. However, her personal fears were forgotten when she saw his head begin thrashing from side to side, then heard him start to moan and mumble as though he was in the middle of a nightmare. Concern for him grew and she rose from the chair, deciding to go closer to the bed but hesitated when she heard him muttering.

At first, she couldn't make out any words but after a while she heard him mention his mother and someone called Penelope. His sister, maybe, Meg thought. Perhaps it would not help to disturb him in the middle of a dream. Then she heard him mumble something about a widow and someone called Jeanette. His comments seemed so personal that, at first, she assumed Jeanette was his wife, until some of his other comments made her conclude that this Jeanette was more likely to be a widowed lover!

Meg tried not to let his coarse language disturb her, as he cursed his fate in no uncertain terms. But when his arms also began thrashing about, she was afraid he would open his wound, and decided she had to try and restrain his movements, talking softly to him while lightly holding his arms still.

"Shh," she said soothingly, "it's all right. Try to be still. Please."

Her words must have had some effect as he went still for a moment, but then began moving restlessly again. She tried repeating her pleas for him to rest quietly while also increasing the pressure on his arms. Again, he went still, and after a while she decided that he was quiet enough for her to return to the chair.

But as she started to withdraw from him his arms suddenly shot out, grasping hers, pulling her closer, making her lose her balance as she struggled to keep her feet on the floor. His arms then moved to her back, effectively imprisoning her body to his. "Oh no," she cried, both in protest and surprise, and then, to make matters worse, she lost her balance completely, landing on top of him.

She was instantly and acutely aware of the dangerously intimate position she was in, her upper body pressing down on his while her lips were disturbingly close to his own. She was also acutely aware of the way her body was reacting to the situation.

She could smell the brandy on his breath, the smell of soap on his warm skin, and a masculine scent which seemed to overpower all the other aromas, leaving her strangely aroused despite her fear. The fact that the top half of his torso was completely devoid of clothing except for the bandage, and that she could clearly feel his heartbeats pounding as rapidly as her own, simply made her senses spin. She knew she must do something to get him to release her but feared that if she pushed herself off him, his wound would suffer, so she chose instead to stay where she was, hoping he would soon realise the inappropriateness of what he was doing and would release her. She didn't dare utter another sound in case it made things worse.

Gradually, his firm hold on her did begin to weaken, but not enough to get free, and so she decided to repeat her soothing words, this time adding that he should now go to sleep. Sensing him relaxing a little, she started to believe that her ploy was beginning to work. He was still holding her too tightly for her to slide off him, so she decided to try to calm him further by reaching one hand up to stroke his forehead even though it brought her body to rest even more heavily on his.

Unfortunately for Meg, this action seemed to have the opposite effect from the one intended. He must have taken her actions as an invitation, because instead of letting go of her, his right hand moved to the nape of her neck while gently easing her lips towards his own, moaning, seemingly not from pain this time, but from desire!

This unexpected new onslaught caught Meg totally unprepared. And what was even worse was the way her body instantly responded to his caress. Even as she stiffened in resistance, a tingling of desire was coursing through her veins and a warmth was spreading from her head right down to her toes, whilst a throbbing began between her legs. She had to act to stop this. Immediately!

She opened her mouth to scream, only to find the sound immediately smothered by his mouth closing over hers. Then, to her horror, his left hand reached to caress her breast, shocking her so much that she no longer cared whether he was hurt or not. Gasping in surprise, and using her hands and arms for leverage, she pushed away from him with all her might. But instead of hearing him cry out in pain, the man tightened his hold on her and laughed. A deep, guttural chuckle!

Goodness gracious! Was he imagining he was with a lover who liked rough play? She could think of no other reason for him to laugh like that. She supposed anything was possible with him in such a befuddled state, but when he confirmed her suspicion by pulling her close for another kiss, this time plundering her mouth, using his tongue to delve into her hot, wet, warm depths, she was so shocked, she found herself unable to respond, neither withdrawing nor submitting to this scandalously pleasurable onslaught!

Moments later, her sanity returned, and she knew she had allowed the situation to get out of hand. He could not be aware of what he was doing. She was sure of that, but she had to get him to stop. Not so much through fear of what he might do to her – he was an invalid after all - but more from the realization that her body was again responding to him. His hand by this time had succeeded in making her nipple hard with desire, and she moaned with dismay as her body overruled her mind, allowing this sweet assault on her senses to continue. A sense of shame now mingled with all her other emotional responses, while her head desperately tried to keep some semblance of control.

Suddenly, he rolled over, taking her body with him until she was beneath him, causing her to cry out in alarm as he began kissing and licking her throat, whilst his clever hands undid the front fastenings of her bodice without her even being aware of it.

Surely someone would hear her and come to her aid, she thought, before remembering that all except her mother and daughter were off duty, enjoying their midday meal. And, even if her mother were not too far away to hear her, she would be unable to help. That only left Emily, wherever she was. Please don't let Emily come and see me like this, she begged silently, the thought stopping her from screaming for help.

Once again, he seemed to be mistaking her body's responses for acceptance of his actions, and before she knew it, he had pushed back her clothing so that her upper body was covered only by a thin, almost transparent chemise. Her hands stilled when she heard him groan as he opened his eyes, looking down at her over large breasts, not with revulsion as she had expected but with something approaching reverence!

She knew this should not be happening but seemed incapable of taking any action. And then she found herself moaning when he used his mouth to capture first one nipple through the material, then the other, suckling them in turn. She was dumbfounded. Not only by his actions but by the pleasure he was causing her to feel. She knew she should resist, but what he was doing to her just felt too good!

Somehow, his hands were completely dominating her body, roaming wherever they chose to go. She felt one circling on her thigh, knowing that with each caress, her skirts were rising higher, until his hand reached its goal; the junction of her thighs, where her wetness and heat could clearly be felt. Tears pooled in her eyes at the near ecstasy she was feeling but also from shame. This was so wrong, she knew that, and yet nothing she had ever experienced had aroused her as much! But it had to stop.

He had just managed to dip his finger into her honeyed centre, when she tried to buck him off her with a last, desperate effort. Her distress at last seemed to reach his brain, and, though he was confused, his better nature must have prevailed, for he withdrew, rolling to his side, and then cried out with the pain that must have ripped through his shoulder and back.

Meg took the opportunity to scramble off the bed and dash across the room, mindless of his condition, as she fastened her gown with shaking fingers, straightened her modesty shawl while trying to get her breathing under control. She smoothed her hair and her skirts as best she could, then turned with her head held high and her shoulders set back, as she mentally shook herself back into control.

"You should be ashamed of yourself sir," she complained in a croaky voice she barely recognised. "I suppose you thought I was your mistress." As she said the words, she knew they were untrue, for she had distinctly heard him call her Margaret several times between his kisses, when he had whispered his apparent admiration of her body.

God, but he seemed to like her breasts, she thought. Yet she knew they were ugly. Hadn't her husband repeatedly told her so? And her mother always hinted that they were too large. Like a cow, Lucas had said. She always wore either high-necked gowns or modesty shawls for this reason, but they didn't seem to hide what she thought of as her disability as much as she would have liked. In winter it was easier, for she was able to cover them with a thick, large shawl, but the current warm weather made that impractical.

She pushed these thoughts aside, however, and sat down on the chair again, now eagerly waiting for Jenkin's return. She looked closely at the earl and noticed that he was lying on his back once more, his eyes closed. His breathing still seemed to be laboured, though, but no blood was seeping through the thick bandage covering his wound, thank goodness. She decided that he had most likely already forgotten his actions or would believe they were just a dream. He had made no attempt to reply to her complaint, so perhaps it may be better to say nothing more. After all, she would hate for anyone else to know what happened.

Unfortunately, saying nothing more and thinking nothing more were two different things. Her thoughts refused to be so easily managed, and she became more and more distressed as time passed. She tried telling herself that her response to his attempted seduction, or rape, or whatever it was, had been fear and fear alone, yet knew that was not completely true. But if she admitted, even to herself, that part of her had loved his expert attentions, his words of love, and his hard, warm body pressing against her own, what would that make her?

Exactly what she had been accused of being, all those years ago, she thought. A slut. And she hadn't been a slut. She hadn't even liked mating with her husband. She certainly would never have thought of taking a lover. Yet that was what she had been accused of. And the evidence had all been against her. For hadn't one of her husband's best friends been found in her bed!

Despite not wanting to, she seemed powerless to prevent her thoughts from drifting back through the years, to the dreadful night when her marriage had ended. She still remembered that time with horror. Her husband and his friends had been carousing late into the night - nothing unusual in that or the fact that she was neither willing to be in their company nor wanted there - and she had retired early. Only to awaken in the middle of the night being fondled by a man; a man far too large to be her husband. She remembered screaming in panic, at the same time trying desperately to escape from under his body. He was so heavy, she recalled. He also reeked of whiskey, and, as her hands flailed in the air, striking his body again and again, she began to be aware that he was also completely naked!

She remembered shouting for her husband to come, and how relieved she had been when he and his friends, plus two servants, arrived in the room. But then, instead of calling it a rescue, they all seemed to be suggesting that she had been screaming in the throes of passion! And her attacker had the nerve to agree, saying that, indeed, they had arranged this lover's tryst!

No one seemed interested in her side of the story, and the next day, she had been left alone with only servants remaining in the household, her husband giving them strict instructions to ensure she stayed on the estate. Even her baby daughter had been taken from her. There were to be no visits and no visiting. The housekeeper was told to send a report on his wife's movements to him on a weekly basis. She was a prisoner in her own home!

Weeks later, she had learned her husband was seeking a divorce or an annulment. It was rumoured he was claiming that she had been having similar affairs for at least two years reluctantly forcing him to conclude that she would not be a suitable mother to give birth to his heir, or to bring up their daughter. His parents had agreed with him, adding her father's sins to her own to satisfy their claim that the two families should never have been aligned in the first place. Her daughter, Emily, was reported to be living with his parents, and she feared she would never see her child again.

It was a terrible time, too terrible to revisit, even now. Meg managed to drag her thoughts away from those painful memories, thinking instead of her father, who was born with all the advantages that came with being the heir to a prosperous earldom. But reflecting on her father was also painful. After he had become the earl, he had lost no time in squandering his inheritance. Meg had since come to consider him as a foolish and rather weak man, but not an evil one, and had fond memories of him. But he loved to gamble and soon became addicted to it, eventually losing everything he owned. Then, on the night he lost the family estate in a card game, an estate that, for some reason was not entailed, he shot himself, ashamed to confess the loss to his wife.

Yet, even after doing that, Meg had never hated him for his weaknesses, believing that had it not been for Ellen's accident and her subsequent withdrawal from life, her father would not have abandoned them, leaving to live in London where he apparently frequented the gaming hells almost every night.

But the Greene's were not as understanding it seemed, adding his scandals to her own supposed sins to prove her an unsuitable wife and mother. Why, she did not know, because, after all, the Greene family had been fully aware of the scandal involving her father before arranging her marriage to their son.

The wrangling over the attempted divorce went on for two years. Two years without her daughter. Two years of virtual imprisonment, with only bad news reaching her ears. Only her mother's letters to keep her sane, assuring Meg of her love and support. And for those letters she would always be grateful. She loved her mother and would always try to be patient with her. Together they shared their shame and their sadness. Together they would take on the world, if necessary, for Emily's sake. In a few more years when Emily was a little older. But, in the meantime, Meg knew she must control these new, disturbing, destructive feelings.

She had to concentrate on the present and decide what she must do. Whatever else happened, she knew that she must make sure she would never again be alone with the earl. She was not afraid of him, she reasoned, and was sure now that it was his inebriated state which had caused him to act in that strange way. Yet, although she was convinced that he would never attempt to kiss her again, she also thought it wise to ensure that he would never again be given the opportunity.

She had to be sensible. She had to resist the part of her that wanted to rebel. The shameful part of her that had welcomed his seduction. The part of her that knew she would very much like to explore her feelings for this stranger.

There seemed only one way to ensure that she could resist the temptation he posed. She must keep him at a distance. His servants would just have to cope with him. She must protect herself from her own folly. For, if she didn't, she would be ruined.

Long ago she had vowed to have nothing to do with men. A vow that had been easy to keep until now, with no man stirring her interest. And she had wholeheartedly believed she was immune to masculine charms. How wrong she was!

She was still in a flustered state when Jenkins reappeared, and he must have noticed how distressed she was, because he apologised for taking so long and suggested that his lord must have embarrassed her with some of his expletives. Meg shook her head in denial but was in such a hurry to leave the room that he hardly had time to express his thanks for the meal and for her kindness in staying with the patient before she was gone.

While Meg had been dealing with the earl, Emily had spent the time chatting with her grandmother. It didn't take long before the earl was mentioned.

"Grandmama, I think the earl is someone on an important mission, don't you?" Emily ventured to suggest. She didn't wait for an answer, quickly adding, "I think he must have been struck down by his enemy. Do you think he has been followed and that we may, at any minute, be attacked?"

"Don't be foolish, you silly child. Enemy indeed! Your mother has already told me that he was just travelling back to London after a visit with a Lord Frome. Weren't you there when he told her?" Then, without giving Emily time to reply, added, "Though why he was riding when he could have travelled in a perfectly good coach, I *don't* understand."

"Oh, *I* do, Grandmama. Coaches are so stuffy, whereas riding is such fun."

"You would think so, you silly chit. But you haven't ridden long distances, have you? Most uncomfortable, I can assure you. Can you imagine having to ride all the way to your other grandparents?"

Emily gave her grandmother's words some thought and conceded that it was probably a bit too long a ride. "Mind you, when I am older, I am sure I will be able to do it," she added, not to admit total defeat. "As long as I continue to practice. I hope to be able to ride with the earl before he leaves."

"I don't see why he would want to ride with you, child."

Emily could see no way she would be able to persuade her grandmother to support her wish for a ride with the earl, so reluctantly gave up on the idea. "What would you like us to talk about now, Grandmama?" she asked.

"How about giving me a rest from your endless chatter, child?" Ellen said with a smile.

"You love my chatter," Emily replied confidently. "And I bet the earl will want cheering up after all he has been through. It is simply dreadful being stuck in bed when you are ill, with nothing to do. Do you think I should go and see him this afternoon?"

"Absolutely not," was Ellen's retort. "He'll need to rest for a few days, and you, young lady, are anything but restful. No, you stay away from him. And, while we are at it, I don't like your language. 'I bet' is not a suitable expression for you to use. Wherever did you pick that one up from? Jed, I presume."

Emily was about to protest when her mother rushed into the room.

"What's the matter?" they both asked in unison.

"Nothing is the matter. Whatever made you think something is wrong? My hair, I suppose," Meg said, smoothing her unruly curls again. I've just been with the earl and left him resting quietly. I came to see if you were both ready for luncheon."

"You shouldn't have to attend to the man," her mother complained. "Hasn't he got three servants with him? They should be able to look after him without your help. And anyway, Alice could have taken over for a short spell if it became necessary. It's not up to you to wait on him."

"Everyone else was having lunch, Mama. But you're right. I won't be offering my services again. He was very restless, and really needed a man there to watch him."

"Restless? Well, I hope you didn't try to control him."

"Of course not," Meg lied. "I wouldn't have had the strength in any case."

Meg was thankful that she seemed to have been believed, her mother only commenting that the sooner they would be able to get back to their usual routine, the better. When Meg agreed, her mother smiled and the subject was dropped.

After they had eaten, Meg drove Emily into the village to see Mr. Bennett, the local shopkeeper, who assured Meg that he had done as she requested, and it had been no trouble at all to ride to Selby as he had to go there anyway and was able to kill two birds with one stone.

Meg didn't really believe his story about the need to go to Selby anyway but knew he would not have wanted Meg to feel indebted to him. Mr Bennett was such a kind man and always seemed to have a smile for her. He was aged in his mid-forties, had a wife and four children, and was renowned for his friendly, helpful disposition. He once confided to her that he had never believed the stories about her, and she knew he had been telling the truth. She also suspected that he thought she was short of funds, and while not true, she knew her lifestyle gave that impression. Meg was aware that he would be affronted if she were to insist on rewarding him for going to Selby, so thanked him instead for his generosity.

After leaving the village, Meg and Emily drove on to Tadcaster, where they visited the circulating library before buying some material to make Emily some new dresses. Meg felt the need to do some sewing to keep her mind off a certain visitor, and anyway, Emily was growing so quickly, her present dresses were getting far too short. Meg could tell she was likely to be almost as tall as her father. He had been tall and lean, and Emily remained skinny no matter how much she ate. Seeing how generous her mother was being, Emily took the opportunity to persuade her that she needed a new riding habit, saying her own no longer fitted and was sadly out of date.

By the time they reached home, Meg was in a much better humour and Emily was very pleased with herself. After changing for dinner, they spent the remainder of the evening happily, without a cross word being uttered, even by Ellen.

Upstairs, Alex had spent most of the afternoon and evening of that day trying to solve the puzzle of Margaret Greene. He had eventually shaken off his inebriated state and although still feeling decidedly weak, he didn't feel like sleeping. Jenkins had assisted him to bathe and later had helped him to eat. Alex didn't exactly know how late in the day it was but had told his valet, Jenkins, that he didn't want or need anyone to be confined to sitting in a chair watching over him every minute of the day. After insisting that the earl call him if he was required, Jenkins retired to the adjoining room, leaving Alex with his thoughts.

After a while, Alex felt strong enough to make the effort to sit up, but pain shot through his shoulder almost making him cry out. Luckily, he managed to limit the noise to a groan, as though he was just adjusting his position. Otherwise, he knew that Jenkins would have come running to his side, and at that moment, he preferred solitude.

As he lay there trying to piece together all that had happened to him since being shot, he attempted to gather his memories together to form some kind of cohesive whole. He remembered slumping in the saddle and realising that he had been shot, but little else until Lady Margaret had come on the scene. Of course, he didn't realise it was her at first, but now he knew who she was, he could think of little else but her.

He kept picturing her in his mind. She had held him up, and she had stood by his bedside at some point. He remembered both those things and had to admit to himself that she confused him. She just didn't fit the picture he had formed of her when he had been listening to his cousin, Percy. She dressed demurely, acted without artifice, and blushed delightfully!

While she had been embarrassed by his scrutiny as she had stood by his bedside, he was sure she had also been attracted to him, just as he clearly remembered his body's reaction to her. And then he frowned, remembering her voice soothing him. When did that happen? Or did he imagine it? Did she come to him in a dream?

He almost called out to Jenkins to ask him if Lady Margaret had sat by him at all, but then an even more disturbing memory surfaced. He had kissed her!

He knew it had happened, but when and how it had happened, he did not remember. Sometime that morning, he was sure. No way was it merely a dream but was something that had definitely occurred. Oh Lord, he thought, he must had taken advantage of the woman when she had come to soothe him. Would she ever be able to forgive him? How could he had acted so badly?

He lay back, the hand of his good arm going to his forehead as though that would help him remember, and after a while, the images began to form. One after the other darted through his mind. She had been on the bed with him, and he had done more than kiss her! Was she perhaps a strumpet after all? But no, he instinctively knew that was not true. No matter what had been said about her in town.

How did he know that? Because she had seemed very inexperienced in the art of kissing! Memories of her resisting him arose making him feel utterly ashamed, but he also recalled that for a moment at least she had responded to his caresses. But in such an innocent way, he would have sworn she was still a virgin if he hadn't known she had a daughter.

He was sure she had no idea what to do with her tongue when being kissed with passion, or even of the desirability to part one's lips! He must be wrong, he argued. She must have been resisting him because she was horrified by what he was doing. But no, he knew she had responded, at least for a while.

She was supposed to have had numerous liaisons with men, but all he had observed about her contradicted such a scenario. She didn't look the part and didn't act the part.

Percy must have been mistaken, but how and why such false tales were being circulated, he did not know and couldn't guess. How could she seem so innocent and yet be the same person Percy had described? The way she lived also supported his theory that the stories couldn't have any truth to them. Her servants and her daughter were obviously devoted to her, and she cared for them in an honest, gentle way. Not artfully or selfishly, traits she would likely have displayed if Percy's words had been true.

The other thing confusing him was his response to her! Never had he felt so drawn to anyone; she completely enthralled him. Just thinking about her made his pulse race and his loins ache. But more than that. He desperately needed to see her again. To touch her. To have her like him. No, damn it. To have her in his life! For some incomprehensible reason, his fondest wish was now to be her friend and lover. Which he knew would be a big mistake. For wasn't he already betrothed to Penelope? As good as, anyway.

No, this attraction could not be real, he told himself. His accident must be affecting his emotional state. He hardly knew the woman for goodness' sake! And even if he admitted to being attracted to Lady Margaret, there was no way a relationship between them could have a future. No way at all. Especially after the way he had behaved towards her. She would likely want to slap his face when next they met. Or worse!

He had a huge apology to make and had no right to expect forgiveness. She would want nothing from him but his departure from her life, and he didn't blame her. She would never look kindly on one who had treated her with such disrespect.

Just as well, he told himself. He had no right to feel attracted to anyone else but Penelope. He was no longer a free man.

Thinking of Penelope, he wondered whether he should write her a note, but decided against it. He had not yet formerly asked her to be his bride and thought it may be presumptuous of him to assume he had the right to send a communication to her.

He then admitted to himself that he didn't want to write to Penelope anyway. Not while his infatuation with Lady Margaret continued to dominate his thoughts. How long would he have to wait until he saw her again?

Two days later, he was still waiting. Not once had she stopped by to see how he was, and he, of course, was in no position to go in search of her.

Chapter Six

Outwardly, Meg believed that she had succeeded in appearing calm and unruffled during those two days, but inside she was a jumble of nerves. And all because of the man who had sought her help in his hour of need. No matter how hard she tried, she could not seem to put him from her mind. Oh, during the day she managed reasonably well, except when passing the door of his bedchamber, or when she saw one of his servants. But at night, when she lay in her lonely bed, it was an entirely different matter.

For the past three nights, sleep had eluded her until well into the early hours. Instead of getting her much-needed rest, her thoughts had drifted time and time again to the intimate moments when she had lain beneath Alex - as she now thought of him - her breasts exposed to his view through her thin chemise, and she would recall every detail of their encounter. In her mind's eye, she could conjure up not only his actions but also the way she had responded, reliving every glorious, dreadful moment!

Her body tingled every time her imagination replayed the scene. At times, she could almost feel his touch and the way he kissed her in that strangely exciting, very intimate way. Pleasurably intimate, so unlike the intimacy she had shared with her husband. For a start, she had no memory of her husband kissing her in any way at all. Perhaps on their wedding day he had pecked her on the lips in the church after they had been declared man and wife, but she couldn't recall it. Nor could she recall any other kiss taking place between them. He rarely if ever touched her at all except for the almost ritual mating, and even that had ceased as soon as he knew she was pregnant!

And the mating had not been pleasurable, either. It had always been a hasty affair, with her husband coming to her long after she had retired for the night, usually when she was already asleep. He would come up behind her, pull her body to his and enter her from behind almost brutally and with no preliminaries.

But with Alex, she knew instinctively that the experience would be entirely different. Even though he had been under the influence of drink at the time, he had not hurt her. And despite her fear, when Alex had touched her, she had felt a steadily mounting surge of joy wash over her and knew her body was aching for more. She had felt an unfamiliar pleasurable throbbing between her legs, in the place which, to her knowledge, had no name, and all over her body her nerve endings had tingled. She had never experienced such sensations in her life.

When Alex's body had covered hers, she had felt for the first time that a sexual relationship could perhaps be something wonderful. Something so breathtaking that the two lovers could become as one. For that was what she had experienced, albeit for only a moment. It was as though the two of them had merged into one. How she longed to go to him, to lie down beside him, to touch him and feel his warmth, his hardness, and to feel him caress her body.

With thoughts such as those swimming round in her head, no wonder her hard won peace of mind had been shattered, she thought. The earl had arrived five days ago, and she hadn't seen him since the Unfortunate Incident, but even now, sitting as she was trying to concentrate on her sewing, she couldn't put him from her mind.

He was not for her, she knew that. A man in his position would not want someone like her for a wife. It was out of the question. He probably didn't even like her. He certainly didn't know her. He was just a lusty young man who, under the influence of strong spirits, couldn't resist the chance to fondle what he no doubt assumed to be an available female! All she had to do was stay away from him as much as she could and see him on his way as soon as possible. Out of her life, so the memory of him and his kisses could have a chance to fade, eventually to be forgotten.

She had enough trouble just coping with life as it was, seeing to her mother and her daughter. Preparing for the day when Emily would be introduced into society. Nothing and no-one must deter her from her path.

While Meg was restless downstairs, Alex was also feeling restless. His wound was healing well, but he was stuck in one room with no other company but Jenkins. He had been resting obediently for over two days now, but enough was enough. He felt his strength returning, and wanted to breathe in fresh air, and not just through the window of his room.

The weather was fine, and he longed to be able to walk and ride about the countryside, not just rest in bed, or sit in a chair as he had now progressed to doing. Yet he still experienced dizziness whenever he stood, and his legs were hardly able to support his weight. And yes, drat it, he admitted to himself, he still desperately wanted to see Lady Margaret. If anything, his need to see her was becoming even more acute. This enforced imprisonment was not helping his temper, either. Jenkins had had to suffer it on more than one occasion during the past days, and he was still in a foul mood when he heard a quiet knock on his door.

"Come in," he bellowed. Slowly, the door opened, and Emily peeped in, a little surprised to find the bed empty and him sitting by the fireside.

"Oh, there you are! I've come to see you," she told him, stating the obvious, but not knowing what else to say.

He beckoned for her to come and sit in the chair opposite his. "Come and see me then. I am sorely in need of company, I'll admit."

"Oh, I thought you would be. I hate it when I am ill, and no one comes for ages and ages. But Grandmama and Mama told me not to disturb you, so I stayed away. But I was right, wasn't I? You don't mind me coming to see you at all, do you?"

"No, I am grateful for your thoughtfulness. Unless," he added, "you are trying to get out of the schoolroom."

"Oh no, sir. I don't have lessons or a governess. And Mama is presently busy sewing. Otherwise, we would be out walking, I expect. That's what we usually do most mornings."

Alex was surprised at her words. "You don't have a governess or lessons? Whyever not? You are clearly old enough."

Emily shrugged, apparently not offended by his attitude. "Mama says I am learning well enough without spending hours in a schoolroom. Although perhaps that may change soon because she and Grandmama keep saying that I am going to need to learn how to become a lady." Her disapproving expression let Alex know what she thought about that idea!

Alex wondered about the real reason behind Emily's lack of a formal education but knew it was nothing to do with him how the household was run, and maybe she didn't have a governess for the simple reason that her mother couldn't afford to employ one. However, the child did like to talk, so why not take this opportunity to learn more about this dysfunctional family?

"How is your grandmother?" he asked, changing the subject.

"Oh, well enough, I suppose. She is well enough to tell me off if she finds out about me disobeying her by coming here."

"In that case it had better be our secret," he said, smiling warmly at her, and saw her visibly relax.

"Jenkins told me your grandmother cannot walk," he commented, feeling a little guilty for using the child in this underhand way. Still, he consoled himself, she had sought *him* out, not the other way round. And if she was willing to talk, then what was the harm?

"That's right. Her legs don't work."

"And has she always been like that?"

"Oh no, of course not, silly. She used to ride for miles and miles when she was younger. But now she can only talk about it." She thought for a moment, and then asked, "You ride for miles and miles, don't you, Lord Tenby? Would you ride with me when you are better?"

"It would be my pleasure, young lady. But not for a day or two, I'm afraid. I am getting my strength back quite quickly, but maybe I should try getting about the house before I venture further afield. Do you like to ride, then?"

"Oh yes," she replied enthusiastically. "I have a lively little mare called Dolly, and she likes me to ride her every day. Sometimes she even pulls the little cart which Jed made for me."

"You sound a lucky little girl. And do you sometimes ride with your other visitors?" he asked her, knowing he was wrong to question her in this way, but unable to stop himself.

"Oh, we never have visitors. That is why I am so excited to have you here."

"But surely, sometimes people call?"

"No, unless you count Uncle Damien, and he hardly visits us at all," she replied thoughtfully. "Why?" she added, "Is that unusual?"

"No, of course not. I just thought ..." He didn't know what he just thought. He wondered who this uncle was. Could he be a real uncle or was "uncle" a courtesy title only? But more than one person was supposed to have visited. A whole stream of them, in fact. Then he had an idea. "But I was sure a friend of mine mentioned visiting here a year or so ago. Have you no recollection of such a visit?"

"No, you must have got it wrong. No one comes here. I go to visit my other grandparents once a year. Otherwise, we are on our own. No one has been here for years, except Uncle Damien. Oh, I remember, once a gentleman did call, years ago, but he didn't stay. He upset Mama and Jed sent him away. Would that have been your friend?"

"No, Emily," he replied, frowning in confusion. "No, as you say, I must have got the story wrong. It must have been someone else he was talking about. By the way, who is Uncle Damien?"

"Uncle Damien? Why, he's Uncle Damien, of course! Mama's brother. But he doesn't visit us anymore. Mama and he don't get on, you see, and Grandmama takes Mama's side, and they argue and argue. I like him though. He is always nice to me. Brings me presents and lets me ride his horse. I wish he would come to see us again. And he is very handsome, you know. But I get a headache hearing them argue, so perhaps it's just as well he doesn't come here anymore," she said sadly.

Time to change the subject, he thought, and carefully steered the conversation to safer, more pleasant topics. They continued chatting for some time, but Alex found it difficult to concentrate on the conversation, his thoughts trying to come to terms with her earlier words. No visitors. Damien was obviously Lady Margaret's brother. So how could the stories of her passionate liaisons be true? Did she meet the men in the village? No, that was not the answer. It was clear from Emily's chatter that her mother stayed at home, even when her daughter visited her grandparents. Maybe it was during those visits when she saw her lovers. Emily wouldn't know if she wasn't there. But it just didn't add up. He was certain she hadn't used those occasions to meet her lovers. It would mean planning very carefully and that didn't fit in with Percy's story. No, he was sure the stories were untrue. But then, why did such stories exist?

Emily left to see her grandmother when Jenkins came to change the dressings on Alex's wound, telling her about her visit to Alex, proudly claiming that Lord Tenby had welcomed the visit, and so she had been right all along, when they had been wrong. He *had* wanted visitors.

"It is not right for you to visit a gentleman in his bedchamber even if he allowed it," Ellen scolded.

"But he wasn't in bed, Grandmama, He was sitting in a chair and is quite well again."

"It was still his bedchamber. But if he is out of bed now, perhaps he should join *us*, instead. I will suggest it to your mother. He may be happy to join us for dinner this evening. But you were very naughty to visit the earl without permission."

"But I told you, *he* gave me permission, Grandmama!" was the cheeky reply.

Ellen hmphed. "Go and tell your mama that I would like to see her," she said, shooing Emily from the room.

Ever since the earl had descended on their doorstep, Ellen had made it her business to find out all she could about him, shamelessly questioning Alice and Jed about all they knew. Which turned out to be quite a lot. Apparently, Jenkins had spoken to Alice and Jed quite openly, seeing no reason to keep any secrets from them about Alex's impending engagement or what he knew about the Wilde family. Not that he knew all that much, he told them, having worked for the former earl until recently.

When her daughter returned with Emily, Ellen told her about the earl's apparent recovery and suggested inviting him to join them for dinner. "I don't think that is a good idea, Mama," Meg replied, looking ill at ease.

"Why not? You surely don't expect him to stay in that room for the next two weeks!"

Meg could see her mother's point. "I suppose not. But it will mean a lot of extra work for Alice."

"What has that to do with anything?" her mother argued. "I have heard that he is a nice young man and I want to meet him."

"Very well, Mama, I will inform his valet of the invitation and if the earl is agreeable, we shall have him join us this evening."

Ellen smiled. "You know he is engaged to be married?"

Meg felt the colour drain from her face. "What? How do you know that?"

Ellen shrugged but observed her daughter closely. "Servants talk," was all she offered. "I hope the news doesn't bother you."

Meg had inwardly flinched on hearing of his engagement but believed she had managed to mask her feelings from her mother. Apparently not. "Of course not," she protested. "I am only surprised that he didn't mention the fact. He made no request to send the lady any message, only writing to his mother."

"Well, maybe I got it wrong then," Ellen commented.

Meg turned to leave the room. "Before I speak with the earl's valet, I had better go and see what Alice thinks of your idea," Meg said, glad to escape her mother's probing eye.

Alice seemed to favour the idea, so Jenkins had been approached next. He put the suggestion to his master, who agreed without hesitation, and the message was passed back down the line. And so, Alice set about preparing a more elaborate meal to be served in the dining room (which was hardly ever used, the three usually having their evening meal at a small table in the parlour) and organising for Peter to come in from the garden to act as footman. An ill-fitting uniform was the best that could be found for him on such short notice, and Peter was subjected to a crash course on etiquette and his role in the proceedings, much to his chagrin.

Meg saw no way to prevent the earl from joining them that evening and therefore pretended to be pleased at the prospect of having company for a change. She noted that Emily seemed particularly excited to be dining with the earl, and soon had her mother and grandmother smiling when she confided her hopes of him riding with her and becoming her friend for ever.

And although Meg smiled at her daughter's reaction, it made her wonder if her daughter may be lonely. Emily only had one friend of her own age, Laura, and she a servant's daughter who came with her mother on laundry days. Even though Emily always seemed to be a happy child, and didn't want for love and affection, Meg accepted that it would be good for her to be allowed to enjoy the company of their uninvited guest.

Everyone in the household seemed to be involved in the preparations for the evening, and even Meg played a part. While rushing round from one task or another, she found herself wondering if the earl realised that he was the cause of such a commotion!

Eventually, everything seemed to be ready, and the time came for the family to assemble in the drawing room. Ellen was the first to arrive. She had asked her maid, Sally, to make an extra effort that evening. Over the following two hours, the two women had enjoyed deciding on every aspect of the challenge, beginning with dressing Ellen's greying hair in a more fashionable style with a central parting and ringlets at each side of her head. Ellen even had Sally use a little rouge on her cheeks and lips.

The gown Ellen chose to wear was of midnight blue silk which was cut low at the neck and was decorated with puffed sleeves. To complete the ensemble, she carried a fan made of ostrich feathers which had been dyed to match her dress. When Jed arrived to carry her downstairs, he made sure to compliment her on her looks, which seemed to please her immensely. He took care not to disturb her hairstyle as he deposited her in the drawing room, settling her on a sofa.

Meg, on the other hand, had dressed herself as usual, simply changing into another demure, muslin day dress, this one being light grey in colour, its plainness relieved only by a white, embroidered lace modesty shawl. She wore no rouge or other adornments. However, she had taken extra care with her hair, and was pleased with the result. Her thick chestnut locks glowed with health, dressed with curls being left to hang carelessly down her back, controlled only lightly by a ribbon. She had decided to forego wearing a cap that evening, something Emily noticed when Meg went to collect her from her room. She found Sally there, brushing Emily's hair.

Emily looked at her mother. "You look nice. You look much younger without that silly cap."

"Thank you dear, but it is not a silly cap. It is what matrons wear. But more to the point, why aren't you ready for dinner?"

"I got engrossed in my book and forgot the time. And anyway, Sally said she would stop by and help me dress up. I will come down as soon as I can" she promised.

When Meg entered the drawing room, she looked at her mother and sighed. "It seems that you and Emily have decided that having the earl join us for dinner is a special occasion."

"Well, it is certainly out of the ordinary. For us, anyway."

"You look very nice, Mama."

"Thankyou. I can return the compliment by telling you that your hair looks very attractive, Meg, but it is a pity about your choice of gown. Have you got time to change it?"

"I don't intend to change it, Mama. It is not as though the earl is an invited guest."

As if on cue, moments later, Alex appeared in the doorway, and Meg found her heart going into overdrive. Flustered, she plonked herself down on the sofa next to her mother.

"Good evening," he said in greeting, glancing briefly at the older lady before fixing his eyes on Lady Margaret. Ellen's smile faded, clearly aware that her efforts had been wasted. He only had eyes for her daughter.

Meg had been feeling nervous while waiting for the earl to arrive, but when she met his eyes, the intensity of his gaze unnerved her completely. He obviously liked what he saw. As did she. The moment he had appeared in the doorway, all coherent thought had vanished, and she could do nothing but drink in his beauty. He was not wearing a jacket because no doubt it had been too painful to don, but his crisp, white linen shirt was covered partly by a beautifully tailored waistcoat, and he wore an expertly tied cravat at his neck. His tight-fitting, light brown breeches showed off his muscular physique so clearly that Meg's breath caught in her throat. She forced her eyes to lower demurely, allowing her to take in his manly shaped calves, covered as they were by fashionable silk stockings which were decorated at their sides with an embroidered pattern in silk, known as clocks, before finally resting on his flat-soled shoes.

She knew she was blushing furiously. Heat was radiating through her body, and not from anger, even though after their last meeting she knew she should be furious with him. It was not from embarrassment either. Not completely at any rate. No, her heart was galloping for an entirely different reason.

"Good evening, Lord Tenby," Ellen responded as he approached the sofa. Meg said nothing. Apparently, she had lost her ability to speak!

Mentally shaking herself, Meg forced herself to look up at him. She knew she should be introducing him to her mother, not sitting there like a demented fool. He was still looking at her, she noticed, but this time his eyebrows appeared to be raised in a silent question, as though he was asking her what was wrong, and though colour sprang again to her cheeks, she at last found her voice and managed to make the necessary introductions. Quite calmly. How she would never know. Especially as she had to explain that her mother, while still a countess, preferred not to use her title, choosing instead to be addressed as plain Mrs Searle, which was the family name. For a moment, Alex had looked confused, but quickly seemed to accept the situation for what it was.

To Meg's relief he then took over, first addressing her mother, bowing over her hand, and kissing just above her fingertips as prescribed by polite society. Meg heard him say something gracious, no doubt complimenting her mother on her appearance, although Meg was still feeling too flustered to take in his words. Ellen apparently made an appropriate reply, after which he turned to her, addressing her as Lady Margaret, saying equally flattering words she was sure, even though they seemed to her to be meaningless, automatic nonsense, just said for the sake of it.

Her insides were trembling, but she knew she had to continue to try to conceal her confusing emotions from both him and her mother. Unfortunately, she doubted that she was being very successful. Having always prided herself on being level-headed and in control, she could not understand how this man was able to destroy her composure so utterly without even trying. She knew she had done her best to prepare herself emotionally for this evening, knowing she was bound to feel embarrassed when they met again. For most of the day she had been both dreading and longing to see him again after their last encounter, but she never expected to feel quite so utterly devastated by his presence.

She might have coped better had embarrassment been her only reaction, but this overwhelming response to him, this longing, seemed somehow shameful. She had to pull herself together!

Knowing it was her turn to respond, she searched her mind for something to say, but without success. Even worse, her lips began to tremble, and she tried to smile to disguise her discomposure, failing miserably. All she could do is turn to her mother with a silent plea.

She found that her mother was looking at her with concern, no doubt wondering about her strange behaviour and lack of manners, but luckily, she came to Meg's aid, responding instantly by taking charge of the situation, addressing Alex as Lord Tenby, inviting him to sit in the chair opposite the sofa. Alex thanked her, taking the designated seat, saying that he also would prefer that his title not be used, asking that they refer to him by his first name.

"That is very kind of you, Alex," she said with a warm smile. "And I am sure that such informality should be mutually applied. My daughter likes to be called Meg, a diminutive of Margaret, don't you know. And my name is Ellen."

"Thank you, Mrs Searle. But while I would be honoured to be allowed to address your daughter as Meg, I would feel uncomfortable addressing you so informally. Perhaps I may address you as ma'am?"

"That will be fine, Alex," she told him before turning to the rather badly uniformed, slightly nervous young footman who had admitted Alex to the parlour, telling him it was time to see to their drinks. Peter stammered a little at first but did a creditable job of taking their orders. Alex opted for sherry, and Ellen requested the same. Meg asked for a glass of water. Something her dry mouth suddenly needed very badly!

"You have had quite an ordeal," Ellen remarked to Alex while they waited for their drinks to be served.

"And I dread to think what the outcome would have been had my horse not led me here. I owe you all my life."

"My family were happy to be able to assist you. And I am glad to see you are now firmly on the mend. The worst is over."

"Yes, I should soon be able to leave you all in peace."

"Not for another week, I was told. And don't think for a minute that you are imposing on us. You have livened us up. Our household is usually rather a dull one."

"Thank you, ma'am. I hope to be able to repay you one day."

"Oh, as to that, we have been shamelessly making use of two of your servants, so please don't speak of debts owed."

Meg still hadn't said a word, but she had listened to him speak, loving the sound of his voice. She had no idea how she was going to make it through another week of meetings like this one!

She was thankful when Peter returned with the drinks giving her something to do as she sipped at her glass of water.

An awkward silence then seemed to settle over the three, and for a while they simply smiled at each other and sipped their drinks. And then suddenly the door burst open, and in strode Emily. "Sorry to be so late, but I just couldn't decide what to wear!"

Her words caused the three to laugh, and the atmosphere in the parlour no longer seemed as strained. Meg was at last able to snap out of her trance-like state and explained Emily's presence to Alex. Normally, in households such as this, young children would be confined to the schoolroom for their meals, but here, there wasn't even a schoolroom.

Emily pulled a stool over to the chair where Alex was seated and wasted no time in asking him about his horse and all the places he had visited during his life. Meg and Ellen eventually joined the conversation and before long, they were all happily sharing childhood memories with one another, although nothing too personal was said.

Emily was not the slightest bit shy and continued asking questions whenever she had the chance. Alex told her that he was sorry to have to dispel her belief about him being on a secret mission for the government but instead, related some exciting tales of his time in the Peninsula, to which they all listened in awe.

Yet, throughout the evening, which was enjoyed by all, it became obvious to Meg that she and Alex were constantly aware of each other. Meg turned away whenever their eyes met but knew that the attraction was mutual. It was agony trying to pretend it didn't exist. She found her hand was shaking when she picked up her glass, and her lower lip began trembling again, especially when she looked at him, trying to form a smile. She knew he was looking at her and she tried to appear unaffected by his scrutiny, but doubted she was very successful. Once, she even knocked her wineglass over in her flustered state. She just hoped that neither her mother nor Emily guessed what was wrong with her. And especially not the earl!

Chapter Seven

But of course, Lord Tenby had noticed. He had been aware of every move Lady Margaret – Meg as he now thought of her - had made, every word she had spoken from the moment he had entered the drawing room. He had hardly noticed her mother when he had joined the ladies, giving her only a glance before his gaze was drawn to Meg. He drank in her loveliness, while also observing the way she was reacting to him. Not with anger or hatred, as he had expected, but with admiration and interest.

His body had jumped to attention, his heart and loins responding immediately on a more basic, carnal level; a response that had intensified the moment their eyes had met. Heat seemed to radiate between them, and although Meg had looked away almost instantly, he was sure that some sort of understanding had passed between them in that moment.

Yet, seconds later, his certainty had begun to fade. She looked so distant and uncomfortable sitting there on the sofa, he was made to wonder if he had not misread her message and that she had been more embarrassed than enamoured, remembering what had occurred when last they met. There was no way to solve the dilemma until they could speak privately, of course, but as the evening progressed, he became more and more certain of their mutual attraction.

He observed her carefully, drawing conclusions as he went. He noted everything about her; how she was dressed and how she acted, including her frequent blushes. He became convinced that she was experiencing the same mixture of joy and agony at being near each other as he was, and as each hour passed, it seemed as though an intimacy continued to develop between them, even without any physical contact taking place.

He just had to find a way to be alone with her. He doubted she would initiate such a meeting so he knew he would have to watch out and seize any opportunity that presented itself. That very night if possible.

When the meal ended, they moved to the drawing room but since by then it was time for Emily to retire, she did not join them. He hoped Meg's mother would also choose to retire early, but that did not happen. She seemed only too willing to engage him in conversation. And anyway, he reasoned, Meg would probably leave at the same time as her mother. At least he would be in her presence for a while longer if he humoured the older woman.

Without Emily's presence, the conversation quickly turned to the accident Alex had suffered. He learned that Ellen was an avid newspaper reader, and listened as she voiced her opinion on how lawless society was becoming.

"How alarming it is when even a Prime Minister can be assassinated. I was shocked when I read the report, I can tell you," she said.

Alex raised his eyebrows in surprise. He had not seen a newspaper for days. "Perceval has been assassinated? I have heard nothing about it."

"I am not surprised, young man. You have had your own problems to deal with."

"When did this happen?" he asked.

Ellen clasped her hands together, obviously only too happy to fill him in on the details. "It happened a few days ago, on the eleventh of May. He was shot in the lobby of the houses of Parliament by a John Bellingham. I will ask Jed to pass the recent papers on to you if you like so that you can read the story for yourself. But meanwhile, I will tell you the main points of the story. After his arrest, this John Bellingham gave his side of the story, blaming the government for his economic woes and swearing to everyone that he had acted alone, but others have disputed his version of events, believing he could not have planned it without help and it must have been part of a bigger plot. I suppose they were thinking that those dreadful Luddites could have been behind it. Anyway, whatever the truth, instead of being jeered by the crowds as he was taken away to Newgate prison, it was reported that the spectators had openly cheered, several of them even managing to open the doors of the coach he was travelling in to shake the prisoner's hand! What do you make of that!"

Without waiting for a response, she continued. "I don't know what the country is coming to, with shootings becoming so frequent. Look what happened to you! Perhaps you were shot by one of those Luddites thinking you were an enemy. They are causing trouble almost on a nightly basis, and nobody seems willing to do anything about it. Just as no-one has been to see us about the attack you suffered. It is scandalous!"

A lively discussion ensued, with Alex agreeing with Mrs Searle about the lack of action by the authorities but thought the trouble was they didn't know what to do. "I know that many magistrates have employed squadrons of dragoons and troops of yeomanry to quell the actions of the Luddites, but they seem to have had very little success to date. In my case, I have no idea who was responsible for the attack on me, but since it occurred during daylight hours, I think it was more likely to have been a footpad. There is certainly no shortage of them during these troubled times, and the odds of discovering the perpetrator would have to be very long indeed."

"I suppose you are right," Ellen conceded, settling the matter. The conversation then drifted back to more personal matters, with Alex remarking on Emily's determination to ride with him.

"You mustn't pay any heed to her forward behaviour," Ellen stated. "She is a naughty miss to be pestering you with her nonsense."

"Really ma'am, I shall be delighted to comply with her request if you are both agreeable to the idea. But not tomorrow, I'm afraid. Jenkins insists I follow the doctor's advice to wait for another day or two before engaging in any such exertions, and I suppose he is right. No doubt you will be relieved to see the back of me, but I should not wish to disappoint young Emily before leaving you all in peace again. I shall try not to outstay my welcome however and shall be on my way as soon as I am able. I cannot express my thanks often enough for your kindness to me and my servants. I shall be forever in your debt, and only hope you will accept my hospitality one day soon."

Ellen looked at Meg before answering, "I'm afraid we don't get about much. For myself, well, you can see why, and I know Meg prefers to stay with me."

Alex nodded, as though he knew he had made the two women uncomfortable. He let the subject drop and shortly afterwards, Ellen announced that she was ready to retire for the night. Jed was duly called and soon Alex and Meg were the only ones in the room. The evening was over.

As he had expected, Meg went to follow her mother but was stopped in her tracks when he touched her lightly on her arm.

"Please spare me a moment," he whispered, drawing her back into the room as he quietly closed the door.

"No," she replied softly, as though she had guessed what he wanted to say. "We must not ..." But she didn't finish the sentence, shaking her head instead.

"Please," he begged. "I am aware that I behaved with the utmost discourtesy the last time we were alone together, and that I owe you more than a sincere apology."

"No," she cried. "You were not yourself. I understand, and I know you would not normally behave like that. I just think we should try not to be alone together again."

"I promise to behave myself, Meg. It is just that we both know what happened and I will never forgive myself. But I compromised you most dreadfully, and I must put that right."

"I was not compromised my lord. I am a twenty-six-year-old widow, not a young virgin!"

For a moment he just stared at her, not saying anything. How could she dismiss his sexual attack on her as though it did not matter? It was as if she was telling him that she did not mind what had happened. But the fact that she had been avoiding him told a different story. His behaviour had unsettled her. Greatly.

"I don't know how you can dismiss my behaviour so easily, Meg. *I* certainly cannot. When I came down to dinner this evening, I expected you to look at me with hatred, but instead your eyes welcomed me. I believe that an instant attraction sprang up between us. When we looked at each other I am sure that I was not the only one who felt captivated. I *felt* you respond to me. You cannot deny it."

"I can and I do," she cried. "Stop speaking this way, Alex, and let me go."

He dropped his hands to his sides. "I am not preventing you from leaving, Meg. I just need you to listen to me for a moment longer."

"All right," she agreed eventually, sighing in resignation. "But only for a moment."

"Can you deny that you feel something for me? All I want is for you to spend some time with me so we can explore our feelings."

"That is something I must not do."

"Because you know what is happening between us."

"No. Nothing is happening."

"But it is happening. I have never felt this way before, Meg. This instant connection. I want to have you in my life. I need to have you in my life. Will you do me the honour of becoming my wife?"

For just a second, Meg faltered, allowing him to see the longing in her eyes. And then she shook her head emphatically, almost shouting her answer. "Impossible," she cried, before turning to quit the room.

But before she could reach for the knob, his hand reached out to her again, gently grasping her arm. "Why is it impossible?"

She turned to look him in the eye and opened her mouth as if to speak, but then closed it again and shook her head, her eyes turning away as though she was unable or unwilling to meet his. He noticed that his hand was still on her arm, but instead of withdrawing it altogether, he turned it over and used the back of his hand to stroke her arm. "Please Meg, answer me," he begged as he took a step towards her.

The next moment was vitally important. He could sense her uncertainty and knew that everything rested on what she did next.

Seconds passed, maybe minutes, with them just standing there. He still had his hand on her arm, and gently lifted his other hand, touching her other arm. She shuddered in response, and he was fully aware of it. A smile curved his lips as he slowly, very slowly, drew her closer to him, and instead of pulling back, her feet moved closer to him as though they were obeying his request. They were now standing so close together that they could feel each other's warmth, and then her eyes met his. A feeling of triumph flowed through him which must have been obvious to her, and he couldn't stop himself from gathering her in his arms, gently pressing his lips to hers.

Alex could feel the pressure of her full breasts against his chest as she swayed towards him and delighted in the warmth of her response. He was sure she was totally unaware of the effect she was having on his senses.

"Part your lips for me," he urged, silently encouraging her by nipping her bottom lip and using his tongue to urge her to respond. He heard her moan as she opened for him, but when he darted his tongue into her mouth, she stiffened and gasped in surprise. At least she hadn't withdrawn, he noted, so he gradually deepened the kiss further, finding her responses all he could have hoped for. She relaxed into the kiss, letting her own tongue join with his, and soon they were both lost to the all-consuming sensations as they ravished each other's mouths without constraint.

"Oh, my darling," he cried, as his passion grew, and his senses reeled. He had seduced many women in his time, but never had any affected him so deeply. This was beyond his experience, and he knew instinctively that what they were sharing was more than mere lust. "We both feel it, don't we? This need? This feeling of belonging? We both know what it means."

His words didn't have the desired effect, however. Quite the reverse, in fact. Meg suddenly realised what she was doing and pulled away from him with all her strength, shaking her head in denial. "No ... no, it's not true. It cannot be true. We cannot do this."

Meg decided she must have lost her mind. Why had she not left the room when she had the chance? Before her body's reactions had made leaving impossible. But he had looked at her with such longing, as though she meant the world to him. And he had declared his feelings for her, pleading with her to admit she felt the same. It almost seemed as though this were a matter of life and death to him. As though he truly wanted to marry her. Which she knew was out of the question. But she wanted him as she had never wanted anyone in her life.

She needed to explain things to him. Somehow, she had to make him understand.

He still had not withdrawn his arms from her, but now she felt them on her sides, just below her breasts, his fingers exerting a gentle pressure to urge her body back to his. She knew with all her being that she had to resist him and pushed down on her heels whilst leaning backwards away from temptation. She had to fight this attraction, this longing. "Surely I have suffered enough," she cried. "This cannot be happening to me. You will destroy me if you continue. If I surrender to you."

"Suffering and destruction? What nonsense is this?" he queried, sounding so very angry, but he also released her after making sure she had regained her balance. He looked as though he was not used to rejection. She had clearly offended him. But what else could she do?

She wanted to run. To run away as far and as fast as she could. If he felt for her anything approaching what she was feeling for him, the situation was dire indeed. Yet running would do no good. And she knew that she owed him an explanation for her outburst.

After taking a few deep breaths while straightening her hair and her clothes, she tried to look at him. But he looked so hurt and confused, she nearly succumbed to the temptation to touch his beloved face and smooth away his frown lines. To stop herself, she took another step backwards, resting her hand on the chair back for support, for her legs were threatening to give way, they were shaking so much.

But her voice was deadly calm. "It is not nonsense. You must listen to me."

He nodded, raking his hands through his hair. "Yes, please do explain it to me."

By now, she was wringing her hands. "I cannot deny feeling a strong attraction for you, Alex. I think that is obvious now, But, you see, I am not able to get involved with anyone. I should never have allowed you to touch me, for I am not strong where you are concerned, it seems. And although I believe you when you say that you also feel desire for me, you must accept that there is no chance of a future for us. If I allowed myself to love you, all would be lost. Not just for me, but also for you." She put up her hand to stop him from interjecting.

"Please allow me to finish. You see, I have been involved in the most damning of all scandals. A divorce. And although the divorce did not take place, I am considered a pariah by all respectable people. Everyone knows of the circumstances. Everyone who was in England at the time, anyway. But you obviously have not heard about me, or you wouldn't be thinking of associating with me. And anyway, I have been told about your betrothal. You are no freer than I. You must get well and leave as soon as possible. Go back to your life and forget me."

"Meg, it is all right," he said, "I do know about your divorce case. But all that is in the past. We are here, in the present. And we want each other. No, it is more than mere wanting. On my part at least. I feel we must have been destined to meet. That we belong together. I cannot simply deny how I feel. And neither should you. I can see it in your eyes. You want me."

Meg wanted so badly to believe his words, for he was right; she did want him. She was falling in love with him. She wanted nothing more than to fall into his arms and surrender to his kisses, letting her body be possessed by his. But life was not a fairy tale where everything worked out in the end. He may be besotted now, but when faced with the reality of the situation, he would soon regret his decision. And then another thought struck her. If he already knew of her divorce, that meant that...

She paled as the truth hit her. "You know of the scandal? And yet you pursue me? ... Oh, my God! Now I see what you are about. You want me and are saying all these things to me so that you can get your way. I have heard such honeyed words before, my lord, and they do not stir me. What a fool you have made of me. You think you can simply enjoy my body and cast me aside. After all, I can hear you thinking, she must be willing. Isn't she an adulterer after all? That's what you're thinking, isn't it? Well, I am not an adulterer!" She then covered her face with her hands and sobbed.

"How can you say those dreadful things? You must believe me when I tell you how I feel. You know I am telling the truth. This is not just lust, for God's sake. Meg, listen to me."

Alex tried to touch her, but she fought him off.

What could he do to make her believe him? To make her see that his feelings for her were too strong to put aside. He had never felt this way before; didn't even imagine it was possible to feel like this for someone one he barely knew. Yet he did. He couldn't deny it. Nor could he deny the word that would describe these feelings. Love. It would break his heart to walk away from her, for somewhere along the way, he now knew that he had fallen in love with her.

Why had he been in such a hurry to propose to Penelope? He did not love her. And while a betrothal seemed inevitable, it was not yet a fact. He had been surprised to hear Meg mention his betrothal, having no idea how she had learned of its existence, but for the moment, an expected betrothal seemed unimportant when compared to their relationship. He had to make her see how right this was. He had to make her know that he considered her past to be immaterial.

"Listen to me. I believe you, Meg. I believe you, my darling. You are no adulteress. I know you too well, even though only a few days have passed since we first met. I realised the gossip was untrue the moment I saw you with your family. But you must also believe *me*, Meg. You are the only one who matters to me now. Come back into my arms, I beg you."

He went to touch her again, but again she shook him off. "Listen to me, for God's sake!" he pleaded.

But she wouldn't listen. She put her hands over her ears, moaning her rejection like a wounded animal while she shook her head repeatedly. He said nothing more, but just watched her as though he was trying to think of a way to comfort her.

Slowly she stopped moaning, although her hands still covered her ears, and then she felt his hands cover hers, gently coaxing her to let him remove them, all without words. She let him take her hands in his and watched as he lowered them until he was holding her hands between their bodies. He was caressing hers gently.

He finally spoke. "Meg, please listen to me. We need to talk. To sort this out. But not tonight. You needn't shake your head at me anymore. I can see you need to come to terms with this. Let us sleep on it. You'll agree to do that?"

She just stared at him, neither agreeing nor disagreeing, her eyes bright with tears.

He took her arm, saying, "Come Meg, let me see you to your room."

He wanted to say something more, but neither spoke as they made their way to her door. It was as though she was in a trance. Then, as she reached out her hand to grasp the doorknob, he could stay silent no longer. He had to make her know that this was not the end of the matter. Turning her towards him, he looked deeply into her eyes before he spoke. "I have no intention of giving you up, Meg. I never thought I would ever feel this way about another human being, but I do. And now I have found you, I cannot let you go. We will work something out, you'll see. Even if we must wait. One day, we will be together. This feeling is for ever; I am not going to change my mind about this."

"You don't understand, Alex, but I accept your words and thank you for believing in my innocence. Emily must be my only concern, but for your sake as well, this thing between us cannot be. You cannot marry me, and if you did, you would be made a laughingstock. And I cannot be your mistress. Emily's only hope is for me to live a blameless existence. I will not jeopardize her future. Or yours." And with that quiet pronouncement, she removed his hands from her shoulders, slowly turning away from him and entering her room. The door closed behind her. For some reason, her calm words frightened him far more than her tears had done.

Chapter Eight

Meg almost felt at peace as she prepared for bed that night, knowing she had managed to survive her encounter with Alex, and knowing also that she now had the strength to win the battle she was having with herself.

Long ago she had resigned herself to her fate. Emily was all that mattered. All her hopes now were for her daughter. She had never wished for a second marriage, knowing that she was financially independent. If possible, she would also like for her mother and herself to be allowed readmission to polite society, to be accepted as equals by other widows and maybe to make some close friendships. Her reaction to Alex was therefore unwanted and unwelcome. It could only bring ruin to herself and to her plans.

She had never considered that Emily would benefit by having a father in her life. After all, hadn't her own father ruined, not only his own life, but also that of his family? And her husband, although fond of his daughter, had lived the kind of life that would, ultimately, damage his own, and his family's, reputation.

For a while, as she lay waiting for sleep to claim her, Meg allowed herself the indulgence of imagining herself living a different life. One full of love and happiness with Alex as her husband, with Emily as their child.

But she found these thoughts too unsettling. Emily was not his child and Alex needed a different wife, not her. And much though she may wish for a life in which Alex played a part, Meg knew it was not a realistic possibility.

He was destined to marry elsewhere. Society expected it. Expected him to marry a young virgin. He was already promised to another. As for her, if even a hint of a relationship with Alex reached her father-in-law's ears, she would lose Emily. He had made that perfectly clear.

Alex, on the other hand, found sleep impossible. Too late, it seemed, he had found the one person he could truly love. He ached to hold Meg and to make her his own. Never had he thought that a woman could mean so much to him. And in such a short space of time. Until now, he had taken advantage of the charms of many women and had even cared for some, such as Jeanette. But he had never been in love until now. He knew this was different. This was true caring for another human being. It surpassed even his love for his mother, although that love was great indeed. But Meg was now his love, his life, his destiny.

Was this love to be denied? To be unfulfilled? Somehow, he had to work out a solution. But first, he had to define the problem. Meg had told him enough to know that she had been wrongfully accused of adultery. However, the scandal existed, as did the fact that she was still talked about as a lightskirt, a trollop, at least in some quarters. God, even the thought made him feel sick with anger. Yet the stories were all untrue. He believed that with all his heart.

She had a brother, presumably the new earl. What was his part in all this? He must find out about this Damien tomorrow, he vowed. What sort of man must he be, for God's sake, to stand by and allow his sister to be slandered?

Then there was the problem of his own engagement. He hadn't yet proposed to Penelope, but everything else was settled. He could not now withdraw his offer. Not if he wanted to keep his own honour. Somehow, he had to find an honourable way of withdrawing from the contract he had made with the marquess for Penelope. He couldn't marry her now. He wouldn't marry her, but at the same time, he didn't want to damage either her or his own reputation if he could prevent it.

But an inner voice protested that nothing mattered more than his need for Meg. Neither honour nor logic. Why could they not defy all for their love?

He contemplated this option for a while. Emily was the key. He knew Meg would do nothing to harm her daughter. Yet her daughter would undoubtedly benefit from his protection. She would be *his* daughter then. The daughter of an earl. A wealthy earl, which was more to the point in these days when wealth seemed to open most doors.

Even if society frowned on them, there would be many who would ignore the gossip. The Prince Regent himself, for one. He had accepted many reprobates into his circle, and his own way of life was far from blameless. Some of the gossip surrounding the prince would make Meg's situation seem commonplace!

But that was only away from court life. In London Society, it was a different matter. He and Meg would not be welcomed at court, or in any of the more respectable establishments or drawing rooms. And Emily's prospects would therefore be affected. But would she be able to contract a marriage with a member of one of the more respectable families anyway? Scandals may fade from conversation but are rarely forgotten. And, although Meg was unaware that her name was still being defamed, the fact remained that it was.

What could he do about it? Should he tell her about it, for he supposed she had a right to know? No, he decided eventually, it would hurt her too much. However, he vowed that, even if he could not have her, he would do everything he could to stop the rumours and lies. That must be his priority.

Eventually, he decided he had examined the problem as much as he could for the moment and that he should try to sleep but could find no peace. Thoughts kept circling round in his head, and he heard the first cock crow to welcome a new day before he was at last able to fall into an exhausted sleep.

The next day, he joined the family for lunch, but Meg sat as far away from him as she could and rarely looked at him. Emily was her usual cheerful self, telling him about her morning which she had apparently spent out of doors with her mother. He did his best to involve Meg in the conversation, but she spoke as little as possible during the uncomfortable meal. Emily was the first to ask to leave the table. Her friend, Laura, would be waiting for her, she told them.

Meg then also gave her excuses and left the room without a backward glance. Alex watched her go and noticed how unhappy she looked by her obvious decision to avoid him. With only himself and Ellen now left in the dining room, Alex wondered if perhaps she may be able to help answer some of his questions, but soon abandoned the idea. They engaged in a rather stilted conversation about London, discovering that they had very few acquaintances in common, after which Alex excused himself stating that he still needed to rest in the afternoons.

On returning to his room, he decided to enlist the help of his valet. Without giving any details, he explained to Jenkins that he needed to find out about male visitors to the house over the years. Excluding Lady Margaret's brother, Damien.

"Oh, I already know most of what has gone on in these parts for many years past," Jenkins informed him.

"Really?" Alex was dumbfounded and didn't know whether to be angry or eternally grateful.

"Oh Lordy, yes," Jenkins continued. "Great talkers round here, you know. Rob and Tom found out most of the gossip down at the village alehouse. But Jed let slip a few things as well. Very protective of her ladyship they all are round here, or so it seems."

"Well, it seems to me that those in my service have been engaging in gossip rather more than they ought," Alex exclaimed, feeling his hackles rise. The thought of his men gossiping in the village about Meg alarmed him. Yet, while he hated the thought of anyone gossiping about her, he needed to know what was being said. A bit of a conundrum!

"Do you want me to tell you what I have heard or not?" asked Jenkins, looking offended, as though he had been rebuked without cause.

Alex waved his hand in an expression of dismissal. "Of course, carry on," he said, adding that he was sorry for acting like an ass.

"Well, I can tell you that shortly after settling here, over five years ago it was, a fellow from London arrived saying he had come from the earl, her brother. Even so, Lady Margaret was very wary of the man for some reason, and only with great misgivings did she allow him to stay. Pity she didn't send him packing there and then, but I suppose she thought she had better not turn him away if he truly had been sent by her brother. Anyway, it transpired that he was telling a pack of lies, and was really after Lady Margaret herself, thinking her fair game. Thought she would fall into his arms, or so the story goes. When his wooing failed, he lost his temper, apparently, and got mean, saying she was not likely to get a better offer, being what she was, and she should be grateful that someone was willing to offer her marriage. It got quite nasty, it did."

By this time, Alex's fists were clenched so tightly, his knuckles had turned white. But his voice was deadly calm. "And how do the servants know all this?"

Jenkins shrugged. "Listening at doors, I expect. Anyway, Jed intervened apparently and saw him off the premises, but they say that Lady Margaret was in a dreadful state for weeks afterwards.

It was obvious the fellow was only after her inheritance, and this was confirmed the next time her brother arrived, begging as usual. He often comes begging, I was told. And gets what he wants, it seems. Soft as butter, is Lady Margaret, so they say.

"Anyway, this time she and her brother had words, but as usual, he somehow managed to soften her up. Jed heard him admit his blame in the matter saying that the man was more of an acquaintance than a friend and that, most likely, the fellow found out about Lady Margaret's financial status when he - that is her brother - was in his cups one night, after losing badly at the gaming tables. He said he vaguely remembered mentioning something about appealing to his rich sister to pay his debts, and then confessed that when his friends had seemed mighty eager to know more, he had started to brag, telling them more than he should have. Lady Margaret was very angry with him but, as I said, she came round eventually and agreed to settle his debts. Something she still does, apparently. It is thought that all he must do is go to see her man-of-business in London whenever the need arises."

From knowing virtually nothing about the reasons for Meg's predicament, Alex now understood so much more. He was simply stunned by what his valet knew. My God, her brother had much to answer for! Was there anything more that Jenkins had not yet told him?

"I should be angry with you for talking about her ladyship behind her back, I suppose, but as it's what I have just asked you to do, I would be being a bit of a hypocrite, wouldn't I? Thank you, Jenkins. What you have told me helps me understand a lot more than I did. I didn't realize she had inherited money. A fortune, you said. She certainly doesn't live as though she had a fortune. Still, that's none of my business. I want to help her, you see. Did you hear anything about any other callers, by any chance?"

"Well, when I mentioned to Jed that I would have thought it likely that more than one would have been interested in trying their luck with her ladyship, he told me I had guessed the right of it. But he was determined to prevent her ladyship from suffering through any more such visits, and so, from then on, Jed and the others watched out for any other unscrupulous varmints.

"Whenever any likely candidates asked for directions to this house, they were given false directions, and a message was sent to Jed. He then intercepted these visitors and asked their business. Not one to be fooled easily, is that Jed. He has sent several potential bothersome individuals on their way over the years. As far as I know, no one else has managed to upset her ladyship like that first fellow did."

"Thank you, Jenkins. I must speak to Jed and find out if he remembers the names of any of these fellows. I think I shall be paying them a visit."

* * *

Alex's plans to speak to Meg and Jed did not meet with success that day, and the following day seemed to start without much hope of success either. But Emily was to get her wish and she and Alex set out for a light canter after breakfast.

Alex's mount, Firefly, was restless at first, having had little exercise for days, but he reined him in and kept to Emily's pace. He would have thoroughly enjoyed listening to her chatter had he not had so many other concerns to consider. He was astounded, therefore, when she confronted him with a direct question about her mother.

"What did you say?" he asked, whilst slowing his horse to a walk.

"I said, why don't you marry Mama?"

"Why should your Mama want to marry me? She hardly knows me," he managed to say calmly, despite being both unsettled and stunned at her words.

"Oh, what has that to do with it. I know you like each other. And I would so like you to be my papa and be with us forever. And then Mama would not be so lonely, you see. And Grandmama would be able to live in a large house again. One like she used to have and misses so much. You do have a large house, don't you?"

Alex laughed, at last getting himself under control. "So, this house is not large enough for you. Is that it?"

"Oh, it's plenty large enough for me. But Grandmama and Grandpapa Greene live in a much bigger house, and I think Grandmama must have lived in one like that. She looks so sad when she talks about it to me. And anyway, that is not the reason I think you should marry Mama. I think Mama wants you to stay, and she sighs when I talk about you staying. Before telling me off for being foolish, that is," she added with a broad smile. "I know she likes you a lot. And I have noticed how you look at her. Just like Peter looks at Sally. And he is in love with her. Everyone says so. So, you see, I think you love Mama. And people in love should marry, shouldn't they? And have children. I think I should like a little brother or sister," she added, "as long as they didn't break my toys!"

"My word, you've got it all worked out, haven't you? Well, much as I would like to agree with you, in this case, I'm afraid I am not able to." How could one so young be so perceptive, Alex wondered. He had no idea who this Sally was but did remember that Peter was a young man in Meg's employ. Yet as far as he knew, neither he nor Meg had acted in such a way as to invite speculation about their mutual attraction. Quite the reverse, in fact. But this young lady seemed to believe that he and her mother loved each other! While this was true from his perspective at least, he knew he had to deny it.

Seeing her frown, he continued, "You see, it isn't possible to wave a magic wand to make things happen as you want them to. People must do things they don't want to do sometimes. Other people must be considered. For instance, your mother wouldn't want to do anything that you or your grandmother didn't like, would she?"

"Oh yes, she would. She is always stopping me from doing things I want to do. And she and Grandmama often argue. That means they don't agree with each other, doesn't it? So, you see, Mama doesn't always do what we want her to do. And anyway, I *do* want you to marry her!"

Alex laughed at her delightful ingenuousness. "But will my fiancée feel the same?"

Emily frowned. "What is a fiancée?"

"A lady who has agreed to become my wife."

"Oh bother. That does mess things up. But she won't mind if you really love Mama, will she?"

"I'm afraid it doesn't work like that, Emily. And anyway, you are assuming that I love your mother. I owe her, and you, my life, and I shall always be in your debt. But love, now, that's another thing. I have become very fond of you both and I hope we shall always be friends. But you must not try and make things happen just because you would like them to happen, Emily. And this conversation is not a suitable one for young ladies to pursue, you know, so let's change the subject, if you don't mind. Your mother would be horrified if she knew what we were talking about."

Emily frowned but seemed to accept his edict, as she then asked him to promise not to tell either her mother or grandmother what she had said. Receiving his promise, she cheered up considerably, challenging him in a race back to the house. He was only too willing to oblige, and they set off for home. Alex made sure he lost the race which made Emily whoop with joy, and she ran off to boast of her victory to anyone who would listen!

Alex entered the house in a much more sombre mood having realised that it was now time for him to go. He had recovered enough to allow him to travel, at least as far as Selby, and knew it would be unwise to remain in the house any longer. Meg had been trying to avoid him, and he acknowledged that there could be gossip if he stayed. Having a male invalid in the house was one thing, but having a healthy, lusty male guest in a house without a male host would be inviting comment. But he was determined to speak to Meg again before he left. He just had to have one last attempt to convince her of his love, and to see if she would allow him to hope.

He ran into Jed in the stables and asked if he had time to stop and talk. Jed could tell from Lord Tenby's tone that the matter was of some urgency and immediately left with him, walking towards the paddock.

They talked about horses for a while, and it was Jed who eventually broached the subject uppermost in the earl's mind, by saying, "If I may say so, my lord, I believe you wish to ask me something about my mistress. Am I right?"

Alex nodded, and Jed continued, "I also think I can guess what it may be. That Jenkins of yours seemed mighty interested in finding out about Lady Margaret's private life. Especially about men. Well, I would like to ask you a question first if you don't mind, my lord. Why do you want to know? I doubt you would mean her harm, but she has suffered enough, if you will excuse my impertinence. She is a truly good woman and deserves to find happiness. I won't do or say anything to harm her."

"You are a good man, Jed. Lady Margaret is lucky to have you in her household. And you are right. I do want information. But to help her. For no other reason. If I tell you something in confidence, can I be sure it will go no further? Not even to your Alice?"

"I have never betrayed a trust, and I won't start now. Yes, you can trust me to keep your secret. I hope that assurance will satisfy you, for I can do naught else to convince you."

"Thank you, Jed. Yes, your word will do nicely. You see, before I came here, I was told something of Lady Margaret. You wouldn't want me to repeat the slanderous lies, but there are those who have boasted of receiving favours, and I need to know the names of these braggarts so that I can shut their mouths once and for all. I am told you have sent more than one man on his way, having become suspicious of their intentions towards your mistress. I would have their names, if you know them, or, failing that, their descriptions."

Alex's words had caused Jed's face and neck to go red with anger. "Those bastards," he cried. "I should have killed them when I had the chance. Those, wicked, evil, useless fops. Harmed my mistress, have they? It makes me want to mount a horse and go tearing off to London to deal with them."

Jed then looked into the eyes of Lord Tenby, and saw he was thinking along the same lines. "But you are more likely to succeed than I am, aren't you? You have the means, being of the same class."

"And I have every intention of succeeding," Alex confirmed.

Jed nodded and scratched his head as if deep in thought. "Well, I remember two of the names but the third managed to keep his name to himself. But I can give you a description, for it was only last year that the last of them arrived."

Alex received this intelligence with gratitude and with some surprise. Hadn't Percy implied that there had been many who had claimed to have carnal knowledge of Meg? He would confront Percy with this as soon as he could and hoped Percy would be able to identify the third villain from Jed's colourful description. Then his eyes glittered dangerously at the thought of his interview with Percy, for he realised with a jolt that, since Percy had also slandered Meg, he may have to call his own cousin out over the issue!

Chapter Nine

After his talk with Jed, Alex was even more impatient to be alone with Meg, but knew he should first inform her mother of his proposed early departure. Unfortunately, he found that Emily was with her grandmother and was reluctant to announce his decision to leave Wharfe House in front of the child. He had to wait until after enduring another uncomfortable lunchtime before he found himself alone with Meg's mother.

Once again, Meg had sat as far away from him as she could, and the thought of leaving her made his food taste like sawdust! She looked so demure sitting there with her eyes lowered, her frilly, lace cap covering most of her hair. But he couldn't help but notice that one or two strands of hair had escaped, lending a softness to her otherwise rather austere outfit. She had chosen to wear a high-waisted day dress made of a pale, blue cotton with long sleeves and a demure apron front.

He would never tire of looking at her, he thought. Why was it that only this one woman had touched him as no other had before? The thought of leaving her caused a pain to his heart that hurt far more than the bullet to his shoulder. Nor would it ever heal. But he knew he had to go. Would she receive the news of his departure with relief? He would soon find out. As soon as possible after the meal,

Meg and Emily left together and Alex took the chance of offering to assist Meg's mother to the sofa.

"That is very kind of you, Alex," she said, watching him take the seat opposite to hers. He lost no time in announcing his imminent departure explaining his reason for leaving so soon.

She smiled at him. "I see you are a gentleman of refined sensibilities, as indeed you should be. You have been more than welcome here, my lord, but, you see, we need to be incredibly careful of gossip. We have Emily to think of."

"I know." He wanted to tell her so much more about his plans where Meg was concerned, but knew the time was not right. Rising from his chair, he excused himself. "I had better go and instruct my valet to pack. I would also like to tell Lady Margaret of our decision."

"Yes, you should. I believe you will find her in her sitting room on the next floor, third door on the right. She should be on her own as I believe that Emily is writing up her journal in the library, so please leave the door ajar while you are with my daughter."

Alex went straight to Meg's room and lightly knocked on the door, unsure of his welcome and unsure he would be able to control his emotions. His innate good manners had always managed to guide his behaviour in the past but being alone with the woman he loved was a very different matter, especially as she had made it abundantly clear that she wanted nothing to do with him. He wanted to say so many things, do so many things, and only hoped he wouldn't make a complete hash of it.

He found Meg sitting on a window seat, with a sewing basket at her side. She had been doing some mending, he guessed, but when she saw him, she visibly jumped, pricking her finger in her surprise, then stifled an exclamation as colour suffused her face and neck.

Alex saw her struggle to compose herself as she lowered her work to her lap before inviting him to take a seat indicating the comfortable, leather chair near the fireplace.

He moved to the chair as she requested, noticing that she still looked flustered, so he smiled as she moved to join him, sitting in a similar chair to his on the other side of the hearth. Only then did he take his own seat.

He had better get to the point, he decided, even though he would much prefer to reach out for her, remove her silly cap and kiss her senseless!

The feelings she evoked in him were completely foreign to him and he had no idea how to deal with them. He had never found it so hard to bid a woman goodbye, yet leaving Meg was near impossible to do. It would be like tearing himself in two. The tension was unbearable and when he spoke, his words were more abrupt than he intended.

"I came to inform you of my departure," he began, before her reaction made him wish the words unsaid. She had visibly paled, and her look of sadness mixed with despair almost made him change his mind. The urge to reach out for her became even more difficult to resist, but he knew he had no choice but to leave her. And he had to tell her so now, without wavering. "I am feeling much better and, as you know, this morning I rode with Emily with no ill effects. Indeed, my energy is returning more rapidly than I had thought possible. And to accept your hospitality any longer would be unfair of me."

"But the doctor said ten days. Surely you should do as he says, my lord. And you must know you are welcome here."

"Am I, Lady Margaret? You have given me the distinct impression that you wish me to the devil!"

"Oh, please don't say such a thing, Alex. I wish you nothing of the sort. It's just that I have been busy. We have ... enjoyed having you here. All of us. And we shall be sorry to see you depart. Especially Emily."

He had hoped she was going to admit that *she* had especially enjoyed his company but knew she would never do so. And why should she?

"Yes, Emily has enjoyed my visit. And even your mother, I venture to suggest. But you, Meg. You have been made to feel uncomfortable. Which, I confess, is my fault entirely. If I had not declared my true feelings for you ... but I did, and whilst I would like nothing more than to have you respond to me as I believe your heart would wish ..."

She interrupted him. "Please stop. I cannot let you continue. We have said all that needs to be said. There is no future for us, so perhaps you are right to go now, while we can still resist temptation and I can begin to learn how to ... how to forget you."

Ah, so now we are getting to the truth, he thought. "Meg, my darling..." he began, then paused when she opened her mouth to protest the endearment, putting up his hand to still her unspoken words. "I *shall* call you my darling Meg, for that is how I think of you."

"I am not your darling, or even your Meg. I can never be your Meg. You are betrothed to another, or have you conveniently forgotten that fact?"

Alex knew she was getting angry, but also knew that her anger was tinged with despair.

"No, I have not forgotten. But she has not yet accepted my offer, and if I speak with her, I feel there is hope that she will release me from my promise."

"You must do no such thing! It would be most dishonourable. I cannot be your wife; you must realise that."

"Why can't you be my wife? You are free to marry, and I hope soon to be. Yes, I do want you to be my wife. I should be honoured for you to be my wife."

Tears sprang to her eyes as she shook her head. "Oh Alex, if only it were so simple. But nothing you have said has changed my mind. Listen to me, please. If you do not proceed with your betrothal, you will not be honoured for long. And if you did that and married me, you would find yourself being cut in the street, at your club and by the best families. And before long you would start blaming me for ruining your life. Even if you are not concerned for yourself, think of me. How do you expect me to live with the knowledge that it was because of me that your life was ruined?"

"You are more important to me than any of those people, Meg."

"Well then, and what about your mother? Would she thank me for marrying you? She would be ostracised as well, you know. And I would have to suffer her disapproval, for she *would* disapprove of me, you can be sure. I am not the kind of wife she has in mind for you. You must face facts, Alex. I wouldn't be welcomed into your family. I have first-hand experience of how the system works, and none of you would like it, I can assure you," she said bitterly.

Alex didn't want to listen but when she mentioned his mother, he saw that she had a point. Not about his reactions, but he did understand her reticence, and knew she was right about how much his mother may suffer. "But there has to be a way for us to be together."

"If you think I will become your mistress, you can forget it."

"That's not what I was thinking, but if it was, so what? Surely, if society forbids us our love, we can meet discreetly. After all, society allows for widows to have discreet liaisons. But I am still planning on marrying you. We could go abroad. You have nothing to keep you here, after all. Buried as you are in the country, never seeing anyone. We could marry and leave England."

"Now you are being reckless, Alex. You left the army because it was your duty to take up your inheritance. Nothing has changed. You know that. And even if I agreed, where could we go? The war in Europe has put a stop to us living on the continent. But my answer would be no, anyway. Emily is English, and I want her to be brought up here. When the time is right, we will re-join society. I am not penniless, you know. I will be able to set up an establishment worthy of my former status and will try to win the goodwill of some of the matrons in Bath. Then, hopefully, we will slowly gain acceptance.

So long as I continue to live a blameless existence. That means no romances. No discreet liaisons. No male escorts even when I begin to attend functions again. I am determined to do all I can to ensure that Emily will have a chance for a good future. She will have money, and I am sure, beauty as well."

Alex felt like telling her that she was fooling herself, and that her present reputation was anything but pure. That she was still being talked about as a loose woman. But he did not do so. To do so would only destroy her. He had to pretend the future she was painting for Emily was a possibility. Otherwise, she would feel she had no hope. And maybe, if he could put a stop to the rumours, her plan would have a chance. In any case, he didn't think telling her would make her any more likely to accept his proposal.

"You are making it very hard for me," he said, his shoulders slumping in dejection. "How can I just say goodbye to you? I love you, Meg Greene. I love you."

"And I love you," she responded, almost in a whisper, before adding, more strongly, "But it cannot be. You must accept that. But know I shall treasure your words for ever, and shall continue to hope, that wherever you are and whatever you are doing, some part of you will still love me. I know I am being selfish, but in that way, your love shall become my solace. My comfort. It will be with me always, even though you cannot. Let us part in agreement, please, Alex. Accept your fate as I have learned to accept mine."

Never, his whole being cried, but he did not voice his thought. "Oh Meg, this is so damned hard," he said, rising from his chair. "All right. I will accept what you say for now and won't try to change your mind even though I think most of your reasoning misguided. But please Meg, let me at least hold you once more before I leave." Holding out his arms in invitation, he urged her, "Please come into my arms, my love."

She did not immediately rush to his arms, but he knew she wanted to. He waited patiently, and his heart nearly stopped when she uttered a soft cry, rose, and went into his embrace, resting her head on his chest.

They silently held each other, swaying gently, as if to soothe away their pain. He breathed in her scent and could feel her warmth as he gloried in the feel of her full, soft breasts pressing against his chest and in her unspoken trust as she clung to him. He knew he would remember this moment all his life. The love and the feeling of belonging that passed between them as they held each other was indescribable and unforgettable.

Time stood still for endless moments until slowly but surely the bliss they were feeling was replaced with longing. Alex tightened his hold on her and kissed her temple. He could feel her breasts begin to swell, her nipples begin to harden, and her heartbeat begin to quicken, and he knew she was becoming as aroused as he. His hands began to roam at will over her back, her neck, her buttocks. Their breathing became even more laboured and his erection by this time was hard, urgent, and painful. He silently cursed his bodily reactions, not wanting to frighten her away, but in the next instant, it became apparent that she was anything but frightened.

Her body changed position, and she raised her arms so that her hands could caress his shoulders and head, while her body moved closer still and she raised herself up until their very centres were pressed hard against each other. His arousal must have been obvious to her, but she seemed to glory in it, rotating her hips gently to both give and receive pleasure, while looking into his eyes, as though inviting him to claim her lips in a hungry kiss.

He obliged, moaning as he plundered her depths with his tongue. She answered by mirroring his actions with her own mouth, sucking, nipping, and exploring his mouth in return, as if communicating to him all the love and passion she was feeling. By now, his heart was racing while he gloried in the bitter-sweet delight of her newfound responses. She had not only learned well from their earlier encounter but was trying out some new ideas of her own! Ideas that were driving him crazy!

He realised that soon it would be impossible for him to stop, and he was not at all sure she knew what she was doing. So, gently but firmly he drew back, taking her face between his hands as he gazed into her eyes. She was breathing heavily, as was he.

"I need you, Meg," he told her, "But we must stop before I lose all control. I want to make love with you, but I don't think you want that, do you?

"What? Oh my God! I'm so sorry Alex. I didn't know. I just felt so free, as if I had been released from my bonds. As if I had escaped. But nothing has changed. I know that. I just got lost for a while in the wonder of you and the feelings you evoke in me." She also stepped back but looked as if she would have preferred to throw caution to the winds.

And then she made a confession. "I too may have been unable to stop, but where would that leave us? I must be strong because of Emily, but it is not easy for me."

"You want me?"

"Yes," she acknowledged at last, her breathing still laboured. "I now understand what you mean by your need for me, I am also burning up with need. I need to lie with you. To feel you take me. I never enjoyed the sexual act with my husband, Lucas, yet, somehow, I know it would be different with you. I feel so much when you touch me. Even a look can make me shiver in anticipation. And whenever I think of you, a warmth flows throughout my whole body. It has been hell trying to appear calm in your presence. At luncheon and in the evenings, my heart does somersaults whenever you enter the room. I suppose I shouldn't tell you this, but I need to be honest with you. You are leaving because you must, and I want you to go with a clear conscience. We must resist doing anything to jeopardize that."

Alex nodded, accepting her decision with reluctance, and bit down the words he wanted to say. He was going to spend one more night in her home and the thought of spending it with her in her bed would be his dearest wish, except for the fact he respected her too much to take advantage of her vulnerability. Yet, at the same time, he was not ready to end things between them. He kissed her lightly on her trembling lips. An almost chaste kiss. He smiled and watched as tears flooded her eyes.

"Your smile has undone me," she cried, and he held her close while she sobbed. When eventually the tears subsided and she had used the handkerchief he had offered her, he stroked her hair - her cap had long since fallen from her head - saying soothing words to convey his own emotions.

"Have we time to talk, Meg?" he asked. "I would like you tell me about your marriage if you would honour me with your confidence. I very much want to understand what happened and the kind of husband he was."

She nodded and they returned to their seats rather shakily, keeping in contact by holding hands. Even that limited touching burned him to the depths of his soul.

"And I want to tell you, Alex. I have never told anyone else the whole story about what happened between the two of us, not even my mother. I said only what had to be said, but now I want you to know. To understand. I know I can trust you with my innermost secrets. That you will not condemn me."

"Never," he cried.

And so, looking down at their joined hands, she began her tale.

"Well, I was only fifteen when we wed, and I thought I loved him. He was so handsome and gallant. And I thought he loved me. He said he did. Told me I was the only woman he would ever love. I went into the marriage willingly. But on the wedding night he seemed more interested in his friends, and I went to bed alone.

That was to be the pattern throughout the months ahead. Until I became pregnant."

"Go on. What happened on your wedding night? Did he eventually come to you?"

"Sometime in the middle of the night I awoke to find him about to enter me from behind. When I screamed, he stopped for a minute, but said he was trying to make things easy for me and urged me to lie still. So that is what I did, for I had been warned to obey him in all things. Mother had told me something of what to expect and had told me that my wedding vows were sacred. But he hurt me and when I cried out, he cursed me, even as he was pumping away inside me. Eventually, he groaned loudly, stiffened, and then went limp. I couldn't bring myself to move. I was so horrified by what had happened I suppose I was suffering from a kind of shock. I couldn't look at him or speak. I only knew how grateful I felt when he left me and returned to his own bedchamber."

Alex realised he was squeezing her hands with the tension her words had evoked. He wanted to kill the bastard, but knew he was already dead. He forced himself to relax his grip and encouraged her to continue.

"The following morning, I tried to talk to him about it, but he told me in no uncertain terms that it was not appropriate to discuss such things. He seemed kind enough during the day, but most nights I had to endure that unpleasant ritual. It never lasted long, thank goodness. And I never felt like kissing him. Which is just as well, for he never kissed me." She looked at him then, for the first time since beginning her story, and saw him nod.

"I gathered as much from your inexperience in that area," he responded. "And while I hate what he did to you, I am also overjoyed and honoured to be the one to awaken your sensuality. He could have scarred you emotionally for life." *Or is that another reason for her drawing back from me,* he wondered for a moment before rejecting such a notion. She had a passionate nature and when the time came, he knew it would be good between them. *If* that time ever came.

Pushing that thought aside, he then asked her to continue with her story. "What happened after you became pregnant? And why was a divorce considered? Or is it too painful to talk about? I don't want to press you but would like to understand."

"It's all right, Alex. I want to tell you. As soon as my pregnancy was confirmed, he left me alone. Went to London without me. When he did visit for a night or two, he never spent time with me. Said my appearance disgusted him. He hated fat women, he said. I felt terrible, as you can imagine. Unloved and unwanted. But I had a child inside me and I think that was what kept me from total depression. That and the letters my mother wrote me.

"She was still with my brother Damien at the time. We had lost our home, you see. But that is another story. She was living in London, supervising Damien's small, rented townhouse, and trying to curb his excesses. Without much success, I fear. I asked for her to be allowed to stay with me, or at least to be allowed to visit, but Lucas refused to permit it.

"Anyway, after Emily was born, he returned for a while. He seemed very taken with his daughter even though she was not the son he had hoped for. But then, she looked so like him. Black hair and deep brown eyes. He tried to have sex with me again, but told me my large breasts made me ugly and said he couldn't abide ugly women. I don't know why they grew so big. They weren't like this before I became pregnant. I was almost completely flat when I married."

Alex felt his anger rise again. "There must have been something wrong with him then, for your breasts are magnificent. I have never seen lovelier."

"Really? I have noticed you looking at them admiringly but couldn't understand why. Even my mother thinks they are too big."

"Jealousy. It must be. That, or she knows the effect such luscious breasts have on men and worries for your safety." How could her mother add to her misery, he thought? At least he could reassure her about her beauty.

"Anyway, I believed him and from that time on have always felt they were ugly. I cover them whenever possible with a shawl and never wear fashionable, low-necked gowns."

"And I suggest you keep doing that. Or I shall be jealous!"

She laughed and squeezed his hands, and Alex knew that she at last felt completely comfortable with him. Just as he felt comfortable with her. Somehow, a miracle had happened. Somehow, they had found each other, and love had strung up between them. He was honoured beyond measure that she felt she could trust him with her secrets.

After a while, she continued with her story. "Alex, I felt so unloved and undeserving. Yet I didn't hate him. He couldn't help how he felt, I suppose. And his mother was forever scolding me, telling me what a dreadful wife I was, not to allow my husband in my bed and that it was my duty to produce an heir. Lucas must had told her I was the one at fault, and she wouldn't listen to me. Anyway, he spent more and more time away from me, coming home with his cronies for a few days every now and again, when he tried to do his duty, but couldn't. Oh, how I cried! How ugly I felt. I only felt happy when he was gone, and Emily and I were alone together. I knew by then that I was trapped in a loveless marriage. It was obvious that his love for me had been a pretence from the start and I came to realise that I had made a terrible mistake in imagining myself in love with him."

Alex knew of course that it was general knowledge that she had taken a lover and was discovered, but now knew she would never have done such a thing. He also knew that there was something different about her husband and was beginning to suspect what it was. "Yet despite being in a loveless relationship, the idea of the divorce did not come from you."

"Of course not! I had Emily by then and would never have thought of taking such a drastic step even had I known that such a thing was possible."

"So, what did happen?"

Meg lowered her eyes for a moment, a frown forming between her brows. "This next part is difficult for me to speak of. It is very shocking."

"But since you know that I have already heard some of the tales, it is surely better that I now hear the truth."

Nodding in agreement, she took a deep breath, then continued. "Emily was two when it happened. Lucas came home with his friends for one of his visits. That evening, I went to bed early. My presence was obviously not wanted any more than I wanted to be in their company. Lucas seemed so different when they were with him. Or maybe he had changed. I was hardly ever alone with him so how would I know? But he now seemed so cruel and frequently taunted me openly in front of his friends.

"I didn't expect him to come to me that night - he rarely did any more - so when I awoke with a naked man on top of me, I jumped and screamed in alarm. Almost immediately I realised that the man on top of me was not Lucas - this man was much bigger and heavier than him - and so I screamed even louder and struggled to be free, terror stricken and fighting for my life.

"I was so relieved when help came, but not for long. At least Sir Blewett - the man in bed with me - was prevented from completing his rape, but Lucas stormed at me, accusing me of adultery, and saying he had had enough of my depraved behaviour. I was so shocked I could only gape at him! He ranted on about me not being fit to produce his heir, that he would never be sure if the child was his. His friend apologised profusely, saying it was the wine that had caused him to succumb to my seduction. Two servants heard all this as well as several of his friends. Lucas ordered everyone from the room, before leaving himself, locking me in!

"The following morning, they all left, taking Emily with them. I just couldn't believe what was happening. But worse was to come. I was a prisoner; my daughter was gone and then I heard he had started divorce proceedings.

"As you know, the only hope of getting a divorce was if he could convince parliament that I was unfit to be his wife or to bear his children. So, my crime had to be great indeed. But to think of these lies being made public only increased my sense of shame. I even felt guilty for a while. After I recovered from the shock, I began to understand his behaviour. He obviously wanted to divorce me and only did what he had to do. He and Rodney Blewett must have planned the whole thing. No doubt he had already chosen his next wife, but I never heard of any other woman. And I never saw him again. My main concern was my daughter. I knew she was with his parents, but worried about her constantly.

"After his death, the following year, his parents sent their man-of-affairs to discuss my future with me. I was told that I had inherited five thousand a year and that a generous dowry had been set aside for Emily. Lucas had not changed his will, you see. I suppose he never gave death a thought. Luckily, his parents could do nothing about it. Lucas had money of his own, inherited from his maternal grand-parents, and was not dependent on his parent's wealth. The divorce bill was, of course, dropped. I had to move from my husband's estate as it was part of the Greene inheritance and was encumbered. His parents did not want to give me shelter. They wanted me gone and had arranged for Lady Greene's younger sister and her family to be installed in my place.

"However, they also owned this modest country house. I don't know how it came to be in their possession, but it was not an entailed property, and they had no great attachment to it. In fact, it had been left unoccupied for some time. They allowed me to purchase it for a sum far below its estimated value and advised me that if I agreed to live here quietly without a breath of scandal, they would relent and return Emily to me. I immediately arranged for my mother to join me. She was the only one to support me throughout my troubles, and I knew she would be happier with me than with Damien. And that's about it. You know the rest, I think."

"You have been so abused, my love. And I can see that you still live with the threat from his parents hanging over your head. I assume your father-in-law is Emily's official guardian?"

She merely nodded.

He thought then about the rumours circulating about her. What if Lucas' parents should hear of them? Would they carry out their threat to take Emily away from her? It seemed imperative for him to find a way to expose the lies without causing more speculation. Without causing Meg more harm. Aloud, he said, "But you have not told me all. I would like to know about this brother of yours. Did he not stand by you?"

"Damien? He has also been hurt, you know. Our father gambled away his inheritance, you see. After father's death, Damien had a mother and a younger sister to support, but no home and no money. He was only two and twenty at the time and must have resented having such a responsibility placed on him. When he received the offer for my hand from one of his friends it must have seemed a godsend to him. The Greene's did not even require a dowry, but instead, settled an enormous amount of money on me, whilst also settling Damien's considerable debts. At that time, you see, I was greatly valued."

She laughed, but without mirth. "Ironic, isn't it? For Lucas could never have loved me, could he? But Damien was forever in his debt and continued to live on Lucas' goodwill. So, when the scandal broke, Damien found himself in a difficult position. He could hardly bite the hand that fed him. And afterwards, what could he do? He talked to me about how lucky I was to be rid of the scandal at last, and to be such a rich widow. Of how fortunate I was to have come out of it so well. He really did not understand. And still does not, I fear."

"And now he lives off *your* goodwill," he finished for her.

"I suppose he does," she conceded. "I offered to buy him a commission, you know, but he would not hear of it. Told me he wasn't the type to forfeit his life in honour of his country. But he doesn't seem to be the type to do anything else, either. He is now over thirty, and seems quite happy to live an idle life, coming to me to rescue him from his creditors when the need arises."

"And why do you continue to rescue him?"

"Simply because I must. There has been enough shame surrounding my family already. We don't need any more. And Damien never does anything too dreadful."

"You hope," he added dryly, silently adding Damien to the number of problems to be dealt with.

"And is that the end of it? Nothing else to trouble you in all these years?"

"No."

"Am I your first admirer then? Have no others tried to court you?"

Meg looked down at their hands. Very quietly, she sighed and told him of the man who visited her five years before.

"Who was he, Meg?"

"Sir Rodney Blewett."

Alex heard the name in disbelief. How could that varmint dare to face Meg after what he had done to her? Let alone insult her with his advances and curse her when she rejected him? He hoped he was still alive, for he dearly wanted to be the one to kill him. But to Meg, he simply nodded his understanding, saying, "The swine. After all you had suffered. I hope you sent him on his way."

She laughed. "Oh, Jed took care of him. You should have seen him, Alex. I almost felt sorry for Sir Blewett in the end. I knew I was safe from him then. He would not dare to show his face here again." Seeing Alex was not amused, she added, "Don't look so angry, my love, it is all in the past. He cannot hurt me anymore."

But I can hurt him, he thought.

"So, until I came, you were content? You feel safe here, is that it?"

"Yes. To both your assumptions. Although, the trouble with the Luddites bothers me a little, even though I know they won't attack this house. I have neither a farm nor a factory. But I worry about the lawlessness sometimes. What happened to you could happen to any of us."

"I think you will be safe. But if you ever need to move, please come to me for help. Apart from loving you, I owe you my life, and will always come if you call. I now know how much you risked by allowing me into your home, and it makes me even more determined to remove myself at once. I will leave tomorrow. No, don't look like that, or I will forget all my good intentions and come to your room tonight!" For Meg had looked so lost and so heartbroken at his words, gripping his hands with such force that her need had been transmitted from her body to his, once again awakening his scarcely controlled passions.

"Oh Alex, I know you must go, but so soon? Surely, the doctor's advice should be followed?"

"No, you are risking too much. When I was unable to get about, you could only be said to be doing your duty to a sick man. But a man able to go riding is another thing. People have nasty minds, and they will think if I am able to ride a horse, I am also able to ride a ... well, you know what I mean!"

Meg looked confused, and he laughed. "You are so innocent, Meg. And I would so love to show you what I mean. I know it would be wonderful between us."

She coloured suddenly as the meaning became clear.

"I'm sorry if I have shocked you. I forget you have been living the life of a nun. But you have a passionate nature, and if we were free to love, I should soon have you rejoicing in your sensuality. And, as for me, I would be your besotted husband with your happiness my only concern. I will always love you, Meg. Can you honestly say that you are prepared to reject our love?"

"Yes, for I must. Even though it breaks my heart. But Alex, in a way you will always be with me. For you are already a part of me and, far from rejecting your love, I shall cling to it, and to my own fairy tale, where all things are possible. Where I can treasure your words and can pretend that you are sharing my life. In my dreams we shall be together, free to love each other."

"Oh Meg, why are you so strong? So able to turn me away? I cannot accept your rejection, you know. For now, I will give you what you want. But I shall be waiting. Only if I knew for certain that you wanted no part of me, would I try to forget you. Then you would never hear from me again. But if - no, when - circumstances allow us to be together, I shall come running. That I promise you."

Meg shook her head. "Don't make promises you cannot keep, Alex. For you shall marry your Penelope and have lots of children. I shall become but a fond memory."

He could see it was no use arguing with her. She had made up her mind. But he vowed that his relationship with Meg Greene was not about to end. Somehow, he had to have her in his life.

"We shall see," was all he replied.

Chapter Ten

The Debutante

Back in London

As her maid put the finishes touches to her hairstyle, Miss Penelope MacDonald surveyed her image in the mirror and liked what she saw. She was enjoying life, perhaps more than she ever had before. She considered her position to be perfect. Betrothed yet not quite betrothed. She had the option of accepting Lord Tenby's proposal, but for the moment was still free. Free to enjoy the pleasures of the Season while being feted by Society as the future Countess of Tenby, for everyone seemed convinced that her engagement was imminent. And the pleasures of the coming evening of gaiety included attending the theatre before proceeding on to Lady Dakin's rout which was expected to last until the early hours.

She had never felt so in control of her life. When she had first been introduced into society by Lord Frome, she had been full of trepidation. She had wanted to repay the kindness shown to her by her guardian by making a good match, aware of how much she owed him, Yet, how had she repaid him? By almost getting herself ruined!

She had found herself attracted to a dangerous married man. Dangerous to her, that was. Whenever she had been in his company, he had pursued her relentlessly and she had known that she was in fear of succumbing to his charms. All she had wanted was to be away from Yorkshire and temptation. Now here she was, an almost engaged lady, being tempted yet again!

But things were different now. She was no longer being treated as a husband-seeker or a timid little mouse. Her anticipated engagement to Lord Tenby had put her in this glorious position. And she knew that whatever she did, the earl could not honourably withdraw his proposal. Only she could do that. How powerful that made her feel!

Lord Tenby had been gone for well over a week now and she had just learned from Cousin Celia about him taking the time to visit with some friends in the north, meaning that she was free from his attentions for a little while longer and she intended to make full use of this joyful, in-between period of liberty and approbation. After that, she would accept his proposal, marry him, and settle down to become a good, faithful wife. She owed him that.

Smiling to herself, she thought of the several harmless flirtations she had engaged in during that very week, and especially of the one she hoped to engage in before this evening was over.

She certainly hadn't bargained on becoming besotted with yet another scoundrel! Yet even thinking of him made her pulses race and he was rarely out of her thoughts.

To her, he seemed the epitome of sophistication and good looks, but appeared to be rather bored with life and with the women who flirted so openly with him. He stood taller than most men and dressed superbly, and while Penelope had tried to ignore him, she found that was simply not possible. She loved looking at him, especially at his face, or more particularly, at his wide, sensuous mouth and arresting deep grey eyes.

Of course, she knew of his dreadful reputation and knew he would never be considered a suitable husband for her. Even if she could get him to propose to her, which she strongly doubted. Men like him took what they wanted from a woman but felt no responsibility towards those they seduced.

She had first seen him when she had been attending a soiree shortly after she had arrived in town. She remembered feeling ashamed when he had caught her looking at him and had returned her gaze with a smouldering one of his own. She had stood transfixed, unable to tear her eyes from his, until he released her with a sardonic smile and a slight nod of his head. She had quickly turned away, hoping no one had noticed her unseemly behaviour, or heard her frantically beating heart, but Lady Dawson had leaned towards her ear, saying, "He's not for you, my dear. A very disreputable man, from a very disreputable family. Although he is handsome, I grant you!"

Nothing more was said, but it was enough. From then on, whenever Penelope had found herself in his company, she had made sure she was as far away from him as possible. Of course, she was always aware of his presence, but she hoped she never betrayed to others her awareness of him or the effect he had on her whenever she thought of him, her body tingling in anticipation of something unknown but wonderful. Somehow, the more she saw him, the more she wanted him!

At least, by always pretending to be shy, she had managed to give the impression of being a demure young girl without strong passions or thoughts unbecoming a young lady. If they only knew! And she had used that shyness to discourage both him and other, less interesting suitors. She had also used it to conceal her inner thoughts from Celia Dawson. Penelope owed her and her brother far too much to betray their trust.

Then she had met Lord Tenby, who had already been described to her as a suitable candidate for her hand. She had therefore made up her mind to try to like him and was more than pleased to find that he was attractive. Moreover, he seemed to like her and so, from the moment of their introduction, she had encouraged his attentions and had even enjoyed flirting with him a little whenever they were on the dance floor. At other times, she had made sure she always acted as she believed Celia would wish.

She soon persuaded herself that Alex was going to be the one to save her from herself. For surely, she reasoned, a husband would protect her virtue and satisfy these inner longings? Alexander Wilde was agreeable and seemed to care for her enough to want to make her his wife. And, maybe, if she tried hard enough, she could eventually come to care for him in return, and even perhaps, to love him.

On the other hand, if she were to refuse him, she didn't know what the future would hold for her. She knew she needed to come to terms with her own nature. For some reason, she seemed to be attracted to irresponsible rakes and womanisers rather than their steady counter-parts. Most women would have been thrilled to have been chosen by Lord Tenby to be their wife, so why was she unhappy at the thought of settling down to a life of luxury with a titled husband? After all, she told herself, she had no title of her own. It was only through the generosity of Lord Frome consenting to become her guardian that she had been given the chance to marry so well.

When Celia Dawson had talked to her after speaking with Lord Tenby, telling her of his wish to propose to her, instead of feeling delighted with her success, she remembered feeling trapped and frightened. Her reticence had obviously been noticed by Celia who had responded by expressing her disapproval of this initial hesitation in no uncertain terms, telling her that Lord Tenby was by far her best chance of contracting an advantageous marriage and that to even think of rejecting his offer would be the height of foolishness.

Penelope knew her cousin was right and apologised for her initial reaction adding that she would happily accept Lord Tenby's offer when it was made. This seemed to appease Celia, who nodded, saying that she expected Penelope's reticence was simply due to nerves, rather than to any opposition to the match. She then lost no time in discussing the happy news with Alex's mother and a few other close friends.

From that time on, Penelope found that she was treated differently, and it didn't take her long to understand why. Everyone, it seemed, was aware that she was about to become betrothed to an earl, causing them to treat her with more respect. She suddenly felt empowered to act as she wished.

No longer did she feel it necessary to pretend to be what she was not, and, since Lord Tenby's departure, she usually found herself surrounded by admirers. Her dance card was always full within minutes of arriving at a ball, and she had even dared to waltz with the man who frequently disturbed her dreams. And now she knew his name. Lord Hawkeswood. Another earl!

What she found even more exciting was the fact that he was to be one of her party that very evening. How he had managed it, she did not know. But he had whispered his intention to her before parting from her the night before. She felt utter exhilaration at the thought of the dangerous and disreputable earl opening flirting with her. Celia would likely be horrified when she found out he was to accompany them both to the theatre as well as to Lady Dakin's rout.

But Penelope's main thought as she prepared for the evening was that he had at last noticed her and found her desirable. She also felt secure enough to allow herself to respond to his flirtation, at least a little, as all now considered her future settled. She experienced such joy just by remembering the previous evening when he had shown a marked interest in her. He had noticed her long before he had requested a dance, casting her admiring glances and then, whilst they whirled around the floor, she had gloried in his honeyed words and the pressure of his arm holding her a little too firmly and too closely to his own body than was considered acceptable.

Penelope knew she had drawn disapproving glances from several of the matrons present but had not cared. Nor had she been surprised when Cousin Celia had scolded her on the way home last night. Her cousin had apparently witnessed what she termed fast behaviour from her charge during the evening, stating that it was her duty to admonish Penelope for acting in such an unseemly manner. Penelope acted contrite but inwardly, nothing could dampen her spirits.

She had taken the utmost care with her toilette that evening and was wearing a high waisted Empire chemise style gown with a fashionably low square cut decolletage. The material was white satin and had short, puffed sleeves. To keep out the chill of the evening air, she had recently purchased a beautiful lilac, satin spencer with a high standing collar edged with ermine and had had a turban and reticule made to match. She took one last look at her reflection and sighed with approval. No need to pinch her cheeks, she decided. A feeling of excitement was making her skin glow and her eyes sparkle.

The invitation to the theatre and the rout came about because of her friendship with the Honourable Sarah Weston. Celia had expressed her delight when Penelope had become friends with Sarah, who was the daughter of the late Viscount Sawley, saying that she considered her to be a most suitable companion. Penelope knew that part of the reason Celia encouraged the friendship was because she got on so well with the girl's widowed mother. Celia and Lady Sawley seemed to share a love of the theatre, which was what prompted Lady Sawley to proffer the invitation for them to join her small party to see the comedy *A School for Scandal*, explaining that her son, the current viscount, would act as their escort.

The evening began with both the young men paying attention to Penelope, much to Celia's obvious displeasure. She had even gasped when she saw Lord Hawkeswood was one of their number, and Penelope knew exactly what Celia was thinking.

However, when Penelope realised that her friend Sarah was also enamoured with Lord Hawkeswood, she wisely chose to pretend indifference to both her admirers, staying close to her friend instead. She knew from Celia's demeanour that this strategy was the right one, for that lady visibly began to relax her vigilance, eventually giving her attention to her new friend and the play.

But while Penelope was pleased by Celia's apparent acceptance of the situation, she herself was feeling anything but relaxed. She was aware of Lord Hawkeswood the whole time, even though he did not sit near her. She forced herself not to look at him, promising herself that she would get close to him sometime that evening even if that was only whilst dancing. For now, she had to settle for the delicious feelings coursing through her body at the mere thought of him being nearby. The viscount didn't interest her at all, but she forced herself to accept his arm when they left the theatre, trying hard to quell her instant jealousy when Lord Hawkeswood offered his arm to Sarah.

The comedy was well performed, but the short farce which ended the evening was hardly suitable for polite company, being decidedly risqué in places. Cousin Celia had expressed a desire to leave before it began but had acceded to the rest of the company's wishes.

Lady Dakin's rout was in full swing by the time Penelope's party arrived, and as their hostess was nowhere to be found, a footman announced their entry as loudly as he could. They slowly made their way through the crush, and were eventually greeted by their hostess, who apologised for her tardiness, and led them to a relatively quiet corner of the room. After many compliments were received and given, she indicated towards the salon where dancing was taking place, and towards another, smaller salon in which card tables were to be found.

Lady Dakin was an attractive woman in her mid-forties, accustomed to entertaining on a lavish scale, and her suppers were renowned for their extravagance. After pointing out some of her distinguished guests she introduced them to her guest of honour, George

Gordon, Lord Byron, whose writings were known throughout the land, making him a most sought-after guest. Especially popular at that moment were the first two cantos of his long, imaginative poem, entitled *Childe Harold's Pilgrimage,* which had been published in the spring of that year.

It was reputed that his sexual charisma and his smouldering "under-look" made women of all ages feel faint when in his company. And when he bowed over Penelope's hand, she did indeed feel a small frisson of excitement, but was struck more by his pallor and the thought of how extremely bored he looked. Nevertheless, she found his presence captivating and found herself watching him as he moved about the room, always surrounded by a group of women who gazed at him as though he were a god. Sarah had also been struck by the young poet, and clung to Penelope's arm, giggling nervously, and sharing her views with her friend.

As the evening progressed, Penelope began to fear that her wish to dance with Lord Hawkeswood was not to be realised. He had danced with Sarah on two occasions and with several other young, unattached females. When it was time to be taken into the supper room, she looked around hoping to capture his attention, but was approached instead by a young army captain who had partnered her in one of the sets. She reluctantly agreed to his request and was even more disappointed to find Lord Hawkeswood accompanying Sarah! When Captain Forster left to fetch a plate of delicacies for his partner, Penelope took the opportunity to greet her friend.

"Oh, there you are," Sarah exclaimed. "We wondered what had happened to you, didn't we, my lord? Come, sit with us," she continued, patting the seat next to her.

"Captain Forster is at this moment getting me a plate of food, Sarah, and I should go back and wait for him," Penelope said modestly.

"Nonsense. You must bring the young captain over to join us," Sarah insisted.

Everyone present echoed this suggestion, and so it was that the captain joined their party. Penelope felt more and more forlorn as the evening progressed. All her plans and wishes were coming to naught. Lord Hawkeswood seemed to have forgotten his words of the previous evening and was paying her very little attention. I must not let my dismay show, she told herself. But all the joy had gone out of the evening. An evening which had begun with such promise.

Two hours and many dances later, Penelope was wondering how much longer she had to stay and endure this torture, when her tormentor at last requested her to honour him with a dance. She tried not to show her joy, but knew her eyes betrayed her, since both knew that the dance in question was a waltz.

"So, you do care for me," he whispered in her ear as he guided their steps through the masses of couples crowding the floor.

She again tried to appear cool and unaffected but could not think of a thing in reply. She knew she shouldn't gaze up at him in such a stupid way, but he seemed to find her manner totally captivating. He tightened his embrace, drawing her closer, until they seemed to become one, their limbs moving in complete accord.

"We are safe here, amongst this crowd," he added, seeing her concern, "and as we have not drawn attention to ourselves throughout the evening, no one will think anything of us enjoying one dance together. In fact, I think your chaperone is now more concerned about the young captain."

"Are you telling me that you have ignored me to allay suspicion only? You did not really wish to pay such attention to my friend?"

"As to that, it would not be politic of me to say. But if you cast your mind back to earlier in the evening, it was you who made it plain you wished nothing more to do with me. Or don't you remember cutting me so cruelly?"

"Indeed, I did not! I was simply aware of Sarah's interest in you and did not wish to cause her to feel jealousy."

"Very noble of you, I'm sure. And what about now, Penelope? Or should I continue to address you as Miss MacDonald?"

Penelope chose to disregard his last question, liking so much to hear him call her by her first name, but not feeling it prudent to say so. "Sarah has already danced with you on two occasions. This is my first, so she has no reason to feel jealous. Quite the reverse, I assure you," she said hotly.

He laughed. "You should not give yourself away so easily, sweeting. Are you confessing to having tender feelings for me? A young lady so soon to be betrothed to another?"

"Oh, of course I am not."

"Not what? Not in love with me or not about to be betrothed?"

She was so mortified by his outrageous words, she struggled in his arms, trying to move away from him, but he held her even more firmly, and laughed.

"My Lord, you are as wicked as I have been told. How dare you speak to me in that way?"

"But you knew my reputation when you first met me," he replied calmly. "I heard your chaperone warning you about my character weeks ago. Yet you dance with me, and I believe have encouraged me to think that you find me attractive. Do you find me attractive, Penelope? Do I please you, even a little? For I must confess that you have already succeeded in capturing my heart."

"You must not speak so, my lord. A lady cannot discuss such things."

"Ah, maybe a lady ought not do so, but a woman can. And I think you are becoming a very beguiling young woman, Penelope MacDonald."

"And I think you are trying to humiliate me!"

"Quite the contrary, my little one. I assure you that my intentions are entirely honourable. I know, however, that you would never risk your reputation by becoming involved with me. But please don't blame me for revealing my weakness for you."

His weakness! she thought. What about her own? She was finding it almost impossible to resist him but made one last desperate attempt, forcing herself to reject his honeyed words.

"I think we should not dance with each other again, my lord, or seek the other's company in any way. As you say, you are not someone with whom I should associate. I have made a mistake if you have come to think I have encouraged you in any way, and I apologise."

Penelope looked so sad when speaking these words that Lord Hawkeswood's embrace became more of a comforting caress. "I understand you perfectly," he said after a long pause, and completed the dance in silence.

When the music stopped, he led her back to her cousin, and withdrew to the card room. Penelope felt so wretched, she wanted only to retire to her bedchamber and shed the tears she knew were threatening to fall. Before dancing with him, she had also felt miserable, but then, her misery had been tinged with anger and jealousy. Now she felt only despair. For though he had confessed his feelings for her, there was no hope of a future together. No hope at all.

Had he been telling her the truth? At the time she had believed him because his eyes had conveyed his meaning even more than did his words. And when he had walked away, he had looked hurt. If that were the truth, then he could not be a complete cad. People must have misjudged him. Perhaps he was not a rake at all but someone who was not accepted by society for some other reason.

One thing she did know was that she could no longer engage in a light flirtation with him. He meant too much to her and she knew she was in danger of falling in love with him. Before, she had longed for his kiss, but now, she felt as if his kiss would destroy her completely. She would not be able to resist his caresses. Even thinking about him caused her to feel faint. Somehow, she had to pretend not to care. No one must suspect or she would disgrace herself and her cousins.

Celia chattered about the evening on the way home and congratulated Penelope for taking her advice to heart. "No one could have criticised your behaviour this evening," she told her. "You always acted with the utmost decorum, favouring no-one in particular, just as you ought. I did notice that you danced one dance with Lord Hawkeswood, but it would have been rude to refuse, and you parted company with him as soon as you could. No, I was very pleased by the evening, although you look a trifle down if I may say so, but I suppose all that dancing has tired you."

"I have a bit of a headache, that is all," Penelope replied.

The following day, when Penelope used this same headache as her excuse for not accompanying her cousin on their usual round of visits, Celia initially expressed her concern, but on questioning her charge further, seemed to conclude that Penelope's low mood was more likely due to fatigue and Lord Tenby's extended absence.

"I can see that your spirits are low, my dear, but all will be well soon. I know that Lord Tenby's continued absence must be unsettling for you, but he will be in town again shortly, and you will be the first person he will visit. You'll see. And as soon as your betrothal becomes official, we shall have to decide what to do. I propose that we stay in town a little longer so we can arrange a new wardrobe for you, and of course your wedding gown. You shall enjoy doing that, I'm sure, even though most will have gone away for the summer by then."

When Penelope did not seem to respond with enthusiasm as most young girls would at the thought of a whole new wardrobe of clothes, Celia looked perplexed, but seemed to decide she needed to say more to lift her charge's spirits.

"Hopefully, Lord Tenby will also stay in town for a while longer. And when it is time for you to return to Yorkshire, we can ask him to accompany us, for I shall certainly not leave you to travel back without me. I still think it was wrong of Claude to permit you to travel all the way up to London in the company of Mr and Mrs Jackson, nice people though they seemed to be. They have no connection with the family at all. But what's done is done, I suppose. I know my duty and anyway, it's been an age since I last saw Claude, you know."

"Thank you for your concern, Cousin Celia, but you really needn't worry about me, you know. It is just that the Season is beginning to tire me, I expect. I shall be glad to get things settled, though, between myself and Lord Tenby. Maybe he will return tomorrow."

"If not tomorrow, soon anyway. I can't think what's keeping the man. It is some while since I heard from Claude that all was settled. He is certainly spending a long time with that army friend of his. I hope he doesn't intend to go off and leave you alone on a regular basis. That won't do at all."

"Oh cousin, we aren't even betrothed yet. He could hardly have taken me with him, could he?"

"No, of course not. Forgive me, my dear. I'm sure he is a most thoughtful young man. I am beginning to think his friend needed some help, you know; I am sure he would not have remained away so long otherwise. His mother also thinks there is more to the story than the one he told her in his note. She told me as much the other evening."

"I am sure you are right."

Celia looked at her charge closely. "I think we had best take a break for a couple of days from our engagements, Penelope, so you can rest. Perhaps Lord Tenby will be back by then."

Penelope simply nodded her agreement.

The next event they attended was a ball being held to celebrate the betrothal of Sir Joshua Weldan's youngest daughter, Claire, to her childhood sweetheart. Celia had hoped that Penelope would herself be betrothed by this time, but Lord Tenby still had not returned to town and, despite the rest, Penelope was still looking listless and forlorn.

"Smile," Celia told Penelope as they were waiting to be announced to their hosts. Penelope frowned instead but did manage a weak smile while they were being greeted and she kept the smile on her face as she and her cousin made their way into the crowded ballroom, only to fade in an instant when she scanned the ballroom. She almost gasped as her eyes rested on none other than Lord Hawkeswood, her heart thudding in alarm! And then it raced as she became aware of the incredibly beautiful woman he held in his arms!

They were dancing a waltz, and Penelope's eyes burned as she noticed how cosy they seemed together and how much they seemed to be enjoying each other's company, laughing together in a most familiar way. What a wretched sight!

How could she pretend to be unaffected when she felt as if her heart was breaking? After their last encounter, she had cried herself to sleep until she thought she had no tears left. And now to her shame, she felt her eyes glistening with tears once again. So much for thinking that she could handle the situation! she chided herself. What a fool she was.

Somehow, she managed to converse normally to those of her party and to others of her acquaintance and even allowed her young admirer, Captain Forster, to partner her in the next set of country dances. Yet all the while she was acutely aware of Lord Hawkeswood. She knew when he was near without even seeing him. One of her senses must be alerting her to his presence, she thought, before rejecting the idea as ridiculous. It must just be a coincidence that whenever she felt him near, she would look and find that it was so.

Something was even at that moment compelling her to look towards the balcony doors. She resisted the impulse, knowing instinctively that she would find Lord Hawkeswood there, looking at her, but eventually could resist the urge no longer. She nearly lost her balance when she saw him standing in the doorway, confirming her suspicions.

As soon as she saw him, he beckoned her to go to him. Not in a blatant way it was true, but the invitation was unmistakable, nonetheless. Then as she watched, he slowly walked through the opening onto the balcony beyond.

Everything cried out to her to follow him. But how, without making a spectacle of herself? Fate seemed to be on her side, however, for without consciously staging anything, and probably more because of her agitation, she really did lose her balance when her partner went into a turn in the dance and would have fallen were not the captain's arms there to steady her.

"Miss MacDonald, are you ill?" cried the young captain, releasing his grasp as soon as he was able, while guiding her to the side of the room.

Realising that this was her chance, she took it without hesitation. "Oh dear, I do feel a little faint. So many people," she explained, "Could you take me outside for a breath of air?"

She saw him flush as though he considered her request some kind of invitation before he stammered his reply. "Your s-servant, ma'am." And so, offering her his arm, he guided her across the crowded ballroom and through the French doors onto the dimly lit balcony. She observed a couple enjoying the warm night air, standing at the railing, but did not see Lord Hawkeswood. Maybe I got it wrong, she thought in dismay. Maybe he went in again through the other doorway. The captain guided Penelope to one of the many seats provided for guests and drew up a second chair next to hers. He took one of her hands in his and looked earnestly into her eyes. "Are you feeling any better?"

"A little, I think, but perhaps a drink of ratafia would help me. I don't like to put you to so much trouble on my behalf, but..."

"Thing nothing of it," he interrupted, jumping up immediately and saying he would be honoured to be allowed to fetch her a drink. "But it may take me a while," he added, "it is such a crush here, is it not? Hopefully I will see a footman and get back to you quickly. I shall do my best."

She smiled up at him, and he almost fell over his chair in his haste to be gone on his errand.

As soon as he had disappeared through the doorway, Penelope stood up, then walked the length of the balcony. At the far end was an alcove, unseen until she was almost upon it. She could see cigar smoke drifting from that direction and stopped in her tracks. Whoever was there most likely did not want to be seen. She was about to retrace her steps when a hand stayed her, and a voice which had become so dear to her heart spoke her name.

Without thinking, she moved towards him and was drawn into his arms. She could feel his warmth and smell the scent of his cigar, mingled with other scents. Of brandy, of aftershave and of him! Never had she realised before that each person had a unique scent of their own. But she knew this scent and her body responded to it instantly. And to his heat and his blatant masculinity.

He released her just enough to be able to discard his cigar, explaining that it was only his excuse for being there in case he was discovered by anyone else.

"We only have a moment," she said hurriedly, "My dancing partner is just procuring a drink for me. What did you want to say to me?"

"What I have to say will take more than a moment. Let him come. You can hide behind me. He would not dare look past me if I did not permit it. I will deny all knowledge of you."

"Oh no, that will not do. Quickly tell me what you want," she begged.

"I want *you*, Penelope MacDonald. I have tried to keep away from you, but you are in my thoughts both night and day. You are driving me insane. I know I am only giving you proof of what a scoundrel I am, but I cannot keep away from you any longer. There must be a way for us to be together. That is, if you want it as much as I."

"It didn't look to me that you were suffering too much when I first saw you this evening!" she said in an accusing tone.

He smiled ruefully. "Ah, so you noticed me dancing with that renowned flirt. She means nothing to me. And I haven't danced with anyone else since you arrived. When you are in the room, I have eyes for no one else. And I think you also notice me. Admit it."

"No," she said defiantly, but when he raised his eyebrows in disbelief, she sighed.

"Alright, I also think of you. Far too much for my own good."

"Then we should be honest about our feelings. I love you, Penelope, and I want you to be mine."

The joy of his declaration swept through her, but at the same time she shook her head. "That cannot be, yet I know you can see what is in my heart. What do you propose, my lord?" This is madness, she thought. Yet I want to hear him out. I cannot leave without hearing what he has to say.

"You have not yet accepted Lord Tenby's offer, I understand. I wish you to refuse him and come away with me. It is no use me approaching your guardian for he would dismiss any offer from me out of hand. And quite rightly so. For I have no prospects, my family and I are steeped in scandal, and I have no fortune behind me, living from day to day. The only thing I have is an empty title, a modest residence, and a wardrobe of clothes, most of which have not yet been paid for. You would be mad to agree to what I am suggesting. Yet I am selfish enough to ask. I can promise you nothing but my love. But still, I am foolish enough to hope. If you agreed to this mad scheme, we could be married in Scotland. Then we could go to my sister. You see, while I have no wealth of my own, I do have a wealthy sister. If you agreed to elope with me, we could throw ourselves on her mercy. She has never let me down, and I know she would love you in an instant and would let us stay with her until your guardian relented and gave us his approval, as he would eventually be forced to do. It is not much, and I know it is the last thing I should be asking you to do, but I cannot help myself. Please think about it Penelope. At least we could be together."

"Oh, what can I say? Can I believe your words? Do you really love me?"

In answer, his hands cupped her face and his lips gently glided across her own. "Yes, Penelope, believe it. Inconvenient though it is."

His fingers slid to her throat, caressing her gently until she tilted her head back to give him greater access, accepting his kisses as they moved lower, his lips following his fingers in their exploration. She shivered and moaned as her head involuntarily fell even further back in complete surrender.

Drawing her body ever closer to his, he continued his assault on her senses, nuzzling her and kissing her over and over, his head dipping lower and lower, until he was kissing and licking the smooth, warm, white, fragrant flesh between her breasts, then the soft swell of her breasts as they rose and fell with her quickened breathing. She heard him moan and murmur, "You are irresistible, simply irresistible."

So lost was Penelope to these new but delicious sensations, she gave no thought to the possibility that she may be discovered, or any possible aftermath. Nothing else mattered but being in the arms of the man she loved. Having him hold her, kiss her, love her. Even when he gently ran his fingers along the low decolletage of her gown, so low that he was soon able to expose one hard, pink bud which he promptly took in his mouth, she did not protest.

She was slightly shocked it was true, and even stiffened for a moment before giving herself up again to his lovemaking. But his gently coaxing words of passion soothed her, even when he confessed his needs and promised her how wonderful they were going to be together. He made her feel weak with desire, and had he taken her there and then she would have been powerless to stop him. The sensations he was making her feel were just too wonderful, too exciting to resist.

Lord Hawkeswood seemed to sense that she was his for the taking, and moved his hands to her buttocks, hauling her centre hard against his erection. Her reaction was instinctive. She cried out, clinging to him in desperation, her head spinning and her body a mass of molten heat as it throbbed with desire, knowing that she would be in danger of falling if he were to release her.

At that very moment, she heard the captain calling her name. Slowly, her sanity returned. Lord Hawkeswood loosened his hold on her, and she struggled to steady herself, holding on to his arms. "I must go," she whispered.

"No. Stay. Stay with me now. Have the courage to follow your heart."

"Not now. Please. I must go. Let me think about what you have said. You have confused me badly. Let me go now, I beg you. I will give you my answer tomorrow."

Reluctantly, he released her and helped to straighten her clothes and hair. She tried to look composed as she moved away from him, making her way back along the balcony towards the captain. Suddenly, she turned, and whispered into the darkness. "I heard Viscount Sawley address you as Hawk, but would you tell me your real Christian name?"

"Damien," came the reply.

Chapter Eleven

◆——————•——————◆

Penelope did not speak to Lord Hawkeswood the following day. Nor did she wish to. For by the end of the morning, she was formally betrothed to Lord Tenby and was thoroughly disgusted by her behaviour of the previous evening, feeling nothing but loathing for the Earl of Hawkeswood.

Penelope had spent a restless night grappling with her feelings and with the quandary she was in. But she was awakened early by Lady Dawson herself.

"Lord Tenby is back in town," she exclaimed, rushing into the room unannounced. "He has sent word that he will be calling on you this morning. Hurry child, there is not a minute to lose."

But instead of the expected response, Penelope became overwrought, causing Celia to look at her askance.

"Whatever is wrong with you, Penelope?" she asked. "You are about to become engaged, for goodness' sake."

"But I am not!" Penelope blurted out. "You see, I now know that I must reject Lord Tenby's offer."

"What did you say?" cried her cousin. "You must be mad! Everyone assumes you are already betrothed! You cannot cry off now!" When Celia got no response, except for Penelope to visibly flinch, Celia continued, "And why, may I ask, do you wish to do so? You seemed to welcome his attentions before. Now it is too late for you to change your mind, I tell you. Think of Claude. Think of me. Think of yourself, for goodness' sake."

"But would you to wish me to marry him if I found out I loved another?"

"Loved another? Loved another! What is this nonsense? Really, Penelope, what has got into you? I thought you were more sensible. You know you are fond of Lord Tenby. Many marry without even that, you know. And as for love? Love is not something that comes in a moment. Love develops over time and will come to you eventually if you work at it. In a few years, you will look back at this moment and see how silly you were to even think of refusing such an offer. And anyway, who is this person you think you love? Don't tell me you have fallen for Captain Forster? He has no title, no prospects either. Claude would be most displeased if you ditched an earl for a mere captain!"

"And what if the one I chose instead also had a title? Would that make a difference?"

Celia's eyes narrowed. "What are you saying? Which member of the aristocracy has been paying you attention? Not an honourable one, that is for sure. For all know you are promised to Lord Tenby."

No reply was forthcoming. Celia was looking very closely at her charge obviously trying to think who it could be, and then suddenly she exclaimed, "It's Lord Hawkeswood, isn't it? That blackguard! He deserves to be hung and should not be welcomed in polite circles. No respectable mother would countenance him as a suitable candidate for a daughter's hand. If you think Claude would allow you to associate with him or his family, you are mad.

"His father lost everything but his title then shot himself. He associates with a most unsavoury set of characters, none suitable for you to meet, and his sister is a whore! Want to align yourself with someone like that? Over my dead body! If he has been trying to seduce you, tell me now. I shall inform Claude immediately. And Lord Tenby. They will sort him out. For you can be sure of one thing, Penelope. Lord Hawkeswood is not an honourable man. And he would soon tire of you. His reputation with women is legendary. If he has trifled with your feelings, you must tell me."

With every word her cousin uttered, Penelope's shame and humiliation grew. And by the time Celia had finished speaking, Penelope felt raw and exposed. Her cousin's words had devastated her. She had been more than stupid. She had been exposed for what she was, a wanton fool. Unable to resist the seduction of a rake. Just like in Yorkshire. No, this was worse. Ten times worse. For this time, she had really humiliated herself.

Should she tell Cousin Celia everything? So that her punishment would be complete? For some reason, she still wanted to protect her seducer. Even though he proposed taking her to stay with a whore! What must he think of her to suggest such a thing? He must have recognised her true nature, for had she not behaved exactly like a lightskirt? No doubt he never intended to go through with the marriage. After all, what would be the need? Once she had ruined herself, she would have had nowhere else to go.

She had to save herself. She had others to think of besides herself. Somehow, she had to get herself out of this mess.

"We have done nothing to be ashamed of, believe me. But I must admit to being fooled by his smooth compliments. What must you think of me?" She hoped her words sounded convincing but couldn't prevent the tears from forming.

"There, there," Celia crooned as she took Penelope in her arms and comforted her. "We are all young and silly sometimes. Better now than later, eh? And no harm done. You are sure he has not compromised you in any way?"

"No, just words whilst we were dancing. I have never been exposed to such flattery, and it must have gone to my head." Her fingers were crossed as she uttered her lies.

Celia hoped Penelope was speaking the truth but thought it wisest to leave matters where they stood. She just needed to know one more thing. "And now, Penelope, may I ask what you are going to say to Lord Tenby when he asks you for your hand?"

"I shall accept him, cousin. And gladly." Penelope spoke these words with absolute conviction, knowing how much she now needed Lord Tenby's protection.

* * *

Alex had arrived back in town late the previous evening, tired but determined on his course. As soon as he had refreshed himself and changed his clothes, he set out immediately to call on his mother despite the lateness of the hour. He knew she would have arranged to stay at home, confident that she would have received the message he had sent on ahead the day before to alert her to his impending arrival. He also knew he was in for a scold.

It wasn't as bad as he had feared, however. She was too glad to have him back to be angry for long. And after hearing his story about being shot, she knew he had only been trying to protect her from distress. Alex related all the details of his journey and his accident but left out any reference to his stay with Lady Margaret. He had no intention of giving anyone further cause to question Meg's morals. Soon, he vowed, he would seek out all those who had spread lies and rumours about her and get them to recant. Until then, her name would not pass his lips, although the memory of her was his constant companion. He was glad that his mother did not question him too closely but was not so pleased when she brought up the subject of Penelope and the now expected announcement of their betrothal. He didn't want to lie to his mother but tried to lower her expectations by reminding her that Penelope had not yet accepted his suit.

"But she will, Alex, you can be sure. Everything was settled satisfactorily between you and the Marquess was it not?"

He could only assure her that it was, telling her that he would call on Penelope first thing in the morning and that if he were accepted, she would be the first to know.

Penelope had to refuse him! he thought to himself on his return to his house late that night. He couldn't bear to marry her now. His heart belonged to another.

While preparing to retire, he remembered the last moments he had had alone with the woman he *really* wanted to marry - Meg Greene. It had been the morning of his departure. Emily had just left him after hurling abuse at him about people who thought they could just decide to leave their friends whenever it suited them. She had stalked off, her head held high, telling him to go, to leave them alone, that she didn't care if she never saw or rode with him again!

Alex had known she was upset but was sure she would soon recover. Unlike himself, he remembered thinking. But he had decided to let Meg know of her daughter's tantrum in case she stayed away from the house too long. He had walked from the parlour, nearly bumping into Jenkins who had been arranging for the portmanteaux to be loaded on the coach and gathered from him that Lady Margaret was to be found in the kitchen.

Alice and Meg had been busily arranging the meals for the day when he entered and informed them about Emily. "But please don't punish her. I think it was just her way of saying she was going to miss me." he had said.

"More likely she was cross because you had yet to see her in her new riding habit," Meg had replied. "The naughty minx. But I'm glad you understand that she didn't mean what she said. She has few friends, and I know she hoped you would be staying for several more days. I shall speak to her about her lack of manners after you have left."

He had noticed that, although her words were uttered brightly enough, she had a forlorn look about her, and her eyes were red-ringed as though she had been crying. He really didn't want to leave her like that, but knew it was time to go, so, after a stilted conversation thanking both women for their generosity, he forced himself to make his exit, moving towards the front of the house. He hadn't looked back, so had been unaware that Meg had followed him. She had to touch his arm to gain his attention.

"May I speak with you for a moment," she had asked, turning to make her way towards the library. It was like receiving a reprieve from the hangman's noose, he remembered. He was being granted another moment with his love. His knew his eyes must have clearly mirrored his thoughts, as he followed her into the library, shutting the door behind him.

Looking at the face of the woman he knew he would never forget for as long as he lived, he had let out a sigh and then had gone to her, taking her in his arms. "Meg, oh Meg. This is so hard. You know I don't want to leave you." he remembered saying to her, just as he remembered all the other things they had said and done during those last moments together. He remembered her softness and her scent as his lips brushed her ear. And her rapidly beating pulse. Yet her words were cold.

"Please Alex, we both know you must go," she had pleaded, stepping away from him. "Please don't make this any harder than it already is."

"Then why did you ask me to come in here?" he remembered saying, almost angrily.

She remained silent for a moment but then reached out for him, tears in her eyes. "Because I could not bear to see you go without kissing you one last time," she confessed. "I admit it. If you hadn't taken me in your arms, I would have found it hard to think of something to justify asking you to come in here. I know this is madness. I shouldn't have done it. It is just making things harder to bear. But I couldn't stop myself. And I admit to almost coming to your room last night. I couldn't sleep, knowing you were about to leave. And that I would never see you again. And I wanted you so badly. I told myself that no-one would ever know, but I would have known, wouldn't I. And so I did not come to you, knowing that I can't have you."

"You can have me, as you put it, whenever you like. My God, to think I was lying awake longing to hold you and you were lying awake thinking the same as I! And now you tell me! When I am about to leave. If I found an excuse for staying one more night, would you let me come to you?"

"No. No. Please Alex. I shouldn't have said anything. I had my chance at happiness years ago and made the wrong decision. I can't do anything about that now. But I can make sure Emily has her chance. And you, my love. You must not do anything you will later come to regret. Promise me you will try to be happy?"

"I promise to try, Meg, since I can see that you are not prepared to let me into your life. But will you also promise me that if you ever change your mind, or if you ever need help of any kind, you will write to me?"

"Gladly. Oh Alex, I'm going to miss you so much. Please, please … kiss me once more, before I go mad!"

Alex had needed no further prompting, and soon they were only aware of each other, giving and receiving, exploring, and surrendering, inflaming, and savouring.

Even now he gloried in remembering her warm response, knowing that she was prepared to give herself to him. He had known she had no resistance left and he should have stopped, but, instead, he had deliberately taken her words for consent and was in the process of lowering her to the carpet when there was a sharp, loud knock on the door. "Excuse me, Lady Margaret, but your mother is asking for you. I think it's urgent." Alice's voice.

They had pulled apart, thinking Alice about to enter. I should have locked the damn door, Alex remembered thinking as he had tried desperately to get himself under some sort of control, but had kept his thoughts to himself. Instead, he had given Meg a rather wobbly smile and had shrugged his shoulders. "I'm sorry, Meg," he had told her then, as he released her, letting his hands fall to his sides. "I wasn't intending to do that, but ...." He could find no words to express his regrets.

Meg had looked mortified. And, oh, so very beautiful, with her swollen, well-kissed lips and her wide-eyed stare. Her hair had looked as though she had just awoken, and, in a way, he knew she had. Desire had still been clearly visible in her eyes, and he had wanted her so badly, he was in physical pain. Even now, reliving the scene in his mind, he felt himself harden and his pulse quicken at the thought of her and how she had looked in that moment.

He knew Alice had deliberately interrupted them to protect her mistress, but even though he liked and respected Alice, at that moment, he had wished her to the devil.

His time with Meg was over, but he would never forget her final words to him. She had raised herself up and kissed his lips softly, saying, "Goodbye my love. Godspeed. Remember me." Then, tears in her eyes, she had opened the door and was gone.

Alex had stayed in Selby for two more nights before feeling fit enough to head for home. His shoulder still pained him greatly at times, but it was healing well. More quickly than his heart, he thought wryly. But, during the days of rest and travel, he had formulated a plan of action. Firstly, he would make Penelope cry off by painting himself as so unworthy a soul that she would feel compelled to reject him. Then he would track down Damien and the others. What he would say or do to them, he was unsure, but was determined to make Damien stand up for his sister, and her slanderers to retract their lies. It would then be time to speak to his mother about Meg and convince her of Meg's virtue and inform her of his intention to marry her. And lastly, he would have to talk Meg round to accepting him.

His campaign began the morning after his return to town, when he called on Lady Dawson. She was expecting him of course. News of his return had quickly spread through *the ton*. Lady Dawson was even waiting for him in the hall. "Welcome back," she said, greeting him warmly. "Miss MacDonald is waiting for you in the drawing room, and I know you wish to speak with her alone."

He was then escorted to the door of the drawing room by Lady Dawson who wished him luck before heading away. Luck? He certainly needed it, he thought, even though he had prepared all his arguments against the match in advance. Perhaps Lady Dawson thought that Penelope had doubts if she thought he needed luck. That would definitely make things easier. He relaxed slightly and entered the room.

He found Penelope sitting demurely with her head bowed, not even glancing at him, almost as though she was unaware of his entry. He stood for a moment observing her. She looked so very young and appealing in her modest long-sleeved day dress of pale blue cotton with its double neck frill. He also realised she looked sad and even a little afraid. Yes, he was sure her hands were shaking in her lap. Maybe she is as unprepared and unwilling for this meeting as he was. Maybe he would be able to extricate himself from this abominable betrothal without causing her too much distress. He hoped so.

Penelope looked up at that moment and searched his face. He was nervous, she could tell, but he hid it well, standing there, looking more like an earl than she had ever noticed before. He was resting his weight on one leg, his hands clasped behind his back. In one way, he was just as she remembered him. He looked splendid in his grey day-coat with the fashionable "M" cut velvet collar, white stock and waistcoat, and snugly fitting fawn pantaloons. Very masculine despite his obvious unease. But in another way, he looked different from before. She wasn't sure what that difference was, but there was something about the way he was looking at her that caused her unease.

"Please my lord, pray take a seat," she said shyly, indicating the velvet covered wing back chair opposite her. Then she waited.

When he was seated, he leaned forward, resting his forearms on his slightly open thighs, and cleared his throat.

"Miss MacDonald, I have come to apologise to you for being unable to call on you sooner. I believe you are aware that I left town to visit your guardian in Yorkshire, but my return was delayed due to an unforeseen accident."

He proceeded to relate a version of his adventure to her, explaining merely that he had fallen from his horse, injuring himself to a degree that required a period of rest. He finished by repeating his apology for not calling on her for a while. "I hope, however, that you will forgive me," he finished.

Was this how he intended to propose, she wondered. He sounded so formal. Wasting time talking about his journey and his silly accident when both knew why he was here. But then again, what if he has changed his mind? He certainly doesn't look particularly happy about his mission, she observed. Maybe his mother has told him something to make him doubt her. Maybe that is why he was looking at her in an unfamiliar way. She visibly paled at the thought. No, he cannot cry off now, she assured herself. Celia said he was committed, didn't she? But to make sure, she decided to precipitate matters.

She smiled warmly. "You are more than welcome, my lord, as you very well know, and there is nothing to forgive, I assure you."

He didn't return her smile, frowning instead, and he looked decidedly uncomfortable. He looked as if he wanted to bolt rather than to propose! Oh dear, she thought, this *really* isn't going well. He wasn't shy, was he? It was more likely that he had changed his mind. That wouldn't do at all!

She took a deep breath, clasped her hands together tightly and using his first name, looked him directly in the eye.

"Dearest Alex," she said, "if this is difficult for you, perhaps I can help by saying that I am honoured by your visit, and by your offer, and that I return your affection wholeheartedly."

She watched as his frown deepened. "That is very kind of you Miss MacDonald, but I don't deserve your affection." She noticed that he was wringing his hands and waited for him to continue, getting more nervous by the moment.

"I am unworthy of you," he told her. "You deserve someone who enjoys the things you do. Like parties and balls. I hate dancing and intend to retire to my estate for most of the year. You wouldn't like that, you know. I have been selfish in the extreme to expect someone like you to share my life. Really, I am a soldier at heart. And I have a brutish temper. I don't expect I shall settle easily into my new role and will likely be very difficult to get on with at times. You are far too good for me. I fear I would only make you miserable."

"Oh Alex, please don't berate yourself so." By this time, Penelope was sure he had heard something and was trying to make her take him into dislike. Well, she would stop this nonsense right now.

"I will be proud to be your wife, my lord. You are everything I want. I, too, love the country more than town life. We shall suit each other perfectly."

At that moment, Celia entered the room. No doubt she has been listening, Penelope decided, and has come to help. Just as well. "Oh cousin, such happy news. I have just accepted Lord Tenby's proposal of marriage. We are betrothed."

Chapter Twelve

Damn, damn, damn! Alex swore to himself as he entered his club later that same evening. How could it have happened? Betrothed! And no way of getting out of it without causing one hell of a scandal! He knew he had no option now. After his visit with his mother, he had been persuaded to put the announcement in *the Gazette,* so the news would be all over town in the morning.

Alex had clung desperately to the hope that he could persuade Penelope to cry off, but instead, she and that so-called cousin of hers had staged a scene worthy of the worst melodrama. Alex felt he had been trapped but knew in his heart that it was he who had made the proposal originally and had been accepted by Lord Frome on Penelope's behalf.

The scene that morning had been merely a formality and he knew now that it had only been a wild hope of his that Penelope could have been persuaded to reject him. He had been fooling himself. Meg had been right all along. The only way out would be to go abroad or to run away with Meg. And oh, how he would love to run away with Meg!

But he knew she would not go. Not with Emily to think of. And he had his mother and his inheritance to consider. The family name! What a world he lived in! Where unwritten rules governed one's life to the extent that a man - or a woman - had to live without love for the sake of others. Yet he would defy them all if Meg would have him.

Instead, she had rejected him, thinking their love would die slowly but surely without the approval of his mother and society. And what she thought was what really counted. For the sake of her daughter, she would not take the risk. Yet it was not a matter of lacking courage. Quite the reverse. She was a woman who had enough courage to defy the world for the sake of her daughter or for anyone else she loved or cared for, and she was prepared to deny her own happiness to protect them from hurt. That was the problem. It was not that she didn't love him enough. Alex knew now that she did love him. It was just that her daughter's welfare would always come first with her.

So, was it the end for them? He couldn't bring himself to accept it. He loved her too much. The pain of their parting was still almost unbearable. What would his life be like without her? Empty. Meaningless. Without hope. There had to be a way for them to be together. One day.

Meanwhile, he had other fish to fry. Someone at his club must know where the Earl of Hawkeswood resided. Unfortunately, that someone was not likely to be his cousin Percy this time, since he was almost sure Percy was once again out of town. A shame since he would dearly like to get his hands on his cousin!

But Percy would have to wait. To begin with he would concentrate on dealing with Lord Hawkeswood, after which he would make it his business to track down and expose the lying curs who had maligned Meg's name, especially Sir Rodney Blewett.

Alex's mood was solemn as he entered his club, looking around the room, acknowledging those he knew but not stopping to chat. He went into the card room hoping to find Lord Hawkeswood there, or at least someone who knew him; perhaps even one of the other men he was eager to confront. He asked the head waiter but without success. No doubt the gaming at Boodles was not enough of a challenge for

Lord Hawkeswood and his cronies, Alex surmised. He would have to try one of the gaming hells.

Two hours and five gaming hells later, he finally made a breakthrough. At first, as he scanned those present through the smoky haze that permeated the room, disappointment once again was his first response, being told by those he approached that none of the names mentioned were present. As usual, the place was full of elegantly clad players, who, beneath their expressions of ennui or faded amusement, lay the anxiety and excitement that accompanied each throw of the dice or turn of the cards. Empty bottles and full glasses lay testament to the fact that, almost to a man, those present seemed determined to drink themselves senseless - assuming, of course, that they had any sense to begin with.

Then, thanks to a contretemps at one of the tables, when voices were raised, Alex heard the name Rodney mentioned. He looked over to the table, his eyes drawn to a man he recognised as someone his mother had described as a particularly dissolute, debauched character, notorious for his drunkenness and gambling. A man tolerated by society simply because his father was a duke. Lord Iain Blair, third son of the Duke of Gaister. It was he who was speaking and who had mentioned someone called Rodney. Could that Rodney be the one he was seeking? He had to find out.

As he watched, Alex saw Lord Iain stand up, pushing at the table as he did so, swaying unsteadily and swinging his arms about him, shouting that the game was rigged and that he would have the law on them all. He then took a step backwards, unfortunately for him forgetting the existence of the chair, which caused him to lose his balance. He crashed to the floor, landing unceremoniously on his back, his legs sprawled in the air for a moment before they came to rest on the upturned chair, then he went quiet. He had knocked himself out.

"Trust poor old Iain," bellowed one of the players, not seeming in the least worried about his so-called friend. "Can't take his drink and can't accept defeat graciously. Take him away, someone. We have a game going here. No time to waste on that silly blighter."

Alex saw his chance and went to the man's aid, helping him to his feet as he slowly regained consciousness.

"Hello, old boy," he said to Alex, even though the two had never met before. "Where am I? Deuce knows what I'm doing here. Was supposed to go to my sister's soiree tonight, don't you know. Take me there, will you, old fellow?"

Alex grinned at him. "Certainly, Iain, old boy. It would be my pleasure." To the others, he asked, "Do any of you know his address? I'll happily see him to his home. Being a friend of mine, it's the least I can do."

"What? Oh yes, that would be most kind of you. Twenty-seven, Liscombe Square, I believe. Is that right?" said one of the group, addressing his cronies, who reluctantly took the time to confirm his guess. They then went back to concentrating on their hands, completely forgetting Iain Blair and his threat. They're as bad as each other, Alex concluded.

Alex hoped that the man was not too drunk to answer a few questions, while also hoping that his inebriated state would prevent him from becoming suspicious. After all, they did not know each other. Soon, the drunk lord would remember that fact. But before he did, maybe he could be persuaded to confirm that he knew Rodney Blewett, and perhaps divulge another name or two; even, with luck, some other pertinent details.

"Well, old friend. You have landed in the suds again I see," Alex said cheerfully. "Still, I'll see you home."

As soon as they reached the exit, Alex asked the doorman to summon a hackney cab.

"Good man. Good man," muttered Iain Blair. "Friend of mine, are you? Can't think of your name for the life of me."

"Alex Wilde. Met you at the races. My mother knows your mother. Old friends, I believe," Alex lied. He decided to throw out some names. "Also know some friends of yours. Rodney Blewett, Damien Searle, Clive Chillingworth, John Kendle and Neville Oakley. And the late Lucas Greene," he added for effect.

"Poor old Lucas," Iain said softly, shaking his head. "A good friend, he was. Died in that stupid race. He should never have made the bet …. not against Lord Burt. No one ever beats Lord Burt. Renowned as the finest whip in the land, he is. But we couldn't make Lucas see reason. He believed he had something to prove, you see, and just because he thought Lord Burt had accused him of being faint-hearted, although none of us had heard Burt say any such thing."

So, Alex thought, this drunken lord is going to be talkative. Good. And more to the point, he was a crony of Lucas Greene. This could be the breakthrough he was looking for.

As soon as he had deposited Iain Blair's large frame in the cab, and had taken the seat opposite, he asked innocently, "Wasn't Lucas married to Damien's sister?"

"Who?" asked Iain Blair, seemingly having forgotten the conversation in his effort to enter the cab.

"We were speaking of Lucas Green and Damien Searle," Alex reminded him. "Wasn't Lucas married to Damien's sister?"

"Ah, yes, you're right, and a damn fine-looking filly she was too. But married far too young, you know. He should have waited to see if they suited. It was a rotten thing he did, trying to get out of the marriage. Should never have said those things about such an angel. Did you ever meet her?"

This is interesting, Alex thought. "I heard about the divorce, of course. And I didn't believe the story myself. Lies, was it?"

"Oh yes. But the only way to get out of a marriage, don't you know. Unfair, but there it is. As I said, he shouldn't have married her in the first place."

"And is it common knowledge that the evidence was rigged?"

"Don't know about that. But his friends knew, of course. Never liked that Rodney Blewett, you know. Probably because he took too many women off me," he said chuckling at the thought. "Handsome devil, he is. Know him as well, do you? S'pose you went to Eton and King's College like us, did you? Can't remember you, though."

"Yes, I do know Rodney," Alex lied again smoothly, "And no, I didn't go to Eton. My mother decided to keep me at home. Had a tutor instead. A dead bore it was, but you know how protective some mothers are."

"Gad yes. No father to look out for you, then?"

"No. He died before I was born, I'm afraid. In the Americas."

Alex decided he was getting off the topic. "As a matter of fact, I have just returned from duty in the Peninsula and wanted to look up Damien and Rodney and the others. Perhaps you could help me locate them."

For a while, there was no reply. Iain seemed to be about to go to sleep, his head nodding, but then he suddenly sat up straight, looking almost sober. "No trouble at all. See them regularly. Damien lives in town all year, you know. Owns a place in Bloomsbury. Cannon Row, number thirty, I think. Rodney, now that's a different matter. Married a rich cit's daughter about three years ago and has moved to Henley. Built a large house on the river and regularly holds house parties. As a matter of fact, he has one planned for the week after next, as I was telling my friends a little while ago. I can get you an invite if you like. Most of the others you mentioned should be there, I imagine. Usually go to these affairs. But not Clive, I'm afraid. I think he was one you mentioned. He went to India quite a while back, and I haven't heard anything about him since then."

By this time, they had reached Liscombe Square, and the Hackney stopped at Lord Iain's town house.

"Here we are. Come in for a drink?" offered Iain, completely forgetting that he had been engaged to attend his sister's soirée. Alex declined, but helped guide Iain to his door, leaving him in the capable hands of his butler, who looked as though he was used to this routine. Alex handed him his card and said he would call to see how his friend fared the following day. He meant to remind Iain about the invitation to Rodney's house party. No need to quiz the fellow about the name of the unnamed cur. Alex was confident that he would be able to identify him if he should be at the house party. But before visiting Iain again, Alex intended to confront Lord Hawkeswood, and now he had his address.

He arrived at the unfashionable Bloomsbury address a little after eleven the following morning. The exterior of the building looked as though it had seen better days. The row of off-white stone houses formed an attractive, gently curving semi-circle. Each house looked identical, each with six steps up to the front door, columns on either side, also painted off-white, but with the paint peeling away in places. All had shiny, black front doors with brass door furniture and had window boxes at the ground floor windows, most of which looked sadly neglected.

The door was opened by a badly dressed, small, thin, bald man with a wrinkled face and shaky limbs. He did not speak. Just stared at Alex vacantly. Alex introduced himself, handed his card to the fellow and requested an audience with Lord Hawkeswood. The old man examined the card at close range, turning it over, then back again, then looked back at Alex. After a moment he seemed to make up his mind and beckoned Alex to enter, moving aside and then closing the door behind them.

"Wait here," he said, leaving Alex standing in the hallway while he slowly made his way up the creaking staircase. Alex watched the man until he disappeared and then took in his surroundings. He noted the dark panelling on the walls, the decaying mirror, and the various portraits and landscapes. All looked as though they could do with a good clean. The portraits seemed to have been painted a long time ago, judging by the fashions worn. The men wore wigs and the ladies had powered hair, their gowns tightly laced and low cut. Alex vaguely wondered if any of them were related to Meg. After several minutes the old man reappeared and coughed to attract the visitor's attention. "Come," was all he said, beckoning for Alex to follow him up the stairs.

Alex found a man he assumed to be Damien sitting in a leather armchair seemingly engrossed in reading a book. His first thought was that Damien appeared to be slightly posed. Could he be worried about something? Then Alex took a moment to examine the man's physical features, and could not remember ever having seen him before, even though they must have attended many of the same social events. He was certain they had never been introduced.

As though slowly becoming aware that he was no longer alone, Damien looked up at his guest, rose politely to his feet, putting his book next to his glass of ale, then strode across the room, smiling and extending his hand in welcome. Well, he has charm all right, Alex thought, I'll give him that. His smile could lure the birds from the trees. Alex also noted several similarities between Meg and her sibling, somewhat to his surprise.

The colour of Damien's hair was the same deep chestnut, but whereas Meg's was fine and curly, Damien's was coarse and wavy. Like Meg, he had a full sensuous mouth, straight nose, and square jaw, but Damien's nose was larger and more dominant. In physique, of course, they were very different. Instead of a long slender neck, Damien's was thick and corded. He had very pale skin, but this was countered by broad shoulders, strong thighs, and a flat stomach, suggesting that he engaged in physical pursuits on a regular basis.

"Don't believe I've had the pleasure, Lord Tenby," Damien said, shaking hands firmly. Damien's hands were cold and slightly unsteady, Alex noted, again wondering why the man seemed on edge.

"No, but I needed to speak with you on an urgent matter. I hope you will excuse my rudeness in calling like this," Alex responded.

"No rudeness, I assure you. Please, come and sit down. Potter will get you an ale, won't you, Potter?" Damien said, turning to Potter who was lingering in the doorway.

Potter touched his index finger to his forehead, bowing slightly before exiting the room.

"Silly fellow. Hardly says a word. But he and his wife come cheap, you know, and look after me well enough."

Alex took the seat opposite to the one Damien was using. He decided it was time to state the purpose of his visit. "Lord Hawkeswood, I've come to talk to you about ..."

"Penelope. Yes, I know," Damien interrupted, his hands clasped together nervously.

"Miss MacDonald?" Alex almost stuttered, so surprised was he by this misunderstanding. Why on earth should Damien think he had called about Penelope?

Chapter Thirteen

Had Alex but known it, Damien had received the news of his visitor with considerable trepidation - in fact, frantic with worry may be nearer the truth. As soon as he saw the name on the calling card, he immediately assumed that Lord Tenby had discovered about himself and Penelope and had come to call him out for insulting her with his attentions.

He hoped Penelope hadn't told him everything, but doubted she would have gone into too many details. In fact, he was surprised that she had dared to even mention him at all.

But why else would Lord Tenby call on him?

Deciding to start by denying everything and if that didn't work, to apologise and admit to a little harmless flirting, he would state in his defence that her betrothal hadn't been announced at the time and he hadn't heard anything about it.

His next decision was on how to greet the earl. Should he stand, ready for the confrontation, or remain seated, thereby conveying a demeanour of innocence, of not being bothered in the least by what his visitor had come to say? He decided on the latter option, leaning back in his leather armchair, and picking up the book he had been reading, which is how Lord Tenby had found him.

Damien immediately noticed Lord Tenby's stern expression confirming in his mind the reason for the visit, but he went through the motions of welcoming his guest. He hoped that by adopting a friendly attitude and behaving like a gentleman, he may have a chance of keeping the conversation civil, thereby avoiding a full-on confrontation. But when his visitor said he had come about an urgent matter, Damien knew he was in trouble. He began to panic, which was probably the reason why he finished Lord Tenby's sentence for him. At first, he did not register the stunned expression on his visitor's face, so intent was he on trying to formulate his defence.

"Yes," he continued, "And I know what you must be thinking. But you have nothing to worry about, I assure you. She repulsed me, you know. And told me about you. I would never have approached her if I had known ... "He stopped in mid-sentence, at last becoming aware of the surprised expression on Alex's face and realising that he may have incriminated himself without cause. "Uh ... it seems I may have jumped the gun a bit. You are not here about Miss MacDonald?"

Lord Tenby did not reply immediately, and Damien watched as the earl's eyes narrowed ominously as though he were considering his opponent anew. Damien sat up straight in his chair, preparing himself for whatever came next.

He watched as Lord Tenby altered his position, leaning towards his opponent, his expression grim. The earl's index fingers were brushing his lips as though he were deep in thought before cupping his hands and resting them against his chin. And then he spoke, his tone as severe as a judge delivering his verdict.

"Well, I *wasn't*," his visitor began, a glint of challenge appearing in his eyes, "but now it seems I have two reasons to call on you. And I'll begin by asking who gave you leave to refer to my fiancée by her Christian name?"

"Well ... no-one, actually. It's just that I think of her ... thought of her... quite a lot ... at one time." Damien's thoughts rushed ahead, trying to guess the other reason for the earl's visit, but forced himself to concentrate on the issue at hand. Although flustered at first, he soon recovered and used his well-honed skills for extricating himself from awkward situations. "But no longer, I can assure you. I know now that she is your intended. No disrespect meant."

Alex sat unmoved, clearly unimpressed by the confession. "I am not sure you know what the word 'disrespect' means, Lord Hawkeswood. You and your friends have a lot to answer for."

That made Damien sit up even straighter, his colour rising as he gripped the arms of his chair as if to rise. What on earth? "How dare you, sir! You don't even know me. What makes you think that you have the right to come in here and insult me and my friends. What is going on here?"

Alex put up a his hand in a calming gesture. "I am afraid the mention of my fiancée has caused me to lose my temper, and I am sorry for it, because the matter I really called here to discuss with you is far too important for me to back away from now. Any other matters between us will have to be dealt with later. You see, it is not *your* reputation I have called about, but the reputation of another member of your family."

"Another member of my family?" exclaimed Damien, genuinely perplexed by this turn in the argument. Was the earl intending to drag up all the old family scandals? Hadn't he suffered enough because of the disgrace caused by his father? And anyway, what did this man know about his family and friends?

"I don't know what you are talking about. I suppose this must have something to do with my reprobate of a father dying and leaving our family with its standing in tatters, or about my current way of life. I will even admit that some of my friends have less than pristine reputations, but we are not shunned by Society entirely and are still welcome in most drawing rooms. And as far as I know, my lifestyle has not harmed any other member of my family."

"I think most people would condemn a man for selling his own sister."

Damien blanched. Was this about Meg then? He had long felt guilty over his treatment of his sister even though he had tried to rationalise his actions as being justified in the circumstances. But what had this man to do with his sister? And what was the reason for this unexpected attack?

Damien's hackles rose. "God, I could call you out for that slander! I may have arranged the match, in fact I admit that I *did* arrange the match, but my sister wanted it. No one forced her, least of all me. And what's all this to you? I thought you had come here to talk about Pen … Miss MacDonald. I thought you were concerned about your fiancée. How can you have got yourself involved with my family's affairs? And what gives you the right to interfere? In fact, who the hell do you think you are coming in here like an avenging bloody angel?"

Then another thought struck him, and his eyes narrowed. "And, while we're at it, what's my sister to you?"

Alex put up his hands in mock surrender.

"Ho! Not so fast, my friend. No need to jump to any nasty conclusions. I can understand your anger and your suspicions, but you have no cause to be alarmed or to call me out. I had occasion to meet with your mother and sister briefly when I recently visited Yorkshire. They were a great help to me when I was taken ill, and I owe them a debt of gratitude which I mean to repay. For even though they live quietly and are well thought of in the community, I have learned that lies have been circulating about your sister; lies that have disturbed me."

"Don't tell me people are still circulating those old stories? Goodness gracious, no good can come of keeping them alive. My advice is to ignore them. The least said the better, so to speak."

"Such heartless comments," Alex remarked, obviously still bristling with indignation. "But we may be speaking at cross purposes. I believe you may not be referring to the same 'old stories' as myself."

"What are you talking about then?"

"Perhaps we should start again, and both calm down and I will tell you exactly why I am here."

Damien nodded his agreement and leaned back in his chair, trying to look as though he didn't have a care in the world. "Please do."

"I have come here for information and to learn more about you, your motives, and your views. About how much you know and why you have acted as you have. Then, and only then, can I decide how to deal with you. So, let's start at the beginning, shall we? I want to understand what you said about your sister wanting to wed this Lucas fellow. You say she was for the match, but didn't you consider how young she was at the time? She was only fifteen. A child. Surely, you should have considered her best interests and waited until she was older."

Damien frowned. He did not like the way this conversation was going, not one little bit. Especially about the implied threat in the earl's statement. What was the fellow talking about? The scandal surrounding the divorce? But that was old news. So why the threat? He'd like to get rid of the fellow but sensed that would neither be an easy nor a wise thing to do.

He also found that for some reason, he wanted to put his case to the earl, whether to salve his conscience or just to defend himself, he did not know, but for whatever reason, he was determined to say his piece. The earl had made him angry. "I *did* consider her best interests, damn it! What chance did she have of making a good match? Our family was penniless. Our father had shot himself, the coward! I am sure you can imagine the scandal. And then Lucas offered for her. And she wanted him. Don't doubt that."

"But she was just a child. It was you who gained the most. Right?"

"I gained. Yes, I admit it. Why shouldn't I? But she gained as well. *And* mother. We would have starved if it hadn't been for Lucas."

Damien remembered with dismay just how he had felt at that time. He had only been twenty-two when his father had blown his brains out after losing the family estate in a game of hazard, leaving him the head of a family without a home and without funds. Oh yes, he was the Earl of Hawkeswood, but it was an empty title. There were no wealthy living relatives as far as he knew, and none offered to help. He had a few good friends, but they were either dependent on their families without any wealth of their own or were unwilling to loan money to someone who was unlikely to be able to repay the debt.

His mother was an invalid and had lost contact with her friends, so she could not help. All the money she had brought to the marriage had long since disappeared to her husband's extravagances. So, when Lucas Greene offered him that lifeline, he had grabbed it with both hands.

"So that is why you didn't defend your sister when he arranged to slander her name, and divorce her?"

"Is that what all this is about? I thought as much. But that story is old news."

"No, that is not what all this is about, it is just the beginning. But the scandalmongering began there, and as I told you, I need to establish the facts so that I know what I am dealing with. I am determined to right the wrong done to your sister, you see; something, to my mind, that you should have seen to yourself. I suppose I can understand why you did nothing when her husband still lived, although I cannot approve of your lack of action. However, I appreciate that your financial position depended on his goodwill. But since his death? Since you started to rely on your sister's goodwill? Surely, it must have been in your own interest to stop the gossip and lies?"

"You seem to know an awful lot about the relationship between myself and my sister. Has she been telling tales about me?"

"She talked about you, yes, but not in any derogatory way, I can assure you. She is very fond of you, I believe. But you should know as well as I do that personal information has a way of becoming known by others."

"No doubt those servants of hers. But she is not the angel you seem to think her, you know. Nor is she as generous as you believe. For example, I don't suppose you learned about her trying to send me off to get killed on the Continent, or that she only settles the most pressing of my debts. Luckily, I don't often lose at the tables."

He considered himself an expert card player and did not rely on luck alone. Instead, he took delight in staying sober whilst his fellow players imbibed freely, thereby giving him the edge. He also possessed considerable skill, gained over many years, and rarely left the tables without being ahead. It was how he made his living. But he gambled for huge stakes, and, on the few occasions he did lose, he lost in spectacular fashion, thus requiring a visit to his benefactor, first Lucas, and, since his death, Meg. He was not proud of having to go to his sister, cap in hand so to speak, and had therefore tried to limit his need to depend on his sister by moving to this unfashionable address, allowing himself few luxuries, apart from his clothing. One had to keep up appearances, after all.

As to her idea of buying him a commission in the army, he had refused her "generous offer". The army had never appealed to him, especially the officer class. To him, they appeared to be the most foolish of men. Risking all, heading the charge into battle, and often being the first to die. It was not for him!

"If I didn't know better, I'd say she was the older of the two of you. You're sounding like a spoiled schoolboy, if you only realised it. Far from trying to get you killed, it seems to me she was trying to get you settled in a career, since you don't have an estate to look after. Isn't it time you learned to stand on your own two feet? Or, if that is beyond you, maybe you should look around for a wealthy wife? Ah ... now I understand. You thought Miss MacDonald was an heiress!"

The injustice of that last statement infuriated Damien. "I did no such thing!" he shouted and was about to add more when he thought better of it.

Alex raised a dubious brow but continued calmly, "We seem to have strayed from the topic. Whatever your interest is, or was, in Miss MacDonald, I won't hold that against you for now. But if I hear you failed to behave honourably towards her at any time, you will answer to me on the subject, you can be sure. However, what I want to do now is get back to the subject of your sister and how you and your friends have mistreated her. Shall we start with Rodney Blewett?"

"What do you know about Rodney Blewett?" Damien asked. He had been about to take the earl to task for accusing him of mistreating his sister, but at the mention of Rodney's name, all else was forgotten.

"I know all about Rodney Blewett, from the role he played in the divorce scandal to his visit to your sister after her husband's death. What I want from you is to know what *you* know about Rodney Blewett."

"Well, I know why Rodney Blewett went to see my sister, if that's of interest to you. He wanted to marry her, you know, and, to my mind, she should have accepted him. After all, it was his name that was used in the divorce. Would have made everything right then, wouldn't it? And everyone believed she and he had been lovers, anyway. Nothing I could have said would have made them believe differently. They would just say I was defending my sister. They wouldn't have believed me. Didn't see why I should get myself killed for no reason."

"No reason? Your sister's honour? You don't deserve to be called a man. Just as I said, you're a spoiled boy. Well, *I* will call you out. How about that, my friend? Didn't you know that an Act of Parliament has been proposed that would make it a criminal offence for a couple named in a divorce case to marry? *Make it right*? Nothing but the truth will make it right. And the truth is that nothing happened between Rodney Blewett and your sister. And you know it!"

"All right. I do know it. But it would be my word against everyone else and as I say, who would believe me? However, I do agree with you that it would have been better for the truth to have been told. But not the whole truth. Even you would not want that."

"What are you saying?"

"That the truth would hurt too many people. Especially Emily. What would it do to her to learn that her father was a man who was attracted to his own sex rather than to women. A pansy, many would call him, although worse labels come to mind. Yes, you can look surprised. He only fancied Meg before her body developed. She looked more like a boy than a girl in those days. Rode astride as well. That was how he first saw her, you know. Riding astride her mare, with her short hair and her tanned complexion. I knew his preferences, of course, and knew what he was thinking. His parents were pressuring him to marry and produce an heir. And he thought Meg was the answer. But to tell you the truth, he fancied me more than he fancied her!"

Alex looked horrified by this twist to the story. "Well, that certainly explains a few things. How could you marry your sister to such a man! You should have prevented it at all costs. But instead, it suited you to keep quiet and fool yourself with the thought that you were acting in the family's best interests."

"I told you. She wanted the match!"

"And I remind you that she was just a child." Alex took a deep breath, obviously trying to calm down.

The two men looked at each other, both standing their ground. Damien was the first to look away. "Well, all right, but that is in the past and cannot be changed. What's done is done. Talking about it is not going to get us anywhere."

"Except I am determined to understand what led to your sister being alienated from society. So let us now turn to the divorce. I need to know all the facts if I am going to be able to help your sister. Not only about Rodney Blewett, but also about the others."

"What is the point. It will only make matters worse. Meg never guessed the truth about Lucas, you know. I can't believe it would help anyone to revive the old scandal, let alone create a new one."

Alex looked thoughtful. "Because something must be done to put things right. But I now understand you a little better and accept that things are not as clear cut as I had hoped. Yet while I am beginning to understand why Lucas decided to marry your sister, I still don't understand about the divorce," he managed to ask in a reasonably calm voice.

Damien sighed in frustration. "I can see you won't be satisfied until I have told you all. Why the divorce you ask? The same reason as for the marriage. Pressure from his family again. Particularly from his mother. He felt he had to try again, but he couldn't stand Meg after Emily had been born. She had developed quite nicely if you understand me. He told his mother that it was Meg who had spurned him, and after a while his mother told him in no uncertain terms to do his duty, even if he had to rape his wife. Of course, he couldn't do that. Couldn't perform with Meg however he approached the act, and so he hatched this plan where he asked a friend of his, Rodney, to seduce his wife and get her with child; a child he would claim as his own. It was the only way he could think of getting his mother off his back! "

"And you knew about this plan?"

"Not at first but eventually I learned what was intended to happen. I even went to see him. That's when he told me what a mess he was in, confiding everything to me. And you were right. I *was* dependent on him, as was my whole family. I could do nothing except plead with him. But he was just as much a victim as Meg. He told me he had to do something, and I believe he hoped that Meg would welcome Rodney's attentions. But I swear to you that I knew nothing of the alternative plan. What Lucas had decided to do if his initial plan failed. I had no idea that, if the worst came to the worst, he thought to ensure that Meg and Rodney were found in bed together, giving him the evidence he needed to denounce her as an adulterer and divorce her. Or of his plan to tell his mother that while Meg spurned his advances, she didn't spurn everyone. In short, she was having affairs. He knew his mother - a strong woman, as you will have guessed by now – would decide that divorce was the only answer. Poor Lucas! He never meant things to go that far, but that is what happened. All because he just wanted to be left alone. It was a ghastly mess. I was horrified when Lucas confided the full details to me, but I couldn't act, even though killing him seemed mighty tempting in that moment. But, you see, the truth would have been worse than the lies."

"You should have acted much earlier," Alex said, deep in thought. He was obviously still very angry. "So, let me get this straight. You kept quiet and betrayed your sister and after Lucas's death, you advised your sister to marry Rodney Blewett."

"Yes, I did. He really liked Meg. He would have made her a good husband. He certainly has settled down to marriage now. Seems the devoted husband. Mind you, his wife's father makes sure he stays that way, so I've heard."

"He liked your sister so much, he agreed to rape her!"

"No, I don't believe he would have done that. If she didn't respond to him as he hoped, he knew that he would just have to be found in bed with her for the plan to work."

"Well, maybe you'll be interested to know that she woke up to find him on top of her."

Damien clenched his fists in defence at both Alex's aggression and at the thought of Meg's suffering. He rose from the chair and began pacing the floor.

"God, how awful. I never knew the details ... no wonder she was as mad as hell when I told her I thought she should have accepted Rodney's offer. Why didn't she tell me?"

Alex remained silent, but Damien knew he was being closed observed as he paced the floor. Could the earl see how full of remorse, anger and confusion he was?

After a while, Alex added quietly, "And why do nothing when you heard the lies told by your other friends? Clive, John, Neville and ... who was the other one?"

"What? Oh, so at last we are coming to the supposed lies told by my friends that you spoke about. I thought you were referring only to the divorce scandal and the lies that my friends told to aid Lucas. What other lies are you talking about?"

"Are you pleading ignorance of what your friends did? I find that hard to believe."

"What are you talking about? What have my friends done?" Unfortunately, he was beginning to see where this conversation was heading. He decided to sit down again and listen to the rest of what Lord Tenby had to say.

"Have you not heard about your friends boast of their visits to your sister?"

Suddenly, Damien looked decidedly embarrassed. He hated to even think about his sister in that manner and had avoided any mention of her visitors in her presence. It was nothing to do with him what his sister got up to, was it? But he didn't pretend not to know to what the earl was referring.

"And you are saying they were lying?" he asked. "I assumed she had welcomed their visits. Meg never mentioned them visiting her, that is true, and I certainly never brought up the topic. Not my place to pry into her personal life. It was none of my business and what if she did entertain lovers occasionally? A young, lonely widow. Can't expect her to live like a nun! But my friends should have been discreet about their visits, I grant you that. I suppose you are thinking I should have protected her, and I would have if she lived in town. I told her she was making a mistake hiding herself away in the country for so long. With all that wealth, she could live in town in style and defy all her critics. But, no, she allowed herself to be intimidated, which has not helped any of us."

"All your sister's fault, is it? You don't seem to appreciate just how deeply she has been hurt. She has more courage than any woman I have ever met, and the reason she lives in relative isolation is to protect her daughter's future. Which also accounts for why she doesn't live a lavish lifestyle, I might add. I don't think she considers the money she inherited on her husband's death to be hers, you see, but as money to be held in trust for Emily. As for why she didn't mention those visitors to you, it was simply because she was unaware of their visits. They never reached the house. Jed and others protected your sister when you failed to do so and, to make things worse, it seems that you also did nothing to stop them from bragging about their supposed successes with your sister."

Damien almost rose from his chair again but gripped the armrests instead. "Damn it, that's not true. Told them to button their lips or they would answer to me. But they apologised, and, as far as I know, said no more. How was I to know they were telling lies? God, wait till I see them!"

"Now, that's more like it. Maybe you will be of some use after all."

Damien looked closely at Alex for the first time and calmed down enough to begin thinking about this unusual conversation with this uninvited visitor.

"And maybe I'm not so averse to this visit of yours, after all."

Alex smiled. "Good. Now that you can see why action is needed, perhaps we can begin to work out a strategy. Between us, I believe we could do a lot to help her." One aspect of this "help" made Alex uneasy, however. Somehow, he had never envisioned the ultimate outcome of clearing Meg's name, that of her taking up her rightful position in society. Now Damien had made him face that fact, he didn't know if he could bear to have Meg living in or near London, being able to see her and yet being unable to acknowledge his feelings for her.

But he had gone too far for his resolve to waver, and so he outlined his plan of action. "It is vital that we get these so-called friends of yours to retract their lies in public, leaving us and the gossip mill to take care of the rest. But should any of them refuse, I tell you now, I intend to challenge them on the field of honour."

"No. That is my right and my responsibility," Damien said vehemently. "But it shall be done, you can be assured of that. I should have acted before; I see that now. But I honestly didn't know they were lying, nor did I know how widely their lies had spread. Thought they had confined their tattle to our small circle. I really believed they had listened to my threats and stopped. But I should have realised that once gossip gets started it is impossible to control it. Well, thanks to you, I realise it now. Better late than never, they say. I'll start with Rodney Blewett. That wife of his could be a help there. If she has any idea about the sordid affair, that is. Otherwise, maybe a little blackmail could come in handy."

Alex felt he had said enough for the moment. He could see that Damien was warming to the task, and it would certainly be better for any challenges to come from him. And, although he still had some matters he would like to pursue, like the name of the unknown slanderer, he decided it would be wiser at this point to work amicably with Damien in the effort to restore Meg's good name. And so the two continued to plot their strategy for some time, and when Alex finally went on his way, he felt a measure of relief that the two were friends of sorts instead of enemies.

Alex did pay Iain Blair the promised visit later that day, but no longer pressed for an invitation to Rodney Blewett's house party. He would trust Damien to take care of that side of things. After all, it would have been somewhat awkward to explain his absence from town so soon after his return and the announcement of his engagement. He knew it was his duty to squire his fiancée to all her planned entertainments, and the house party wouldn't have been considered an appropriate function for Lord Frome's ward to attend, even if it didn't clash with their other commitments.

He only wished this development made him feel happy. But it did not. Meg was still denied to him. Marriage to Penelope now seemed a certainty.

Chapter Fourteen

◆————————◆————————◆

Shortly after Alex had left him, Damien scribbled a quick note to Rodney Blewett accepting his invitation to the house party, which was only ten days away. He had intended to convey his apologies, not wanting to spend four days out of town so near the end of the season. Especially as a guest of a rather prudish hostess who would undoubtedly ban gambling for high stakes. By remaining in town, he would have access to far more interesting entertainments. Then again, Penelope being in town was both a drawcard and a drawback. Seeing her every evening would be wonderful but seeing her with Lord Tenby would be torture.

At least going to the house party would save him having to watch her hanging on to Lord Tenby's arm for a few days, but until then, he would just have to do all he could to avoid seeing them together. She and Tenby were bound to be the centre of attention with everyone wishing them well; there would also no doubt be a celebratory ball, a thought he found nauseating!

Jealousy was an emotion Damien had never experienced before. It was completely foreign to him, and he didn't like the feeling one bit! No woman should be able to do that to a man, but here he was, being eaten up with envy and resentment!

Damien couldn't understand why she had such an effect on him. Most women were his for the taking. Even married ones. Especially married ones! Virtuous women usually bored him, even if they had hidden, sensual depths, like Penelope. On occasions he may have toyed with the idea of bedding one of them, but only for a moment. Forbidden fruits had never appealed to him. So, why had Penelope enthralled him so much? Without her even trying!

Oh, he knew she was attracted to him, but he was accustomed to that. He would have understood it better if she had repelled him, giving him the thrill of the chase. But somehow, she had captivated him to the extent that he now found himself caring for someone other than himself! It made him feel vulnerable again. And he didn't like it.

Shortly after his father's untimely death, he had decided the only way for him to survive what life threw at him was by making sure he didn't give a damn about anything or anybody. And yet, here he now was, caring not only about Penelope but also about his own family. And, he reflected, as he sealed and franked the note to Rodney, somehow, for some unknown reason, he felt better about himself than he had for years.

He was now on a mission and attending that dratted house party was the centrepiece of his plan. Mind you, he had plenty of ideas on how to keep himself occupied until then. He was going to go hunting, not for four legged animals, but for men. That very night, he intended to pay a visit to Pauline's; a discreet, clean brothel and gaming hell he frequented, where men could experience both heaven and hell in a single night. It would be a good place to start, he surmised, and if he couldn't find those he was hunting for there, he knew of many other venues to try. Anywhere would be better than to go where Penelope and her intended were likely to be found.

Defending his sister's honour now had to be his priority anyway. It was strange, this feeling that had been generated by Lord Tenby. A man he should loath. Somehow, despite all the insults he had hurled, he had succeeded where all else had failed. Instead of considering himself the victim of a cruel fate, one that had robbed him of his birthright, he now felt empowered for the first time since his father's death. How strange!

It was quite late when Damien arrived at Pauline's. Earlier in the evening he had attended a most boring soirée, one he had been committed to attending, and had been mightily relieved to note that neither the earl nor Penelope were present. He had scanned the room, but none of the friends he was seeking were there either, so he had tried to amuse himself by flirting outrageously with a married lady of his acquaintance. Unfortunately, his heart had not been in it.

But now the evening had begun in earnest. Here at Pauline's, eager to begin his new crusade, he felt sure he would find at least one of the men he was after. He almost hoped it would be necessary for him to issue a challenge to them all. One at a time, of course. Damien was both an accomplished swordsman and a notable shot, just two of the skills he had learned to keep the boredom of his life at bay. And he fully anticipated to be exercising those skills over the ensuing days, maybe even as early as the following dawn.

Of course, Rodney would not be there, nor Clive, but he hoped to see at least one of the others. Failing that, he planned to spend some time at the tables, after which he hoped his favourite whore, Verity, could relieve his sexual needs with her clever, experienced, delightful mouth.

Damien had barely settled into a game of faro, when he saw John Kendle enter the card room. He continued to play, keeping a careful watch on his friend's movements. Neither acknowledged the other, it being the custom to leave players undisturbed. John had joined a game at one of the other tables and looked fairly settled. As soon as there was a break in play, Damien excused himself, gathered up his winnings and strolled casually over to the other table, resting his hand gently on John's shoulder.

"Just the man I was looking for, old friend," he whispered. "Need a word when you have a moment."

"Oh, hello Damien. Haven't seen you around for a while. Give me a minute and I'll join you downstairs. My luck seems to have deserted me anyway." John smiled up at Damien, clearly delighted to see an old friend, and not at all annoyed at the interruption.

Downstairs was a series of lounges, all sumptuously decorated and furnished, where lightly clad, beautiful young women entertained their customers. Pauline was always present, making sure that everyone was satisfied, helping newcomers to feel comfortable, and checking to see that her girls and the customers followed the rules of the house.

She was well past her prime, her figure no longer slender. She wore a sequined, low-cut, sleeveless gown, exposing dimpled fat on both her upper and lower arms. The sparkling material of the gown hugged her generous curves, revealing a wrinkled neck and cleavage, as well as rolls of fat. Her laugh was loud and raucous, her lips and eyes were over-painted, and her cheeks were over-rouged, making her seem more like a circus performer than a society matron or even an actress.

Damien helped himself to champagne, his first drink of the evening, but, even then, he only sipped at it. He had serious work to do, after all. He noticed that Verity was not in any of the rooms, and spoke quietly to Pauline, asking if she was working that night. Pauline teased him a little, knowing his preference, and then assured him that Verity would be able to see to him shortly. Damien informed her that he needed a quiet word with a friend first and requested the use of a suitable room.

"Anything is possible for a price," she told him, then called over one of her footmen, instructing him to show Lord Hawkeswood each of the possible venues.

A little over ten minutes later, John Kendle descended the stairs, and Damien ushered him into a small room at the back of the house. It was a sort of office, but also stored many large boxes which were piled up along one wall. The furniture consisted of only two hard-backed chairs and a desk, nothing like the furnishings in the rest of the building, except for the numerous pictures on the walls. There, as in the main salons, were pictures of nudes; some in suggestive poses, others quite explicit; some featuring only one figure, others with two or more bodies entwined. Both men found their gazes wandering from one picture to another, noting the erotic scenes depicted, before Damien confronted his former friend with his challenge, deciding not to try to reason with him first.

"By God, Damien, what in hell's teeth has got into you, man?" John responded, his astonishment obvious. "You must be drunk. All that happened years ago. And I only told you and a few others."

"But it wasn't true, you lying sod!" cried Damien, warming to the task. "And even if it was, I should have challenged you at the time. I was stupid then, I admit, and only now have heard that your story is the talk of the town. Damn you, John. Meg is innocent and you know it."

"I think you must be touched in your upper works, Damien. What makes you think I fabricated the story? She say anything to you about it? Is that why you are acting like a madman?"

"How could she? You never even got to see her, you lying whelp. And neither did the others. Except Rodney. And he didn't have any success either."

"What? Are you telling me that your sister has never taken a lover? Come off it!"

"Are you calling me a liar now?" Damien all but shouted, his face so close to John's that the threat behind his words was crystal clear.

John suddenly backed up, and almost fell into the chair behind him. "All right, I admit I didn't get to see her, and I can tell you, I was feeling pretty peeved about it. After all, I went all that way on the strength of those stories and got thrown off the place. Literally. By some giant bodyguard. How would you feel? I only wanted to court her. Offer her marriage, for God's sake."

Damien still stood, his posture even more threatening, if that were possible. "After her money, you mean! Well, now you can pay with your life. Name your seconds and we can make the arrangements."

"No, by heavens. I won't. You can't make me, damn it. Damien, I have admitted I lied. What more do you want?"

"Your blood. It's as simple as that. Eventually, we all have to pay for our crimes. Your time has now arrived."

"You're mad. Absolutely mad. You can't meet me after all these years. Why don't you sit down so we can discuss this. There must be another way. Oh, I know you're a better shot than I am, and I wouldn't stand a chance. But what about the others? Clive could beat you, and Howard would stand a good chance, too. And, anyway, Rodney is the main culprit. Caused us all to make up the tales in the first place. Have you challenged him yet?"

"I'm saving Rodney for last. Make him sweat. When he gets to hear about your fate, he'll be wetting himself in fright. I've arranged to go to his house party and will see to him then. But you are first. Simply because you are here. And Rodney may be the main culprit, as you put it, but you made up your own mind to lie about my sister, to besmirch her honour."

"But that's just it. I didn't besmirch her honour. It was already besmirched. I only lied about my success with your sister because of the others who had claimed that they had succeeded before me. I wasn't going to look a fool to my friends by telling them what really happened."

"Nevertheless, it is your lies, and those told by the others that have caused my sister to have a reputation as a lightskirt. And it seems she has never been with anyone but her husband. I can't restore her name, being her brother. No-one would believe me. But I can, and

I will, do what should have been done years ago, and defend her honour with my own life."

"And where will that get you? Or her, for that matter. Use your head, man! There must be a better way to fix this. Why not let me help you? I am willing to confess that I lied about your sister to everyone I know and tell them what really happened. And I am sure that Rodney, being happily married now, would like the world to know he was innocent of any crime. And so would the others, I'm sure. After all, it's water under the bridge now, isn't it? People won't take much notice really. They'll tease me for a while I expect, but nothing worse than that. And your sister's good name will be restored. What do you say, my friend?"

Damien almost smiled at how well his plan was working, but genuinely regretted that he would be denied seeking revenge on the field of honour. He wanted to avenge his sister. He stood for a while longer, breathing heavily, but eventually took a seat. He knew John had a point.

When Damien agreed to discuss the possibility of avoiding a duel, John let out a sigh of relief. It took a while, but the two finally came to an acceptable understanding, John agreeing to begin confessing his sins that very evening while stating that Margaret Greene had been sorely wronged.

The two eventually shook hands before parting. But just as John reached the door to leave, Damien called his name. John turned, and his face hardly had time to register surprise before Damien's fist connected with his jaw.

"Think yourself lucky that that's all I intend to do to you. And if you don't do as promised, or if you don't succeed in having your confession believed, then I shall be back to take care of you."

John tried to smile from the floor, rubbed his jaw, saying, "I deserved that, didn't I? And I don't blame you, really I don't. Would have done at least as much if it was a sister of mine. And I shall make sure I am believed, you can be sure," he promised.

Damien looked at him, uttered an indistinguishable sound, something between a laugh and a cry of anguish, and left the room.

He now needed to avail himself of Verity's considerable skills even more than before and headed off towards the main salon. Pauline intercepted him and asked if he had successfully concluded his interview, looking past him to see if the other gentleman was there.

"He'll be along in a minute. Don't worry, Pauline, I haven't killed him. Not yet anyway."

"And not here," Pauline countered. "Don't bring your quarrels into my house in future, my lord. Or you won't find your usual welcome."

"After our long and profitable association? Shame on you, Pauline. But you can be assured about one thing. I will never cause you any embarrassment. You should know that by now."

Pauline nodded. "I believe we understand each other. You are a good patron of my establishment, Lord Hawkeswood, and have never mistreated my girls or made a scene. And I know you use the card room more as a place of work, earning money whilst enjoying the game. But then, you often pass on some of your winnings by employing Verity or one of the other girls. So long as everyone sticks to the rules, we can all be happy."

* * *

Two weeks later, Damien found that his crusade had all but evaporated. He hadn't had the satisfaction of even one duel. Rodney Blewett, Neville Oakley, and Howard Ramsey - the one name Jed had not known - were all present at the house party, and, after a late-night session when the truth became known, all saw the necessity of confessing that they had lied. Rodney had spoken at length to his wife, Julia, and she had become their staunchest ally after castigating her husband severely, that is. She seemed determined to attempt to right the wrong done to Lady Margaret by inviting her to stay with herself and her husband before it was pointed out to her that it would be unlikely to help matters if Lady Margaret was seen to be friendly with her supposed former lover.

Damien only wished his rented home was suitable to house his mother and sister but knew he couldn't ask them to stay with him. Yet he understood Julia's argument. He must persuade Meg to visit London later in the year, giving him time to ensure that the gossip mill had finished its work and that she would not be subjected to cruel innuendos or abuse. By that time, most of the *ton* would have returned after the summer break and the entertainments would have recommenced. Then the last of the rumours should die, as Meg would undoubtedly be seen as the naturally graceful, virtuous, and charming lady she truly was.

He hoped he was not being too optimistic, but if he was successful, and she saw that she was once again accepted by polite society, perhaps he would be able to persuade her that it was time for her to re-establish herself in society by moving back to London, and maybe even to buy a country estate not too far from town for herself and her daughter. Then the family honour could finally be restored. Which would mean attending to his own, sullied reputation as well, he realised. One almost completely undeserved, in his own opinion, at least in comparison to some he could name!

As he began to consider all these possibilities, he began to dream that if only Penelope could be his, he would then be the happiest of men. But that was one dream he knew would not come true.

* * *

During that same fortnight, Alex went through the motions of being a devoted beau, but knew his eyes lacked sparkle and his smile was forced. The only time his eyes had shone was when he had confronted his cousin, Percy, going to his home the moment he had heard of his return to town.

Alex had never intended to hit him, but as soon as Meg's name was mentioned, Percy had laughed, making some remark about Alex enjoying her charms. Alex saw red and couldn't help himself. The action was instinctive. His fist moved so quickly, it connected with Percy's jaw before either was aware of the force behind the punch. Percy landed on his backside, blood dripping from his cut lip, the smile gone from his face, replaced by a look of shock rather than of anger.

"You deserved that," Alex had said, even as he helped his cousin to his feet. He then explained the situation and a bemused Percy listened in astonishment, becoming more and more ashamed of the part he had played. In the end, he agreed to do all he could to help, which Alex assured him was considerable, and they eventually parted amicably.

And then there was the ball given in honour of their engagement. Alex did his best to smile at his fiancée and his guests, dancing with Penelope whilst gazing into her eyes, but his heart wasn't in it. He knew he was living a lie. How on earth was he to stand a lifetime of this torture? Hurting not only himself, but also Penelope. For he knew he couldn't give her what she wanted.

She was not the shy, young ingénue he had first thought her, but a dazzling, flirtatious beauty who attracted the admiration of all the men she met. Including Lord Hawkeswood, it seemed. Yet she seemed so content with their betrothal, he did not for a minute think she was enamoured of anyone else. *Maybe she really loves me*, he thought. But if that was meant to make him feel better, it didn't. She would be tying herself for life to someone who could never love her in return.

He was sure his mother had noticed his lack of enthusiasm. She had given him some odd looks lately, he noted. And her attitude towards Penelope seemed to have changed perceptibly during that fortnight as well. She no longer spoke about Penelope in glowing terms as she had done earlier. In fact, he now realised, she hadn't said anything complimentary about his fiancée since he had returned from Yorkshire. He must have a word with her, he decided, and find out if there was anything amiss between the two women.

But before he had a chance to bring up the topic of his engagement with his mother, she surprised him one afternoon by bringing Meg's name into the conversation. Penelope was spending the afternoon in Bruton Street seeing her modiste, leaving Alex time to see his mother on her own at her home in South Street, an opportunity that was becoming more and more rare. They were enjoying discussing the latest gossip concerning the royal family. Charlotte, the royal princess, was almost of marriageable age, and her name had been linked with the exiled Prince of Orange.

"Such an odious looking creature," his mother exclaimed. "I find it hard to believe that the Prince can be thinking of marrying his daughter to him."

Alex commented that, as usual, politics would be the main consideration in the choice of a husband for Charlotte and that, according to the gossip, Charlotte was behaving in such an unsuitable way, she should consider herself lucky to find anyone willing to take her on. "It's a good job she is a royal princess, if you ask me," he concluded. "Otherwise, she may not find it so easy to attract a husband."

Princess Charlotte was sixteen but had already caused gossip due to her coarse language and her dangerously forward behaviour with men. It was common knowledge that her father had recently reacted by restricting her activities severely.

"Yes," his mother agreed. "No man wants soiled goods. But we should be careful when we hear gossip not to condemn without proof. Which reminds me, Alex. I heard a new rumour about the Greene's. I don't suppose you know anything about the family." She looked at him briefly, saw his stunned expression, and continued. "Well, from the look on your face, you have never heard of them and wonder what on earth I am talking about." She then filled him in on the basics of the case before getting to her point. "To think, all *the ton* assumed the story about Lucas Greene's wife was true. Why else would he go to such lengths to try to divorce her? But it seems we were wrong. She was set up, or so the story goes. She was as pure as snow. So it goes to show, doesn't it? Gossip can be cruel. We should resist the temptation, even though I know it is almost impossible to do so."

For a moment, Alex was simply too stunned to speak. His mind was in a turmoil. Was his mother castigating him for gossiping about the princess? It seemed so. But she was using gossip to prove her point! And what gossip! Her mother had heard about Meg.

He was sure the colour must have drained from his face when his mother spoke of the Greene family. Luckily, he hadn't been holding a drink at the time, or he was sure he would have spilled it all over himself. Getting himself back under control took a while, but he had to take this unexpected opportunity to further Meg's cause.

"Actually, mother, I do know the story," he said as calmly as he was able. He knew he mustn't rush things. He had to be sure of his ground. "What makes you think this latest gossip has any truth in it? After all, as you say, gossip can be most unreliable."

"Well, apparently, the man accused of having the affair with Lady Margaret confessed all," she told him, warming to the story. "Seems that Lady Margaret's brother is at last taking an interest in his sister's affairs. Oh, what a bad choice of words that was," she added, giggling at the double meaning.

"Go on, Mother," Alex prompted, not joining in her amusement.

Prudence Wilde looked at her son for a moment, wondering at his interest in the story and lack of humour, then shrugged. "Well, Sir Blewett admitted trying to help Lucas Greene to get enough evidence to divorce his wife. Said Lucas told him she couldn't have any more children, and he needed an heir. Something like that, anyway. I've heard of such things happening before, so can quite believe it. It's not fair on the poor girl, though, is it?"

"Indeed, it is not. And she isn't the only one to be hurt. There is a daughter as well."

"Really? How old is she?"

"Nine, I believe."

"Oh yes, I remember now. Thought it was funny at the time. He accused his wife of having numerous affairs, but never once questioned his daughter's paternity. And they hadn't been married all that long."

"He married her when she was only fifteen, then kept her in the country."

"And there she has stayed, it seems. And no wonder. When I think of how she was treated when she came to London after her husband's death! No wonder she didn't stay long. I am just as much to blame as anyone, you know. I didn't go out of my way to befriend the girl. It was wrong of me to accept the story as true, especially as I knew such things happened sometimes. I never should have believed it. After all, I knew what a ne'er do well her husband was. But I had never met her, and so couldn't make a judgement. At least, that is my excuse. But I should have made it my business to meet her. You know, someone ought to encourage her to try again. Give us another chance to act decently towards her. I must have a word with her brother, when next I see him. Or maybe I could write to her."

Alex smiled, seeing his mother getting involved. She was known as someone who was willing to take on Society to help and befriend those whom she considered worthy of her attention and patronage. But she obviously hadn't yet wondered how Alex knew so much about the Greene family.

"Mother? You haven't yet asked me how I know so much about Lady Margaret."

"No, I haven't, have I? How *do* you know so much about her?"

"I met her on my recent visit to Yorkshire. After I was shot, Firefly carried me on to her land. It was she who saved my life."

His mother looked at him, open mouthed. Her mind was working furiously, trying to decide why he had not mentioned this before and why now? And what part he had played in this new development? For she knew her son, and now guessed that he was involved in this somehow.

"And you wanted to help her," she finished for him. She put up her hand to prevent him denying it. "Oh yes, I can see your hand in this, Alex. Lady Margaret saves your life. You see she is not as she has been painted and you make it your duty to repay her by clearing her name. Very noble! And I thought it was her brother who had come to her aid. But tell me, what did you have to do to persuade Sir Rodney Blewett to retract his earlier words?"

"Very little, I promise you. You were right, her brother *did* come to her aid. All I did was simply explain things to him. You see, he hadn't questioned the story either. Though I agree with you that he should have. And there were other rumours that you obviously haven't heard about. Some of her brother's friends had been spreading false rumours about her after failing in their attempts to bed her. Probably to get revenge, or just to protect their egos and pretend that they are irresistible to women, I suppose. Anyway, Damien now understands the situation and is determined to put matters right. So, you see, I did nothing but make her brother act as he should have at the time."

"Hmm. I am now wondering what happened between you and her brother."

"Nothing to worry you, mother. No fighting and no duel. I can assure you he saw the sense of my argument immediately."

"You wouldn't do anything to endanger your life, would you, Alex? Promise me you won't go that far?"

"Mother, it is all over. Meg ... I mean Lady Margaret, has had her name cleared. That's all I intended to do, and I have done it. My debt is paid. The end. You have no need to worry, I assure you."

"In that case, I am greatly relieved. And I hope you are right when you say that Lady Margaret has nothing to worry about either. You know, I hope, that I am willing to do whatever I can to support you. Even to the extent of exaggerating a little. Would that please you?"

He smiled and caressed her cheek. "Yes, mother, very much. I knew I could rely on you."

"And now, how are you enjoying been betrothed to Miss MacDonald?" she asked, changing the subject. Alex did his best to satisfy her that he was happy in his choice of wife and then asked if she had any concerns over the match. She seemed to be a little disconcerted for a moment, but quickly recovered herself and assured him of her full support and approval. Nevertheless, Alex suspected from her hesitation that she had reservations about Penelope's behaviour, perhaps even to feeling guilty about encouraging the match so enthusiastically. But both knew that it was too late to change things now.

Alex was glad when they moved on to other topics, happy to discuss their plans for the next few weeks. The Season was as good as over, and soon Penelope and her cousin would be leaving London. Alex wanted to return to his estate as soon as possible, but also planned to escort Penelope back to Yorkshire. Alex's mother offered to accompany them if a chaperone was required, for she knew that Celia was keen to return to Bath.

"Maybe we could drop in to meet Lady Margaret on the way home," she suggested. "I would like to meet her. I will write to thank her anyway but would much prefer to be able to thank her personally for all she did for you."

Alex's heart almost stopped when he heard those words. It brought back to him only too vividly the memory of Meg and his desire to hold her in his arms again. To see her beloved face and to tell her of his undying love once more. Yet nothing really had changed. He may have made people begin to think more kindly of her, but she knew nothing of that. All the arguments she had used to refuse him still stood. More strongly than ever. He was now formally betrothed to another.

He knew he could not see her again. Neither he nor Meg would be able to cope with another meeting. Meg had made him promise not to return, convincing him that such a visit would be unbearable. To see him and not have him. And Alex knew that if he ever saw Meg again, he would be sorely tempted to make her his own, no matter what the consequences.

It would be impossible to simply stand by, uttering commonplace pleasantries, while his love for her consumed him. No, he must never see her again. He knew he could seduce her, could make her lose her ability to resist him. He had almost made her his own at their last meeting. But in doing so, he would be destroying her. Her image of herself would be tarnished forever.

"Alex," his mother repeated, "You seem so lost in thought. And so sad. Will you tell me what's wrong?"

Alex gave himself a mental shake and smiled warmly. "Nothing is wrong, I assure you."

"And my idea of visiting Lady Margaret and her family? Is that not a good idea?"

No, it is not! his inner voice screamed, but outwardly all he said was, "We'll see, mother. We'll see."

Chapter Fifteen

Four weeks later

"What do you two intend doing this morning?" asked Prue, Alex's mother. She was addressing her son and his fiancée, Penelope, as they ate a hearty breakfast at the Marquess of Frome's seat in Yorkshire. They had been there for two days, and were feeling more rested now, having recovered from their long journey from London. As expected, Lady Dawson had jumped at the chance of returning directly to Bath, knowing that her charge would come to no harm if Lord Tenby's mother accompanied them on the journey.

"We thought we'd exercise two of Lord Frome's horses, since he so kindly offered them for our use," Alex replied.

"I suppose you are regretting your decision not to bring your own mount on this journey."

"No, I chose to leave Firefly behind because I knew you would expect me to keep you company in the carriage."

"Well, I am sure Lord Frome will be grateful to you for giving a couple of his horses a bit of a run. Why he keeps a stable of so many horses, I just can't understand because he never seems to ride himself. All he seems interested in are his confounded inventions!"

Alex laughed. "Come now, mother, he's not that bad. He is doing his best to be a good host and you couldn't want for better accommodations or food even if he does eat at a rather unfashionable hour. And as for his interest in inventions, I'm sure you are appreciating having a bathroom attached to your bedchamber. His inventive nature is the reason you are so comfortably housed, you know."

"I suppose so," she conceded. "But I don't want to spend any more time talking about, or looking at, his inventions. Now, his excellent library, that's another matter. Maybe while you two are out riding, I'll spend some time looking at some of his first editions. He has an excellent collection, you know."

"Then you won't mind if we stay for another day or two?"

"On the contrary. I wouldn't want to set out on the return journey just yet. Another day or two will suit me fine. Anyway, we couldn't leave before tomorrow. Not when Claude has been kind enough to host a party for us so that we shall be able to meet with some of his neighbours this evening. And if the evening goes on until late, as I expect it will, I shall be feeling tired tomorrow, so I'll want to rest. Apart from that, we can head for home any time you say."

Alex was pleased to see how well his mother and Lord Frome got on together despite her complaints. The two had quickly become on easy terms, even to the point of engaging in several friendly arguments. They were treating each other as though the two families were already joined, which, in a way of course, they were.

If only he felt as much at peace with the situation, Alex thought. Even though he loved riding, he found he had little enthusiasm for this particular excursion with Penelope. It is not Penelope's fault, he reminded himself as they rode side by side. He had condemned himself to this life and he would just have to make the best of things. At least the horses were thoroughbreds and his mount seemed lively enough. And Penelope was an excellent horsewoman, he noted with relief. Maybe she was merely speaking the truth when she had told him of her love for the country. She certainly seemed to enjoy riding.

They spoke little as they rode along, Penelope seemingly content to canter along, looking at the countryside and breathing in the clean, fresh air, commenting occasionally on the scenery. When they passed a farm or other landmark, she made a point of informing Alex of the names of the farmers if she knew them, or the names given to various landmarks. Otherwise, she remained silent.

She was a pleasant companion, he noted, which confirmed his mother's stated opinion. He supposed he should be pleased that the two women appeared to get on, especially as he intended to offer his mother a permanent home at Knopton Manor. Not that he would suggest she sell her own home if she didn't wish to, but it seemed only sensible to him to have his mother near as she grew older.

When he had taken her to visit Knopton Manor, shortly after he had inherited, his mother had freely commented on the need to redecorate and refurbish many of the rooms. He had asked her to take on the task, which she had agreed to willingly, enjoying the challenge. They had discussed the need for her to have her own apartment, and she had thanked him, but, other than that, nothing had been settled. He wondered whether to bring up the topic now with Penelope, but then discarded the idea. It would be better for the three of them to sit down together to discuss the matter. Not that he was any more enthusiastic about the future than he was for this ride.

Ever since he had inherited the title, his life had seemed plagued by one change after another. And none that he wanted. The only change he wanted was to make a life with Meg, but that was to be denied him. All the other changes were just inconveniences. His life had been decided for him and there seemed to be nothing he could do to change things. It was his duty to marry, and it was no use prolonging the agony of living in hope that something might happen to prevent the marriage and permit him to have his dream.

For a moment, he allowed himself to conjure up Meg's image, envisioning her by his side, imagining her scent, and her softness, but the pain of such self-deception was too great, so he shrugged and blinked quickly to rid himself of this torture. Nothing was likely to happen to save him, and he knew he must put a stop to this unhealthy dreaming as soon as possible. His fate was sealed. He must accept things as they were. Penelope must not be made to suffer because he could not love her as he should.

His thoughts were interrupted when Penelope turned to him, telling him about the crops growing in the field beside the track, and he nodded and smiled at her, commenting that they must like the mild, warm weather they were having. Penelope smiled back, and suddenly urged her horse to take the lead as the track narrowed.

"You obviously know this area well, Penelope," he shouted to her. "Where are we headed?"

"There is a ruined castle at the top of the next rise," she shouted back. "All this land belongs to Lord Frome, you know. These farmers are his tenants."

"I guessed as much," he replied. "We also have tenant farmers at our seat in Surrey, but our lands are not as vast as those of the Marquess. A mere fifteen hundred acres. We must have already travelled more than four miles. I hope this castle is not much further, or the horses will tire before our return."

"We are nearly there. Just a minute or two more," she replied, glancing over her shoulder. She quickened the pace even further, and nothing more was said until they reached the top of the rise.

Penelope had been daydreaming, and when Alex had smiled at her, tears had sprung unwillingly to her eyes. She had raced ahead to prevent him seeing her distress and managed to stem the tears that were threatening to fall. For she had been imagining that, instead of Alex at her side, it had been Lord Hawkeswood, or Damien as she now thought of him.

Even though she now knew how dishonourable he was, brazenly suggesting that she run away with him, throwing themselves on the mercy of his whore of a sister, she still could not rid herself of his memory and her infatuation for him. He had sounded so sincere, whereas he was just trying to seduce another victim. She knew that. Yet in her heart she still yearned for his touch!

No man had made her feel so alive. Her breasts tingled and a warmth spread downwards to her centre just thinking about the night he had held her in his arms and had caressed her so intimately. No man had dared to take such liberties with her before. Oh, to feel such rapture again! Would Alex be able to arouse her passions in the same way? She doubted it, for, while she did not shrink from his touch, she did not feel any spark of passion either.

Naturally, Alex had never attempted to kiss her on the lips. He was too much of a gentleman for that. He had held her in his arms, but only whilst dancing, and he had kissed her fingertips on occasions, but only when it was permitted to do so. And at no time had she felt herself responding like a lover. Maybe she would have to close her eyes and imagine that it was Damien making love to her! Her body was responding now, just thinking erotic thoughts about Damien doing wonderful things to her. She felt her breasts becoming swollen and tender, her nipples hardening into buds, whilst the movement of her mount and her position on the side-saddle caused her to experience the most delectable, pleasurable, but unsettling sensations between her thighs!

Penelope allowed herself to continue experiencing these sensuous feelings whilst at the same time trying to convince herself that a life with Alex was what she wanted. Acceptance in society. A title. Children. Wealth. Yet she had been willing to consider throwing all that away for a rakehell named Damien. He had a title, equal to that of her fiancé, but no wealth. Not even a proper home to call his own. And no doubt he would quickly squander her small annual income, derived from the money left to her by her parents and her late aunt. She knew her guardian would never have sanctioned the match and would have been most displeased with her had she chosen to reject Alex in favour of Damien, likely washing his hands of her.

And anyway, although Damien had talked of marriage, she was now convinced he never would have honoured his words. No, she thought, his words had merely been a part of his seduction. No doubt he had hoped to make her feel sorry for him while, at the same time, make her believe him sincere. And he had succeeded more than he could possibly know!

How loved and desired she had felt as he held her and whispered his words of love to her. She had come so close to surrendering herself and losing all respectability! If he was suddenly to appear in front of her now, she knew she would be helpless to resist him. Her body was burning for his touch. Taking a deep breath, she forced herself to face reality. She must marry soon. Before she was tempted again!

The horses eventually came to a standstill by the castle ruins, and the two dismounted, Penelope making sure she had dismounted before Alex had a chance to help her. She couldn't allow him to touch her. Not then. Not when she was still recovering from her fantasy. When her feet reached the ground, her legs almost gave way beneath her, but luckily, she managed to control herself before Alex noticed anything amiss. Even had he noticed her stumble, he would only assume it to be a normal response after riding such a distance, she told herself.

She stood looking at the landscape, only vaguely aware of Alex when he came to stand at her side. Silently, they gazed at the views surrounding them, the clear air letting them see for miles in all directions from this vantage point. After a while, she became aware that Alex had turned away, and saw that the groom had arrived. She watched as Alex approached him, and listened as he asked the groom if he had a blanket with him. The groom was able to oblige, soon spreading a thick, woollen blanket on one of the few areas of level ground before moving away to tend to the horses.

Alex smiled at her and asked if she wished to rest, indicating the blanket.

"Oh, thank you, Alex," she said, smiling warmly and moving towards him and the blanket. But when they sat, she made sure she left as wide a space as possible between their two bodies.

While Alex leaned comfortably back on his elbows, Penelope sat stiffly upright, not even turning in his direction as she spoke about discovering the ruins shortly after coming to live with the Marquess.

"They quickly became one of my favourite places," she explained. "It is so peaceful here, and I would often sit here, reliving happy times in my life and reflecting on my past and present."

Alex looked around him and asked Penelope about the history of the place.

"I don't know it," she replied. "I just enjoy riding here and looking at the views and at the ruins," she said. "I sometimes imagine what life would have been like back in the days of the Normans, but not enough to discover the truth. Perhaps I don't want to know, in case the truth is less inspiring than my imagination!"

Alex smiled at her. "And does that mean you prefer to keep your illusions about people as well, preferring to take them as they are rather than to delve into their pasts in case you may discover unsavoury secrets about them?"

"Maybe," she replied, smiling. *I wonder what he is hinting at,* she thought. "Why?" she added in a teasing voice. "Do you have any unsavoury secrets in your past that I should know about?"

He laughed. "No. At least, none to bother you. But I suppose we all have things in our past we would prefer to forget."

This had the potential of turning into the most intimate conversation we have had, she thought in alarm. Normally, she found it easy to prevent conversations from becoming over personal and liked to keep her deepest thoughts strictly to herself. She had grown up without any siblings and without her mother to confide in. Her aunt had discouraged confidences and she had become used to keeping her own counsel. This marriage business could change all that, she suddenly realised, not liking the idea. She wanted Alex to respect her need for privacy.

Luckily, in most of the marriages she had seen, the husband and wife led quite separate lives. Except in the bedchamber, she supposed. She blushed at the thought, then dragged her attention back to the present. She would have to learn to handle her husband with care, she decided, starting from right now.

She forced herself to smile in a flirtatious way. "Like all the times I should have been learning history when, instead, I persuaded my governess to let me go riding?"

"If that is all you have to regret, you must have had a happy life indeed," he responded. "But I know you have also had much in your life to cause you unhappiness. Parting from your parents, and then having to move again when your aunt passed away. I hope you will come to feel that Knopton Manor is your home, Penelope. We will be starting out together, you know, learning about the place and making it into the home we want. It isn't as though it has already been my home. Even though I have spent as much time there as I could since inheriting, I do not know the place intimately."

Oh dear, Penelope thought, he wants a close, loving relationship, with them working side by side. She knew she should have been delighted with his words, but instead, the picture he painted alarmed her. He was far too good for her!

"Come. I will show you around," she said, jumping to her feet. Alex raised his eyebrows, obviously wondering why she wanted to cut the discussion of their future short, but complied.

As they wandered around the ruins, Alex commented that the castle had obviously been built by the Normans, probably originally in the eleventh century when it would have likely been constructed mainly of timber, later to be strengthened using stone, enabling it to withstand invasions by other warring barons.

"You seem to know a lot about it."

"I know a little," he confirmed. "You can tell from the ruins that it was of a simple design, consisting of at outer wall and a square keep. The way castles were built before they discovered that circular walls provided better protection against invasions. It is a pity that so few of the remaining walls are of any height, but if you look, it is still possible to make out where the great hall had stood."

"You are starting to sound like my guardian!"

"I'm sorry but I thought you may have a better chance of imagining what could have taken place here if you knew more about the structure."

"Hmm, I suppose so. Perhaps if we stood in the middle of where the great hall used to be, I might be able to imagine it full of people eating and dancing."

"Come on then," Alex said, putting out his hand for her to hold. But she pretended not to notice and held on to her skirts instead as she moved to follow him.

Alex frowned as he stood in what would have been the centre of the great hall, fully aware that Penelope was avoiding looking at him. He wondered if the fault lay with him, but it seemed that they were both pretending. He knew she was trying to be pleasant company, but it was becoming more and more obvious that she wanted to avoid contact with him, and even seemed to be unwilling to discuss their future together. She was so defensive in all her conversations with him. So untrusting, whatever she may say to the contrary. Unwilling to let him really get to know her. But then, wouldn't a marriage where he and Penelope kept their distance from each other suit him better?

Or, better still, no marriage at all! Could it be possible that Penelope was beginning to have second thoughts? Perhaps he should sound her out on whether she would like a long engagement before marrying. If she welcomed the idea, it might confirm his suspicions that she was having doubts about their suitability. Oh, if only that were true...

Alex's thoughts were at that moment abruptly halted, and he whirled around, the most peculiar sensation of being watched coming over him. Not a friendly watcher, either. He felt a malevolent presence behind him, wishing him ill, making the hair stand up on the back of his neck. But no-one was there. His eyes scanned the whole area, his ears pricked to hear the slightest sound. Nothing.

I must have imagined it, he thought, deciding that the ruins must be stirring his imagination as well as hers. After all, there was a good likelihood that all manner of bloodthirsty deeds had been committed there during medieval times. On the other hand, perhaps it may be just that his guilty conscience was getting the better of him or some natural phenomenon had been the cause of his feeling of unease. He looked over at the groom, who was still sitting with his back against a stone wall, his cap over his eyes, oblivious to all. Not him, then, Alex surmised.

An unexpected, chilling breeze then took them both by surprise, making them shiver.

"Time to start back," Alex suggested. "Not only has it turned colder, but we have a fair way to go, and the horses should be rested by now."

Penelope smiled her agreement, immediately calling the groom and setting off to where the horses grazed.

The return journey was uneventful except when a rider approached them from behind, galloping as though the hounds of hell were behind him. Alex instinctively pulled his mount to the side of the track, but the approaching rider slowed as he drew near, guiding his horse to ride alongside Penelope.

"Good day to you, Miss Penelope. And welcome back to Yorkshire."

Penelope looked back at Alex, who was being completely ignored by the intruder. "This is Stanley Thorpe, Lord Frome's steward, Alex. Stanley, may I introduce you to..."

But Stanley prevented her from completing the introduction. "I know who he is," he interrupted, his disapproval of Alex clear in his tone, "but it was you I wanted to see, Miss Penelope. Mother wants to see you. She asked me to give you this note," he added, pressing a crumpled bit of paper into Penelope's gloved hand. "Told me to tell you to visit her as soon as you can. She has something important to show you." He then rode on without hearing her reply.

Alex drew alongside an obviously startled Penelope, noticing as she folded the note and pushed it inside the palm of her glove. "If you hadn't smiled at him in such a friendly way, I would have floored the rude fellow!" Alex began. "Lord Frome's steward, is he? What makes him take such liberties with you? Handing you notes and addressing you by your name! He made it sound as though you knew him and his mother very well. And he certainly didn't approve of me. Perhaps you should let me see that note."

Penelope smiled a tremulous smile. "Oh Alex, it's nothing. Really. Perhaps I should explain. You see, Stan and Mrs Thorpe helped me enormously when I first came here, not knowing anyone. I know he seemed rude just now, and I'm afraid it may have been because of your presence. He was always very protective of me. I don't know why. Anyway, as I was saying, his mother is the local herbalist and is the daughter of the old rector. Quite learned in fact. But she fell in love with Stan's father, who was a tenant farmer on this estate, and would have no other. She brought Stan up to believe himself to be the equal of any man. She also saw to his education, making sure he could have a better life than her husband, and is proud of his success. She has been a good friend to me, Alex, and has taught me a lot about herbal cures."

"I have never heard of this Stan Thorpe or his mother until now, Penelope. Does Lord Frome know of your association with them?"

"Of course, he does."

Alex was not sure that he believed her. She was being defensive again. "Why should she want to see you now? And why did her son slip you that note?"

"Oh Alex, the note is of no importance, believe me. No doubt she gave it to Stan out of convenience. I expect she wants to share the recipe for a new potion with me or something like that. As I said, she is very fond of me. But I won't visit her until after you have left if you don't want me to. And please don't mind Stan. He is not usually so rude, you know. In other circumstances, I think you would like him. But I'm afraid he thinks of me as some sort of princess. In his eyes, no-one would be good enough for me. No doubt he thinks I'll be leaving here now and is concerned for his mother. She doesn't take to people easily, and he doesn't want to see her upset."

"I'll be surprised if that is the only reason he doesn't like me. No doubt he fancies himself in love with you. It doesn't do to encourage unsuitable young men to dream dreams that cannot come true."

Her face flushed with anger at his words. "Encourage him? I have *not* encouraged him. What a dreadful thing to say," she replied indignantly.

"I don't mean you actively encouraged him. But just by becoming friends with the two of them, you will have given them the impression that you consider them as equals."

"Well, I *do* consider them as friends and equals. I haven't got a title like you. And her father is the younger son of a baron, if you must know, so she has as much claim as me, if not more, to be considered a member of the upper classes."

Alex was surprised by this vehement defence of Stanley and his mother and found himself suddenly feeling defensive. "I wasn't born with a title either," he countered.

When she raised her eyebrows at him, he continued. "Don't look at me like that. I also can claim many commoners to be amongst my friends. But, Penelope, you are a young, vulnerable young woman, and must be more careful of the people you make your friends. Just because her grandfather was a member of the aristocracy doesn't mean she would be accepted in society, and you know it. You say Lord Frome knows about your friendship with these people. But does he know just how much time you used to spend with them?"

The look of Penelope's face confirmed his suspicion that Lord Frome knew little about this friendship with the Thorpe's. "Don't worry, Penelope, I'll say nothing of this to Lord Frome. Your secret is safe with me. And if you wish to visit with Mrs Thorpe, please do so. As far as I am concerned, you can see her as often as you like. But not Stanley Thorpe. That I cannot condone. It would be most unwise of you, my dear, to continue with that friendship."

"Are we having our first quarrel, Alex?"

"Only if you disagree with me."

Penelope lowered her head, apparently contrite. "I don't. And I will do as you say, of course. I want to make you a good wife, Alex. I hope you believe that," she added demurely.

Alex felt a stab of remorse for speaking out as he had, wondering if the fellow's rudeness had influenced his words, so said with as much good humour as possible, "I have complete faith in you, my dear. And should I ever become ill, I shall now expect your knowledge of herbal remedies to enable you to make me well again instantly."

Penelope laughed in relief and the conversation ended. She had not told him quite the whole truth, but she had only been fifteen when she had first come to Hoddam Hall and had been flattered by the attentions of the good-looking Stanley Thorpe. He was the first man who had treated her as a desirable female, at a time when she desperately needed to be loved.

She remembered trying out her instinctive feminine wiles on him and of being delighted by his response. Until he had started talking about marriage, that is, when she had realised her mistake, and had tried to extricate herself from the embarrassing situation. Since then, she had made sure they were never alone together, and, slowly, he had seemed to understand that he had read too much into her earlier responses to him, for, from that time on, a more formal relationship developed between them, albeit a friendly one.

Penelope didn't want to open the note Stanley had thrust into her hand. Not in front of Alex. Something in Stanley's expression had made her wonder if the note was from him and not from his mother. Yet, surely, he would not try to capture her attention again, after all this time, would he? No, of course not. The note was undoubtedly from his mother. It must be. He would never dare give her his own note in front of Alex! But she would wait until she was alone, just in case. She was glad Alex had told her he trusted her, for after saying such a thing, he could hardly then demand to see the note!

As soon as she reached her room, Penelope pulled off her gloves and read the message. Her worst suspicion was then confirmed. The note was from Stanley! It was short and to the point:

I must speak with you. I know something about
your fiancé that you should be made aware of. Come
tomorrow morning at seven to our special place
and I shall reveal all. Tell no-one else about this
or my life would be in danger.
Stan

What rubbish! she thought. What was he trying to do? Make her think Alex was a murderer or something? How melodramatic! How ridiculous! She would destroy the note immediately and forget the whole thing. Taking it to the hearth, she used the flint and steel to light a spill and held the note to the flame, watching it burn in her hand, until the flames caused her to drop it to the hearth. Then, after watching the final flames fade away, she pushed the ashes into the grate until no trace of the note remained. She would think of it no more.

After changing out of her riding habit, Penelope joined Alex in the breakfast room, where they had decided to take a light repast, having returned too late to join Alex's mother and the Marquess for luncheon. They had found Prue busily involving herself in the preparations for the evening's entertainment, while Lord Frome had made himself scarce, as usual. Probably tinkering with his inventions again, they correctly surmised.

Alex introduced the topic of his plan to return to London and then to Surrey. He also broached the subject of their marriage, asking Penelope if she wanted to wait until the following year as suggested by her cousin, Celia, or whether she would prefer to be married in the autumn.

Penelope grasped at the suggestion of bringing the wedding forward. More than anything else she felt the need to be safely married, when she could leave behind all her past mistakes and live under the protection of an honourable man.

Alex nodded and went off to find Lord Frome, leaving Penelope to help her future mother-in-law.

By the end of the afternoon, Penelope and Prudence had conversed more than they ever had before, but without any real attachment evolving. If anything, a tension had developed between them that hadn't existed previously. Penelope began to suspect that Prudence might have changed her view about the marriage after witnessing her behaviour when Alex had been out of town and now thought that she was not good enough for her son. If that were the case, the less the two of them saw each other after the wedding, the better.

Penelope therefore became quite alarmed when Prudence raised the possibility of her having an apartment at Knopton Manor, something that Penelope hadn't until then considered. But the idea that both she and her future mother-in-law might end up residing in the same household on a permanent basis did not please her at all!

Eventually the two women parted to make their preparations for the evening ahead, and Penelope found that her relationship with her future mother-in-law was not the only thing on her mind. She found herself also thinking about the note she had received from Stanley that morning. Despite her intention to give it no further consideration, its contents kept bothering her. What if Alex did have a secret in his past? Wouldn't she like to know what it was? It would be nice to have some leverage over him.

Yet, what could Stanley possibly know about Alex? Had Alex perhaps killed someone on the field of honour? Being a former soldier, he would certainly have the necessary skills. And then she recalled the conversation she had had with Alex earlier in the day when they were at the castle ruins. Hadn't he asked her whether she preferred to take people on trust, ignoring whatever was in their pasts? At the time, she was sure he had been talking generally, or, at worst, had been talking about *her* past, but, what if he had been referring to his own?

Most likely, there was nothing to tell, she assured herself. Stanley must be just trying to stir up trouble because he was jealous or because he had taken such a dislike to Alex, she reasoned. But her niggling doubts refused to die. What if Stanley did know something? Maybe about another woman? A mistress, perhaps? Wouldn't she like to know? Oh yes, she most certainly would like to know. Then, if, or when, he became domineering again, like he had earlier in the day, telling her who she should see and who she shouldn't, she would be able to use his past to defend herself against him.

Her thoughts went round and round, getting nowhere, and she was eventually brought back to the present by her maid, who was chattering on about the evening, and about how lucky Alex was to have such a lovely bride. All the servants knew that the party was being held to celebrate her engagement and to introduce Alex to the local gentry.

Penelope was determined to enjoy herself that evening and considered that her maid had been right when she had told her how lovely she looked. Her dress was the height of fashion; a white, high-waisted affair with puffed sleeves and low neckline that revealed an expanse of smooth, pale skin and the swell of her small bosom. Her hands and arms were covered by long evening gloves, and the only jewellery she wore was the gold locket containing miniatures of her parents that never left her neck and the pearl earrings given to her by Alex at her engagement ball in London. Her maid had dressed her dark brown hair becomingly in the Grecian style with plaits coiled high on her head, the whole effect softened by short ringlets along the nape of her neck and on the sides of her face.

When she saw Alex, she thought that he looked equally as splendid in his plain, but exquisitely tailored evening attire and couldn't help but think what an impressive couple they made. She felt proud to be standing next to him, aware that he was receiving many admiring looks from the ladies present, who were no doubt appreciating his impressive physique and good looks.

Lord Frome had certainly pulled out all the stops to host a memorable occasion. Despite his reputation for being frugal with his wealth and for preferring his own company, his generosity or hospitality on this night could not be faulted.

He had arranged for the meal to be held in the great dining hall where all twenty-four guests could be seated with ease at the long table, which was weighed down by the best crystal glassware money could buy, together with silver cutlery and four large, ornate, silver candelabrums atop the linen and lace tablecloths made by the gifted Nottinghamshire lace makers.

Then there was the meal itself. Eight courses in all. Enough to keep them all seated for several hours. Extra staff had been hired for the occasion ensuring that each guest had their every whim attended to while also making sure that the food was still warm when it reached the table.

The cream of the local gentry was present, and, because they shared common interests yet rarely got together, there was no shortage of congenial conversation. Penelope had met them all before but didn't count any of them as friends. Not even Sir David Telford, a baronet who had paid her particular attention, tempting her to indiscretion.

Penelope had dreaded meeting him again but was both surprised and delighted to find that he did not affect her as he had before. Not even when he attempted to rekindle the flirtation at the first opportunity by coming up behind her as the guests began to move to the dining hall, lightly touching her bare shoulder when no one was looking, whispering words of love into her ear, and making a most improper suggestion! Any feelings she may have had for him had died completely, she was glad to say. She just flushed angrily and gave him a blistering glare before moving away from him.

She had already made sure he was not seated too near her at the dining table but knew she could not avoid him completely. Yet she now knew he posed no threat to her happiness. To her, he now appeared as a rather shallow, insensitive individual, incapable of experiencing any meaningful, deep emotions. And instead of suffering from her usual pangs of jealousy, Penelope was surprised to find herself feeling sorry for his poor wife.

Lady Telford was not present as she was *enceinte* with their fourth child after only six years of marriage. Penelope hoped Alex didn't use *her* simply as a brood mare, for that was how she saw Lady Telford's fate. She also silently hoped that soon, perhaps when she had been married a while, she would get over her feelings for Damien just as easily as she had those for David.

Before the ladies withdrew at the end of the meal as custom dictated, leaving the men to their port, many toasts were made to Alex and Penelope, and during his own speech, Alex smiled down at Penelope, and presented his future bride with a beautiful five-strand pearl bracelet, much to everyone's delight. Penelope found she was the centre of attention in the drawing room, the matrons offering her advice and the younger women envious of her success.

After the men finally joined the ladies and the customary tea had been served, Penelope entertained the guests on the pianoforte before card tables were set up for whist.

The parson was the first to leave, and by then it was well past midnight. The remaining guests took their leave reluctantly, thanking and praising Lord Frome for his generosity and repeating their congratulations to Alex and Penelope. When the Marquess and the others at last climbed the stairs for bed, it was understood that no-one would be stirring until at least noon the following day.

Chapter Sixteen

It was exactly seven o'clock, but it might just as well have been before dawn, for no-one disturbed the peace of this quiet place. Penelope sat on a felled tree trunk, hugging her shawl to her to keep the chill of the morning at bay. She had obeyed Stanley's summons after all.

Somehow, she had wakened at dawn, and couldn't stop his words from whirling round and round in her head. She just had to find out what he knew about Alex. After all, what did she have to lose? She knew that he wouldn't hurt her. Stanley was fond of her. He had never kissed her against her will, and, when she broke things off with him, he had accepted her rejection without rancour.

She had walked to this spot, not wanting to disturb the grooms at this early hour. And it was only half a mile from the house. Yet few came to this clearing by the lake, preferring the other side, with its manicured lawns and carefully landscaped gardens. Often, she and Stanley had met here in the early days of their friendship, having first encountered each other during one of her lonely walks on the estate. Here they had shared their worries and their dreams and had allowed their new-found friendship to develop into something warmer, more intimate, granting themselves the freedom of holding hands, which naturally progressed to caresses and kisses before Penelope decided to end the affair when it became obvious that Stanley wanted more from her than she was prepared to give.

Where was he? she thought, looking about her. Eventually she stood up, rearranged the shawl about her shoulders and was just about to head back to the house having decided it was all a joke and that he had never intended to appear, when she felt herself grasped from behind. Her head snapped backwards as a cloth was firmly pressed over her nose and mouth. She couldn't breathe! Panic set in as she struggled uselessly, frantic for air, thrashing her arms about and trying to kick her attacker with the heels of her boots. All to no avail as her struggles and her attempted screams only hastened the inevitable result and she began to sink into unconsciousness.

Vague memories troubled her as she began to regain consciousness. Memories of a sack being placed over her head, of being slung over a horse, and of having something bitter being poured down her throat by strong, somewhat familiar, callused hands.

What had happened? Where was she? What day was it? So many questions, but it was no use. She was frightened and had no idea why this was happening to her. She shook her head in an attempt clear it, but no memories returned. She could not recall anything except the feeling of panic which still assailed her. Then, gradually, everything began to come back to her. She vaguely remembered sitting by the lake waiting for Stanley, gasping as she recalled the feeling of being smothered by someone large. Someone stronger by far than she. And suddenly she knew the name of her attacker! Stanley!

Penelope recalled both his size and his scent. But why did he do this to her? And where was she? How long had passed since her attack? She had no idea. And, to make matters worse, her head was hurting, stopping her from thinking clearly.

Looking about her, she realised that she was lying on a straw mattress on the mud floor of an old, primitive building. No bed, no hearth, no other furniture. Just two shelves on the grey, cold, stone walls, one holding an iron candlestick where a candle was burning. Then she noticed a small window, partly covered with old cotton curtains high on the wall above her head. But no light was entering the room except from the flickering candle.

It must be night, she surmised. Where on earth was she? And why had no-one found her? They must know she had gone missing. After all, a whole day must have passed. Or had she been here for more than one day? And where was 'here'? Perhaps, Stanley had taken her far from the Hall!

Her mouth and throat felt so dry, she could hardly swallow. An old blanket was covering her body and she noticed that by her side, on the hard, damp mud floor, was a pitcher of water and an old, cracked cup. Turning on her side, she tried to pour some water into the cup. That was when she realised that her left wrist was manacled to the wall!

A metal bracelet round her wrist was attached to a heavy chain which was bolted to the wall. She knew it would be useless to try to get free, but she nevertheless went through the motions, tugging violently until she hurt herself. She shouted her frustration, but knew she was unlikely to be heard. Wherever he had taken her would be somewhere isolated. Somewhere where the candlelight would not be seen. But where was he? Was she going to be left here to die?

She lay back on the mattress for a while, trying to calm herself. After a while she remembered her thirst and made a second attempt to pour a cupful of water. This time she succeeded. The chain was long enough to allow her to sit at the edge of the mattress. Maybe it was even long enough to allow her to stand, she thought, deciding she wasn't strong enough yet to try it. But she knew she wouldn't be able to reach the door. That was on the other side of the room. She would just have to hope she would be found soon. Or even that Stanley would appear. Anything but this waiting. Not knowing anything.

She took a sip of water, then finished the cupful. It tasted good and freshened her mouth a little, even helped clear her head. He must be mad, she realised. Come to think of it, he had behaved strangely when they had last met. When he had handed her the note and had been so rude to Alex. But why had he done this to her?

She sat and waited. After all, she had little choice in the matter. Time passed slowly. He would have to come soon, wouldn't he? Surely, he couldn't leave her alone much longer, unable even to relieve herself. Or would she be found dead, soaked in her own urine? A dreadful picture of her dead body flashed before her eyes, making her shudder with revulsion. Why was he doing this to her? She had done nothing to him.

That was when she began to get angry. Very angry. She cried out in frustration, her screams becoming louder and louder until she could scream no more. Panting with exhaustion, she listened. There was no response. She was aware only of the ominous silence returning once more. She felt drained, resigned, empty of hope.

Eventually, her youthful optimism returned; her spirits revived, and she re-examined the situation. She just could not believe Stanley meant to harm her. All she had to do was to be patient. Either Stanley, Alex, or someone else would come soon. Alex and her guardian would be looking for her, she felt sure, and all the tenant farmers would be asked to help. Maybe even the militia.

Hours seemed to pass by and still she was alone. Should she try to sleep? No, she had slept for long enough. She would stay alert for as long as she could. She looked around the room for a weapon but saw only the pitcher within reach. Would she be able to hit Stanley with it while pretending to be asleep or by getting him to look away for a moment? Unfortunately, she thought dejectedly, even if she succeeded, where would that leave her? She would still be chained to the wall.

Looking at the heavy candlestick, she wondered if *that* could be of help, knowing that first she would have to get free of the chain. But she felt she had to consider all possibilities if she were to have any chance of getting away. She hoped the candlestick was as heavy as it looked. Everything rested on that and her ability to get him to release her from the chain. Once outside, she would likely recognise where she was. And, even if she didn't, she should be able to find someone to help her before long.

If Stanley was the first to arrive, which seemed to her the most likely scenario, she would have to soothe him and talk him into releasing her. Then, if she could get her hands on the candlestick, she would take him by surprise. How dare he do this to her? Her anger returned once again, but soon her hunger and her headache made her feel so depressed, she sagged on the mattress, her shoulders hunched in despair until she gave in and lay back on the mattress, covering herself with the blanket whilst she fought back her tears. Soon the candle would go out and she would be left in the dark.

Eventually she fell into a restless sleep but became instantly alert when she heard footsteps approaching. Was it Stanley or was someone else passing by? Without further thought, she screamed as loudly as she could, "Help me! Help me! Please!"

There was no reply. Then she heard bolts being drawn back and eventually the door creaked open. Stanley entered carrying a lantern and a bucket containing what looked like food.

"No use making that noise, Penelope, my love. And no need, either. I am here to help you to escape."

Had she been wrong? Had it not been Stanley who abducted her? "Wha...what do you mean? You have come to rescue me? To take me back home?"

"Not to take you home. No. Not back to your jailers. I have thought it all out. You and I will go away together. Just like we planned."

Penelope was so confused by his words, she rubbed her brow with her free hand. "What are you talking about, Stanley? We never planned to go away together. I know you cared for me but that is all in the past. I have grown up now. Everything is different."

"Ah, but that's where you're wrong, my love. I know you love me just as I love you. And I know why you pretended you didn't care. You were trying to protect me. Trying to safeguard my position. We both knew that Lord Frome would sack me and evict both me and Mother if he found out about us. You were very clever, Penelope. As soon as I realised what you were up to, I knew you were right. We had to bide our time. And then he sent you to London. Away from me. I thought I should go mad with jealousy. But I remembered our kisses and knew you were mine. Only mine.

"Until that man came. I knew what he had come for and knew I had to save you from him. I waited until he left here, then followed him. Or tried to. He rode so quickly he got away from me. I didn't want to kill him until he was far from here, you see, so that no-one would suspect his death was caused by someone on the estate. But he rode so quickly, I couldn't keep up with him. And then I lost sight of him completely. But fate was on my side, you see. I decided I may as well continue to Tadcaster since I was getting hungry, and, lo and behold, there he was. I knew the route he would use from there, and, forgetting all about my hunger, I set off to find a good spot to hide. Then I shot him. Only he didn't die. I really thought he had died, Penelope. Thought I had saved you. But he is here with you still.

Penelope couldn't believe what she was hearing and had no idea what to say as he continued with his confession.

"At first, I thought it must be someone else, but soon realised it was the same man. I will have to kill him, you know. Then, no-one will have any claim to you except me. Your first and only love. But for a while, I will continue to lead them all a merry dance, chasing off in all directions, except here. It should be easy enough for me to arrange for him to have a fatal accident. There are so many possibilities to choose from. Especially since I've been put in charge of the search."

He really was mad, she thought, as she began to believe his unbelievable words. He had shot Alex? He thought she loved him? And he was willing to kill to get her? Would he even be prepared to kill her if she rejected him? These and many other questions whirled around in her head as she tried to come to terms with the perilous situation.

Stanley was claiming that he had shot Alex when he was on his way back to London, which, if true, must mean that when Alex was supposed to have delayed his return from his visit to Lord Frome, saying he was visiting an old friend, he was probably recovering from a gunshot wound. Yes, that made sense. No doubt he had shot Alex. Yet Alex had said nothing of the incident to her. But that didn't mean it didn't occur.

The more she thought about it, the more she became convinced of Stanley's guilt. He was dangerous! Unhinged! He was no longer the same man she remembered. The Stanley she had liked had been gentle and kind. A new Stanley had emerged. Was she responsible for his madness? Did he really love her *that* much?

She now fully realised how stupid she had been to make a friend of Stanley, but she had liked him and thought there would be no harm in enjoying his company in those early days. While Lord Frome had shown her kindness, he was not good company; she knew he was more interested in his inventions than in her. And she had been reasonably honest with Stanley when she had ended their friendship, even if she had tried to soften the blow by using society's expectations as her excuse.

Had she brought all this upon herself? No, she refused to accept that. This was all Stanley's fault. She had been a child at the time. But what should she do about it? She could only think of one possibility. She would have to play along with him until she had a chance to escape.

"If you love me Stanley, and are sure that I love you, then why did you hurt me? Why have you abducted me and why am I chained to the wall? Let me free, Stanley, please. Then, we'll discuss your plans."

"I'm sorry I have had to hurt you and chain you, Penelope. Truly I am. And I'm sorry for having to deceive you with that note. But I know you too well, my love, and I know you would never have arranged to go away with me. You're too obedient. You wouldn't want to do anything your guardian didn't like, would you? Even when it meant turning your back on the one you love. I remember when I asked you to marry me. Do you remember your words? You said you couldn't marry me, not you wouldn't. I knew then that you were refusing me only because of your guardian's wishes. And if I let you go now you would run back to your guardian, sacrificing yourself again. Don't try to deny it, for I know it's what you would do."

Penelope shook her head, about to assure him she would not run back to the Hall, but he held up his hand and smiled.

"There you see. I am right. But I have it all worked out. For a little while longer, I shall have to pretend to lead the search for you and make sure you don't wander about. I can't stay with you all the time. Not yet. But soon, we'll go away together and then everything will be all right. Look. See what I've brought you." With that, he put the lantern and bucket on the floor and took out some bread, a chunk of cheese and some strawberries saying he remembered how much she loved strawberries. He also took out some candles and placed them on the shelf next to the candlestick. "Before I go, I'll light another candle. That should last the rest of the night."

God, what can I do? she thought. Maybe I should plead with him. "Oh, please don't go, Stan. Don't leave me here alone. I don't like it here."

"I know. It's not very nice. Not the sort of place for you. But it's the best I could do. No-one comes here anymore. And I'll make sure only I search in this area. I've organised for the others to search in all the other places."

"What is this place, Stan, and how long have I been here?"

"It's the old hunting lodge, or what's left of it. Lord Frome has never used it as far as I can remember. But in the old days, it was used a lot. Built by the second marquess, I believe. Fond of his hunting, it seems he was, from what I have heard. I don't think you ever found it though, did you, Penelope? The ruins are surrounded by brambles now. I only found it by sheer chance when I was out clearing the land hereabouts. It has been forgotten by everyone, it seems. Very convenient for us, of course, even though I would like to house you in something a lot nicer than this. But a tree fell on the main building, and it has allowed the weather to seep into the rest of the structure, ruining everything. This outbuilding is the best I could find. At least the roof is intact. You are protected from the weather in here. And you won't be here long. Just for a day or two until the search is either called off, or more likely, moves on to more distant places. Then we shall slip through the net and escape to Scotland. There, we can marry more easily, you know."

His words horrified her so much, she forgot to ask more about her location. Stay here for another day or two? Never. Marry him? Never, never. Somehow, she had to get free. "How long have I been here, Stan?" she said more calmly than she would have believed possible.

"Only since this morning. After bringing you here, I went back to work until the alarm was raised. Everyone was so worried, I had to hide my smile. They were all pretending to care so much about you, when we both know the Marquess just wanted to arrange for you to marry someone of his choice so that he could be left on his own again. But the best part was when Lord Frome asked me to organise the search, I then knew my plan was going to succeed. That man you were going to have to marry wanted to do the organising, but Lord Frome persuaded him that I knew more about the area and could call on the local farmers for help more easily. They both played right into our hands."

"Stanley, what you are doing is wrong. You will never get away with it. Whatever happens, you must know that the Marquess will still turn you and your mother away when he learns what you have done. Your only hope is to let me go back, Stanley. I won't say anything about you to anyone. Please listen to me, Stanley. I promise not to marry the earl if you will just let me return home."

Stanley seemed not to hear her. He lit another candle and encouraged her to eat. Penelope didn't think she'd be able to eat a thing but decided to humour him and took a bite of bread. To her surprise, she found it delicious. Suddenly, she realised just how hungry she was despite her ordeal and continued eating whilst he watched her, a smile curling his lips.

"Let me free, Stanley. Please. My wrist is hurting. I'll even stay here if that's what you want. I won't try to run away. I'll wait for you to return if you want me to."

"In a minute, my love, in a minute." Then, to her horror, she saw him take a spoon and bottle from his pocket, pour a small amount of thick liquid from the small, brown bottle on to the spoon. "After you have had this." He then held the spoon to her mouth, forcing her lips to part by holding her nostrils together, and, at the same time, forcing her head back until he was able to put the spoon and its liquid into her mouth, just as though she was a little girl refusing to swallow her medicine. She struggled just as a little girl might, but to no avail. He continued to keep her head back until she had swallowed the sleeping draught, for she was sure it was laudanum that he had forced her to take. Soon she knew she would succumb once again to a drugged sleep.

"How dare you treat me like this," she cried, her anger making her forget her earlier strategy, as she tried to strike him with her free hand. "You have drugged me again, haven't you? First, you lure me to meet you secretly, then you abduct me, nearly killing me, drug me, leave me in this horrid place, chained to the wall, and now you drug me again!"

"Only to keep you quiet. And to stop you doing what you mistakenly believe you should do. I know you want me, but I also know that you feel you must do all you can to escape from here. Just as I knew what would make you come to me. I knew you wouldn't be able to resist finding out something nasty about that man. Then you would have been able to break off your engagement, wouldn't you? But unfortunately, I don't know anything about him that would convince Lord Frome that he had chosen the wrong man. And, anyway, even if we could do that, Lord Frome would never permit you to marry me.

"No, my way is best, you'll see. I will help you to have what you really want, Penelope. Just leave things to me. And don't worry. See, I am releasing you now." He took a key out of his pocket and unlocked the manacle. She massaged her sore wrist with her other hand but made no attempt to attack him. He was still looming over her.

"When I have gone you can use the bucket for your personal needs and sleep until I return tomorrow. Or I suppose I should say, later today. For it will soon be dawn. Then, when I return, I'll make you my own. They will let us be together when they learn that I have already taken your maidenhead, you'll see. Even if they find us before we reach Scotland. You'll be mine then. Too late for them to do anything about it. And even if they throw mother off the estate, it will have been worth it. For you are more important to me than anything else. I was prepared to wait for you, Penelope, but I couldn't stand by and see you being given to another man.

"Now you will sleep, my love. It will not be long before I return to you. I will wait outside until I know you are asleep again, so don't think about trying to escape. You wouldn't be able to open the door in any case. It is thick and is bolted securely. And the window is too small for you to get through even if you were able to get up that high. Once you are mine and you know there is no going back, I won't have any reason to restrain you any longer. I hate doing these things to you, my love, but it is for your own good. And it will soon be over." He then leaned towards her and kissed her gently on the lips. "I love you, Penelope," he said, before raising himself to his feet and leaving.

Chapter Seventeen

Penelope sat gaping at the door after he had left, not being able to comprehend such utter madness. And she had made no attempt to escape, she realised, relying on persuasion instead. But to be fair on herself, she admitted that he had not given her any opportunity to attack him. What was she going to do now? Did he really intend to force himself on her?

He couldn't make her marry him, could he? No-one could compel someone to marry them against their wishes, could they? And, if he truly loved her, there must be something she could say to convince him not to rape her. Oh, what a mess she was in. All due to her own foolishness!

Even if, by some miracle, she found herself free and safely back at the Hall at this very moment, there were bound to be repercussions. She would probably find her reputation already in tatters. Word was bound to get out about this. And goodness knows what the gossips would make up about her and Stanley when they found out that he was behind her capture!

If they even believed that she had been captured. Maybe they would think she had run away with him. And what would Alex think? Would he still want to marry her when this was over? Maybe he would, she conceded, if she was found quickly. But if she didn't get free soon, she was sure to be ruined.

At that moment, she began to feel a little dizzy. She remembered the drug and knew she must try to stop it from taking effect. Firstly, she had to make herself sick, she realised. She forced her fingers down her throat until she vomited up all the glorious food she had eaten into the bucket. She only hoped the drug was gone as well. What a sacrifice!

She then moved the bucket into the far corner and relieved her aching bladder, before pacing the floor, hoping that by moving constantly, she could combat the sleepiness she was feeling. Pacing had also proved useful to her whenever she had a problem to solve. But, this time, the pacing merely seemed to exacerbate her anger, both at Stanley and at herself.

How could I have been so stupid to fall for his trick? she chided herself. Or to think him harmless? Oh, what an odious man! Fancy him thinking she would really have considered marrying him! When she had refused his offer of marriage, instead of trying not to hurt his feelings by using words that could let him believe she cared for him a little, she should have laughed at his insolence. But, at the time, she remembered she had been flattered, if surprised that he had considered their liaison a possibility. She had no idea the stupid oaf thought she still wanted to marry him.

He had never given her any indication that he still harboured feelings for her during the intervening years, and she was sure she had given him no reason to make him believe she still felt anything for him. On the few occasions they had spoken, she had treated him just as she should. She had been very polite but also aloof.

After a while, she forced her mind to concentrate on her escape rather than trying to make sense of what had happened to her. She listened at the door for a while, then went to the small window. There was no way of getting out through either of them. She doubted that anyone would be passing by but wondered if she should scream for help every so often. Perhaps, but not while there was a chance that Stanley was still out there, she decided.

Moving away from the window, she looked at the candle. Stanley must be pretty sure that no-one was likely to come near, she realised. Otherwise, he wouldn't have allowed her to have a lighted candle. Penelope slowly concluded that she would be stuck in that room until Stanley returned. Then she would have to find a way to escape.

Hopefully, he would be expecting to find her still asleep and enter without caution. If she could be ready with the candlestick, she just might have a chance. As no other scheme came to mind, she sat on the mattress, resigned to waiting but determined to be ready when he came. Would he come in the morning? she wondered, before deciding that he must mean to return sometime before midday, no doubt intending to carry out his threat and then probably drugging her to make her go with him without her being in a state to resist him. She shivered at the thought. If she couldn't overpower him by taking him by surprise, her fate was sealed.

She lay down and looked up at the rafters. Perhaps an hour passed before she suddenly sat up, a new idea springing to life. The roof! Of course. If she could find a way to climb to the rafters, perhaps she would be able to escape through the roof!

But how could she get to the rafters? Even when standing on the mattress she could not reach them, and the mattress had no base. Would the shelving help? No, both shelves were too short, and anyway, she wouldn't be able to climb up them any more easily than she would be able to climb the walls! Was her idea to come to naught? Then she saw the curtain rod. It was thick and sturdy, even if it wasn't very long. Would she be able to tie the curtains together to form a rope and then hang them from the rafters somehow, using the rod to act as a makeshift kind of grapnel, securely held behind the struts of the rafter?

Wasting no time, she decided to try. Soon, the curtains were tied together by a series of knots, one curtain still threaded on to the rod. So far, so good. Now for the awkward part. She swung the curtains to the roof, but the only result was that the curtain started to slip out of the rod. Penelope tore some of her clothing to make ties and succeeded in securing the curtain in place. She then tried again. And again. And again.

Each time she tried, she refined her method until, at last, the rod was ledged behind the struts. She pulled on the curtains and knew they would take her weight. But how to climb them? Her first attempts were pathetic, and she soon realised that she would never succeed wearing her skirt and petticoats. She quickly undressed and threw the items to the rafter, one by one. Even that took up valuable time. Dawn was already breaking. She must hurry.

Eventually, she worked out that she would have to leap as far as the first knot, then haul herself up, one arm at a time, gripping on with her legs as soon as she could. With luck, she could then reach the rafter and haul herself up the rest of the way. At least her sleepiness had gone. She was sure now that she had succeeded in escaping from the worst effects of the drug. Now she just needed her luck to hold to enable her to complete her escape.

After several attempts, she managed to reach the rafter, but couldn't pull herself up by her arms. That was when she thought of using her legs. She swung them to the rafters and hung on, upside down, clinging on with all fours. She stayed in that position, panting, until her breathing slowed sufficiently for her to try to pull herself over the top with her arms. She knew she wouldn't have enough strength for too many attempts, so took a deep breath and used every bit of strength she could muster. She did it, albeit with much moaning and groaning.

By the time sunlight was entering the window from outside, she was ready to attempt dislodging the roofing slates. She had dressed herself and had used the curtains to harness herself to the main strut, leaving her arms and hands free to work on removing the slates from the roof. It took quite a time to move the first slate, but, after that, it turned out to be a relatively easy task. Soon the hole was large enough for her to get through and the height was low enough for her to pull herself through the gap without mishap, which was just as well as she had to leave her safety harness behind.

Getting to the ground also proved to be reasonably simple, thanks to an old, gnarled tree which was leaning towards the building, its branches providing a welcoming route to the ground. Her hands and her legs suffered a bit during her descent, but after rubbing them roughly, her only distressing observation was the state of her clothes. Decidedly dirty, with several tears to her sleeves and her skirt. She could wrap her shawl round her to hide her torn sleeves but could do nothing to hide the state of her skirt.

She looked about her but could not see the house or any other familiar feature of the landscape. Was she north, south, east, or west of the house? She was pretty sure the building was not to the west as she knew that part of the estate very well, and to the east was a vast forested area. All around her were gently sloping hills and a few dry-stone walls. So, she was either to the north or to the south of the hall. She must head in one of those two directions.

Luckily, she had seen the sun rise and therefore could get her bearings. But should she just walk north or south hoping to come across something she recognised, or someone? She could think of no other alternative, for she had to get away from the building as fast as she could. But which way? She didn't want to run straight into the arms of Stanley!

The search would likely be starting again soon, if indeed, it had not already begun. Then there should be many people about. She persuaded herself that it would just a matter of time before she was rescued so long as she could avoid being seen by Stanley.

And then there was Alex. She must get help and prevent Stanley from injuring or killing Alex.

Not knowing which way to walk, Penelope said a little childhood rhyme to herself, heading off in the direction indicated by her words. But, after what seemed like hours, she still had not seen anything she recognised and had not seen another soul. Now what? she thought, as she rested under a tree. Turn back or go straight on? Surely, there must be a road somewhere in this Godforsaken place! She was feeling both hungry and thirsty but had not even come across one stream to enable her to quench her thirst. Or a berry to eat. It seemed the best solution was to keep going south. There was a rise ahead, and perhaps the view from the top would give her a better idea of her options. The thought of retracing her steps for hours ending up where she began did not appeal to her at all.

Meanwhile, Stanley, Alex, most of the male servants plus several farmers and their labourers continued the search. Lord Frome had no trouble persuading Alex not to send for the militia to help, both aware that the scandal would then become public, and would quickly spread to his neighbours and to London. No unmarried female could spend a night alone without some malicious gossip materialising.

Alex and Lord Frome also agreed that the rapid recovery of Penelope was paramount, before a second night elapsed. They had reluctantly called off the search the previous evening when it became unsafe to continue, but had resumed at first light, so far without success.

The reason for her disappearance mystified them both. Had she run away? No, they decided, as she had left no note and taken no clothes. It had to have been an accident. But everywhere she might have been had been searched.

Stanley had done a marvellous job, according to Lord Frome. Alex heard how tireless Stanley had had been in giving instructions and in making sure that every inch of ground was covered thoroughly.

Alex learned that the lake had been one of the main areas to be pains-takingly searched, men in boats with poles, hoping to find only mud at the bottom. Men had apparently roamed the forests, keeping in straight lines so as not to miss any sign that may help in the search. Stanley had even had people searching their own farms in case she should be sheltering on one of them.

Alex knew that people were speculating on what had happened with some believing that she must have had hit her head on something, losing her memory and simply wandering away. No-one had mentioned the possibility that she had been abducted or killed, but some began to wonder aloud if she might never be found. Or that her body would be found, devoid of life.

Penelope's decision to keep walking south eventually paid off when she finally sighted another human being. She was so relieved that she almost called out to him, before considering the possible con-sequences of him seeing a bedraggled woman, alone, dirty but obviously young, with no-one to witness any attack. But he looked harmless enough, leaning against a wall, eating bread, and drinking from a flask. She hoped that if he saw her, she would be able to count on his help.

He was obviously a farmer. Probably one of her guardian's tenants. Quite good-looking really, she noted. Strong body, of medium height and with long, wavy, dark brown hair. She hesitated, looking around in the hope that there may be others nearby. But the only other sign of life was the man's horse attached to a haycart. He had obviously been gathering hay, for his cart was piled high with it.

He must be about to return home, Penelope surmised. If she could get on the back of his cart and hide in the hay until he reached his home, he might have a wife or mother there who would help her. It would probably be safer to wait to reveal herself until then. Deciding that this was the wisest course of action, she crept round the wall, running the last few yards when she was sure he couldn't hear or see her, burying herself in the strongly smelling, slightly moist, hay. She hoped she wouldn't sneeze!

It wasn't long before she felt the movement of the cart along the dirt track. At last, she thought, I am on my way to safety. The nightmare will soon be over. But on and on the journey went. Sometimes, the track was so bumpy, she had to cling on for dear life. After what seemed like hours of torture, when she was sure she was black and blue all over, the cart at last came to a stop. Should she leap out immediately? Better wait until she heard a female voice, she decided. Either that or wait until she was discovered.

All went quiet and she couldn't prevent herself from peeping out. This wasn't a farm. She was outside a village tavern! Now what should she do? There must be a woman about here somewhere. Deciding that she couldn't wait here indefinitely, she scrambled out from under the hay, stiff limbed and covered from head to foot with bits of stubble from the hay. After brushing herself down as best she could, she decided to go around the back of the tavern, hoping to find at least one woman in a kitchen or laundry.

There were three young females outside the back of the tavern when she approached, all attending to the washing whilst giggling together, no doubt sharing stories about the guests or about their lovers. When they saw Penelope, they stopped in their tracks.

"Lordy me," exclaimed the first, a young, red-haired girl of about fifteen, on seeing Penelope. "What have we here? Got yourself in a bit of a state, haven't we luv?" she said, smiling at the strange newcomer.

"Ooh, don't talk to a guest like that, Lucy," said the second girl, who had obviously noticed that Penelope was wearing expensive clothes, even if they were dirty. The third girl merely stood there giggling nervously, and partially hiding herself behind Lucy.

"She ain't a guest, Mary," replied the first. "I'd 'ave remembered if 'n she was."

"Well, she's a lady, anyways," answered Mary, turning then to Penelope. "Can I help you milady?" she asked, bobbing a small curtsy. The third girl continued to giggle. "Stop that, May," Mary ordered, swatting the silly young girl with the back of her hand.

Penelope stumbled forward, almost overcome with relief at hearing these friendly words.

"Oh yes, I wish to...to speak to the lady in charge if I may. I find myself desperately in need of her help, I'm afraid."

"Wot 'appened to yer?" Lucy asked, "had an accident or somethink?"

"Yes, you could say that," Penelope replied, finding herself smiling despite her troubles. "I am miles away from home and need to get back there. I have escaped from a madman, you see," she added. "Perhaps I should introduce myself. You may have heard of me. I am Lord Frome's ward, Penelope MacDonald."

"A lord, is it?" said Lucy. "Well, can't say I've ever 'eard the name, but you certainly sound like a lady. Who was the madman? Your husband, maybe?" asked Lucy, apparently getting very interested in this strange woman and her even stranger story.

"Could I sit down, do you suppose?" asked Penelope, suddenly feeling as though the ground was about to come up and meet her.

"Ere, sit on this 'ere stool," said Mary, who then turned to May, telling her to stop giggling and to fetch the missus.

"You're very kind," Penelope managed to say before almost falling on to the stool in relief.

"She's very pale," Mary said to Lucy, "Do you think she's about to faint?"

"Maybe best to put your head down for a bit," Lucy suggested to Penelope. "Git some colour back in yer."

Lucy gratefully followed this advice and didn't stir until the "missus" had heard all that had happened. The older woman, who was in her early forties, her plump body dressed in black but with a slightly soiled white apron covering her clothes, scrutinised Penelope carefully before concluding that she was indeed a lady in distress. She could tell from Penelope's delicate hands as well as from the clothes she was wearing, for, although her hands were dirty, Bella was sure that those hands had never done a day's work in their lives.

"Well, my dear," she began, "you'd better come in with me when you feel able to stand. I'm Bella Hollows, the landlord's wife, by the way. We'll get you cleaned up and fed first, then consider what's to be done. Unless there's a rascal that needs apprehending straight away, that is."

Penelope forced herself upright again, relief once more almost causing her to collapse. "Thank you so very much, and no, there is no rascal nearby," she said, looking at Bella and trying to smile. She wanted to say more but found the words just wouldn't come.

Bella assisted her to rise and led her into the tavern, up the back stairs and into a sparsely furnished, but clean bedchamber. There, Penelope was aided to undress, given water to wash with and a nighty to wear and was then guided to the bed, the landlady persuading her that she needed to rest after such an ordeal, and that she would fetch her some food. She also picked up Penelope's clothes, saying that they would be washed and mended before nightfall.

But Bella's helpfulness came to an end when Penelope protested that she really had to send a message to her guardian at Hoddam Hall.

"Well, as to that, there is a bit of a problem, you see. Unless you have some money with you, that is," Bella informed her. "You see, while I'll willingly let you rest here without payment for the bed, your food, or anything else, I'm not so sure I could persuade anyone to ride all that way without being paid for doing so. I know where the Hall is, but I doubt if anyone is likely to be heading that way. I'll ask, but I know this lot. Won't lift a finger unless there's something in it for them."

"Oh, but whoever goes there will be well rewarded, I can assure you. Lord Frome will gladly pay whatever is asked, and more, for whoever brought him news of my whereabouts. And you shall also be paid," Penelope added, "for your kindness."

Bella blushed with pleasure, saying that no payment need be given her for doing only what was right in helping someone in distress, but adding that most folks would not be as generous. "Money up front is what they'll want, I'm afraid. They won't necessarily believe your story, you see. But I'll ask, anyway."

Penelope had to be content with those words and lay her head back on what turned out to be a rather lumpy pillow. At least the bed was clean, she noted. And at least she was free. And safe. She was certain that someone could be persuaded to take a message to Lord Frome. After all, most would jump at the chance of getting a handsome reward from a lord. Bella was just being cautious, she concluded. All would now be well.

When Bella returned carrying a tray of food, she was smiling, giving Penelope hope that she had found someone willing to ride to Hoddam for her. But Bella's words dispelled that idea.

"It's as I thought," she said, putting the tray on the bed, within Penelope's reach, "I couldn't get anyone to agree to ride to Hoddam for you, I'm afraid. But maybe I can help you anyway. Although the long-distance coaches don't stop here, they do stop at Selby which is a short way south of here. And it so happens that Mr Hollows will be sending young Bert there tomorrow with the wagon to pick up some supplies. He could take a letter there for you if you like. Then, it could go on the Newcastle mail coach run with the rest of the mail. What do you think? It is the best I can offer you, I'm afraid."

"But that could take ages! Days even!"

Penelope couldn't believe that she had come this far and still wasn't safe. She tried telling Bella that she would be able to leave for home the following morning at the latest if a message was sent to Hoddam today, but Bella remained unmoved.

"Eat up," Bella urged, "and then get some sleep." And although Penelope protested that she wouldn't be able to rest until she was back with her guardian, she fell into a deep sleep within minutes of satisfying her hunger and thirst.

By the following morning, Penelope had made up her mind. She would persuade "Young Bert" to take her to Selby. She hadn't met the young man yet but was confident that he would pose her no threat. And she felt she had to do something for herself; not just allow others to help her whilst she sat back and accepted their hospitality. It was a pity the boy wasn't going north though, she reflected. It seemed to be such a waste of time going in the opposite direction to the one she needed to go. But, at least in Selby, she was sure someone would know her at the inn, as she, Alex and Lady Wilde had stopped there on their journey north. She could promise the innkeeper a handsome reward for arranging her travel back to Hoddam as well as one for the person who offered to drive her there. Not everyone would be like these suspicious villagers.

She didn't blame Bella, and would see her well rewarded, but the rest of the villagers? She hoped their crops would fail and their cows would go dry!

Having made up her mind, she dressed in her newly laundered clothes, and went down to confront Mr Hollows, the landlord. She had expected some resistance from him, but found him to be a most timid, polite fellow who expressed his willingness to help her in any way he could - except to take a note to Hoddam, she felt like reminding him. Instead, she thanked him profusely for allowing her to accompany young Bert to Selby, and, full of smiles, set off on her day's journey.

Young Bert was about fourteen and was big for his age but very immature. He had a large, round face, ruddy, sunburnt cheeks and a smiling, friendly countenance. He was inordinately shy and when he did pluck up the courage to address her directly, he spoke in monosyllables. Penelope decided that he and the giggling May were made for each other!

She remained in good humour, despite the lack of stimulating conversation, feeling full of optimism now that she was at last nearing the end of her adventure. The weather seemed mild and the scenery pleasant even if the road was rather too rough for her liking, and the springs on the wagon, if indeed it had any, were doing little to soften the ride. However, by the time she reached Selby, the skies had opened and her smile was long gone.

Chapter Eighteen

Penelope, Prudence, and Alex were not the only ones who had headed north at the end of the London Season. Damien Searle, the Earl of Hawkeswood, was another who had decided it was time to have a long talk with his sister, heading north shortly after returning from the house party at Henley. He would have set off straight away, but his horse had suffered an injury to his fetlock on the journey back to London, making Damien delay his departure for a few days. However, he soon realised that it would be some time before the animal was up for such a long trip, and as he was eager to speak with Meg and make plans for their future, he eventually chose to make the journey using hired hacks.

He was now reaching the end of that journey and had been looking forward to arriving at Wharfe House before nightfall, but the beast he had hired at the last staging post seemed to have no stamina whatsoever. To add to his list of complaints, the weather had turned decidedly unpleasant over the last half hour and the rain was now coming down in torrents, with no sign of easing.

He spurred the horse on, his temper fraying as the overfed creature merely cantered a little faster. A gallop seemed beyond its capabilities. Luckily, he was nearing Selby and would be able to find shelter there. Even though it was only mid-afternoon and Wharfe House was barely more than twelve miles or so away, he had already had enough of the pouring rain and gloomy, overcast skies, so decided to rest for the remainder of the day at Selby, giving his clothes time to dry and his temper time to cool.

The dreadful weather almost made him wish he had delayed the journey by a few more days but needed to speak with his mother and sister even though what he had to say wouldn't be easy. He planned to convince Meg and his mother that, at long last, he was ready to accept his responsibilities, hoping to convince them that the best plan was for them all to live together, preferably on an estate near to the capital, but also to have a London town house worthy of their station. In his opinion Meg should never have shut herself away, believing that doing so had caused more problems for his sister rather than less.

The fact that he would have to rely on Meg's money to build this new life seemed immaterial. After all, he reasoned, she would not have had the money if it hadn't been for him. All right, he conceded, it was a lousy thing to do to marry your immature sister off to someone with Lucas' inclinations, but he had not been that mature himself at the time. He had been desperate, and Lucas Greene had seemed like a Godsend. And from a financial point-of-view, the match had been a good one. Happiness in marriage was never guaranteed, after all. They could have rubbed along reasonably well together. How was he to know how it was to turn out?

But, of course, it had turned out to be a disaster, and he now realised that the time had come to accept his responsibilities as head of his family and do something about it. Even though he was without wealth or property, he was the Earl of Hawkeswood, and ever since encountering the Earl of Tenby, he had come to feel differently about life.

He felt surprisingly good about having at last taken on the task of defending his sister's honour, and now, at the advanced age of two and thirty, he believed he had earned the right to call himself a man. Now, thanks to Lord Tenby, he was ready to move on and make things right with Meg and his mother.

He would have to begin by apologising to them, something he was going to find very difficult, but he knew it must be done. Then, he would have to convince them of his sincerity in being willing to act responsibly in the future. It was not going to be easy; he had no illusions about that. After all, he had little to offer them but his protection, and they no doubt saw him for the wastrel he was, still counting on the turn of the cards for a living. And he had to admit he enjoyed the risks and the excitement associated with gambling, but, if he had to give it up, he was prepared to try living a different life, because restoring his sister's faith in him was now of paramount importance.

By the time he reached the Fox and Hounds in Selby, Damien was feeling thoroughly miserable. He was soaked to the skin, tired, ashamed of himself, and fed up to the teeth with the nag he was riding. Luckily, he was greeted warmly by the innkeeper who remembered him from previous visits, quickly showing him to a private parlour. Damien had stopped at the inn on several occasions in the past but had never stayed overnight. He hoped the bedchambers were as welcoming as his host; a large, jovial fellow of middle years by the name of Bernard Best.

Soon, Damien's greatcoat had been whisked away for drying and a saucy looking serving wench had brought him a bottle of their finest red wine. Even though it was mid-afternoon, Damien had not yet had luncheon, so ordered a full meal to be served. Damien noted the serving girl's flirtatious manner and was sure she would be willing to warm his bed that night. Yet even though this warm welcome raised his spirits, the thought of bedding the serving girl did not excite him, pretty and young though she was.

Could this newfound virtue be causing him to lose some of his interest in sex, or was it, he wondered, because of that witch Penelope, who had remained in his thoughts over the past weeks despite the futility of it? Even his favourite whore, Verity, had failed to please him recently, despite her considerable skill!

The red wine and an excellent meal of several meat dishes including a delicious, raised pie, soon helped to improve his mood and before long he sat back feeling very mellow after finishing off a bottle of excellent wine. He had informed the landlord of his intention to remain overnight and had been assured of the best bedchamber at the inn, to which Damien made the usual joke of hoping he wasn't turning the landlord out of his own room! Bernard Best even laughed as though he had never heard the joke before!

After giving orders for his lordship's portmanteau to be taken to his room, Bernard noted that Damien had no servant with him and offered to find someone to "do" for him.

"Thank you, Bernard," Damien said. "I know the hack is being well cared for by your excellent ostler, but if you could find someone willing to see to the deplorable state of these clothes and boots, I should be grateful. Other than that, I can manage on my own."

"Certainly, Lord Hawkeswood. I'll show you to your room as soon as you are ready and send my man Henry up to attend you. Just pull on the bell cord when you want him," he added, making a polite bow.

"Thank you again, Bernard. I believe I'm ready to go up now," Damien replied, rising from the table a little unsteadily. "Lead the way, there's a good fellow."

They had just entered the taproom when a commotion at the entrance drew their attention. Two very bedraggled young people had just entered, soaked to the skin. Another man was trying to bar their way, thinking them tramps trying to shelter from the storm. As well as being wet through, they were also covered in mud, the young man more than the girl, but even she had smudges on her face and her clothes.

"Let us in, you stupid oaf," she cried, and Damien looked more closely at her because he was sure he knew that voice. It first he dismissed the idea, decided that he was being fanciful. He had been thinking of Penelope and now he was imagining he was hearing her voice. He shouldn't have drunk so much wine with his luncheon!

But as he took in her appearance, he became convinced it was she.

"Penelope?" he said, moving towards her, his heart thudding in his chest as he held out his hand.

All attention turned to him and even the man who was obstructing her entrance looked round at Damien as he approached.

"Lord Hawkeswood?" she said, clearly amazed and stunned to see him. She watched as he approached her, his hand outstretched, and moved forward into the taproom, tears of relief stinging her eyes.

"Who is it, milord?" Bernard Best asked, clearly surprised, and not at all happy at this turn of events.

"Oh, Bernard, this is Miss MacDonald, ward of the Marquess of Frome. But what she is doing here in this state, I cannot begin to guess. However, she clearly needs help." Then turning back to Penelope, "Come Miss MacDonald," he said, taking her hand and leading her to his private parlour as though they were just returning from a gentle stroll. But while appearing calm on the outside, inside, a whole range of thoughts and emotions were swirling through him in rapid succession, not the least of which was desire for this woman, the only one to ever capture his heart.

Young Ben was obviously pleased at being able to enter the inn but then he stood still, seemingly uncertain of what to do next. "Hmm, excuse me..." he said to Damien's back.

"Oh, my Lord, Ben has brought me here. I must thank him," Penelope said, turning to look at the lad. "Thank you so much for allowing me to travel with you, Ben. You have helped to save my life. I shall never forget your kindness and will send you and your mistress a more fitting thanks as soon as I am able," she assured him.

"Oh, no bother. No bother at all," replied Ben, stringing more words together than he had during the whole trip. He then turned to Bernard to state his own reason for coming to Selby, saying he had better be on his way to the stores.

"No, you must accept my hospitality first," said Damien, showing an interest in the lad for the first time. "You have been of service to this lady, and that puts me in your debt. Landlord, please see this fellow is cleaned up and fed and given a bed if he so desires. I'll be footing the bill, you understand."

"Certainly," replied Bernard, "Anything you say, milord."

"Thank you, Lord Hawkeswood," Penelope whispered as she was led to a chair by the hearth. Damien took the seat opposite hers, and now they were looking at each other, seemingly unsure of what to say. Damien knew that by arriving at the inn in such a state, Penelope had attracted the attention of everyone in the establishment and whatever had happened to her would be the subject of speculation. And now there would also be speculation about her connection to him. They were both in a devilishly awkward situation.

But looking across at the woman of his dreams made him forget all of that. Sensations swamped him and he wanted nothing more than to take her in his arms, holding her fast and never letting her go. He recalled their last intimate encounter when she had promised to consider his offer of marriage, only to ignore him when she saw him again. She had physically turned her back on him, he remembered. But she couldn't ignore him now. Nor did she appear to want to.

Since then, he had nursed his disappointment even though he had understood why she had refused his offer. But he knew she was still drawn to him, no matter that she had become engaged to another. Now, here she was, like a bedraggled urchin, and here he was, a knight in slightly tarnished armour! And he loved her, God help him!

Leaning towards her, he reached out and began wiping the mud from her wet cheeks with his handkerchief, pleased to see that she did not visibly shrink from his touch. *Lord, but she is lovely,* he thought. *Even more lovely than she had been in his dreams.* And the look in her eyes told him she was no longer thinking of him with disgust. It would be so easy to take advantage of the situation if he had no conscience, but this new-found virtue of his told him that to do so would be despicable. He therefore did his best to tamp down his basic carnal instincts, concentrating instead on her immediate needs.

However, he recognised that she really had to get out of those wet clothes as quickly as possible, and while his old self would like nothing more than to be the one to take them off her, he knew they were in enough trouble as it was, without courting more. But then another thought struck him. "Are you hurt, Penelope?" he asked.

She shook her head. "No, just a bit battered and bruised perhaps, but I am all right. Oh Damien, it is so good to see you. I am in the most dreadful mess." She then burst into tears.

Damien was relieved and thankful that she was not hurt, but to hear her use his first name and see her weeping undid him. It took all of his willpower to resist taking her in his arms, doubting he would be unable to stop at merely comforting her, so settled for offering her his handkerchief, telling her to be careful to avoid putting mud back on her face. This seemed to amuse her, because she stopped crying with a bit of a hiccup and smiled a watery smile at him, folding the handkerchief over until a clean patch was revealed, before using it to dab the tears from her cheeks.

How am I going to resist her, he said to himself, almost shaking with the need to reach out for her. He gripped the arms of his chair instead and forced himself back under control. "I hope you will allow me to help you, my dear," he said as calmly as he could. "And I look forward to hearing your story but first, let me attend to a few practical matters for you." With that, he rose from his chair and headed for the door, calling "Landlord" as he went.

Within less than a minute he returned to Penelope and drew her gently to her feet, putting an arm around her as he led her from his private parlour. "Come," was all he said as he guided her up the stairs and into a bedchamber. *His* bedchamber.

"I have asked the landlord to take my things to another room so you can rest here," he explained.

"Oh, I don't think I should be here, Lord Hawkeswood," she said, looking around her. "What if someone should see? Can't I use that other room?"

"It is not ready yet and your need is urgent. Please come and sit by the fire, my dear," he said, leading her to a chair. "Anyway, I have the landlord's assurance that he will do everything possible to prevent your presence here from becoming known by anyone else, after I stupidly called out your name when you first appeared in the doorway. He told me that only locals had been present, and they were unlikely to talk, except amongst themselves and he knew his business depended on protecting his patron's confidences. So please don't worry about gossip."

Penelope sighed in relief. "That is good to hear. Thank you again, Lord Hawkeswood."

Damien didn't like her using his title to address him. "I liked it when you called me Damien. Do you think you could do so again? There is surely no longer any need of formality between us."

Penelope looked very unsure, but reluctantly did as he requested and then watched as he added more coal to the fire before sitting in the chair opposite hers. "I have also asked for a bath to be brought up and requested that a change of clothes be found for you. Are you hungry?"

She assured him she was not, and he nodded, confirming that he had also eaten. An awkward silence then followed, until Penelope looked at his clothes. "Oh dear," she cried, "I have made you all wet and muddy."

"Never mind about that. I need to change anyway. I was also caught in the storm. It is the reason I am staying the night at the inn. Look, it might take a while to prepare the bath for you and wonder if you would be willing to tell me a little bit about this mess you say you are in while we are waiting."

At first, Penelope did not reply, and did not even look at him, and he wondered if she may be near collapse, but slowly, he noticed her straighten, and then she smiled. "You are being very kind to me, Lord Hawkeswood."

"Damien, please," he entreated.

"Damien then. And I do trust you, even though I know I should not. But it is rather a long story, I'm afraid, and only hope you don't regret offering to listen."

Penelope was at first reluctant to confide in Damien, but once she had made up her mind to trust him, she wanted to tell him everything. Needed to tell him everything. When she had first seen him turn towards her after calling out her name, her heart had almost stopped. She couldn't believe what was happening. The last time she had spoken to him had been on the balcony after their intimate encounter, promising to consider his offer of marriage. Since then, she had nursed her anger at his deceiving words but had never for a second stopped longing for him. And now, here he was!

What was he doing here? He said he was sheltering from the storm, but why else was he here? There had to be a reasonable explanation. She wanted to ask him, but what did it really matter. He *was* here, and he was helping her. She was safe at last.

He had asked to hear her story and she suddenly realised that he was perhaps the only person in the world she wanted to know the whole truth. What did that tell her?

And so she began, keeping nothing back. Not her feelings nor the details of her mistakes. She answered all his questions honestly, feeling free to talk to him as she had never spoken to anyone else before. And as the telling of her story progressed, she was struck by the realisation that the bond between them was deepening, as though they already knew all there was to know about each other. She knew instinctively that he would understand her and would never betray her trust.

Sometimes, during the telling, she cried, bringing Damien to her side; sometimes, she held her head up high; sometimes her voice was barely a whisper. But, throughout, she looked into his eyes and took comfort from his expression. It was neither condemning nor lecherous. He was looking at her with encouragement, understanding and with affection.

And when she came almost to the end, telling him of her journey to Selby with Ben, when the wagon's wheels had got stuck in a huge, deep pothole, making it necessary for them to walk in the thick mud, getting soaked to the skin whilst pulling and pushing both the horse and the wagon before finally getting it free, Damien smiled at the scene she painted, making her see the funny side of the story as well, until they were both laughing at the absurdity of it.

The bath had been brought up by the time the story had been told, and Damien's things had been taken away. She suddenly felt guilty about what he had organised for her.

"Oh, Damien, I don't intend to stay the night here. It wouldn't be right to impose on you so. I'll be all right after a bath and a short rest. And anyway, I need to return to Hoddam Hall. My ...guardian and ... Lord Tenby ... will be worried about me," she stuttered, finding it difficult to mention Alex to Damien.

"It is out of the question for you to set out for Hoddam Hall today, Penelope. Not in this storm. Not after all that has happened to you already today. But a message should be sent to your guardian, I agree with you about that. How about you write a note and I arrange for someone to take it to Hoddam Hall as soon as it is written?"

"I suppose that would be best," Penelope said dejectedly.

"And as for travelling back to Hoddam Hall, I think we must wait for the weather to clear and for a chaperone to be hired to accompany you. I suggest that in the morning I hire a carriage for us to travel the short distance to my sister's home…"

Her gasp of amazement made him stop to look into her eyes. "What is it, Penelope?" he asked instead. "My sister lives but twelve miles from here and you will be able to rest, change into more suitable clothes - Meg is bound to have something to fit you - and then we can find a chaperone to escort you back to Hoddam Hall, perhaps the following day. What is so dreadful about that idea?"

"Ah, so your sister lives near here. That explains why you are in Selby. I did wonder."

"Yes, I am only here because of the storm. Otherwise, I would have travelled the rest of the way instead of taking shelter."

"But I don't think you should take me to your sister."

"Whyever not?"

"Well, I heard that … your sister is a … a … is not very respectable." She couldn't bring herself to repeat Celia's words.

"Ah, so you have also been listening to the gossip," he stated angrily. "Is that why you rejected my offer of marriage so vehemently? And why you looked right through me on the few occasions we have been in the same room since then? And why you accepted the offer of marriage from a man you obviously don't love?"

"Yes," she shouted. "Yes, yes, yes. You offered me only disgrace. Alex offered me protection and security!"

"And I thought you … Well, it doesn't matter what I thought, does it? But, let me tell you, my sister is not a loose woman. She is probably the most virtuous woman alive. She is certainly more virtuous that those who gossip about her."

His anger was palpable, and she felt his rebuke keenly. But then he seemed to calm, speaking in a quieter, but equally cold, business-like voice. "But that can wait. Come, Penelope, you must get out of those wet clothes before you take a chill. I shall leave you now to your bath, but I will return later, if you will allow such a disreputable devil as I entry, and we shall try to sort out what is to be done. By then, you may have managed to write that note for your guardian, and I'll see that it is delivered. Unless, of course, you cannot trust me even to organise that, and you would rather see to it yourself. After all, I might just tear it up and abduct you myself, mightn't I?"

"Oh Damien, try not to be so angry. Please try to understand. If I believed ill of you and your sister, and I confess that I did, it was only because of what I had been told by my cousin Celia. Can't you see? I only acted as I had to, as society demands. But you must also know what you made me feel for you before my cousin's words poisoned my thoughts. I thought I loved you!"

He looked at her closely for what seemed like minutes, but then she saw the tension easing from his body. "So, you did feel something for me. It is nice to know that I wasn't the only one to suffer from your rejection. But all in all, I know that you were right to reject me. It was wrong of me to even make such a dishonourable proposal. Yet you believe me about my sister now, I hope, and will let me take you to her."

She nodded. "I have been wrong about a lot of other things as well."

"Haven't we all," he commented quietly before rising from his chair and patting her on the shoulder. "I will leave you now to get out of your wet things but will return shortly to organise for that note to be sent to your guardian. After that? Well, that will be up to you and fate."

Two hours later, they were ensconced in his former bedchamber, once again sitting opposite each other on high-backed leather chairs, waiting for a meal to be sent up to the room. Penelope was dressed in a plain, cotton nightgown and wrap, loaned to her by Mrs Best, who was a much larger woman than Penelope, so eating in the parlour was out of the question. It seemed no-one had clothes to lend her, and she only hoped her own could be made to look presentable by the morning.

When Damien had first returned, Penelope had handed him the missive she had prepared for Lord Frome and he took it downstairs to ensure its immediate dispatch. In it, Penelope had stated that she was safe and well, having been abducted by Stanley Thorpe, but that she had managed to escape. She then went on to explain that not knowing her whereabouts, she had ended up in Selby, where she had the good fortune to meet Lord Hawkeswood at the inn, an acquaintance from London who was on his way north to visit with his family. She stressed that Stanley was dangerous and warned that he was intent on killing Alex. She concluded by saying that she had agreed to accompany Lord Hawkeswood to Wharfe House, his sister's home, feeling it wiser to be under the protection of another family as soon as possible and that she would proceed from there to Hoddam Hall as soon as she was able, accompanied by a suitable chaperone.

Penelope had thought that perhaps she should also enclose a message to Alex but was unsure what to say to him. As it was, she felt that somehow her story lacked credibility, maybe to the point of being unbelievable. Even she found it hard to believe she was safely in Selby, so far from her starting point and keeping company with a known rake. What would Lord Frome believe? What would *Alex* believe?

Well, she would just have to tell them the full sequence of events later, she decided, hoping that when the time came, they wouldn't question her too closely. She fervently hoped that her former relationship with Stanley did not have to be revealed to anyone other than Damien.

Damien was with her now at her request even though she knew it would be frowned on by society for him to be alone with her in a bedchamber. But after all that had happened, what would one more questionable decision matter. Anyway, they had much to discuss, and she didn't want to be on her own. Penelope thought that being covered from her neck to her toes in the voluminous garments, her hands hidden beneath the overlong sleeves, would be sufficient to make her feel safe, but now knew she was wrong. She felt very vulnerable, dressed as she was in the presence of the most disturbing man she had ever met.

She looked across at him, the tension in her palpable. He was so beautiful! His eyes captivated her. They were like green moss, but now were darkened with emotion. His sensual mouth looked unusually severe, almost hard. She could see his pulse beating at the side of his strong, corded neck, for he had loosened his collar and had removed his stock. She could even see some dark reddish-blond body hair revealed where he had undone the top two buttons on his white, linen shirt.

As she lowered her eyes to escape from his penetrating gaze, she saw how snugly his brocade waistcoat hugged his broad chest, and how his muscled legs were parted, drawing her attention to his powerful thighs and the bulge between them, causing her to blush alarmingly.

She quickly looked away, forcing herself to meet his gaze once again and found him smiling a broad, self-satisfied smile! Her blush deepened even more as she realised that he had read her thoughts.

"What?" she said defensively, in an unmistakably croaky voice.

"Oh, my dear Penelope, if you could only see what a truly desirable sight you are," he said, visibly relaxing. "I forgive you for all those uncharitable thoughts about Meg. How can I resist such loveliness? You know, Penelope, you're the only woman I have ever proposed to. Marriage, that is. I only wish I was worthy of you and that you could have accepted me. There are many things in my past that I now regret."

If he truly believed what he was saying, and he still wanted to marry her, was it too late for them as he claimed? She knew she was underage and needed permission from her guardian, but if Alex cried off, and there was a strong possibility now that he would do so, then her guardian may begin to think of Damien in a better light. Especially after he had come to her rescue, and they had spent time together. Alone!

Would not the possibility be worth exploring?

However, when she put this to him, he shook his head. "I hope your feelings for me have not reignited only because you need my help at the moment."

"Of course not. My feelings for you have never changed."

"Then we are both in trouble. You are young, Penelope, and need to be protected, even from yourself. We cannot just do as we wish."

"Hmm, and what do you wish, Damien?"

"I wish things were different. I wish I was a man your guardian would approve of as a husband for you. I wish my family had never been unfairly mired in scandal. I wish so many things. But right now? I would like to pretend that all those wishes were granted, and we were promised to each other. Then I would tell you what I would like to do to you if you were mine."

"What would you like to do to me?" she asked, breathlessly.

Without waiting for permission, Damien leaned across to her and took one of her hands in his. "I should allow myself the pleasure of burying my fingers in those soft, velvet curls of yours; of caressing your silky skin, of fondling your beautiful body. I still remember how it feels to have you in my arms, Penelope. I don't think I shall ever forget what it feels like to hold you and breathe in your scent, to feel you respond to my loving.... but I'll spare your blushes and say no more. I know I do not have the right to speak to you so, but then, I have rarely done what was right in the past. It will take me a while to reform, I think, especially when you are here to tempt me."

She wanted to tell him that she would welcome his touch, but before she could, she saw his smile fade as he let go of her hand, shaking his head. "Please forget I said all that. We need to talk about tomorrow, not about what can never be. Since you have agreed to be taken to my sister, I will hire a carriage in the morning to take us to Wharfe house. When you meet my sister, you will know how wrong the gossips are. Whatever you heard about me is probably true, but my sister ... she does not deserve your condemnation."

Penelope was disappointed by his retreat into formality but knew he had been right to do so. She had been silly to think things could be otherwise.

As for her condemning his sister? "I think it is more likely that your sister will condemn me!" Penelope exclaimed. "But I should like to look less shabby when I meet her. Could you take me shopping first, Damien? Even if my clothes are wearable, there are other items I shall need to make myself presentable."

"I think we should have time for that, although there is no need. My sister will welcome you whatever state you are in."

"Perhaps, but I will feel better if I look respectable. I need things for my hair, and …" She was just about to mention stockings and the like but considered she had better not.

The meal arrived at that point, and they ate in silence for a while, occasionally glancing at each other. And then he said something that made her senses sharpen and her heart race. "I know I have no right to ask, but I really would like to know. Tell me, did you even for a minute consider accepting my proposal?"

She frowned. "Before I consider answering that, I would need to know that your proposal was sincere. Did you mean what you said?"

"At the time, I did. Yes."

She forced her mind to recall that night when she had succumbed so easily to his seduction and to her own passion. She had known then that he was the man she wanted, even though he had admitted his unworthiness to her at the time.

"When I thought your proposal was honourable, yes, I confess I did consider you as a husband. I am not penniless, and even though you told me that you would never be accepted by my guardian as a suitor for my hand, I believed that we could live off our joint incomes reasonably well. I am not totally dependent upon Lord Frome. But, at the same time, I didn't *want* to want you. My feelings for you are... were... well, were too dangerous. Based on a wildly beating heart whenever I thought of you; of knowing myself totally vulnerable to your seductive charms. I was frightened of you ... I still am."

"Frightened of yourself, I think you'll find. Of your own sensuality. I know I acted dishonourably towards you that night, and I apologise. And I admit my feelings for you have not changed, but I will do my best to act the gentleman from now on. You are promised to another, and I shall just have to restrain myself. Just as I tried to stay away from you in London after I learned of your betrothal. I should find some rich cit to marry, I suppose. But we would have been good together, you and I. You are as passionate as I, and I think you are going to be very bored with your chosen mate. Or does he also make your heart race?"

She blushed again at his words. "Alex would make me a good husband. But, after this escapade, he may want to cry off. Stanley is bound to say something about me, isn't he? And, even if he doesn't, Alex will probably have his suspicions. Will he think I encouraged Stanley to care for me?"

"If he did, he would be right in a way, wouldn't he?"

"Oh, such cruel words," she cried.

"But with some truth in them. Admit it. You find men attractive. You may be a lady on the surface, but you are a passionate woman beneath. Why should someone like you not have the right to flirt when you feel like it? It is not your fault if we poor mortal men fall at your feet if you so much as glance in our direction! Poor Penelope! Having a passionate nature is a real drawback for a lady, isn't it? You may even be right. Maybe Alex will have second thoughts. Whereas I would understand completely. Of course, I would still kill the man, but I would understand! Mind you, if we were married, you would have to have eyes only for me!"

At last, he had managed to get her to smile. "Oh Damien, what am I to do?"

"Now, there's a question!", he replied. "A month ago, I would have probably taken that as an invitation to seduce you, but now my conscience is forcing me to act the gallant gentleman. And, unfortunately, there can be no honourable future for us. So, the answer to your question is nothing. Absolutely nothing. We'll go to Meg's tomorrow, and the following day, your state of health and weather permitting, you shall travel back to your guardian. What happens after that is anyone's guess. There is bound to be speculation about your disappearance and time away from the hall, but I suspect that your guardian and fiancé will want you to marry without delay to scotch any ugly rumours. I know Lord Tenby is an honourable man and am sure he will stand by you."

"How do you know Lord Tenby is an honourable man? Do you know him?"

Damien shrugged. "We have met, but I also know of his reputation."

Penelope had no idea that Damien and Alex knew each other, but she could tell he didn't want to expand on that topic. He rushed on. "You can take it from me that Lord Tenby will do what must be done. And for what it is worth, please know that you also have my full support."

He sounded so formal and withdrawn and she hated it but was determined to hide her distress. "Thank you," she managed to reply and even smiled at him as she reached out to take his hands in hers.

He drew his away. "No, my dear, do not touch me. I am finding it hard enough to resist you as it is. If you should touch me, I fear I would be unable to stop myself from doing something we would both later regret." He rose. "I had better go now. Rest well, my dear one."

Tears sprang to her eyes as he moved to the door. "Don't look at me like that, Penelope. I must go. I will see you in the morning." Then he flew from the room, almost slamming the door in his haste to escape.

* * *

The following morning, Penelope and Damien visited the local general store, using Damien's funds to purchase petticoats, chemises, handkerchiefs, a reticule, shoes - for hers were irreparably damaged - hair ribbons, combs, brushes and pins and other sundry items. They then returned to the inn, repacked her things before bidding farewell to Bernard Best who apologised for not immediately recognising her the day before.

She laughed. "I don't' think even I would have recognised myself in the state I was in."

"Thank you for your understanding, Miss MacDonald."

Soon they were on their way to Wharfe House in a hired barouche. The storm had passed, and the weather was now promising to remain fine if a little cloudy, but as each mile passed, Penelope became more and more apprehensive. It was time to face her future. She found herself only half listening as Damien talked about the route and other mundane topics, until he must have sensed that she wasn't in the mood for light conversation and fell silent.

Penelope could not stop thinking about their intimate conversation of the previous evening, as well as of all the problems she knew she was going to have to face. Not only about her abduction and escape, but also being in the company of Damien, word of which may already be on its way to London! Despite the landlord's assurances about protecting their anonymity, someone else could have recognised her, either at the inn or while they shopped. And the more she contemplated the future, the more she needed to sound Damien out on the situation.

Suddenly she turned to him. "Damien, if you were my fiancé, would you still want to marry me, knowing all that has happened?"

He turned to look at her, and saw that she was not flirting with him, but was full of concern. He couldn't help squeezing her hand in a reassuring gesture. "Penelope, if you were *my* betrothed, I would probably put you over my knee and spank you for not trusting me, and then I should insist you marry me immediately. But only if you loved me. And, if you loved me, I should keep you so busy in our bedchamber, you wouldn't have the strength to meet someone else at dawn! You would be totally exhausted from making love with me!"

"Shh" she said, glancing briefly at the driver. "Keep your voice down!"

In truth, she hadn't expected *that* response! So much for formality! One minute he was withdrawn and the next he was acting like the rake he professed that he no longer wanted to be.

Penelope's body had instantly responded to his wicked words and to his touch. She knew that her face had become suffused with colour and couldn't prevent her eyes and lips rounding in surprise. She literally tingled all over, and her heart lurched, sending shock waves downwards to her very centre.

But what did his words mean? What was truly in his heart?

If Damien truly loved her and wanted to marry her, maybe she should cry off from her promise to Alex. It would be another scandal to be sure, but it looked like a scandal was unavoidable anyway. So why not wait for a time when she could marry Damien? She let the thought take root. Would she dare risk the condemnation of the whole of society by breaking her engagement to Alex?

She would if she could have Damien in her future.

She just had to know if that was a possibility and decided to push her luck. "Er ... Damien ... I rather like the sound of that! I like the thought of being yours and you doing all you just said, including the idea of you spanking me. How can I marry Lord Tenby when I want you?"

Her words clearly startled him, because any hint of a smile vanished, replaced by a deadly serious expression as he looked directly into her eyes. The formal Damien had returned!

"I like the thought of being married to you as well, Penelope, but believe me, it is not possible. Once again, I am going to have to beg your forgiveness for speaking out of turn. I had no right to burden you with my dishonourable thoughts. I am sorry if I have misled you, speaking so unwisely. It was not my intention. You must face facts, Penelope. The truth is that you are underage, my dear. If you ended your engagement to Lord Tenby, it is likely your guardian would marry you off to whoever would have you to save your reputation."

"Then why should not that someone be you?"

"Because I am the last person your guardian would choose. I have an unsavoury past and earn my living as a gambler. He would prefer you marry almost anybody else! No, if you truly do not wish to marry Alex, please wait until the current scandal dies down before you cry off. The engagement needs to stand until society has something else to gossip about. For both our sakes."

"What are you saying? Are you saying you will never marry me, no matter what happens?"

"No, I am not saying that. But I cannot marry you now, Penelope. Thank you for the proposal though," he added with a smile. "As I told you last night, my reason for visiting my sister is to try to get her, her daughter, and my mother to move to a more suitable home and to accept me as head of the family. I wish things could be different, but it is now my duty to do everything I can to restore the reputation of myself and my family. If I were reckless enough to rush you to the border to marry you, it would be another almighty scandal and I cannot afford that at this time. Neither can you, if you think about things sensibly. You must go back to your guardian and your betrothed. Neither of them would want a scandal and are bound to look for a way to hush things up. They will most likely urge you to bring your wedding forward and I think in time you will see that choosing to marry Lord Tenby was not such a bad idea. He is good husband material."

Penelope was simply stunned by his words. How could he give her hope and then snatch it away? And as for thanking her for her proposal! The cad!

How could he do this to her? Damien had proposed to her first and had declared his love for her, but all that seemed to mean nothing to him now. Had she proposed to him? A sense of shame made her face turn scarlet before being replaced by anger.

Hadn't the same thing happened with Alex? Alex and Damien had both been keen to talk of marriage but had wanted to back off at the last minute. Was she so unlovable? Could she just attract men, but not hold them? Damien's family obviously meant more to him than she did!

She had opened her own heart to Damien and exposed her true feelings to him. But it seemed that while he wanted her, he didn't really want to marry her.

How humiliating.

Luckily, anger once again came to her aid; gave her courage to go on. She had just learned a most valuable lesson. One she would never forget. Never again would she be honest with a man. Never again would she allow herself to be so vulnerable.

"Thank you, Damien," she managed to say, holding back the tears of anger and despair that were trying to form, "for being so *honest* with me. You have saved me from making a dreadful mistake."

She didn't expect an argument from him and didn't get one. Damien, now even more grim-faced, turned away, his eyes on the scenery. After a brief look at his stern profile, Penelope also turned to look at the scenery on her side of the carriage biting back her tears.

They rode on in silence for a while, and when they did speak it was Damien who quietly explained to Penelope a little about his sister and her household. By the time they arrived at Wharfe House, no-one could have guessed that the visitors cared anything for each other, let alone that they were deeply in love.

Chapter Nineteen

◆———————◆———————◆

Meg had spent the time since Alex's departure trying to pretend to herself that he meant nothing to her. That she didn't constantly miss him and long for him. During the daylight hours she believed she had been successful, doing her best to appear happy and was reasonably confident that neither Emily, her mother, nor even Alice guessed how unhappy she really was. But at night she couldn't keep his image from invading her waking moments and her dreams. Would she ever get over him?

Had her sacrifice been worth it? God, she hoped so! She had purposefully rejected the most precious gift one person can give to another. But she had had no choice. She had to think of Emily. Emily, who had also suffered at the loss of this new friend. Yet she knew she had to protect her daughter and Alex from suffering from her hateful past even if they didn't see the need themselves. Emily, because she was too young to know, and Alex, because he had never felt the scorn of others. He had only known what it was to be the beloved son, the successful soldier. And now he must become the respected earl. She could never be a part of his life. One day he would thank her for rejecting him, she knew. But let it not be too soon, her heart cried out. Please God, let him love me for a little longer.

Three weeks after his departure, she had received a note from his mother, Lady Wilde, thanking her for taking care of her son in his hour of need and inviting her and Emily to stay for a while with her in London. Meg had tossed the letter away, thinking only of what he would have told his mother. Not the truth, that was for sure. Otherwise, the sentiments in the letter would have been vastly different! She knew she should write in reply but could not bring herself to do so.

Meg was also aware that his betrothal to Miss Penelope MacDonald had been announced. He had obviously accepted his fate and she tried not to dwell on the thought that, before long, he would more than likely be treating the memory of the time he had spent with her merely as a pleasant interlude. Just as she had urged him to do! But the thought that he might forget her was impossible to acknowledge. She would always cling to the belief that he still wanted her, and loved her, just as she loved him. No, she amended, she did not want him to love her quite as much as she loved him. For if he loved her that dearly, he would be as unhappy as she. And she wanted him to be happy.

Emily and her mother sometimes mentioned him, and she couldn't stop the colour from rushing to her cheeks and her hands from trembling whenever his name was spoken. But she had become adept at hiding her face at these times and was fairly confident that neither her mother nor her daughter suspected how much the mere mention of his name affected her or how much she was missing him, and when speaking about him, she was sure that she always managed to convey the impression that, whilst she remembered him fondly, she thought of him only as a man they had helped.

However, when she was confronted with Miss Penelope MacDonald arriving with her brother, her confusion and agitation was clear for all to see. Did Miss MacDonald know that Alex had stayed in her house? Why had she come and why was she with

Damien? Just the two of them. Why was she so beautiful? Would Alex be arriving soon as well? These were just a few of the questions and thoughts swirling around in her head.

She had no idea what she had said to them, but she must have acted as she should when greeting guests to her home, for Miss MacDonald was smiling and expressing her thanks for being welcomed so graciously after arriving unannounced and in such a state. Damien began to explain the situation, but Meg only grasped a small part of the story due to her perturbed state and so, when they entered the drawing room and Miss MacDonald was introduced to her mother and daughter, she tried to listen more carefully as the story was repeated for their benefit.

When their mother asked Damien why he had decided to visit them at this time, he dismissed the question, saying he would get to that later since what had happened to Miss MacDonald was much more urgent. He then described the account of Penelope's abduction and escape, ending with them meeting up in Selby. Emily was, as usual, full of questions, and when Alex's name was mentioned, she asked Damien how he was involved with the story. "Has my friend Lord Tenby been on some secret mission to rescue you?" she asked Penelope.

Meg immediately knew from the surprised look on Miss MacDonald's face that she knew nothing about Alex's visit or even that they had ever met. Meg, on the other hand, now knew that either she or her mother would have to explain about Alex's visit to them, something she had hoped to able to avoid.

Angry at Emily's interference, and feeling vulnerable at the same time, she shot a scathing look at her daughter. "Emily!" she exclaimed more sharply than she had intended. "Don't keep asking questions. I think you could be more useful by going to Alice, letting her know that we need to prepare a room for Miss MacDonald in addition to the one she is preparing for your uncle. If you wouldn't mind," she added more calmly.

"But I *would* mind, Mama. I want to hear more about this lady's adventure." Emily replied, unwilling to do her mother's bidding.

"Go!" said her grandmother imperiously. "You spoiled little minx. Do as your mother tells you for once."

Emily's face flushed with embarrassment at being reprimanded in front of a visitor, but it was obvious that she understood she had overstepped the mark, for she immediately rose from her chair and left the room.

"I didn't know you and my fiancé were acquainted, Lady Margaret," Penelope said, apparently without much interest. But at the mention of Alex, Meg's heart had lurched alarmingly.

She began to wring her hands together and tried to tell Penelope about his visit, but no words would come out, just a croak. Luckily her mother noticed her discomfort, and quickly came to her aid, answering the question herself.

"Oh yes," Ellen replied, "I'm surprised Lord Tenby hasn't mentioned his visit here. It was after he was injured, you know. Somehow, his horse brought him here. He was barely conscious, I believe." She then explained how they had called a physician and how he had left as soon as he was fit enough to travel to the nearest town.

Meg could tell that Penelope wanted to know more about this, and stepped in, suggesting that she take Miss MacDonald up to her room so that she could freshen up and perhaps see about a change of clothes. Penelope looked at Meg sharply for a moment but smiled her agreement and the two women departed.

Penelope's interest was now well and truly engaged. As they made their way upstairs, she had many questions she wanted answered. The fact that Alex had not mentioned the visit seemed particularly relevant. Why hadn't he mentioned it? Did it have anything to do with his change of heart towards her? Maybe it was not hearing rumours about her fast behaviour that had cooled his ardour, after all. Could it be that he preferred Damien's sister? Surely not. And yet....

Her thoughts were interrupted when Meg opened a door and invited her into what was obviously to be her room.

"You are all being so kind to me," Penelope said. 'Thank you so much for your hospitality. I don't know what I would have done if Da … I mean Lord Hawkeswood hadn't been at the inn. But I shall only stay for one night. Tomorrow I really should return to Hoddam Hall."

As Meg showed Penelope her room, they were both scrupulously polite to each other, but a certain reserve remained. Penelope had the feeling that Meg Greene didn't really like her, which may even be jealousy if indeed she had been attracted to Alex. Penelope was determined to discover the full story of Alex's visit to this house, and if, as she was coming to suspect, this woman and her Alex had been attracted to each other, perhaps they had even acted indiscreetly. Oh, how she hoped so! Then she would not feel so dreadful about her own transgressions!

Looking at Meg, Penelope could see only too clearly why men would find her attractive, what with her large breasts, an attribute always appealing to the male sex, she knew, and those gorgeous, auburn curls, her pale, clear skin and those beautiful dark grey eyes. Penelope wondered why she felt no jealousy towards this woman and realised it was because she did not love Alex and would willingly free him of his commitment to her in other circumstances. Unfortunately, Damien had made it abundantly clear that he did not want to marry her. Otherwise? No. There was no 'otherwise'! If Alex cried off now, she would be in real trouble.

Eventually, Meg left Penelope alone in the bedchamber while she went in search of a change of clothes, leaving Penelope alone. Sitting down on the only easy chair in the room which was a chaise longue, Penelope realised that she still felt a little weak and obviously hadn't fully recovered from her ordeal. She closed her eyes for a moment before glancing around her, noticing how pleasant the room was with its high ceiling and panelled walls, painted in pastel shades of pink, beige and grey. The carpet was thick under her feet, off white in colour and decorated lavishly with an Indian design. The furniture, on the other hand, didn't really suit the rest of the furnishings in her opinion, being made of oak and looking far too solid and heavy in such an elegantly decorated room. Looking at the bed, she saw that it too was old-fashioned, being a four-poster with an ornate canopy and heavy brocade curtains surrounding it. Penelope hoped it would be comfortable.

After a while, Meg returned with Alice in tow, carrying several day gowns for Penelope to select from. Alice told her she would be happy to alter the chosen dress as none would fit well enough due to the difference in bust size and in height, Penelope being the smaller of the two in both of those measurements.

"Oh, Lady Margaret, I can't allow you to alter your clothes for me," protested Penelope, "And just for one night. I can make do with this," she said, indicating her badly mended dress. The seamstress at the Fox and Hounds must have been the worst needlewoman in England, she surmised.

"I can and I will let you have one of my old gowns, Miss MacDonald. I haven't worn any of these for a long time, and probably never will again. I would be handing them on to some-one else anyway. And, after you have changed, Alice will do what she can with your own gown. She should be able to make enough repairs to make it presentable again."

After arguing against the suggestion for a little while longer, Penelope chose a high-necked, high waisted gown of pale blue spotted muslin with long sleeves. Meg left her with Alice and returned to the drawing room, where her mother, daughter and brother were catching up with the news from London.

Damien listened to his mother, who seemed to know a lot about the increasing crime rate in London, as she regaled them with reports of murderous assaults, arson and thefts being committed with alarming frequency, but Damien chose to play down the seriousness of the problem. After all, he was here to try to persuade Meg to agree to at least visit London later in the year. So, he waved away his mother's concerns, charming her and Emily with stories of the delights to be found at the theatres, and about a new museum that had been recently opened in Piccadilly by a Liverpool collector, a William Bullock, named the Egyptian Hall. The facade of the museum was very striking, he told them, with columns, statues and carvings all done in the Egyptian style. And inside, well, there were all manner of things to interest them. Mr Bullock's collection was quite spectacular, he assured them, and simply must be seen to be believed.

Meg returned in time to hear the end of Damien's glowing description of the delights to be found in the city. "What are you trying to do, Damien?" she asked with a scowl.

"He is telling us all about the marvellous things to be seen in London, Mama," Emily answered for him. "Oh, please may we go?"

Damien sat back, smiling at his success, and wasn't at all dismayed when Meg failed to agree with her daughter's request. Time was on his side, he mused, and Emily usually managed to get her own way in the end. Meg gave him a look that could kill, but still he smiled, raising his eyebrows at her obvious condemnation of his behaviour, looking as though he had no idea why she should frown at him so.

Instead of allowing him to continue, Meg deliberately changed the subject, asking how he had come to be acquainted with Miss MacDonald.

"The same way I am acquainted with most of the young debutantes," he replied calmly. "Through contact at the many balls, routs and soireés I was invited to throughout the Season."

"She must have been both surprised and pleased to see you at Selby," she ventured.

"You could say that," he said. "She has had a terrible experience and will probably suffer from it for quite some time. Being abducted is not something one could easily forget."

Ellen voiced her agreement, adding that she was lucky to have escaped physically unharmed. "At least she can go on with her life now. I expect her guardian will have received her note by this time. I'm sure he and Lord Tenby will be greatly relieved to know that she is safe."

"Yes. She intends to return to her home tomorrow, and I plan to escort her to ensure her safety. I have the hired barouche and driver to take us but think it would be better if Penelope was accompanied by a chaperone and hope you will be able to provide us with one."

"Is that why you brought her here rather than taking her straight back to Hoddam?" Meg asked him.

"Yes. Her reputation has to be my first concern. But I must admit I was also concerned about the chap who abducted her. I hope that by delaying her return they will have had sufficient time to deal with the fellow. Penelope told them about the fellow in her note, warning that Lord Tenby's life was in danger. Did you know that it was he who had shot Lord Tenby?" He could see the astonishment on all their faces, and added, "Yes, apparently he followed the earl after he had left the hall, having arranged the marriage settlement, and shot him."

"But Al....Lord Tenby was miles away from Hoddam Hall when he was shot," Meg interjected.

"Well, it seems the fellow lost him, then caught up with him again in Tadcaster and must have decided to ride ahead and wait in ambush for Lord Tenby to pass."

"And I thought he was shot by an enemy of the King!" exclaimed Emily in disgust.

Their thoughts were at that moment interrupted by the sound of a coach coming to a halt in the yard.

Emily ran to the window, turning to inform them that three people had alighted from the vehicle. Alex, a fat man, and an older, very regal-looking lady. "Oh no!" Meg cried out.

Damien stood and looked at Meg in concern, seeing she had gone as white as a sheet, but he was also feeling shocked by this development. Why had they rushed here so quickly? Emily ran past him, clearly intent on being the first to welcome her friend Alex back to her home.

Alex was looking up at Wharfe House when he saw and heard Emily. She ran down the steps, passed Jed, and hugged Alex round his waist, crying, "I knew you would come back. I just knew it."

Alex laughed at her exuberance, saying, "Well, someone is pleased to see me again, at least." He turned to his mother and Lord Frome, adding, "This is Miss Emily Greene, Lady Margaret's daughter, in case you haven't guessed. Let me go, you little imp," he said, gently disentangling Emily's arms from around his body.

She stood back reluctantly but was clearly still excited as she smiled up adoringly at Alex, who, in turn, smiled down at her affectionately before addressing her again. "And Emily, I'd like you to meet my mother, Lady Wilde, and the Most Honourable, the Marquess of Frome."

This time, Emily's manners didn't let her down and she shyly curtsied before the two eminent visitors.

"You may have guessed why we are here, Emily. I understand Miss MacDonald is with you."

"Oh yes, she is, and she has had such an adventure. Wait until you hear about it," she replied, pulling him by the hand and leading him quickly into the house. The others followed at a more sedate pace.

"How is Miss MacDonald?" he asked Jed, who was approaching him to escort the visitors to the drawing room.

"She is well, my lord," Jed replied, "No need to worry. She's just had a shock, that's all." Alex said how relieved he was to hear that and then enquired after Jed's health and that of the other members of the household. Jed assured him all were well.

"No need to see us inside, Jed. Emily will show us the way. I would appreciate it if you would see to the servants though. My mother's maid is still in the coach and will need to rest and be given some refreshments as well as the coachman and footman of course. If you would also show Isaac, the coachman, where he can water the horses, I would be obliged. We won't be staying long, just enough time to rest the horses, then we'll be on our way again."

"Of course, Lord Tenby. And, if I may say so, it is nice to see you again, and looking so well." He hesitated a moment as though he wanted to say something more, before heading off to deal with the three servants.

Inside the drawing room, the atmosphere was strained. Alex noticed that Meg was looking very anxious, and decided to behave as though there was nothing between them, even so far as addressing her and her mother formally. What he really wanted to do was gather her up in his arms and carry her off to some place they could be alone to comfort each other. But that was impossible.

Meg did not rise to greet him, a false smile on her ashen face, and so he and Damien took over the job of making the introductions. Alex noted that Penelope was not in the room and wondered again if she was all right. He dearly wanted to have a private word with her about her ordeal as well as to discuss the parts played by Stanley and Meg's brother, but his concern was mainly for Meg, who had clearly not recovered yet from the shock of seeing him again. Oh God, I shouldn't have come, he thought. Yet, at the same time, to see her again was wonderful; a dream come true.

His mother, Prue, went immediately to sit beside Ellen; Lord Frome was shown to the seat vacated by Damien; Alex and Damien sat on the second sofa, and Emily squeezed next to Alex, looking up at him in adoration.

"I hope we haven't put you out, Mrs Searle," Prue was saying to Ellen, obviously assuming she was the head of the household. "But, as you know, this isn't a social call, even though I am so pleased to be able to thank you all in person for taking care of my son during his time of need. And it seems that my family is, once again, in your debt. Thanks to you, Lord Hawkeswood," she added, turning briefly to address Damien. "What dear Penelope would have done if you hadn't been at the inn at Selby, I shudder to think. She must have been in quite a state after such a dreadful ordeal. How she ended up in Selby, so far from her home, I have yet to fully understand, but I am just thankful that you were there to help her.

"Anyway, the reason we came here, rather than just waiting at Hoddam as Penelope suggested in her note, is because I insisted on bringing her some fresh clothes to travel in and thought it best if she had me to chaperone her on the return journey. I didn't think it right to put you to any more trouble. Then Alex said he would escort me, and Lord Frome insisted it was his place, as her guardian, to go to her if anyone was going. So here we are. I hasten to add that we have arranged to stay in Tadcaster overnight so please don't think we have all landed on you expecting to stay. Fortunately, it didn't turn out to be a market day, or we might have had no alternative but to impose on your hospitality even further. But luckily there was no problem. Where is the girl, by the way?"

"Up ... upstairs with Alice, my housekeeper," Meg replied, her voice a little croaky and unsteady, Alex noted. "They are altering one of my gowns." She then jumped up as though she had come to a sudden decision. "But of course, you must be anxious to see her. If you would like to come with me, Lady Wilde, I will take you to see Miss MacDonald and then Emily and I will see to some refreshments. You must all be tired after your journey."

Prudence willingly acquiesced to this suggestion and Emily and the two women left the room together, leaving the others to discuss the events of the past four days, sharing their thoughts and experiences.

Lord Frome began by relating his side of the story. He told them that after receiving the note from Penelope, late on the night that Penelope had arrived in Selby, he and Alex had called off the search informing the men only that his ward had sent word that she was safe with friends. Stanley had then been sent for, only to find that he had disappeared. Neither he nor Alex had doubted Penelope's word, but Lord Frome voiced his amazement that such a trusted servant, one who had always seemed such a level-headed, quiet man, could be capable of such wickedness.

Alex then took over the story, telling them how, at Lord Frome's suggestion, he had ridden over with a servant to see Stanley's mother the following morning, finding she knew nothing except that she had been concerned about her son for quite a while. Apparently, he had been suffering from violent mood swings for some time, but that during the search he had been quite elated. When he had been home, that is. She informed Alex how he had only returned for food, spending the rest of his time with the search parties. Night and day. When she was told that the search had been called off sometime during the previous evening, she seemed surprised, but then began to share their concern for her son's safety.

Lord Frome interrupted at this point. "While Lord Tenby was visiting Stanley's mother, I got on with organising a search party for the man, stressing to the searchers that Stanley might be dangerous. Most of the searchers know Stanley well, you understand, and must have been shocked by this pronouncement. They had already heard about Stanley's disappearance, of course, but had decided that he must have suffered an accident.

"I told them that I had good reasons to warn them to be careful, suggesting that Stanley may have suffered a mental breakdown, adding that when they found him, he was to be locked up securely and guarded. They still looked sceptical but promised to take my warning seriously and to follow my instructions. One man informed me that he had seen Stanley head off alone to the South of the estate the day before, carrying what looked like his provisions for the day. So, those searching for Stanley also headed South. Hopefully, by the time we return, he will have been found."

Alex then listened as Damien gave a full account of Penelope's ordeal as it had been related to him, leaving out the reasons for her abduction and the fact that she had gone out to meet Stanley the morning of her disappearance, merely mentioning the friendship between Penelope and Mrs Thorpe, Stanley's mother, leaving Lord Frome and Alex to draw their own conclusions. He ended with their decision to send the note to her guardian.

"Damned lucky to find a friend in Selby," observed Lord Frome. "But it seems to me the chit needs to be spoken to about her foolish behaviour. What on earth was she about to go off on her own so early in the morning?"

"As to that, I cannot say," replied Damien. "Probably just for a walk? But she is still considerably shaken, as you can well imagine. I should not be too harsh on her if I were you. I think she will have already learned to take more care in future. The main thing, I think you will agree, is to catch this Stanley and hand him over to the authorities."

"Well, hopefully when we return tomorrow, we shall be able to do that. As to sparing Penelope a scolding, I shall take your advice, Hawkeswood. Never did like that side of being a guardian. If she has acted foolishly, I expect it was probably my fault for leaving her alone too much, and not replacing her governess when that lady resigned. But Penelope talked me out of it. Shouldn't have listened to her, I dare say, but she seemed to enjoy her life at the hall. Didn't know anything about her friendship with Mrs Thorpe though."

"I'm sure you have nothing to blame yourself for," Alex remarked. "Penelope always speaks of you with affection, and I know she is grateful to you for your care of her. And my mother thought her a very well brought up girl. Quite the pick of the bunch, she told me."

"Why, thank you, Alex. It is kind of you to say so. But now, Alex? After all that has happened, are you still of the same mind about my ward? What do you think now?"

"Well, I think there is now even more reason to hasten the wedding ceremony. I know you weren't too keen on the idea when I asked you about it before, but there may be some gossip resulting from all of this, and I, for one, think we should give them something else to talk about." He said this as positively as he could, while feeling that he was signing his own death warrant. But he knew he could not cry off now, or Penelope would be ruined. The pundits would have a field day should their engagement be broken off if details of such an escapade ever reached the public. While he was tempted to take this opportunity, the only one that was likely to present itself to him, he could not do so. Now, more than ever, he felt that his fate was sealed.

"Good man. Knew I could count on you the minute I met you. And I agree with you," Claude said. "I believe a quiet wedding here in Yorkshire is advisable, with few guests, if any. Afterwards, we can host a larger affair to celebrate the nuptials. What do you think to my idea?"

Alex hated the idea but could see no reason to object to this proposal, except that it would break his heart. And so he agreed. The two then began discussing the arrangements, leaving Damien looking decidedly dejected.

After taking Lady Wilde upstairs to see Penelope, Meg left them to speak privately while she, Alice and Emily headed to the kitchens to prepare refreshments. Meg did her best to remain calm, concentrating on the task at hand as best she could, but couldn't do anything about her nervous state. She kept wondering what the others were talking about, dreading what she was going to hear and praying that this ordeal would soon be over. Damien joined them, needing to speak with the driver of the barouche, who was enjoying the hospitality provided in the kitchen, explaining to him that his services would no longer be required, and that he could return to Selby whenever he was ready. He then persuaded Meg to return with him to join the others.

Prue and Penelope descended the stairs just as the refreshments were being served in the drawing room, and Meg forced herself to smile at them in greeting. While doing a creditable job of acting as hostess, inside Meg wanted nothing so much as to disappear completely, feeling that she would be unable to bear the pretence of accepting the betrothal of Alex and Penelope with smiles and platitudes, while her heart was breaking all over again. She was afraid that she would be unable to hide her feelings for long and hoped they would leave quickly.

Her wish was granted, despite Emily's attempt to persuade Alex to remain longer. By this time, Meg was trembling from the effort to keep herself under control, but as she waved them off, the tears she had been holding back broke free, and Damien had to support her as she sobbed on his shoulder.

"Well, fancy breaking down like that," Prue remarked as the coach drew away from the house, "Why would Lady Margaret be so upset at our departure?" But, as she turned to Penelope, she saw that she, too, had succumbed to a fit of tears. "Well, what a pair you two are, to be sure. Come, my dear, rest on me. You, at least, have good reason to cry. After such an ordeal. There there, my dear. Everything is going to be all right." For some reason, those soothing words just made Penelope cry even more.

Chapter Twenty

<hr>

"**N**ow Meg, I'd like you to tell me how things are between you and Lord Tenby," Damien said later that evening.

After the departure of Penelope, Lord Frome and the rest of his party, Damien had comforted Meg until she was able to control her tears, only then returning to the drawing room while she went to her room to wash her face. He didn't see her again until they met with the family for dinner, but he was determined to see her alone as soon as he could to find out why she had been so upset.

At dinner, he had watched her closely, but it was his mother, Ellen, and his niece who did most of the talking. Emily had also been upset to see Lord Tenby leave and complained about his lack of interest in her and her conversation. Unfortunately for her, no-one showed her any real sympathy, her grievances largely falling on deaf ears. Ellen was more concerned to discover the reason for Damien's unexpected arrival. He assured them that he was not in debt but that he had lately come to realise that, as head of the family, he should become more involved with his family's affairs.

Having caught their attention, he went on to outline his proposal in a straightforward way and was not surprised to find that it was met with a good deal of resistance. Except from Emily, who expressed her view that it a splendid idea for them all to live together, somewhere near to London, where she could see all the marvellous sights and visit the Egyptian Hall and the Exeter 'Change menagerie, which was home to tigers and other exotic beasts. They talked at length, and by the time Emily was taken up to bed, Meg and Ellen had promised to consider the matter.

Damien carried Ellen to her bedchamber shortly after the customary evening cup of tea had been consumed, but not before making sure that Meg would wait for his return. He could see she was agitated when he re-joined her, and sat beside her on the sofa, taking her hand before he repeated his request for her to explain her relationship with the Earl of Tenby.

"I don't think it's any of your concern," Meg responded tartly, removing her hand from his. "I am grateful for your comfort, Damien, but would rather not talk about it if you don't mind."

"But I do mind, Meg. You see, when you allowed your feelings to show so clearly, it was obvious to me that you care for Tenby more than you, perhaps, should."

"Yes, well, you have not exactly led a blameless life, have you, Damien? So, if I have made a fool of myself over someone, please leave me to cope with it by myself. You can rest assured I will not disgrace the family any more than I have done already, if that is what is concerning you."

"Please let me finish, Meg. I was about to confess that I, also, have fallen for someone I cannot have. So, believe me when I tell you that I understand what you are going through. And, please, my dear, do not talk about disgracing the family name. Father did that for us, all on his own. I only lived up to expectations. It was dear Lucas who committed the *coup de grâce* when he accused you of adultery. You are, and have always been, completely blameless. I know that, and now all of London is aware of the true facts."

Meg picked up on the word "now". "Now? What do you mean by 'now'? Don't tell me that the gossipmongers are still raking over that old story!"

Damien then had to explain to Meg about Alex visiting him in London, telling her about the unsavoury gossip linking her name with several other men over the years, and all the two had done to redeem her good name.

Meg looked stunned, aghast, and dismayed in equal measure at hearing of this development. "But this is terrible," she cried, putting her head in her hands. "All these years, I have assumed that by choosing to live quietly away from the gossips, my name and my story would slowly fade and hopefully eventually be forgotten. Instead, the opposite has happened. My absence has only caused further scandal, and nobody saw fit to tell me about it. Jed must have known something and spoken to Alex, who had heard about it, and yet, between them, I have been completely kept in the dark. And that makes me furious!"

Damien felt that he was not handling this as well as he should but didn't know what he could have said differently. "I can see how angry you are, Meg, but Alex was only acting in your best interest. Any anyway, thanks to him, it is over now," Damien assured her.

Meg stayed silent for a long time, obviously thinking through this new development. "Is that why you want me to return to London?" she said eventually.

Damien was glad she had chosen to concentrate on the future instead of the past, and that she had seemed to calm down. He took her hand and smiled at her. "In part, yes, it is," he replied. "Lady Wilde will befriend you and I know of several others who will. You mustn't dwell on what happened when you visited London after Lucas' death. This time, you will be welcomed. I promise you things will be different, Meg. And think of Emily. She needs to mix with others of her rank and age."

"Think of Emily?" Meg cried, snatching her hand back. "Think of Emily? I have done nothing but think of Emily. If I didn't have Emily to think of, Alex and I would have become lov...." She stopped, evidently aware of what she had nearly blurted out.

"Have become lovers, I think you were going to say," Damien finished for her. "Thank you, Meg. You have just answered all the questions I have wanted to ask about the relationship between you and Alex. But before you tell me to mind my own business again, I will confide to you that it is Penelope who has captured my heart, but, quite rightly, she rejected me in favour of Alex. So, you see, we are both losers."

"Oh Damien, I am so sorry," Meg said, grasping his hand. "It was because of the gossip about me that caused her to reject you, wasn't it?"

"Oh no, Meg, don't take the blame for that as well. I keep telling you, you are the blameless one. No, I have no reason to blame anyone but father and myself. If I had accepted the commission you offered to buy for me - assuming I had survived, of course - maybe I would have been a little better placed to win her hand, but I am my own worst enemy. Instead of trying to live honourably, I did the opposite, only confirming what Society thought of me. But then, even as a youngster, I had never been inclined to live a virtuous life, preferring to spend my time seducing pretty girls. It is a wonder the local area was not littered with my bastard sons!"

"And are you sure it isn't?" Meg asked, horrified at the very idea that her brother could have acted so dishonourably.

"Apparently not, or father would have heard of it, to be sure. To be fair to myself, I mostly confined my amorous exploits to those who already had a reputation for being more than willing."

"And have you never been in love before?"

"Not really, though I remember thinking myself in love with the daughter of one of the tenants in my youth," he added with a wry smile.

"What happened?"

Damien then proceeded to tell her how he had "fallen in love" at first sight with this girl and had met her secretly on several occasions before one day being discovered by her father in a most compromising situation. "Father was furious with me and forbade me to see the girl again. I think he made things sweet with the girl's father by paying him off. I remember sulking for a long time, believing myself heartbroken. I even tried to see her again, but her family made sure that didn't happen."

"Do you know what happened to her?"

Damien shrugged. "Oh, she married sometime later, I heard, and I assume she is happy with her lot. After that, I confined myself to those who were more than willing. But of all my sins," he continued after a pause, "my greatest was marrying you to Lucas, knowing what he was like, and not telling you."

Meg looked at her brother in a new light. She could tell he had not revealed the full truth about his youthful infatuation to her, but understood how badly he must have been hurt at the time. Perhaps that was how he came to adopt the "devil-may-care" attitude to life which he always seemed to exhibit. Yet, underneath, he was just as vulnerable as she.

He had made mistakes, to be sure, but then, who hasn't? Especially in their youth. He had been young when their father had taken his own life leaving Damien to sort out the mess associated with his lost inheritance. And she refused to accept that he had betrayed her when allowing her to marry his friend, aware that she had been only too willing to marry Lucas, believing at the time that, by doing so, she was helping her family whilst gaining happiness for herself.

But she did blame him for not accepting her offer of an army commission and was pleased to hear that he was beginning to acknowledge that he may have made a mistake by doing so. She also put equal blame on them both for not talking so openly about their thoughts and dreams before.

"Damien, I married Lucas because I wanted to and because I felt I could be happy with him. And I do not regret marrying him, because without the marriage I would not have Emily, and she is the joy of my life. But I wish you and I had talked with each other like this before. You have been carrying a great burden and are not nearly as devil-may-care as you would have me believe. I think we should have made the effort to get to know one another better long before now."

"Yes, I agree with you that this conversation is long overdue, but, you see, I was so ashamed of what I did to you. You may forgive me for what I did, but I cannot, for I allowed you to be the sacrificial lamb. I traded your happiness for money and every time I looked at you, I felt guilty, which is not a pleasant feeling, I can assure you. And so, I stayed away and led my debauched life, leaving you to rot in Yorkshire and only visiting you when I was forced to. I can't tell you how grateful I was when you arranged for me to see your agent for funds instead of coming here to beg.

"But all that is in the past, ever since Tenby made me see that I had been acting selfishly and stupidly. Called me out, if you must know, or threatened to, anyway. But then, he was prepared to call out the whole of London to redeem your good name! By gad! That means that he loves you as well!" Damien then burst out laughing.

"What's so funny? I can't find anything to laugh at in this whole mess."

Damien sobered. "I'm sorry, but don't you see? It just struck me what a farce this is turning out to be. Unfortunately, in this case, there seems no hope of a happy ending. But the elements of a farce are all there, nevertheless. I love Penelope. Penelope says she loves me. You love Tenby and he loves you!"

"Penelope loves *you*?"

"Yes, I can see why you should doubt me, yet I can assure you she has told me so on several occasions."

"But... but that means... means that Alex and Penelope don't love each other! Oh, how dreadful. Their marriage will be one of convenience only, as so many are, but with the added problem of them loving elsewhere. Are either of them aware of it, do you think?"

"I doubt it. Do you think we should tell them?"

Meg did not think that question deserved an answer, saying instead, "I can't come to London, Damien. I couldn't bear to see him again. I felt like dying today. If it were not for Emily, I know I would rather die than face life without him. But don't ask me to be there when they marry. When they have children. It would be intolerable."

"Then you have already chosen death before life, Meg. You have buried yourself already."

"But I plan to live in Bath when Emily is older. Gain acceptance there. Then I shall do what I must for Emily."

"All right. Let's talk about Emily and what is best for her. Let's forget our own unhappiness. Emily is nearly ten. She needs more than you can give her here, Meg. You must see that. She would be better off if you lived in a manner befitting your status. I really am ready to fulfil my obligations as head of the family, even if you find it hard to believe. If you bought an estate in one of the home counties, I am convinced we would all be happier. You wouldn't have to come to town if you didn't want to. Emily should be with her whole family, should have friends of her own, a governess, trips to town. All the things others of her class have. Please consider it, Meg. But not tonight. I think we both need a dreamless sleep after all we have been through today, don't you?"

* * *

Meanwhile, at the inn in Tadcaster, Penelope was finding sleep impossible. Too many thoughts were tormenting her. She knew she did not love Alex, and now she was sure that Alex did not love her. She had noticed the way he had looked at Meg. And Meg had clearly been disturbed by Alex's presence. Her suspicions had proved to be correct. Alex had changed his mind about marrying her after his stay with Meg and her family. By closing her ears to his protests and insisting that their betrothal be confirmed she now found herself coming between two people in love.

But what to do about it? Her guardian and Alex had told her about their plans to proceed with a rushed wedding designed to counter the inevitable gossip about her disappearance. They were intending to visit the registry in the morning before leaving Tadcaster to procure a license so that she and Alex could marry quickly and quietly without the need for banns to be called in the local parish church near Hoddam Hall.

She had to stop it. Even though she knew it would ruin her in the eyes of society, she could not do it. But she knew they would not listen to her, and she feared her resolve would weaken when they explained the necessity of an early wedding to her. How could she stand firm against such a logical solution?

As the hours ticked by, she wrestled with her conscience She tried to imagine what her life with Alex would be like, comparing it to what her life might be like if she refused to marry him. She knew she would be foolish not to marry him. Marrying him would be the only way to protect her reputation. Marrying him would also provide her with a title, with wealth, with security and with children. Without him, she would only have a small income from her father's estate and an even smaller income left to her by her aunt - she was sure Lord Frome would not help her out if she chose to go against his wishes, for why should he? He was only a distant relative, after all. But then, she was only Miss MacDonald. Why should she expect to be treated like an aristocrat?

Surely, she could be happy living in the simple cottage in Enfield which her aunt had left her? She had been happy there and had been made welcome by the local community. London society would reject her but so what? Living in Enfield wouldn't be such a bad life.

And maybe, there would be a young man willing to marry her if she decided she wanted children.

But unfortunately, she knew that she didn't really have the option of being independent. At least, not yet. She was underage and in the care of her guardian. He would never permit her to go back to Enfield to live on her own, even if she agreed to hire a companion. So, what was she to do? She could not return to Hoddam Hall. Stanley was there. Shame was there. She would be forced to marry Alex when he wanted another. It was all so wrong.

The more she thought about everything, the more she realised that she had to get away. She couldn't face Alex or her guardian. She needed a plan, eventually deciding that she would have to leave the inn as soon as Alex and Lord Frome set out to obtain the marriage licence on the pretext that she needed some ribbons or a book; pawn or sell some of the jewellery Lady Wilde had thought to bring her which included the pearls Alex had given her and her mother's brooch, which alone was worth a pretty penny, giving her the necessary funds to manage on her own for a while, including to buy a ticket on the London Stage.

She realised that leaving the inn to board the coach may pose some problems since she would be on her own, but there were others who were staying at the inn for the purpose of catching the coach, and perhaps she could pretend she was with one of them. If successful, she could make an excuse to leave the coach at Enfield where her friend, Amanda, lived. She had often visited with Amanda's family in the past and remembered that they had expressed the hope that she would return one day to stay with them. Amanda was the same age as herself, and she knew she and her family still lived in Enfield, because the two girls corresponded regularly.

Lord Frome would probably not think of looking for her there as he would likely assume that she had travelled to London. But eventually, she knew that if, or when she was found, she would have to go to Bath, to Celia. She knew Celia would not welcome her with open arms but was equally sure that she would not be thrown into the street! Enough time should have passed by the time she was found to ensure that she would not have to marry Alex, and she could beg Celia to shelter her if Lord Frome refused to release her from his guardianship. With her reputation in tatters, she should be safe from any unwanted suitors, and she doubted that Lord Frome would force her to marry someone else against her wishes. He was too nice a person to do that.

Deciding that the plan had enough a chance of success to make it worthwhile trying, she began to write letters to both Alex and Lord Frome, explaining the reasons for her actions, and begging them not to follow her. She would have to leave the notes with the landlord before taking the stagecoach south, hoping that he would follow her instructions and not hand over the letters before she was well on her way. The stage left at ten o'clock, and she would just have to pray that the two men were kept occupied for as long as possible.

Chapter Twenty-One

"Where the devil is she?" Alex asked as he paced the floor in exasperation. "We were hoping to be well on our way by this time. What on earth could she be buying that would take her this long?" he asked his mother. "She should never have been allowed to go shopping on her own."

"I agree with you, Alex, but I wasn't down when she left as I have already told you. I heard about it from the landlord's wife who informed me that Penelope had left here very early, saying she had a few personal items of clothing to buy. Goodness knows what, considering all the things I brought for her as well as the shoes and other necessaries that Lord Hawkeswood paid for when he took her shopping in Selby. Perhaps you had better go and have another look for her. She can't have gone far."

"Lord Hawkeswood took Penelope shopping and paid for everything? You should have told me, Mother. But I'll have to deal with that later. Penelope's current whereabouts are presently of more concern. Neither I nor Lord Frome caught any sight of her when we were out this morning. And anyway, as you say, there seems to be little reason for her to have gone shopping in the first place. I tell you, Mother, I'm beginning to get worried."

Lord Frome listened to Alex and Lady Wilde discussing the problem and nodded his agreement. "I am also beginning to wonder what has happened to the silly chit. I think I had better have a word with the landlord," he said, "Perhaps his wife could tell us more than she already has."

He stood with some difficulty, huffing and puffing as he did so, encumbered both by his weight and his gout, which was beginning to trouble him again. He left the parlour and leaned on the counter in the taproom waiting to attract the attention of a passing servant. Luckily, Betty, the landlord's wife, appeared as if on cue, and he asked her if she could add anything to what she had told Lady Wilde earlier about Miss MacDonald's whereabouts.

"Well, as I said, she went out early, saying she was going shopping. The only other thing I can tell you is that she briefly returned with a large shopping bag, went to her room, and then went out again, saying she had forgotten something. I don't think that could be important, though, could it? I remember suggesting that she leave the shopping bag in her room or with me, but she said she was in too much of a hurry and that she'd be all right. Seems a bit strange to me, now I come to think about it, but it wasn't my place to question the young lady's behaviour, now was it?"

"What time was it when she left the second time?"

"I can't rightly remember. I am busy at that time of a morning, seeing people off on the stage. Oh, yes, she went out at the same time as those boarding the stagecoach for Selby. Must have been just before ten. Always leaves on time, does the coach. My husband was outside, now I come to think on it, helping the guests with their luggage. Proper hectic it is when the coach comes. But perhaps he'll have seen which way she went. Shall I ask him?"

"Yes, if you wouldn't mind. That would be most helpful. I'll be in the parlour, awaiting his answer."

Claude was looking both confused and worried when he returned to Prue and Alex. "I'm afraid to think what she is up to," he confessed. "Apparently, she returned with some shopping and then went out again almost immediately. Prudence, my dear, were you down before ten?"

"Yes, I was. But I didn't see her. I was in here, eating breakfast. I wonder what made her go out again?"

At that moment, Betty came rushing into the room, bearing two letters. "Oh my goodness, you'd better read these," she said breathlessly, holding out the letters. "Howard's just given them to me. They're from Miss MacDonald, addressed to you two gentlemen. Howard says she got on the coach and asked him to hand them to you just before you left."

"What!" bellowed Lord Frome. "Give them to me immediately. Why in heaven's name didn't your husband see fit to give them to us straight away? It should have been obvious to anyone that something was amiss."

"Well, that's what I told him, but he says how was he to know different. She was in the company of Mr and Mrs Lennox, and he just assumed that we knew she was going."

"With Mr and Mrs Lennox? We don't know a Mr and Mrs Lennox! She couldn't have had any luggage with her either. She had very few clothes with her. Never mind why. Why did your husband not notice that she was setting off without any luggage?"

"As to that, you need to appreciate that things get a bit hectic like at coach time, like I told you. The boys do most of the loading of luggage. Howard would just have assumed she had luggage with her. Why would he think otherwise?" she said, sounding defensive.

Alex saw her square her shoulders and realised Lord Frome had upset the woman. "Could I see the letter addressed to me," he asked the landlord's wife quietly.

Claude looked at Alex and calmed down enough to request the letter addressed to himself. "Well, yes, I suppose you are right. The answer will no doubt be here, in these letters. I hope I can rely on you to keep this matter confidential?" he said to Betty, taking out a five-pound note and handing it to her.

She almost snatched it from him. "Of course, milord, and thank you. Howard and me, we're very discreet. You can count on us to say nowt." With those words, she backed out of the room, clutching the five-pound note to her bosom.

With Prudence looking on, Lord Frome and Alex proceeded to read their letters in silence, both with deadly earnest expressions on their faces.

Alex couldn't believe what he was reading.

Dear Lord Tenby,

I am releasing you from our engagement. I know you had changed your mind about me some while ago and I should never have accepted your proposal in the first place. Please forgive me for making you unhappy. If we married, we would both have regretted it. But I have had to leave as I could not face you and Lord Frome in person. This way, you won't have to pretend you want me to change my mind.

Thank you for doing me the honour of asking for my hand in marriage. I shall always have fond memories of our time together. But I know you love another, and I confess to you that I, also, love someone else. However, I ask you not to mention this to Lord Frome or anyone else and trust I can count on your discretion.

Please do not try to stop me. It will only cause more scandal and end up harming us both. I am so sorry for all the trouble I have caused.

Penelope

In her letter to her guardian, Penelope had thanked Lord Frome for taking care of her so kindly and so generously, apologising for appearing to be ungrateful by running away. She was not ungrateful, she vowed, but felt she had no alternative except to run. Otherwise, she would have had to marry Lord Tenby, and that she couldn't do, telling him she had explained why in the accompanying note to Alex.

She informed Lord Frome that she was intending to head to Bath as soon as she reached London, hoping to stay with Cousin Celia, adding that she would then stay with her cousin until she could persuade him to end his guardianship of her. It would be best for them both, she assured him, saying that, as soon as she was able, she intended to move into the home bequeathed to her by her late aunt and live on the money left to her by her parents and her aunt. She neither wanted, nor expected anything more from him. She asked that he not try to stop her, saying that such action would only cause more gossip, hurting everyone.

Please don't feel I have betrayed your trust, she begged him in her concluding paragraph, *for I know the debt I owe to you. I tried to live as you wished me to do but am not prepared to marry Lord Tenby. I am sorry to be such a burden to you but hope that you will forgive me eventually. It is better this way for all of us, of that I am sure. Penelope.*

"Well, if she wanted to make a point, she certainly knew how to do it," Claude said, handing the letter to Prudence to read. "But of course, we must get her back. If she really thinks she can head off to Bath, then go to live in Enfield all on her own, then the silly chit has less sense than I credited her with. Does she really think she can get her parents' or her aunt's money? She is only eighteen and doesn't get control of her inheritance until she is twenty-one or until she marries, whichever is the sooner. The usual sort of provisions. Doesn't she realise that? Doesn't she realise that I couldn't end the guardianship even if I wanted to?"

Prue looked up from reading the letter. "She must be feeling very unhappy. It seems to me that she has tried to live up to what she believes others want for her, even though her heart lies elsewhere. The poor girl. What did she say to you, Alex?" she asked.

Alex folded his letter and put it in his pocket. "Later, Mother. The priority now is to find her and bring her back."

"Exactly," Lord Frome added. "She must be stopped. Will you go, Alex? She obviously doesn't realise how slow stagecoaches are, rarely managing to go more than four miles in an hour. Besides, she will have to change coaches in Selby, I think, and will have to wait for the coach from York to arrive, which should slow her down even more. You can easily overtake her on horseback if you travel across country, even though she has nearly a two-hour start on you. I shall make sure that I hire the fittest and fastest horse the landlord has in his stables for you. But I'm afraid we had better forget the wedding. For now, anyway. I shall have to accept her decision, silly though I think it. A pity, I would have welcomed having you into my family. She certainly won't find a better man."

"Thank you," replied Alex, still shocked by Penelope's actions and words, "I had better make a start immediately. But I won't intercept a moving coach. Far too dramatic, that would be. I would prefer to take my time and aim to meet the York coach when it arrives in Doncaster and quietly explain the facts to her. As soon as she knows that we are not going to press her into this marriage, I am sure she will agree to return to your care. I assume you will be heading back to Hoddam Hall?"

"Yes," Lord Frome confirmed. "I think it best if your mother and I return there as planned. And since it will not be possible for your mother to act as chaperone, I would like you to hire a chaperone to accompany Penelope on the way back if you can. We don't want any further speculation."

Alex nodded. "And if you don't mind, I shall make a quick detour back to Lady Margaret's home to repay Damien the money he spent on Penelope. It should not cause too much of a delay and needs to be done."

"A good idea, Alex. It does need to be done and I'll be glad if you will see to it for me. I don't like feeling indebted to anyone. A pity we didn't think to discuss it while we were all together. But I'll pay of course, both for what you give to Hawkeswood, and for any expenses you incur. You no longer have that right, you know," he added with a smile.

* * *

While Alex made his way across country on his way to Meg's home, he was reminded of a similar journey he had taken which had ended with him getting shot by Stanley. A journey that had led him to Meg.

Alex wondered what Meg's reaction would be when she learned he was now free to offer her marriage. Would she still refuse him? Yes, he was sure she would offer up all sorts of reasons for rejecting him again. But this time, she would meet with more resistance. He had no intention of allowing her to wallow in exile any longer. Somehow, he would persuade her to become his wife.

Meg's daughter, Emily, was fond of him, and had even suggested the match, so she would not object to having him as a new father. A father! There was a thought. But, on reflection, he had to admit he quite liked the idea!

Meg's mother would likely offer him her support as well. He knew from the time he had spent in their house that Lady Hawkeswood, or Mrs Searle as she preferred to be called, wanted a more fitting home and a better life for her daughter and granddaughter. Meg would like Knopton Manor, he was certain. And Alice and Jed would also be offered a home on the estate if they wanted one, enabling them to continue to serve Meg in any capacity she and they desired. Oh yes, things were going to be different now.

And Damien? Could he become a problem? Alex wondered what his reaction would be. Why had he travelled to Yorkshire at this time? Was he in debt again or was he there to tell Meg of his recent efforts on her behalf?

Alex also gave some thought to Penelope and her note to him. She had mentioned that she loved another. But who? Not Stanley, that was sure. Someone in Yorkshire or someone in London? In London, he decided. He recalled the first time he danced with her, remembering that she had looked around as though she wanted a particular person to notice her. Could it be that she had decided to use Alex to make someone jealous?

Even Damien had admitted to being attracted to her, he remembered and no doubt there were many others. Someone had obviously captured her heart, but why then did she accept *his* proposal? The man she loved must not love her. Either that or was not suitable. Or available! He made up his mind to find out who this man was and see if he could help out in any way.

Meg's house was only a few miles south from Tadcaster and soon he could see the isolated white building looking very picturesque, bathed as it was in the morning sunshine, surrounded by gently rolling green hills and fields, with stands of trees adding interest to the view and with the river flowing gently past its eastern boundary. As he approached the bridge across the River Wharfe, he noticed a man on horseback coming towards him. He soon recognised that the lone rider was Damien.

After greeting each other, Damien turned his horse and the pair set off towards the house. Alex could see that Damien was surprised by his unexpected second visit, and quickly explained what had happened to Penelope.

"I'm glad you thought of coming to me first," was Damien's surprising response to hearing this news. "If you don't mind, I should like to accompany you to Doncaster. I think I could help."

"Well, I would be happy to have you come with me and am sure it would be better for two men to meet Penelope, rather than just one. I shall hire a woman to attend her, of course, as soon as we reach there, but gossip can start so easily, as you know. I must admit, it is a ticklish situation. Why she had to make matters worse than they already were by running away I'll never understand. Am I such an ogre?"

"She is young, Alex. She must have thought it easier just to disappear and leave you a note. I shall have a few things to say to her, I can tell you. You are sure she will be on the coach to London?"

"Yes, the landlord saw her leave on the connecting coach, and she stated that she was heading for London in her notes. We shall be waiting for her. I wonder if she is suspecting that I might be there? She must know by now that I could easily catch up with her. I expect she is feeling really frustrated by the slow pace of the stage. As to you speaking to her about her behaviour, I can only say that I wish I could hand over the responsibility to you, but I'm afraid that I shall have to do the honours! It is not your concern, Damien. Unless …" Alex stopped what he had been going to say, certain that his sudden suspicion could not be correct. No, Damien had taken her under his wing when he rescued her and now feels responsible. That must be it.

"Unless?" Damien prompted.

Alex shook his head. "Nothing. I don't really understand why you wish to go with me at all but will be glad of your company. I suppose you want to make sure she is safe after all you did for her. Which brings me to the reason for stopping here before heading off to Doncaster. It was not, as you supposed, to relate the news of Penelope's flight to you all, but to repay you for coming to her assistance in Selby. Namely, to repay you for the money you spent on her."

"Can I be honest with you, Alex?" Damien said in so serious a tone that Alex looked round in surprise. The expression on Damien's face was beset with tension and his eyes mirrored his anxiety. Both reined their horses to a standstill.

"Shall we walk for a while?" Alex suggested, and at Damien's nod, both dismounted and led their horses along the rough track.

Damien slowly disclosed his feelings for Penelope and the reasons for not offering her marriage. He also stated that he believed Penelope returned his regard and that, if Alex truly meant to give her up, he intended to approach Lord Frome in the hope that recent events may soften the old man's opinion in his favour.

"Do I stand a chance, do you think?" he asked in conclusion.

"She said to me in her note that she loved someone else," said Alex simply. "That someone is obviously you. I see it all now. I suppose I should be feeling angry and hurt by all this. But to tell you the truth, I am only relieved. Yes, in answer to your question, I do believe you will stand a chance. Especially after rescuing her. Lord Frome is now in your debt. But I believe you should not have been so hesitant in the first place. Lord Frome does not concern himself with gossip. You, being an earl, would have been seen as a good catch for Penelope. Maybe not by her cousin Celia, though. But Lord Frome is her guardian, not Cousin Celia. And the fact that she loves you would add to your suitability. My concern is whether you will make her happy. You sound sincere, but your past is against you. Do you truly intend to put her happiness first, Damien? Before all else?"

"I shall try. This is the first time I have felt this deeply about a woman, to be honest, and I am a bit scared by it all, if you want to know the truth. But yes, I only want to see her love for me reflected in her eyes, and I shall do all I can to ensure it stays there."

Alex nodded as the relief he was feeling washed over him. Now, he could concentrate on dealing with his own future.

Before long, they had reached the front of Meg's house and had no time to continue their conversation. Emily called to Alex from the door and came running to greet him. Damien didn't wait to see to the horses, or to greet his niece, but strode purposefully to the drawing room, where Meg and Ellen had been discussing Damien's suggestion of moving nearer to London. Emily ran for

Peter who took charge of the horses and then took Alex's hand as they made their way to the drawing room. By that time, Damien had already managed to inform them of Alex's visit and the reason for it, as well as stating his intention of accompanying Alex to Doncaster.

Meg was on her feet in a flash when Alex appeared, but instead of moving towards him, seemed rooted to the spot, her eyes staring into his.

Well, *she* might be feeling hesitant, but he wasn't! Alex smiled at her, dropping Emily's hand and strode to Meg, taking both of her hands in his, drawing her to him, and breathing in her scent whilst kissing her lightly on her lips! Tears filled her eyes as quickly as the colour flooded her face.

"Oh Alex, what a terrible thing to happen," she managed to say, referring to the news about Penelope. "You must get her back and make her see reason."

"Oh no," he replied, smiling down at her. "Oh, well, I will stop her running away, of course, and I shall return her to her guardian, but I will not force her to marry me. She loves another, Meg. I hope you were referring to Penelope when you said it was terrible, and were not referring to my kiss, because I plan to do a lot more of that, my love. For I am now free to tell you publicly that I love you and ask you to marry me."

She shook her head and put her finger to her pursed lips, lightly whispering "ssh", obviously attempting to silence him from speaking so intimately in front of her family.

While Ellen stared in amazement, Damien's reaction was to shake his head while smiling broadly. "Ha, if I had had any doubts about Alex's true feelings for my sister, they are now dispelled. This farce may have a happy ending after all!" he added, more to himself than to the room in general. But Emily had heard, and turned to him, asking him what he was talking about.

"Well Poppet," he said, crouching down in front of her, "Don't you see? Your mama loves Tenby here, and now he says that he loves your mama!"

"Oh Alex," cried Emily, turning to Alex, who was still gazing into the eyes of her mama, "does that mean that you will be my new papa, just as I wanted?"

Alex reluctantly tore his gaze away from Meg to respond to Emily's question in the affirmative, but before he could say a word, Ellen interrupted them.

"Children! Children," she cried. "Haven't we forgotten something? Emily's guardian. Henry Greene may have something to say about all this, Meg, or have you forgotten that it is in his power to take Emily from us? He is her official guardian and stipulated the terms for allowing Emily to return to you, also stating what would happen if you broke those terms."

"Mama is right, Alex. Sir Henry Greene would take Emily from me if we announced our betrothal. He has that right, I'm afraid. He wants me to keep his family name, you see. I must remain his son's widow, in name as well as in fact, or he will take Emily back. And you should not be seeking someone like me to be your wife. Your countess. Your mother and Society will expect you to marry someone who has not been married before. Someone without a scandalous past or a scandalous family background. Someone without a child already. Penelope's actions do not change those facts."

"My mother will love you, just as I do," Alex prophesied with utter confidence. "And Society can think whatever it likes. But I knew I would have trouble convincing you to accept your fate. I shall succeed this time, though. I am determined. Somehow, I shall persuade Sir Henry Greene to change his mind and then we shall be free to marry. Before the month is out if I have my way. And once we are married, I predict that we shall be welcomed in the homes of even the most illustrious families. In the end, you see, it is position and money that counts, and we have both.," he insisted. "But for now, Damien and I must make haste. We need to be waiting for Penelope when she arrives in Doncaster."

Meg shook her head, obviously still not yet ready to accept his view of things but smiled at him anyway and kissed him farewell.

* * *

When Penelope alighted from the coach in Doncaster and saw two men standing side by side waiting for her, her mouth gaped open in disbelief. She could have sworn her heart had stopped beating and found herself neither able to move nor breathe.

Earlier, while waiting to change coaches in Selby, she had anxiously paced up and down, truly fearful that, at any moment, Alex would appear to prevent her escape. The coach had taken so much longer than she thought it would, and with each mile she had become more and more certain that Alex would catch up with her and force her to go back with him. She had even contemplated what she would do in such a scenario, including accusing him of being a kidnapper but had thought better of the idea when she had envisioned the probable consequences.

But by the time the passengers for the London coach were told to board, she had begun to relax, and as each mile passed, she became more and more certain that she was now safe from discovery. She had not even bothered to scour the area for signs of a familiar face before alighting from the coach. So, when she saw Alex and Damien standing with arms crossed, waiting patiently but with scowls on their faces, the shock simply rooted her to the spot.

As the other passengers were scurrying to the inn and the ostlers were attending to the team of horses, Penelope was aware only of the two men, their scowls slowly changing to smiles, sure now that they had succeeded in trapping their prey. She was so stunned, she didn't pause to think why Damien was with Alex, being aware only that the man she loved and the man she was supposed to marry were here where they should not be.

Penelope watched with amazement as Damien began moving towards her, slowly and deliberately, with hooded eyes, lowered head, and a wicked smile of success on his lips. Why him and not Alex? she wondered as her mind started working again. And what was he intending to do?

Then she felt his hands on her shoulders and visibly trembled at the contact. Her whole body was suddenly suffused with heat, and she found breathing even more difficult.

"It's all over, Penelope," he said calmly but with intense emotion making his voice deeper than usual. "You and I have a lot to talk about and very little time in which to do it."

"Why?" was all she managed to ask.

"Because, firstly, I have to convince you that I love you, and then you and I, my dear, have to persuade your guardian to arrange for us to marry before the week is out," was his unbelievable reply.

Epilogue

Meg lay looking at her husband of nearly three years and marvelled at how wonderful her life had turned out to be. She now had a future she had never envisaged and looking back on all the fears and insecurities she had to overcome to get to this point, she knew how truly blessed she was to have Alex in her life.

He was still asleep in the bed they shared every night. His bed. She rarely used her own bedchamber, and then only if one of them was ill.

Meg was aware that the servants at Knopton Manor knew of the unusual sleeping arrangements, but no-one said anything, and if their smiles were anything to go by, they were pleased to work in such a happy household. No doubt some wondered if their lord's ardour for his wife would ever cool, but Meg knew that the love she and Alex shared would never fade.

Thinking back to the events leading to her marriage to Alex, Meg felt so proud of her husband for the way he had dealt with all the obstacles they needed to overcome. Her main fear had been for Emily and what Sir Henry and Lady Greene would do when they heard about her intention to remarry. But Alex had tackled the situation head on, visiting them in the hope of persuading them to accept the situation sensibly. And he succeeded, much to Meg's surprise and relief. The key to his success had turned out to be Lady Greene's vanity!

Any residual opposition to the marriage had collapsed when Lady Greene had been informed that following the wedding, Meg's new mother-in-law, Alex's mother, was planning to apply to the court for the new Countess of Tenby to be presented to the queen. Lady Greene simply could not resist the thought of being invited to court to witness the presentation of their son's widow to the ageing Queen Charlotte at St James' Palace. And so, Sir Henry Greene needed little further persuasion to transfer the guardianship of Emily to Alex, paving the way for all the arrangements to be made.

Due to her family's problems and her subsequent early marriage, Meg had missed out on being presented as a debutante and having a London "Season", and Alex's mother had decided that it was time the oversight was addressed. Lady Wilde had accepted the need for her son's wedding to be a quiet affair, especially as she knew it was what Meg preferred, but she refused to compromise on the need to have Meg presented at court.

Meg smiled as she remembered the formal occasion when she had been garbed in the unfashionable, uncomfortable but necessary full court dress consisting of a richly embroidered crinoline, the bodice and skirt weighed down with pearls and other jewels; her neck, hair, and wrists smothered in the family jewels, her hair piled high on her head in the most elaborate of hairstyles which included the compulsory three white plumes. Then, when she had glanced over at Lady Greene, she had found to her amusement that Adelaide Greene's costume was just as elaborate as her own, or even more so!

Of course, getting the approval of Sir Henry and Lady Greene had not been the only matter that had required a solution. Alex's life had been threatened by a madman. Stanley Thorpe had to be dealt with. Luckily, they did not have long to wait to discover his fate. By the time Lord Frome had returned to Hoddam Hall, the man was dead, and the mystery of what had happened to him had been solved.

It became apparent that when Stanley had arrived at the hut and found that Penelope was no longer there, he had made his way south, no doubt searching for her, and was eventually spotted by a militiaman on patrol who challenged him because of his erratic behaviour. For some reason no-one now would ever know, Stanley had fired when confronted by the militiaman and had been shot dead in response.

Meg hated the thought that anyone had lost their life because of the events that led to her marriage to the man she loved, but better Stanley than her beloved Alex.

Life without Alex would be unbearable. Soon he would awaken, and she had a good idea what was going to happen then, because the same thing happened most mornings. He would turn to her, and she would welcome him into her arms and into her body. Making love with Alex was magical and had been right from the beginning. She had been surprised to find how responsive she was to his lovemaking, but then he was a considerate, experienced lover.

As if on cue, Alex opened his eyes, looked at her and smiled. "Good morning, my love," he said simply, before their lips met, then opened to allow a thorough mating of tongues and teeth as their need for each other gathered pace. Soon they were both enjoying tempting each other by nibbling, biting, stroking, and probing as the kiss deepened, at times hard and rough, then, by unspoken mutual desire, becoming soft, tender, and loving, only to fire up again into an all-consuming passion.

They made love most mornings and that morning was no different as they came together to experience once again the earth-shatteringly, exquisitely beautiful and fulfilling demonstration of their love. Then, while still joined and with the magic surrounding their lovemaking still lingering, Alex drew back and looked into Meg's eyes, holding her gaze for a moment in loving communion before lowering his head to brush her lips with his. "I love you," he stated simply.

"And I love you," she replied breathlessly.

After lying replete in each other's arms for several minutes, basking in the aftermath of their lovemaking, Meg slowly recovered sufficiently to realise that it was almost time for the daily visit from their son, who would be brought in by his nurse for his morning romp on their bed.

Young Nick, now nearly two, son and heir, was a lively boy, doted on not only by his parents but also by his grandmothers, his half-sister Emily and all the other members of the household.

Meg felt herself to be the most blessed of women. Alex loved her, she was accepted by almost all members of society and her mother-in-law not only approved of her but also enjoyed the company of Ellen, her own mother. Ellen's fate had been another of Meg's worries.

No, life was now so good. Emily was enjoying living at Knopton Manor and was growing up to be a most accomplished and beautiful young lady. She was very fond of her governess who had introduced her to the pleasure of music. Emily was now becoming a most accomplished pianist. Meg, Ellen, and Alex loved listening to her playing and were sometimes joined by Damien and Penelope, whenever they found the time in between their frequent travels and other social engagements.

Meg was glad Damien and Penelope had been allowed to marry. Damien had requested to speak with Lord Frome for permission to marry Penelope shortly after returning Penelope to Hoddam Hall. Perhaps because the Marquess hated confrontations, he apparently quickly accepted the situation for what it was while drawing up a water-tight financial agreement that would provide a generous income for the couple while also protecting both Penelope and their heirs from Damien's possible financial irresponsibility.

Meg had given her brother the gift of a townhouse in a fashionable area of London on his marriage and with that and Lord

Frome's generosity, Penelope and Damien were able to live well, if not extravagantly. The property in Enfield she had inherited had been sold and the proceeds, together with the money left to her, had been put in a personal account for her sole use, allowing her the freedom to ensure that she was not completely dependent on her husband.

Damien still enjoyed gambling, but then again, so did his wife. Penelope had matured into a most dazzling, vivacious, and captivating beauty, who matched Damien in her daring and in her stamina. And their love for each other was clear to all who met them.

Meg, on the other hand, loved the quiet life. She was devoted to her husband and her children. She had no desire to travel, feeling a little uncertain whenever she was faced with new situations. She was happy at Knopton, with only the occasional visit to London, and knew Alex felt the same way. Between them, they were making all kinds of improvements to the estate and their union had developed into a true partnership.

Later that day, Prudence called in to see Alex and Meg about the arrangements for Nick's second birthday party. She had her own apartment at Knopton, complete with a bathroom, but rarely used it, stating her preference to spend most of her time in the home she had shared with her beloved husband. Alex had hoped the Duke of Longford, Prudence's long-time friend and admirer, would eventually persuade Prudence to marry him, but had now accepted the fact that she still considered herself married, and that, one day, she would be reunited with her husband.

Alex greeted his mother warmly, as always, and watched as the three women in his life - his wife, his adopted daughter, and his mother - discussed their plans. They got on so well, his mother's acceptance of his choice of Meg as his bride being such a relief to him. He remembered how she had confided to him before he and Meg married, saying that she had been sorely mistaken about

Penelope and that she considered Meg to be much more suitable. She had then worked hard to ensure Meg's acceptance into society, not only by sponsoring Meg's court presentation after the wedding, but also by enlisting the help of her devoted friend, John, the high ranking, and well-respected Duke of Longford, to lend his approval to the union by joining the family during the celebratory balls. It was his approval that was instrumental in causing even the most inveterate of Meg's critics to rethink their prejudice towards her re-entry into society.

His mother, unsurprisingly, was also a fond grandmother, both towards his son and towards Emily. Emily went to stay with her at least once a year, in addition to her annual visit to her other grandparents. And Alex knew that Emily loved her new grandmother, but most of all, knew how much she adored her new aunt. When she paid her annual visit to Sir Henry and Lady Greene, Emily always travelled north with her Uncle Damien and Aunt Penelope, taking advantage of their own visit to Lord Frome. Emily idolised her new aunt, much to Alex's and Damien's amusement. Whenever they were together, Emily was never far from Penelope's side, looking in adoration at the way she moved, dressed, and spoke. When staying at Knopton, Damien often complained to Alex how difficult it was to get a moment alone with his wife!

Looking at Meg as she chatted happily with his mother and Emily, Alex thought how fortunate he was to be married to the love of his life. Somehow, it made all the heartache worthwhile. Thinking back to their lovemaking earlier that day, Alex marvelled at how he could ever have had any doubt about Meg's ability to overcome her fear of the sexual act. He remembered their wedding night - he had strictly observed the priorities before the wedding, mainly because in those weeks they were never alone, but also because he was determined not to give the gossips any ammunition to hurt Meg any more than they had already.

As expected, the end of his betrothal to Penelope and the two subsequent weddings had caused quite a stir, and Meg, always sensitive to the opinions of others, had needed all the support and encouragement that family and friends could give her. That support, which included having Alice and Jed agree to go to Knopton Manor with them as members of the household, plus her love for Alex and his for her had given her the strength to face the attention her return to society and her marriage had caused.

Alex remembered how nervous he had been on his wedding night; how he had left Meg alone to ready herself for bed, then how he had approached the bed wearing a nightshirt so as not to frighten her. He had been sure that he would have to proceed very slowly if Meg was ever to find joy in the marriage bed. After all, he reasoned, she had been abused and must view the sexual act with revulsion. Even though she had responded so warmly to his kisses and caresses before he had left her home after his gunshot wound, he assumed that she would freeze when it came to the act of sexual intercourse itself. Remembering, he smiled at how wrong he had been!

He recalled now how she had responded to his first caress, moaning with delight and an unspoken invitation to use her body to satisfy his burning desire. He had revelled in her beauty as he had slowly relieved her of her nightgown, gazing with total admiration at her luscious curves and creamy, firm, full breasts, making him groan in anticipation.

What a magical night it had been. He remembered how, instead of shyness, Meg had responded to his initial kiss and exploration of her body by matching him touch for touch, kiss for kiss, coming together for the first time in an explosion of passion. He recalled how she had writhed with pleasure beneath him, almost as if she could meld their two bodies together, and how she had shuddered with the force of her orgasm. It had all happened too quickly, and he had returned almost immediately for a more leisurely joining when his slow movements wrung new heights of ecstasy from her body.

She told him afterwards that she had spent so many nights yearning for his touch that she was more than ready to welcome him into her body. Since then, she had surprised him many times with her instinctive response to his lovemaking, even going as far as to take the initiative, driving him mad with her hands and mouth. Sometimes, in public, she would give him a certain look and he knew that she was lusting after him. He would grow hard just thinking of what he would like to do to her and would become less than the perfect host or guest in his haste to be alone with his wife!

As though she was able to read his mind, Meg looked over to him at that very moment, her eyes sparkling with mischief and invitation! His eyebrows rose in question, and she nodded.

Oh yes, he was a lucky man!